LOVE LOST

by

Mary Minnock

For Mathilde, Nora, Johanne and Ashlinn.

Chapter 1

Dublin 2004

Later, Dennis Byrne would relive the day over and over, recalling every tiny detail so that it stood out in sharp relief in his memory and became the hinge of his life on which hung the before and after.

It was one of those sunny March days—a Friday—that tricks people into believing in summer. But behind the warmth of the direct sun, there was a warning chill.

Dennis parked not far from St. Stephen's Green and walked down Grafton Street. There was a cheery atmosphere among the busy crowd: maybe it was the lifting of the long, wet winter, maybe it was the end of the working week and the start of the weekend or maybe it was just Dennis transferring his own mood to the crowd as he made his way to meet Ciara for lunch.

Even though he hadn't fully sorted out the problem with Pat Casey's faulty clutch, he had happily downed tools and left the garage to join her. Ever since she started college, he didn't get to see her as often as he'd like and he was looking forward to the catch-up.

One of the women selling flowers outside the Westbury called out to him with a cheeky grin, 'Go on, handsome, get some lovely daffodils for her!' The flattery put a bit more pep in his step and he grinned back.

He hurried on past the buskers, past the teenagers hanging around the entrance to McDonalds, past the women laden down with their shopping bags to the end of the pedestrian street. On his right was the front entrance of Trinity College. He was still amazed that his daughter could be going there. When he was growing up, he had thought it only for posh people who moved in circles far removed from his own and yet now, his Ciara was studying physics there. Every time he passed by the impressive old facade, the pride grew inside him until he wanted to stop strangers in the street and tell them.

His strides lengthened as he approached his destination: The Last Drop, a sandwich bar and coffee shop on Westmoreland Street. He bought the newspaper at a newsagent's next door. He knew his daughter well enough not to expect her to be on time.

Still, he took a quick look around to check and, when he was sure she wasn't there, he bought a pot of tea and sat at a table near the window where he could feel the heat of the sun and watch the people passing by. He pushed back from the table to stretch out his long legs underneath. He was examining the inside of the teapot to see if the last of the tea was stewed beyond drinkability when two hands landed on his shoulders and a kiss smacked the centre of the ever-increasing bald patch on the top of his head.

'It's not getting any better, Dad,' Ciara said with the seriousness of a surgeon delivering a difficult prognosis.

'Sit down, cheeky. You're late.'

Ciara threw her coat over the back of a seat, tossed her bag under the table and slid into a chair opposite Dennis, all in one effortless movement, 'Still, look at the bright side. No bad hair days, no sticky gel, just one quick rub to put a bit of a shine on it and you're off.' She leaned in towards him and lowered her voice. 'And I've been told that it drives older women crazy. Reminds them of Sean Connery.'

Dennis ran his hand across the top of his head. 'Sean Connery? That old fella? He should be so lucky! I'm only coming into my prime now.'

Ciara grabbed the menu from the table and studied it intently. 'I'm starving,' she said. 'I had nothing to eat for breakfast. Someone ate all the yoghurts I had in the fridge and the milk was gone off. I love my room on campus but it's a pain not to have my own kitchen.'

'I get the hint. Somehow your purse probably got cleared out too.' A warm familiar glow rekindled in Dennis as it often did when he was with Ciara. Did every father feel like this about his daughter or was he just exceptionally lucky?

Ciara grinned. 'How'd you guess? Lucky I have you, Dad. At least you won't let me starve.'

'Come on, let's get something to eat. Although a bit of starvation might improve your money management skills,' Dennis said and followed Ciara to the counter to order lunch.

Deep down, he didn't care how much of his money she frittered away, he couldn't think of a better way to spend it anyway, but he felt that he should make the point, just for the principle.

As they sat down again at the table, Ciara's plate piled high with about six different kinds of salad, Dennis looked with pleasure at his vibrant, dark-haired daughter. She was wearing a hand-knitted, multi-coloured jumper in wools of different textures and weights with dark-blue jeans that were only barely hanging on to her hips. She wore no make-up as usual but still managed to exude what would always be fathomless beauty to him. Technically, he knew that the dark blue eyes set in a face that never stayed still, the dark hair cropped in a short, choppy style and the pale skin dotted with the freckles she hated, all added up to prettiness rather than beauty but, to his eyes, the whole was so much more than the sum of the parts.

'So, how are things going at college?' he asked. He expected a rambling, witty account of her week; funny incidents from class, minor run-ins with lecturers, outings with classmates, maybe even a tirade against the university's recycling policy but instead her smile dimmed.

She sighed. 'All right, I suppose.'

'That doesn't sound like you. Is there something up?' Dennis examined her face.

'Oh, it's nothing.' Ciara continued stirring her coffee. 'It's not worth talking about.'

'It's not a problem with your studies, is it? If there is anything I can help you with, just ask. You know how physics holds very few secrets from me.'

'Yeah, right, Dad. Don't worry, I'm not that desperate yet.' Ciara laughed as he intended she should. 'At least with physics, I know where I stand. No, this is a personal thing but I'll sort it out. No big deal.' She made an impatient sweeping gesture with her hand as though to brush away annoying thoughts clinging like cobwebs. 'Anyway, that's not the reason I asked you to meet me for lunch.'

'Ah, here I was, operating under the delusion that you wanted to spend time with your dear old dad, make fun of his receding hairline and squeeze some money out of him.'

'Well, of course I do want to do all of those things but the main reason I asked you to meet me is that there's something I need to talk to you and Mam about. I was hoping we could all get together this weekend so we could discuss it.' Ciara paused with a forkful of salad in front of her mouth to look earnestly at Dennis.

'Now you are beginning to worry me. Why can't you tell us separately? Are you devising some kind of diabolical plan to make us fight with each other so that we don't turn on you when you tell us about some hare-brained scheme you have in mind?'

'What an excellent idea! I never even considered that! I'll keep it in mind for another time. But no, this time, what I need to talk to you about has nothing to do with me, well, very little really, it's more to do with the two of you.'

Dennis frowned. 'Ciara.' He could hear the warning tone in his own voice. 'You are not a little girl anymore; you can't matchmake between us.' He caught a glance from an elderly woman at the next table and leaned forward, lowering his voice. 'What happened between me and your mother is over and will never come back. You know we haven't had a normal civil conversation for years and we're not likely to start now. The best thing for everyone is for us to see as little of each other as possible.'

'Do you think I don't know that? Whenever you're in the same room, you're like a pair of stiff, prickly cactuses. Don't worry, getting you two back together is a crusade I gave up long ago. No, this is an entirely different matter altogether. Please come over to Mam's house this weekend? Or even this afternoon? I'm going home for the weekend so what about dropping me off on your way back to the garage and coming inside then?'

'Ciara, I have to get back to work. It's Friday and people want their cars back for the weekend. In any case, I don't like this kind of pressure.' Dennis spoke more sharply than he intended and to compensate, he leaned over and ruffled her hair. 'Listen, it's not a problem to drop you home but I don't want to go into the house, especially if she doesn't know I'm coming. Leave it with me. I'll think about it.'

As they left the café and stepped into the bright sunshine in the street, Dennis felt troubled. This had not been quite the amusing distraction in his working day that he had anticipated. He hated any kind of disagreement with Ciara.

As though reading his thoughts, Ciara gave his arm a quick squeeze as they walked. 'Don't make a big thing of it, Dad. This wouldn't take long and you know I wouldn't ask if this wasn't important.'

With every step, Dennis shook off the burrs of anxiety clinging to him.

'So where is your Golf? Why aren't you driving it?' he asked.

'I leave it out in Mam's during the week. It's more hassle than it's worth to have it in the city centre. I bus or bike everywhere. It's handy for the weekends though if I'm going away. Thanks again, Dad.' She flashed a smile at him.

Dennis's dark green Jaguar XJ6 was parked on a side street where four small boys were hovering around it with transparent admiration. As Dennis and Ciara approached, the sound of the locking system, activated remotely by Dennis, made them jump. The boys took a step back and looked around.

'Nice car, mister,' one cheeky face shouted at him.

'No wonder you can pull the young ones!' Another one with red hair and a mass of freckles shouted, although at the same time he took a wary step backwards, ready to break into a run. Dennis made a sudden movement as if to catch one of them and they scattered like mice. He laughed at their impudence.

He listened with pleasure to the soft click of the smoothly engineered mechanism as he opened the car door and slid into the driver's seat.

'Dad, your safety belt.' Ciara prompted him as he indicated his way out of his parking space.

'I will in a minute,' he said. 'Once we get out on the open road.' He never liked the restraint of the safety-belt; it took away from the sense of power and freedom he felt when he was behind the wheel.

'No, Dad, put it on now.' Ciara was having none of it. 'Don't you remember what happened to Dermot Sharkey?'

'How could I forget? You remind me often enough.'

'Well then, don't be so pig-headed about it. Put it on.'

Not for the first time, Dennis thought that if he had known that Ciara would be as deeply affected as she was by Dermot Sharkey's car accident he would never have allowed her to attend the court proceedings with him. Years before, Dennis had helped with the extraction of the young man from his mangled vehicle and, as a result, had been called to court as a minor witness. Ciara had pestered him to bring her with him, curious to see how a court case was in real life. Her eyes never left Dermot Sharkey who sat at the front of the courtroom between his parents, a metal plate inserted in the back of his head to hold his brain in. He would probably have sustained only minor injuries if he had been wearing his seat-belt, the court found.

Traffic was slow on this Friday afternoon as the momentum of the weekend started to chug into action. The journey to Mag's home in the suburbs took twice as long as it normally would but Dennis revelled in his daughter's company as she explained with passion the dangers of global warming and deplored the minimal efforts being made to counteract them. She had a habit of illustrating the stories she told with grimaces and expressions that made him laugh. It reminded him of when she was a child, when she displayed her inner feelings with expressions that were cartoon caricatures of those emotions.

When she ran out of breath, he asked if her heart was committed entirely to the ozone layer or if there was a corner left over for any mere mortal.

She made a rueful face at him. 'Oh, men! I think I should steer clear. Relationships always get so complicated and I'm no good at sorting them out.' She gave him a nudge. 'Maybe it's a hereditary thing.'

He glanced away from the road at her and she raised an eyebrow. 'Maybe I should go and talk to Sister Dolores, see if she could fit me in.'

Dennis laughed. Despite his belief that the talents of his daughter were limitless, one career where he could never see her was as a nun.

He was almost sorry to see the black wrought-iron gates and cherry trees at the front of Mag's house, the house that had once been his too and where he had lived for almost ten years before they had separated.

'The cherry blossoms will bloom shortly,' Ciara said. 'It's a shame they last for such a short time. Or maybe that's what makes us appreciate them all the more.'

Dennis leaned across her to open the car door on her side. 'Go, go. Philosophise on your own time. I have work to get done before I lose all my customers.'

'All right, I'm going, you philistine.' Ciara gave him a peck on the cheek. 'Please call over on Sunday, Dad. It's important.'

Dennis found it difficult to ever say no to his daughter. 'Let me call you on your mobile. Talk to your mother first. Make sure it's OK with her.'

Dennis paused for a moment to watch Ciara run up the driveway to the house — she never walked when running was an option. She ran past the front door, unlatched the garden gate at the side and, just before she closed it behind her, she turned and waved at him.

And that was the last time he saw her.

Chapter 2

Mag was on her knees in the garden planting flowers in a corner where she had recently created a small rockery. A tall sycamore had stood in the spot previously but it had become diseased and she had been obliged to have it cut down. She had kept a section of the trunk to make a rough garden seat. The earth was moist and dark under her fingers. She plopped the plants into the hollows she made for them. She loved gardening for the moments like this when she felt in harmony with her own little corner of the world. She was leaning back on her heels admiring her work when her daughter arrived in a whirlwind of movement.

'Hi, Mam,' Ciara said. 'How are you? Wow, this looks great. You've done a great job.' She tested out the bench and looked around the garden. 'I know you were sorry to have to cut down that old tree but it does make the garden less dark and shadowy.'

Mag got up and sat beside her daughter. How like her father she was, in every way. She had his dark, impish good looks but she also had his ebullient optimism, his impetus towards the future and away from the past.

'Yes, I'm pleased with the way it's turning out in the end.' Mag brushed the earth from the knees of her old sweatpants. 'Come inside, I could do with a cup of tea after all that.'

They walked up the sloped path which led from the garden to the patio above and went through to the kitchen. Ciara sat at the large, well-worn table, sorting through the post that had come for her over the past couple of weeks while her mother put the kettle on to boil.

'It's good to see you, love, I wasn't expecting you this weekend.' Mag stood by the kettle watching her daughter's face as she opened the envelopes.

'I know but I felt like coming home. You don't mind that I just arrived in on top of you, do you? I wouldn't mind having some quiet time to think about things, sort out what I'm doing with my life.'

Mag looked into her empty mug before speaking but she couldn't keep her voice completely neutral. She tried hard not to interfere in Ciara's life, to let her come to her but it was easier said than done. 'Of course not. You're welcome here any time, Ciara, you don't have to ask. Is there anything wrong, anything I can help you with?'

'No, Mam, it's all right. I don't want to hassle you with this, I'll be fine. I just got myself into an awkward situation but don't worry, I'll sort it out.'

'I have a bit of experience with awkward situations myself.' Mag made a wry face at her daughter. 'Maybe I could help. I'm a tougher nut that you give me credit for, you know.'

'I'm beginning to realise that. Now more than ever.' Ciara gave her a quick, sympathetic smile. 'You are great, Mam. I love you.'

Mag focused on pouring the boiling water into the mugs. 'In any case it's not as if I was planning anything particularly exciting, just the usual hill-walking with Kathleen and the gang tomorrow morning.' She put the mugs on the table and sat opposite Ciara.

'I have a thing on tonight with the Trinity gang. Not sure what time I'll be back but I doubt I'll be awake to hear you leave tomorrow. Maybe we could go out for a late lunch after you get back if you feel like it.' Ciara always held her mug cupped in her two hands as if to draw all the warmth out of it.

'That sounds lovely. Let's do that.' Mag looked out through the patio windows as a ray of spring sunshine arrived in the garden. 'So, will that young lad from your class be there then? Are you still seeing him?'

Ciara shook her head. 'Vincent? No, that's over months ago. It wasn't working out. We had a bit of a falling out but I think we'll be friends eventually.'

'Oh well, take your time, I'm sure one of these days you'll meet the right one.'

'Hmm,' Ciara got up to throw the scrunched up envelopes and junk mail in the bin. 'I think I'd be better off concentrating on college for a while.'

'That sounds very sensible of you. Delighted to hear it. You must have your final exams coming up soon. What are your plans for after? Are you going to be job-hunting or will you take a break?'

Ciara hesitated. 'I don't know yet. It all depends. There's a bit of stuff going on. I'll have to see how things pan out.'

Mag looked at her. She was determined not to interfere. 'You know you're welcome to stay here after you move out of your college room. I'd be delighted to have you.'

'I know, thanks.' Ciara gave her a quick smile. 'By the way, there's something else I need to talk to you about. I invited Dad over here on Sunday. There's something I need to discuss with you both.'

Mag raised her eyebrows. 'And he has to come here to hear it?'

'Only because I want to tell you together. I know I should have discussed it with you first but I saw him for lunch and it made sense to invite him. You don't really mind, do you?'

'Well, I'm not exactly thrilled but I don't have much choice now, do I? So what is it you want to tell us?'

'I can't say now. I'll tell you on Sunday.'

'You're being very mysterious, Ciara, it's not like you. Is there something wrong?' Mag looked at her more closely.

'No, this is good news.' Ciara stopped as if not quite sure of the truth of that. 'Well, I hope that's the way you'll see it.'

Mag felt her stomach lurch. She paused a moment before asking quietly, 'You're not pregnant, are you, Ciara?'

Ciara was obviously surprised by the question but answered evenly. 'No, I'm not, Mam, don't worry, you can put that thought out of your head. Don't start imagining all sorts of scenarios. Just wait until Sunday and I'll tell you then.'

'All right then, if that's what you want.' Mag tried to banish the worries that insisted on burrowing through her mind. She really had to stop being so melodramatic. It was probably nothing. It wouldn't be the first time that Ciara's passionate nature swept her up in some all-absorbing scheme that subsided to insignificance over time.

Ciara grinned. 'Thanks, Mam. I'll explain everything on Sunday.'

'It's been a while since he was here,' Mag mused as she stood up to clear away the table. She shook away the thought. 'Now, what about dinner this evening? Are you eating here?'

'Yes, that would be good. I'm going out after that.' Ciara drained the last of her tea and put her mug in the sink.

Later, Mag would try to recapture every second of that evening, to string together every inconsequential word exchanged as if they were scattered pearls from a broken necklace. While they prepared and ate dinner together, they laughed and talked until Ciara, realising how late it was, dashed upstairs to change.

When she came back down again, Mag thought her daughter looked older and more sophisticated than she had ever seen her look before. She had smoothed and tamed her unruly hair so that it looked pretty and feminine. She was wearing make-up which she rarely did and had put on a denim skirt with a blue-green top. For her mother's benefit, she sashayed down the stairs, as if she were an old-time movie star entering a saloon full of admiring men. Then, she laughed and the pose evaporated.

'Well, how do I look?' the real Ciara said.

Mag longed to reach across this new-found elegance and hug her closely but she held back.

'You look great, lovey,' she said. She heard a jangling noise and picked up her daughter's hand to examine her wrist. 'Oh, it's your grandmother's charm bracelet. I've never seen you wear it before.'

Mag's mother had left the heavy, red-gold bracelet to Ciara. Numerous charms hung from it; a tiny treasure chest; an antlered deer; a die; a revolving disc that seemed to have random markings on both sides but the words 'I LOVE YOU' could be read on it when it was spun. Looking at these familiar pieces drew Mag back to a safe time of loving, chapped hands and sugar sandwiches, a time when her mother was still alive.

'I know. I always thought it was too old-fashioned before but they're coming back into fashion and anyway I like to get dressed up from time to time.' Ciara picked up her battered leather jacket and large shoulder bag and gave her mother a quick peck on the cheek. 'I'd better go or I'll be late. Please don't stay awake for me. I know you do even if you say you don't. Sleep well and I'll see you tomorrow.'

Through the sitting room window, Mag saw the lights of Ciara's blue Golf flash and then diminish as she drove away. The house was quiet afterwards, a quiet that even the senseless babble from the television couldn't chase away.

Chapter 3

Dennis was a deep sleeper. Mag used to tease him that sometimes he fell asleep even before his head hit the pillow. He used to reply that it was the sure sign of a clear conscience. That night, he struggled to haul his mind up through the deep well of sleep towards wakefulness. When he managed to register what was happening around him, he realised that someone was pressing persistently on his doorbell and had been for a while. He fumbled his way out of bed and down the narrow stairs of his small flat above the garage.

When he opened the door and saw the two uniformed Gardaí standing on his doorstep, the wisps of sleep that still lingered were blown away by the cold wind of fear.

'Could we come inside to have a word?' The voice of the Garda was low and wary. He was the older of the two and looked to be about fifty, the same age as Dennis. The other one, at least twenty years younger, seemed ill-at-ease and turned away as if searching for an invisible suspicious presence in the dark, empty street behind him.

'Garda Mullins.' The older man identified himself. 'And this here is Garda Cuff. You are Dennis Byrne; I presume?'

'That's right.' Dennis took a step back into the hallway which was too small to accommodate the three men comfortably. He led them upstairs to the living room. Dim, ghostly shadows created by the light from the street lamps filtered through the curtains. He banished them with a flick of a switch.

'Is there something wrong?' Even as he asked the question, his mind was preparing to move barriers into position to block out what they might tell him.

Mullins removed his cap. 'First of all, you might like to sit down.'

Dennis looked from one to the other. 'No, I don't want to sit down. What's this about?'

The two men exchanged a glance. Mullins continued. 'I'm afraid we have bad news. It's about your daughter, Ciara Byrne. She's been in a car accident.'

Strangely, Dennis felt relief. Hope anaesthetised his mind. It was just an accident. So Ciara was alive. She might be hurt but she was alive. She'd be OK, he'd make sure of that.

'My God, how is she?' Still, he was afraid to know.

'Are you sure you don't want us to sit down?' Cuff looked down at his uniform and tugged at his tunic.

'No, I don't,' Dennis snapped. 'Now tell me how my daughter is.'

Mullins visibly steeled himself before he spoke again. 'I'm afraid she died instantly, Mr. Byrne.'

Dennis stared at him. His mind shut down. A world without Ciara couldn't exist. 'That's not true. No fucking way.' He clenched his fists. He wanted to punch the man in the face. Mullins looked as if he might let him. Cuff was nervous. They were silent. Finally, after Dennis's shoulders slumped, Garda Mullins took his arm and guided him to a leather armchair as if he were a helpless old man. He nudged him to sit.

Cuff made his way to the open kitchen area at the other end of the room. 'Can I get you a glass of water? Or a cup of tea?'

'Water's fine,' Mullins said shortly. He pulled over a chair and sat opposite Dennis. 'How are you feeling, Dennis? Would you like us to call a doctor?'

Dennis heard these words floating towards him, coming from a long distance away. Who were these men who had come into his house in the middle of the night and were behaving as if they knew him?

Mullins continued. 'I'm sorry. I'm so sorry. You can come and make the formal identification now or later if you want but there appears to be no doubt. It's your daughter.'

He wanted to ask how sure they were that she was really gone but a small part of him knew how ridiculous that question was before he expressed it.

'What…? How?' His mind couldn't even formulate the questions he needed to ask. All other information seemed as nothing beside the infinity of the revelation.

The two guards looked at each other and then Mullins proceeded. 'The accident happened in the Dublin Mountains, on the Enniskerry road about two hours ago. She was alone. She drove over the side of the mountain. There was no other vehicle involved.' He paused. 'Death was instantaneous. She didn't suffer.'

Each word was enunciated clearly and slowly as though he were speaking to someone who didn't understand English very well.

Dennis glared at him. 'Where is she now?'

'The investigation team are still at the scene of the accident. They will transfer her shortly to the morgue at St. Vincent's Hospital. You'll have plenty of time to get there before them.'

'Does Mag… Does her mother know?' The thought materialised before him through the mists of his mind and he hung on to it like a drowning man clinging to a life-buoy. It gave him something to do, something to focus on rather than the horrible reality.

'No, not yet. I presume you're divorced or separated. She had both of your names and addresses in her note-book. We were planning to go to see her mother now and tell her…' He paused and his voice softened. 'Was she your only child?'

The use of the past tense stabbed viciously at Dennis's heart.

'Yes, there was only Ciara. I'll tell her mother. I'd prefer if it was me.' Dennis was already out of his seat and heading to his bedroom to look for clothes to wear.

'Of course, if that's what you want but let us take you there. It's not safe for you to drive at the moment.'

'No. I'll take my own car. Then, I'm going to Enniskerry.'

'Do you think that's advisable, sir?' Cuff said. 'You've had a terrible shock. You should take it easy.'

'And what do you suggest, Garda?' Dennis snarled at the man who held up his palms in a pacifying gesture. 'That I should go back to bed? I'll tell you what I am going to do: I am going to tell my wife what has happened and then I am going to see my daughter, whether you like it or not.'

Somewhere in his brain, Dennis registered that he had called Mag his wife for the first time in many years although that is what she still was, officially. In recent years, he had tended to refer to her as Ciara's mother but, with a flash of pain, he realised that this last link connecting them had been cut.

Dennis got into his car. The illuminated digits of the clock glowed 04:43. The streets were quiet, unnaturally quiet, and he quickly covered the two kilometres that separated his garage from Mag's home. It was only when he shut off the engine and the ensuing silence overwhelmed him that he quaked in front of the task he had taken on.

He didn't have long to wait. As he switched off the lights of his car, he noticed the curtains in Mag's bedroom twitch and before he could reach the front door, it opened.

Mag stood on the doorstep. Her soft brown curls were messy but her clear blue eyes were sharp and lucid. She wore a long blue dressing-gown, the same colour as her eyes, which she clutched around her. Her face was white. She said nothing as she stepped backwards to let Dennis in. Mag stood motionless at the end of the stairs. She gripped the bannister. Dennis raised his eyes to the level of her hands but could go no higher. He addressed her gleaming white knuckles.

'She's gone, Mag,' Dennis said. 'Ciara's gone. There was a car accident. She's dead.'

Mag swayed and he thought she was going to faint. He leapt forward to catch her but she stabilised herself and sat down heavily on the last step of the stairs. A whimper of anguish escaped her. She held her head in her hands and, in the silence, he could hear her heart breaking.

'The Gardaí just came to the flat to tell me.' His voice cracked. 'I don't know much. The accident happened on the

Enniskerry road. Apparently, she went off the road on a bend and crashed into the mountain below. I'm going there now. I have to see what's going on. Do you want me to call someone to come and stay with you?'

She took a tremulous breath. 'No, I'll go with you.' She looked at him, her eyes defying him to deny her the right. He hesitated but, acknowledging the futility of resistance, he nodded. He felt awkward; he didn't know how to react with this woman who had once, in another lifetime, been his heart, his soul.

'I'll be ready in a minute,' Mag said. Halfway up the stairs, she stopped for a moment and looked down at him. 'Oh, Dennis,' she said. The sounds emerged with a painful struggle, like bubbles bursting to the surface. He kept his head down, afraid to look at her. They both stood there for a second before her heavy steps continued to the top of the staircase. She returned a couple of minutes later dressed. She ran her fingers through her short curls to put them in order and picked up her bag and coat from the hallway.

'Let's go then,' she said.

Chapter 4

On the way to Enniskerry, the darkness of the night and the silence both inside and outside the car added to Mag's feeling of disconnection from reality. Even though she knew that Ciara was gone, every part of her fought against that truth. It was as though she had created a paper-thin dam behind which she was hiding before the avalanche of emotion swept through it and crushed her. Fear circled over her, a merciless scavenger waiting to pounce.

She glanced over at Dennis. His face was tense and white, his muscles set. He focused on the road with a grim concentration. His hands had small traces of black engine grease ingrained in them. They gripped the steering wheel as if to anchor the car to the road.

They quickly left the city lights behind and took the narrow, winding country roads into the mountains. The night was still and cold. At first, the vegetation on either side was dense and overrun but this thinned out as they climbed the steep grade. At a couple of points, the road became so narrow that if they encountered another car, it would have involved a delicate dance to pass by without incident. At other times, the road shaved the edge of the mountain so closely that there was no protective margin of road, only a sheer drop. The perimeter of the sleeping city was outlined in lights below them but its proximity only emphasised the isolation of the setting. They passed some houses dotted in the landscape, dark and silent for the most part but some had left their outside lights on. To guide their teenagers safely home, Mag thought bitterly.

They turned a final corner and flashing blue and yellow lights became visible. They had not exchanged a word on the journey. Urgent commanding voices carried in the still, early-morning air. Movements seemed to be controlled, economical. There was no panic, no sense that time was crucial, just men dealing with a grim task as efficiently as possible. With a lurch of her heart into her throat, Mag noticed an ambulance. The thought of what awaited her caused her intense physical pain.

Time. What a heartless, merciless creature it was, forcing her inexorably forward, thrusting her into the future with the cold impartiality of an executioner. There was nothing she could do to prevent her own relentless advance and nothing, nothing, nothing she could do to go back to a moment when her own baby girl stood in front of her, laughing, warm, alive.

She wanted to scream, rail at the world, reach up and rip open the sky with her bare hands in search of someone somewhere who could be responsible for this. Oh God, oh God, how could You have let such a thing happen? Why Ciara, of all people? Why not me? Why, oh why not me? It was a long time since Mag had addressed God. She still went to mass at Christmas but more for the social warmth rather than through any real religious conviction.

Dennis pulled up beside a Garda car and jumped out impatiently, slamming the car door. Mag followed. When she caught up with him, he was already in discussion with three Gardaí standing in a group.

'So, what happened?' Dennis was demanding to know.

'Excuse me, sir, but who are you?' A tall, thin Garda shifted position so that his body acted as a physical barrier partially blocking Dennis from the other men. He was holding a large camera in his hands.

'My name's Dennis Byrne. I was told that my daughter was…had an accident here.'

'And I'm Mag Byrne, her mother. Where is she?'

The defensive stance of the men disappeared and they looked at Dennis and Mag in sympathy. They glanced at each other, each hoping that someone else would handle the situation.

'We're very sorry,' one of them murmured.

'She's in the ambulance. They are just getting ready to leave. If you'd like to go over there now you can catch them.' The third Garda spoke gently as if he feared that their mental condition was of a fragility such that even a raised voice could shatter them into a thousand pieces.

As Mag and Dennis walked side by side to the ambulance, Mag couldn't prevent herself from looking down over the sharp drop so perilously close to the narrow country road.

With a heart-thump she could make out the crumpled blue Golf that had given her such pleasure to see on every other occasion. It appeared to have nose-dived over the edge and crashed into the rock-strewn land twenty metres below.

To pre-empt another identity check, Mag addressed a man who was obviously the ambulance driver and a woman who appeared to be a doctor or a paramedic. 'Excuse me, we're Ciara Byrne's parents.'

'I'm Doctor Mannion,' the woman said. 'I'm very sorry about your daughter. I'm afraid that when I arrived there was already nothing I could do.' She touched their arms and guided them a few steps away from the ambulance. 'Did you want to see her? Because if you do, I have to warn you that it may be upsetting. It might be best to wait until later. She would look more like herself, more like your memories of her.'

Memories, Mag thought, is that all that's left now? Memories. It seemed like a strange word to use in connection with their dinner only a few hours earlier. She quickly blocked off that avenue of thought. Now, she had to create some kind of shell of protection around herself if she was to survive this, not that she was even sure survival was what she wanted. Right now, she had to focus on putting one foot in front of the other, breathing one breath after another.

'I want to see her,' Dennis said. The words seemed to be torn, dragged from some deep, ugly place within him. Mag nodded in agreement and in fear.

Doctor Mannion looked from one to the other. 'Give us a minute,' she said. 'I'll call you over when we're ready.'

She returned to the ambulance, spoke a few words to the driver and got into the back. After an agonising eternity, the door opened and she beckoned them forward. Mag climbed up the steps into the ambulance. Her eyes had adjusted to the dim shadowy light of early morning and she felt the impact of the bright glare inside as an aggression.

She forced her eyes to look at the stretcher where Ciara lay, barely recognisable. She had a vicious cut high on her forehead near her hair-line. Blood had poured into her hair which was dark and matted. They had cleaned most of the blood from her face although some dried black traces remained in her eyebrows and on the side of her nose. A shallow scratch across her right cheek stood out vividly red against her waxy white skin. In an instant, Mag could see that she was gone. The essence of Ciara had vanished leaving behind a body that resembled her no more than a watermark resembles the pool of water it was before. She caressed Ciara's cheek with her fingertips and recoiled when she registered its coldness.

A strangled, alien sound, half-gulp, half-scream erupted from Dennis. He left the ambulance, his walk turning into a run as he moved into the relative obscurity of the night, away from the core of activity. He leaned his head against the trunk of a tree but his anguished, body-juddering sobs travelled clearly in the cold air.

The doctor looked at Mag. 'Will he be all right?' she asked.

'I don't know,' Mag answered honestly.

She picked up Ciara's hand. It was cold, clammy and unresisting. She held it between her own two. With a strange rush of revelation, grief overwhelmed her and tears flowed down her cheeks.

With a needle-sharp prick of pain, she noticed her mother's charm bracelet on Ciara's wrist. She swivelled the bracelet around under her fingertips touching each charm as she did, the die, the 'love' disc, the treasure chest. She noticed that the deer charm was missing, the deer with its tiny gold antlers. It had probably come off during the crash.

Doctor Mannion laid a hand on her shoulder. 'Mrs Byrne, we are going to take Ciara to the mortuary in St. Vincent's Hospital now. Would you like to come with us?' Mag looked up, bewildered, unable to think. Before she could answer, Dennis came back. He and Mag avoided looking directly at each other, unable to cope with the grief they would see mirrored in each other's eyes.

'How could this have happened?' Dennis's question was angry and mostly rhetorical but Doctor Mannion tried to answer it.

'That's a difficult question to answer right now. I'm sure we'll know more by the time of the inquest,' she said. 'I don't know if it helps but death was almost instantaneous. A fall of that magnitude with no seat-belt…'

'What?' Dennis stared at her. 'No seat-belt? That can't be.'

'Well, I'm pretty sure that's the case.' The vehemence in Dennis's tone caused Dr Mannion to introduce an element of doubt. 'But if you want to discuss the details of the accident with Sergeant O'Brien, he's over there.' She pointed out a stocky, muscular man with grey, wiry hair who was in discussion with the tall, thin guard Dennis had spoken to earlier.

'I'll do that.' Dennis focused on him like a bird of prey sizing up its quarry.

'Now, I'm afraid we'll have to go,' Doctor Mannion said.

'I'll come with you,' Mag said. She couldn't allow them to take Ciara away from her even though she no longer knew where Ciara was.

'I'm staying,' Dennis said, his tone cold and distant. After his lapse, a shell had hardened around him excluding all outsiders and Mag knew that there was no way she could have reached him. As she left, accompanied by Doctor Mannion, her last sight was of him striding towards the sergeant, a single-minded purpose etched on his face.

1973

Mag was sitting on the upper deck of the number 19 bus to Glasnevin. She leaned her forehead against the cold glass of the window beside her and gazed out the hole she had made in the veil of condensation. It was January and it was an irritable day, blustering people along the street, spitting and squirting rain at them, glowering petulantly at the world. While she sat looking at the people hurrying from one indoor place to another, tears, held back for so long, started to roll down her face, burning her eyes.

She could still hear the recently spoken words of Sister Oliver ringing in her ears, as clearly as if she were sitting beside her.

'Margaret O'Donnell, nursing is the highest calling to which a young woman can aspire.' She had paused to allow her words to embed themselves and take root in this ground of questionable fertility. 'I am deeply disappointed in you that you are incapable of looking beyond your own personal discomfort to the succour you could bring to the suffering.'

It was a subject of animated debate among the student nurses as to whether or not Sister Oliver maintained her stiff, formal posture when she took a bath or when she went to bed.

'Sorry, Sister,' Mag mumbled. She was sitting in the hard wooden chair opposite Sister Oliver's meticulously tidy desk, gazing down at her folded hands. Waves of misery lapped over her but she had no other choice. She couldn't do this anymore. The blood, the pain, the wounds, the anguished eyes, the shaven heads, the silent acceptance were just too much for her to deal with day after day. The day before, she had been assigned to change the wound dressing on the oozing bedsore of an old woman whose every laboured and painful breath further dried and cracked her tongue and mouth. It had taken all of Mag's willpower not to run out of the hospital, never to come back.

'However, the fact that you are unable to do so indicates to me that, indeed, you are probably unfit for this profession.' Sister Oliver was not the worst of the nuns. She was strict and unyielding but she was rigorously fair and never spiteful but she believed with an unwavering conviction in the nursing ideal. This made it all the harder for Mag. She said nothing, her closed lips a dam holding back a flood of tears.

'Furthermore, a significant amount of time and money has been invested in your education since you started your training in September but if you are determined to turn your back on your nursing career, there is nothing further I can or will do to dissuade you from the course you have chosen. You may assemble your personal effects and take them from your room in the nurses' quarters today. Your final week's pay will be made available for you to collect from Wednesday of next week.' Sister Oliver stood and glided to the door, an unmistakable sign that the interview was at an end.

'However, Margaret, I would like to wish you every success in whichever occupation you choose to apply yourself to in the future.' The words belied every other sign that indicated her extreme doubtfulness as to the likelihood of this eventuality.

'Is this seat taken?' The voice took Mag by surprise, jolting her out of her thoughts. A tall young man who looked about eighteen, her own age, was standing in the aisle beside her. His eyes were half-closed and darted from side to side furtively as if on the lookout for some danger although his lips twitched on the verge of a smile. He had dark hair cut very short, brown eyes, long eyelashes and a round impish face.

Mag managed to forget about her anxieties long enough to notice that, despite the few black dirt marks he had on his face, he was, on the whole, very pleasing to the eye.

'No, it's free,' she said, although she did wonder why he didn't sit in the seat ahead of her which was empty.

'Don't ask me my name,' he said in a low voice, leaning slightly towards her. 'Just in case you were thinking of asking. I can't tell you. I'm undercover at the moment.'

'I had no intention of asking.' She looked at this stranger beside her, suddenly conscious of the streaks left on her face by the tears and tried to smooth them away with her fingers.

'Good.' He paused. 'I don't normally travel by bus, you know. Normally, HQ supplies me with a 16-cylinder turbo-charged Aston Martin. But not this time. Secret mission. Top secret. Have to pass myself off as an ordinary fellow. Toughest mission I've ever had.'

Mag decided that she was sitting next to a lunatic and decided to ignore him. She turned back to the window.

'Well, all right, then. You're persistent aren't you? That's a quality we like in the secret service. 006, at your service.' She looked at him closely.

Not a lunatic, just a fool, she thought, but she couldn't help smiling.

'Aha,' he said. 'We're always on the lookout for beautiful girls in the secret service. Can't have too many of them. Looks like you might fit the bill. I could put a good word in for you.'

She opened her mouth to react but he hushed her with a gesture of the hand.

'No, don't thank me,' he said. 'It's the least I can do. I've shaken my tail, thanks to you.' He indicated with a nod two large, middle-aged women carrying two bags of groceries each, their heavy coats wet and steaming, who were at that moment making their way down the stairs to get off the bus.

'Did you see them?' he said. 'The most dangerous agents the Russians could throw at me. But their instructions told them to look out for an outstandingly good-looking fellow travelling on his own. Now that they think I'm with you, they're confused.'

'Right. So now you can get back to your mission.' Mag wasn't sure that she wanted him to go but she didn't want to appear to be giving him too much encouragement.

'Not just yet. You see, that's the difference between a good agent and a bad agent. A good agent has to cover his tracks to the end. If you don't mind, I'll get off the bus at your stop and walk a bit with you, just to get rid of any remaining suspicions they might have.'

'I'm not sure that's a good idea.' Mag didn't feel entirely comfortable with this suggestion but still she hesitated to dismiss it completely. 'Well, which one is your stop?' she asked.

'Oh, mine was three stops ago so it doesn't matter. I'll have to walk back anyway.'

'Well, mine is the next one so do what you like.' Mag reached in behind her feet to pick up her bag containing her few belongings which she had taken from the hospital. Sister Oliver felt far away and the evening didn't seem quite so grey and miserable.

Mag was going to her cousin's flat in Fairview. Anne had said that she could sleep on her sofa for a while until she found another job and a place to stay. On the way to Anne's house from the bus-stop, Mag discovered that the frustrated secret agent was in fact an apprentice mechanic named Dennis.

It had stopped raining but the misty chill in the air reminded them that the rain had not gone far and would be back soon. Mag told Dennis about not being able to continue nursing, about Sister Oliver, that she hadn't told her parents yet. Dennis told her about his dreams to own a garage, to travel to the Grand Prix rallies, to move out of home where he shared a bedroom with three other brothers and get a place of his own.

She had been to Anne's flat once before but the streets looked different in the dim half-light of evening. Dennis, a native northsider, was from the area and took her there quicker than she would have found it alone.

They sat on a low wall outside and talked while the darkness grew, contrasting more and more strongly with the vibrant outpouring of light from the windows and the fuzzy glow of the street lamps. The conversation between them was easy and effortless like a well-rehearsed dance. As they talked, he felt a lot less like a stranger and they rushed to fill this shared space with stories. Every moment was delicious.

The door opened behind them, taking them by surprise. They had thought themselves as invisible to the world as they were oblivious to it.

'Mag, is that you?' It was Anne, her cousin. 'What are you doing out there? Are you mad? Come inside immediately before you catch your death of cold.'

Mag turned to Dennis. 'I'd better go. It was nice talking to you.'

'So, can I see you again?' Dennis asked, less sure of himself now that the stakes were higher.

'I suppose so.' Mag battled hard to suppress a surge of joy.

'There's a dance at the Metropole on Saturday night, if you'd like to come with me. I could pick you up here. You'll still be here, won't you?'

'I will. That sounds nice. I'd like that.' Mag jumped off the wall and picked up her bag.

'So, see you on Saturday then.' He stood gazing at her with his hands in his pockets. His self-satisfied grin was still imprinted on Mag's mind's eye after she closed the door.

Chapter 5

Dennis heard but didn't watch the ambulance leave. He wanted to lash out in anger and frustration at the world but he needed to stay in control to get the information he wanted. Two uniformed Gardaí were standing by the squad car, talking. Sergeant O'Brien was in civilian clothes. His grey curly hair, flattened on one side, gave the impression of someone called recently from his bed. The other man, the tall red-haired guard who had spoken to Dennis on his arrival, was listening intently to him as he spoke. The smoky columns of their breaths were strangely tinted by the flashing lights of the squad car. As soon as he could, Dennis leapt into a break in their conversation.

'Sergeant O'Brien, could I have a word please?'

O'Brien held up his hand to stall him.

'I'll be right with you. We've almost finished here.' He continued speaking to his younger colleague. 'Tom, make sure you stay with the vehicle until it has been entered and recorded at the pound. We'll discuss the writing-up of the report at the station later on today.' O'Brien walked towards

Dennis and indicated for him to come with him as they distanced themselves from the other man.

'How can I be of assistance, Mr Byrne?' He spoke calmly with assurance.

'Can you tell me what happened here? What caused the accident?'

'I'm afraid I'm not in a position to answer that just yet, I can only tell you what we know for the moment. We received a phone call at Enniskerry Garda station at 2.30 this morning from three young people who reported seeing a car that appeared to have left the road and crashed on the side of the mountain. They hadn't seen the accident happen. An ambulance was called and arrived at the scene within minutes of the call.'

O'Brien paused and his voice took on a more personal note. 'I'm sorry to say that your daughter was already dead when the ambulance arrived. From the head injuries, it's more than likely that she died instantly.' He picked up a torch and gestured for Dennis to follow him. 'Come with me.' They walked uphill on the road. Further ahead, on the left, Dennis could make out two stone pillars marking the entrance to a house not visible from the road but otherwise there were no other houses nearby. O'Brien stopped and they turned around. The spot where Ciara's car had exited the road was in a sharp right-hand bend. A narrow verge of vegetation separated it from a treacherous fall.

'Your daughter was travelling towards the city.' O'Brien traced the movement of an imaginary car with the torch light. 'On first impression, it seems that she misjudged the bend and the car plummeted over the edge of the mountain. It doesn't appear that there was any other vehicle involved.'

He led Dennis back to the place where the scraggly bushes and overgrown grasses had been flattened when the car left the road. 'If she was speeding, of course that would also be a factor but we'll know better later once we've examined all the evidence.'

'She wouldn't speed. Ciara's a careful driver.' He paused and felt his heart tear another bit. 'She was a careful driver. I taught her myself.'

'If she had been drinking, that might have affected her judgement as well. Young people often don't realise just how much it does.'

'What makes you think she was drinking?'

'Well, we don't know but we'll run tests. It might explain though why there were no skid marks on the road. She doesn't seem to have applied the brakes before the crash.' At the edge of the horizon, the sun was starting to appear and the outlines of the trees and cars were becoming black outlines against the sky.

O'Brien continued. 'Mr. Byrne, it's normal to want to know what happened to your daughter but I may be making things worse for you by telling you things before our investigation has followed its course. I'm sure that we'll get a better picture later of what led to the crash. Once we get the results of the post mortem we'll know if there was any alcohol or drugs involved or indeed if she had a seizure or heart attack that might have caused her to lose control of the car.'

The two men stood for a moment without speaking. Soon, the sun would rise and the world would come alive, behaving as though it were a normal day although, for Dennis, life would never be normal again.

Dennis broke the silence. 'What about her seat-belt? The doctor said that she wasn't wearing it. Is that true?'

'Yes, that's correct. She certainly wasn't wearing it when we extracted her from the car. But, even if she had been wearing it, it's unlikely that it would have saved her life. The impact of a fall from that height would have been very serious.'

Dennis understood that the man was trying to dissuade him from a pointless, circular 'if only' argument with himself.

'No, that's not the point,' Dennis protested. 'Ciara always wore her seatbelt. I've never known her to go without it, not even a hundred yards. It was almost an obsession she had about it.'

Eamonn O'Brien looked at Dennis, as if weighing something in his mind. A moment passed before he spoke. 'You are probably not in a position yet to answer this question but you might give it some thought at a later stage. Do you have any reason to believe that your daughter might have provoked this accident deliberately?'

Dennis stared at him, uncomprehending. He narrowed his eyes into slits. 'Are you implying that Ciara might have committed suicide?'

'I'm not implying anything. It's just that in the absence of any immediately obvious cause, we have to examine all the possibilities. For example, was your daughter suffering from any particular stress or anxiety at this time?'

'I can guarantee you that this is not a suicide. You didn't know Ciara. She loved life more than anyone else I know and in any case, I met her for lunch only yesterday and she was perfectly fine.' Dennis tried to bury a niggling uneasiness as he recalled her troubled face during their conversation of the day before.

O'Brien nodded but said nothing.

'What about the car?' Dennis asked. 'What are you going to do with it?'

'The car will be taken to the garda compound for examination to check for any mechanical problem such as brake failure which might have contributed to the accident. The car will be released to you as soon as that inspection is complete.'

'There's no way there was a mechanical problem. I serviced that car myself only three weeks ago.' Dennis could hear the aggression in his own voice but he couldn't help it. How could this man even insinuate such things about Ciara?

'I'm sure you're right, Mr. Byrne but we need to check everything out.' He buttoned the top button of this overcoat as a preamble to departure. 'I have one final question for you, Mr. Byrne. Do you know where your daughter spent the evening? Where she was travelling from?'

'I don't.' Dennis had not thought about it before. 'I have no idea. I don't think she mentioned anything to me about it.' Snippets of their recent conversation echoed in his ears but it hurt too much to recall Ciara's teasing voice.

'Well, don't worry about it but if you do find out, please let me know. Of course all of our findings will be presented formally at the inquest but insofar as I can, I'll keep you informed ahead of time.'

'Please do.' Dennis took a business card for the garage with his phone numbers from his pocket.

O'Brien took it and examined it briefly.

'When will the inquest be held?' Dennis asked.

'That depends on the date scheduled for the next hearing. It could be very soon or it might be as far away as two months. We'll try to have everything ready on our side for the next one. Sometimes it helps the families to cope better if it's sooner rather than later.' He nodded at Dennis in parting. 'We'll be in touch.'

Dennis walked back to his car alone. He opened the door and sat inside. The sun had risen fully now: there was no need for headlights. The Jaguar hummed into life and glided forward, cutting through the chilly early-morning air.

1973

One Saturday night, a month or so after their first meeting, Dennis managed to borrow his eldest brother Gerry's car. It was important to impress Mag and she wasn't easy to impress. She came from a fairly well-off family; her father had a good farm in Meath and he could tell from her indifference to material things that prosperity was the norm for her. With her calm manner and quiet intelligence, she seemed to take the good things in life for granted and this made him nervous. Money had always been in short supply in his rowdy overcrowded house but, until now, he had not felt self-conscious about it. In fact, when he thought about it, it was a mystery that she had accepted to go out with him in the first place. As the weeks passed, it became more important for him to match up to her expectations.

He spent ages trying to wrestle control over his hair before eventually overpowering it with a large dollop of Brillcreme. He wore new dark-blue trousers that had cost him half a week's wages and had borrowed a long trendy jacket from Darren that he thought looked like something the Beatles would wear.

Eventually, reasonably satisfied with his appearance, he left to pick her up. He pulled up outside the small, red-brick terraced house that she had moved into a few weeks earlier. She was sharing with two other girls from Kerry who travelled home almost every weekend. She had found work as a clerical assistant in an accountant's office on Baggot Street.

Without opening it, he vaulted over the small gate at the end of the path leading to the front door. He sprinted past the tiny, ragged overgrown garden at the front of the house and rapped on the door.

When Mag opened the door, he bowed low. 'Good evening, my lady. Your chariot awaits.' With a sweep of his arm, he guided her gaze towards the old, dark-blue, faded-in-patches Morris Minor parked on the road.

'Chariot is right,' Mag said. She stepped outside to take a closer look at the car. 'Does it have an engine, at least? Or have you put the horses out to graze somewhere?'

Dennis clutched his chest in agony. 'I'm heart-broken. You wouldn't say that if you knew the duel I had to fight to get my hands on it. Not to mention the barbarians I had to take on just to get an hour in the bathroom so that I could look this good for you.'

She gave him a mock appraising look from head to toe and back again. 'I suppose it was worth it. I hardly recognise you.'

She looked wonderful in a short skirt that showed off her perfect legs and a turquoise blue jumper that set off sparkles in her eyes. 'Well, come on in then.' She stood to one side to let him pass. The house was basic and decorated exclusively in various shades of brown. Why did every landlord he ever knew have a thing about brown? Was it to hide the dirt or to suppress any wild urges in the tenants to throw parties?

'I'm almost ready. Give me five minutes,' Mag said as she ran up the stairs. Dennis sat in an old brown armchair. A broken spring caused him to sink more on one side than the other. He picked up a newspaper. Ten minutes later, Mag appeared, looking exactly the same as when she had left. She stood behind his chair, put her arms around his neck and kissed him on the cheek. His blood did a quick extra lap of his body.

'Well, come on then,' she said, as if it was he who had kept her waiting. 'There's dancing to be done.'

That evening, they went to the Liberty Dance Hall where Phil Boland and his band played cover versions of the latest American songs. There, they met up with Mick and Francis, two other apprentice mechanics who worked with Dennis, along with their respective girlfriends, Martina and Jacinta. They twisted and jived in a whirl of good humour, bright lights and exhilarating rhythm. Shortly after midnight, Dennis and Mag collapsed into two chairs side by side, cheeks and ribs aching from laughter. Their eyes snagged on each other.

'Will we go?' Suddenly, Dennis didn't want to be there anymore. He didn't want to share her with anyone else. They left without saying goodbye to any of the others and walked hand in hand up O'Connell Street. For the first time in their short relationship, words were hard to find. The buzz of activity of the Saturday night revellers around them faded into a soft-focus background and the noisy clamour diminished to a gentle hum. The car was parked by the Garden of Remembrance. As they drove back, they laughed as they recalled Mick's deep-voiced attempt to sing Elvis's Burning Love while Martina rolled her eyes even though it was obvious she was delighted with him, but something was different tonight. Every touch, every glance between them was charged with a mighty energy that they felt powerless to resist.

When the car stopped outside Mag's house, Dennis felt nervous with her in a way that he never had before. He examined the M logo set in the centre of the steering wheel.

'Will I come inside for a few minutes?' He tried to ask the question nonchalantly but didn't quite manage to pull it off.

'Of course,' Mag said. She fumbled with her keys as she opened the door. 'Would you like a cup of tea?' she asked once they were standing in the shabby, brown sitting room.

'No,' The word came out strangely as if it had stumbled over his tongue on the way out. And that awkward 'no', stripped of any shred of artifice of ordinary conversation, propelled them into each other's arms. He kissed her face, her eyes, her lips with a passion he didn't even know he had. She put her arms around his neck. She pressed her body hard against his. Their tongues touched. Like electric eels, they danced and teased each other, sending jolts of ecstasy through Dennis's body. He tried to find skin. He pulled and tugged at her clothes to get rid of the layers between them. She, in turn, scrambled at his. He found a breast. As he held the soft roundness in his palm and touched the small, hard nipple, he had to take a deep breath to maintain a toehold on this precarious cliff-face of self-control. As dearly as he wanted to leap blindly into the abyss, he knew he couldn't, he shouldn't let go now. He rejected the temptation and held on tightly. He buried his nose and mouth in her hair, trying to absorb himself into her by osmosis. He almost cried out when her hand timidly travelled across his stomach and touched his hard penis through his trousers. He kissed her hard.

Suddenly, a huge void opened up in him that yearned to be filled. He pulled her skirt up and touched the lacy edge of her knickers. Now his self-control was stretched beyond endurance. Then, he heard her lungs expel the air in them with a sharp sigh as though she had been unexpectedly punched in the chest. She wriggled to move his hand across so that he could feel the heat and moisture through the silky material. This was the key. He tried hard to distract himself so that he wouldn't give in there and then. They fell on the sofa and made fumbling, urgent love.

For one minuscule, magical second, a miracle happened: their bodies fused and they became one whole. An upsurge of well-being invaded Dennis. So that's what sex is all about, Dennis marvelled when the moment had passed: an escape for just an instant from that feeling of lonely separateness that you become so used to that you forget that it's there.

After a while they started to feel the cold and they moved upstairs to Mag's bed. They made love again and then fell into a deep, motionless sleep. The next morning, they woke early and made love again in a more self-conscious, hesitant way to the sounds of the birds chattering at the windows.

'I'd better go,' Dennis said. 'I have to give Gerry back his car.' And still he lingered, afraid that as soon as he turned his back he'd lose his way to this newly discovered world and not find it again.

Chapter 6

When Mag arrived at the morgue at the hospital, she found herself in the midst of a large family devastated by the death of their mother to cancer. They sobbed and held on to each other, telling each other that everything would be all right in the end because that's what each one wanted to hear. Both their obvious grief and their supportiveness were intolerable to Mag who felt devastatingly alone.

After all the formalities were dealt with, Dr Mannion came back to see her. 'I think you should go home now. I'll call a taxi for you, if you like.'

Mag nodded.

'Let me give you something to help you sleep.' she said. 'Try to get all the rest you can. It will help you cope in the days to come.' She pressed a small, brown plastic tablet container into Mag's hand. It held seven or eight tablets and made a hollow, empty rattle as Mag slipped them into her bag. 'Take one to start with and if sleep doesn't come within an hour, take a second one, but no more.'

The taxi-driver tried to engage her in the standard chatter of Dublin taxi drivers: complaints about the heavy, congested traffic, the ever-escalating house prices, and of course the weather. Mag tried to answer him with the least possible number of words. She would have liked to tell him straight-out that she didn't want to talk, that she just wanted to be taken home but it took too much energy to rebel against half a century of society-imposed politeness. Eventually, a heavy silence fell in the car. They pulled up outside her house, now bathed in the full, cheerful light of a spring morning.

'Good luck, missus. Keep the chin up,' the taxi-driver called out to her as she closed the door of the car.

Mag was weary. Her system had become so overloaded with powerful emotions that it caused a safety device somewhere to click into place, cutting off her access to reality. She walked heavily to the front door and opened it onto a place that was both alien and familiar. It was as though she was looking at her house through someone else's eyes. She took off her shoes and dragged herself up the stairs to her bedroom. She took the sleeping tablets from her bag and placed them on her bedside table. Sitting heavily on the side of the bed, she stared at them, her shoulders hunched. She reached out, took two of the tiny beige pills and swallowed them without water. She curled up on her bed and, after a few minutes, cried harsh, hurting sobs that banged against her ribcage. She didn't think she would be able to let go but somehow her mind escaped her vigilance and she slipped into a muddled, disorientating sleep. A couple of hours later, she woke. The loss of Ciara hit her anew with full force and pinned her to the bed.

Long minutes passed before she managed to drag herself out of bed and into the bathroom. She stood under the shower, feeling the scalding jets jab and tingle her battered body. She closed her eyes and lifted her head so that her face was under direct assault from the sharp needles of water. She stood there for a long time until she heard the phone ring. She paused, wondering if she should answer. Finally, she stepped out, took her bathrobe from the hook and checked who was calling.

It was Kathleen Dwyer, a neighbour and friend. Several years earlier, at a dark point in Mag's life, Kathleen had knocked on her door and asked if she would like to join their hiking group. Mag had accepted. It had turned out to be a lifeline. Before, she would naturally have kept a polite distance from her neighbours and the other mothers at school but over time she discovered a new pleasure in the company of other women. Even now that she was much better, she looked forward to their Saturday morning outings.

'Hello, Mag. We missed you this morning. Nothing wrong, I hope.' Kathleen's strong voice boomed at the end of the line.

Mag braced herself. 'Yes, Kathleen, there's something very wrong.' She paused. 'Ciara was killed in a car accident last night.' The words resonated in the shocked silence. Was there any easy way to say it or hear it?

'My God, Mag. I don't know what to say. I'm so, so sorry. What a terrible loss for you. a terrible loss for all of us. I don't know how I am going to tell Sonia.' Sonia, Kathleen's daughter, and Ciara had been best friends in primary school. They had met on the first day when they were four and had remained friends ever since. She had been a huge support to Ciara during the difficult times of Mag's illness and her separation from Dennis. During those days, Mag had shied away from too much contact with Kathleen, afraid of being judged but over time she discovered that it was she who had misjudged Kathleen who had her own set of difficulties.

'I'll come over straightaway,' Kathleen said. 'I don't know if there is anything I can do to help but please tell me if there is.'

'Your company would be great already, Kathleen. It hasn't properly sunk in. I keep thinking it's all a big mistake and that she'll walk in any minute.'

'I'll be there as soon as I can.'

Mag hung up. Her knees were weak. She sat down on the edge of the bed. She got dressed without any regard for what she was wearing. Even simple movements seemed to require tremendous effort, like wading through deep mud. A few short minutes later, Kathleen knocked at the door. Mag let her in and they hugged. Mag could see that Kathleen had been crying. She looked over her friend's shoulder and saw Sonia standing outside. Her eyes were red and she was finding it hard to look Mag in the eye.

'Come inside, Sonia,' Mag said. Sonia shuffled towards her and burst into tears.

'Come into the kitchen, both of you. Sit down.'

'I don't know what to say, Mrs Byrne. Ciara was my best friend. I just can't believe it.' She blurted out the words through the sobs and running nose. Mag had never seen her so upset. Her calm, deliberate demeanour was the opposite in every way to Ciara's dark, athletic buzz of activity but they had been good for each other and even though they had taken different paths in life after the Leaving Cert, they had still managed to see each other reasonably regularly.

Mag handed her a box of tissues and they sat at the table while Kathleen put the kettle on. With a painful heart, Mag told them what little she knew about the accident and how she had spent the night before. Her explanation was punctuated by Sonia's sobs.

Sonia ignored the cup of tea her mother placed in front of her. When Mag finished talking, she mumbled through her tears. 'I was only talking to her on Thursday. She asked me to go for a drink with her on Sunday night. She said that she had lots to tell me but that she couldn't say anything just yet. I was delighted because she was being so secretive lately that I thought she didn't want to be friends anymore, now that she had the college crowd.'

'I know she treasured your friendship, Sonia. But what do you mean about her being secretive?' Mag asked.

'Just that there seemed to be things that she didn't want to talk to me about. For example, when she was telling me about the party she was going to last night, I asked if there would be any interesting men at it. She just gave me a funny look and said "far too interesting". I asked her what she meant by that but she wouldn't answer me properly.' She broke off to take a slurp of tea and to mop her eyes again.

'What did she tell you about the party, Sonia?' Mag sat forward to focus on what she was saying.

'Not a lot. She said it was in the house of one of her professors. He has a big house up the mountains, near Enniskerry. I think she said his name was McMurray. There was a whole gang of them going from her class. I know that Vincent was going and she was bothered about that.' The words tumbled out as Sonia tried to remember what she had said.

'Why did that bother her? I understood that it was over between them.' Mag's head was spinning.

'When she broke it off with him, he got upset. She said something once about him trying to tell her what to do. They had a big row once. I'm not sure what exactly it was about but I said that she should keep out of his way. She said she had to go to the party even if he was going. I was totally confused but she didn't want to explain. She just changed the subject.' The tissues in Sonia's hand were now a sodden lump although the tears seemed to be drying up. 'I got a bit annoyed with her and said that she should stop being so mysterious and just tell me what she meant. She said she promised to tell me everything very soon. But now she never will.' The tears returned and the last words were lost in the flood.

Mag leaned across the table and took her hands in her own. 'Sonia, did you ever meet Vincent?'

'Just the once. Last October. I went into town to meet up with Ciara and her college crowd for a drink in McDaid's. She was going out with him at the time but he wasn't very nice to her. He barely talked to her, he stayed with the lads at the bar laughing at stupid jokes and only came near her at the end of the night when he was drunk. He started putting his arms around her and showing off. I don't know why she put up with him. I told her to tell him to get lost but she defended him. Said he could be really nice at times, that he was just a bit insecure. Anyway, it obviously didn't get better because she broke up with him a couple of months later.'

'She mentioned something about him yesterday but I can't remember exactly what.' Mag frowned in an attempt to recall her words.

Kathleen put her arm around her daughter to comfort her and Mag felt a stab of jealousy.

At that moment, the doorbell rang. Kathleen offered to answer it but Mag shook her head. Through the column of coloured stained glass running horizontally beside the front door, she could see a tall, dark, distorted shape. She guessed immediately who it was. As soon as she opened the door, she knew Dennis had been drinking. The smell of alcohol drifted towards her carried on waves of animosity.

'We have to talk. We have to make some decisions. Get them over and done with.' Dennis pushed his way into the hall.

'I don't think now is the time, Dennis. You've been drinking.'

'There'll never be a good time so we may as well do it now.' Dennis's voice was raised.

Kathleen and Sonia appeared from behind the kitchen door. Kathleen nudged her daughter towards the front door.

'We'll be going now, Mag. I'll be in touch.' She squeezed Mag's arm on the way out and looked cautiously at Dennis. 'Hello, Dennis. We're very sorry for your troubles.'

Dennis glared at her. Kathleen shepherded her daughter out and gently closed the door behind them.

'Well, thanks for that, Dennis. Chasing my friends away when all they want to do is help.' She folded her arms.

'Oh, for God's sake, how was I supposed to know they were there? And anyway I don't want to listen to them. I'm sick of them all: eejits, full of pity and shite talk. What do they know about anything?' Dennis stumbled against the wall as he made his way into the kitchen. Mag followed him.

'There's no need to behave like that, Dennis. In fact, Sonia was telling me about where Ciara was last night. They had been talking about it a couple of days ago.' Dennis turned and fixed her with a stare. Mag flinched in the beam of his anger.

'So go on. Tell me. Not that you bothered to ask Ciara herself beforehand when it might have done some good. Fat lot of use it is, knowing now,' he snapped.

Mag recoiled. She felt his accusation like a punch in the chest.

'So…go on. Where was she?' Dennis's eyes bored into her.

'She was at a party held in the house of one of her professors who lives up there. McMurray, Sonia thinks his name was. I've heard the name before. I think he was supervising her research project.'

'What else did she say?' Dennis stood over her as if ready to pounce.

'Why don't you sit down, Dennis. You're making me uncomfortable. I'll make you some tea.' She tried to get around him to make her way to the kettle.

'For fuck's sake, Mag.' Spittle sprayed into her face. He mimicked her with a high, mincing voice. 'Let's all sit down and have a nice, civilised tea party. Fuck the tea. Ciara's dead, Mag. Dead.'

Mag winced. 'Dennis, don't use that language with me in my house.' Mag's pulse was racing but she managed to stand upright in front of him. For a split second, she imagined that he might hit her.

'Your house? Your house? Who pays the fucking mortgage? Not you anyway.'

Mag stared at him. Then, her face crinkled and sagged. 'I know you are going through a tough time but so am I. I want you gone out of this house when I come in again.' She slid open the patio doors and walked down the steps to the garden.

'Mag,' Dennis shouted after her.

'Get out, Dennis.' She didn't look back.

1973

She was pregnant. She had feared the worst from the beginning but now she was sure. In one way, the knowing was easier than the agony of waiting and wondering. The certainty banished the jitters and steeled her to find a way out. There had to be one. Her short nursing career had gone some way to make up for the deficiencies in her knowledge of sex, pregnancy and childbirth but right now she felt just as lost and terrified as she had when she got her first period at thirteen.

That night, she had been watching a storm from her bedroom. She opened the window to feel even more a part of the spectacle. Lightning whipped the countryside around their house with white flashes lashing out from behind a shield of black clouds. Thunder bellowed in response. It was right over her head. She jumped backwards as lightning struck close by. Finally, the clouds surrendered and released fat drops of rain, precursors to a deluge. At first she thought that the heavy dragging sensation in the bottom of her stomach was due to the tension in the air but now she felt a wetness. She went to the bathroom and was shocked to find blood. She had been struck by lightning and was bleeding to death. She wondered if it was too late to call for help. She was sitting on the bathroom floor trying to calm down her racing heart when Bernie, her older sister knocked at the door.

'Mag, what's keeping you so long? Hurry up. I need to use the bathroom.'

She opened the door. 'Bernie, come in. I need help. I think I'm bleeding to death.'

'What?' Bernie came in. She laughed. 'What a goose you are, Mag,' she said. 'This is totally normal. It happens to every woman every month. It means that now you can have a baby.'

'What? A baby! When?' Mag was stunned. A baby was undoubtedly a better outcome than death but it was still a shock.

'Not now, of course.' Bernie rolled her eyes. 'It means that you are able to have one after you get married. Now, get out and let me use the bathroom.' Mag suspected Bernie knew only slightly more than her and that she was cutting the conversation short to avoid revealing her own ignorance.

Later, when her mother discovered the panties with the stain Mag couldn't fully remove, she talked to Mag for the first and only time about sex although in such a guarded way that it took Mag a while to realise what she was saying. With her back to Mag, she stoked the fire in the cooker, testing the temperature.

'So you are a big girl now, Mag. You have to be good.' Her voice was muffled.

'What do you mean, Mammy?' Mag knew she was speaking in some kind of code but she didn't have the key to decipher it.

'That's enough now.' her mother said sharply. 'Come and help me peel the potatoes for dinner.'

Now, five years later, at eighteen, the little insight she had gained since then didn't feel very helpful. She understood the mechanics of how babies came about and even quite a bit about the physical changes that took place during the nine months of pregnancy but she had never spoken to anyone about the emotional side of sex. She had always imagined that falling in love would be like falling into something soft and gentle like cotton wool so it had been a shock to discover that it could be powerful and compelling. She knew that she shouldn't have done what she did with Dennis but it was as though she had encountered a force stronger than her. Anyway, it was pointless going over all that now. What was done was done.

One evening, she left work a little early and went to the garage where Dennis worked. She watched him saunter out with two other apprentice mechanics, all three still wearing their dirty overalls. They were laughing and joking, every so often giving each other a playful shove. Dennis spotted her on the opposite side of the street and waved at her. He parted company with the other two and ran across the road to join her. His exuberance quickly died away when he saw her face.

'What's wrong, Mag?' He tried to kiss her but she brushed him away.

'I need to talk to you,' she said, already walking ahead of him.

'It's getting cold. Do you want to go somewhere for a drink?' He was anxious to please.

'No,' she said. 'Let's go to the park.'

They sat on a park bench. Mag began to wonder why she was there. What could he do about anything? Still, she needed to tell him. While he waited anxiously, she searched for the right words. Finally, she just blurted it out. 'I'm pregnant.'

Different emotions fought for space on Dennis's face. 'Are you sure? How do you know?'

'I'm sure,' Mag said, although it was only as she said it that the last shadow of doubt was chased away. 'I'm a month late and I've always been as regular as clockwork. I feel sick in the mornings. My body feels different; I just know it must be that. It can't be anything else. I just know.'

'So what are you going to do? What are we going to do?'

Dennis's questions stirred up her anger.

'Oh, so you are affected by this too, are you? Well, go on then, what do you suggest?' She knew that her anger, masquerading as sarcasm, was unfair but it was beyond her control.

'Of course I'm affected.' Dennis paused as though he knew he was on the wrong footing. He tried to find the right words. 'We could get married and keep the baby.' It sounded more like a question than a statement.

'Don't be ridiculous, Dennis. We are eighteen. We have nothing, not even a place to live. You're only on an apprentice wage. How could we support a baby? My family would disown me. For God's sake, we don't even know each other. I don't even know if I want to marry you.' All Mag wanted at that moment was to rest her head on his shoulder, hold on tight and have him comfort her like a child who fell and hurt their knee but her outburst had the opposite effect. Dennis sat up straighter and took his hand back.

'Fine. You tell me what you want to do and I'll help in any way you want me to.' His voice was cool. Mag felt miserable but a stubborn, self-destructive pride prevented her from backing down.

'I don't know what to do. I just wanted to tell you, so that you would know. I'm going to talk to my sister about it. Maybe she'll know what the best thing to do is.'

'And what about me? Does what I want count for anything? It's my baby too.'

'No, you have nothing to say in all of this. You are not the one who has to have this baby and deal with everything. You're not the one that everyone is going to point at and think 'slut'. This is my problem, not yours.' Mag stood up and walked quickly away, hoping that Dennis would run after her. But he didn't. She even slowed down to allow him to catch up but she heard no footsteps behind her and pride didn't allow her to look back.

The next morning, after a sleepless night, she took the bus back home to Meath but instead of going home, she went to her sister Bernie's house. It was a new, modern bungalow not far from her parent's house, built three years earlier when Bernie had married Tommy, a local farmer. While Mag sat in her sister's overly hot kitchen, Bernie listened intently, feeding her older son a mashed banana with one hand and jogging the new baby against her shoulder with the other arm. Then, as Mag expected and half-hoped, she took control immediately.

'You should have known better, Mag but let's not get into that right now. We have to deal with the situation at hand. Let's think.' Bernie spoke as if Mag were a mere spectator in the drama to be advised rather than consulted. 'It doesn't sound as though this young lad is in any position to marry you and you can't have this baby on your own, it would be the death of Mammy and Daddy. It sounds to me as though giving it up for adoption is your only option. Now we need to sort out how to go about doing that.'

As she listened, Mag envisaged this baby as an unwanted, inappropriate gift which needed to be returned or passed on in the most discreet, tactful way possible. She listened to her sister planning out her future without interrupting her.

'Right,' Bernie said finally. 'We have to go home and tell the parents. They will have to know and now is as good a time as any. We'll just go and get it over and done with.'

Mag nodded dumbly, not trusting herself to speak.

Bernie took Mag back home, taking it upon herself to break the news. In the shocked silence that ensued, she outlined both the problem and the solution. She had thought it all through. Mag would go to stay with their Aunt Lizzie who lived in Offaly for the duration of her pregnancy and then give the baby up for adoption. It was sufficiently far away so that none of the neighbours or the wider family circle would be any the wiser and once it was all over, Mag could get on with her life, having learned her lesson. The solution was so nicely packaged and wrapped up that no one could find the heart to undo it. Mag's father thumped his fist down on the table before leaving to go outside without saying a word. The back door slammed behind him. Her mother's shoulders slumped. She looked instantly older. She seemed to have lost the busy energy that was so much a part of her. Mag wanted desperately to run away from this house, from this situation but instead she just let her head hang lower.

Bernie volunteered to drive her to their aunt's house the following day. Mag accepted with a nod of her head and went to her room as soon as she could. She muffled her cries in the pink candlewick bedspread, wishing she had never been born. When her mother knocked quietly on her door and said in a weary voice that dinner was ready, she said she wasn't hungry. Her mother didn't ask a second time and Mag stayed in her room. The clink of cutlery on plates and the all too infrequent rumble of voices told her that her parents were eating in silence. She tried to block out the sounds by holding her pillow over her head and eventually she fell asleep, fully dressed.

At four in the morning, she woke. She packed a bag knowing that she wouldn't be back for several months and then, feeling the pangs of hunger, went to the kitchen to forage for food. As she took a loaf from the bread bin, the door opened. It was her mother. Her eyes were red and her face was pale.

'How are you, love?' she asked. Mag raced across the room and threw her arms around her neck. Over the past horrible twenty-four hours, it was the first time someone had shown concern for her in the midst of all this.

Mag's mother, slightly embarrassed, pushed her into a chair. 'Sit down there now. I can see you're worn out and is it any wonder? Let me make you a nice sandwich and a hot cup of tea.' She busied herself with the paraphernalia of tea-making while Mag tried to swallow the painful lumps that had formed in her throat.

'Mam,' she started. 'I'm sorry about everything. It's just that...well, I never really meant for it to happen but...'

'Hush now,' her mother said softly. 'You made a mistake. It can happen to the best of us. The important thing is to learn from your mistakes and not make them again. Here, drink up your tea while it's still hot.'

Mag did as she was told.

'Now, don't you mind your Aunt Lizzie. She's not the easiest woman to get on with, she has a lot of rough edges, but underneath it all she's not the worst in the world and she'll look after you. You just keep on the right side of her and you'll be all right.'

Mother and daughter sat together until dawn, talking quietly, drinking tea. At eight o'clock, Bernie arrived, all business, laden down with her two boys and all the accoutrements necessary for their care. After giving their grandmother a list of detailed instructions to follow, Bernie hustled Mag to get ready to leave. Mag's father was nowhere to be seen. As she threw a last look around the familiar surroundings, Mag knew that home would never be the same again.

Chapter 7

Once, when Dennis was about ten or eleven, his father had laid a couple of large rat traps in the shed at the bottom of their tiny handkerchief-sized garden. The next morning, in one of the traps, they found a tiny solitary leg crushed by the iron bar, bloody and raw at the end where the rest of the body should have been attached. Dennis's father explained that the rat, desperate to escape, had finally chewed his own leg off. The sight of that leg had lingered with Dennis for a long time and now he remembered it again. He felt like that rat now. He wanted to lash out and hurt, even himself and maybe especially so.

The morning after Ciara's death, after he came down from the mountains he headed as soon as he could to a pub where he knew nobody and sat on a barstool, dour and silent, pouring whiskey after whiskey down his throat, trying to drown the anguish inside. Sometime in the midst of staring into the contents of his glass, reason abandoned him and a conviction emerged that Mag was not entirely blameless in the whole affair. O'Brien's questions about the possibility of suicide had reminded him of Mag's past and aroused dark, shadowy fears that riddled his thoughts no matter how hard he tried to push them away. If there was any truth to O'Brien's insinuations, then it was Mag's fault. He suspected that he was being unfair but he buried those qualms and allowed his anger to ferment into a desire for revenge. Bitterness and frustration built up inside him until he had to move to relieve the inner tension. He stormed out of the pub to his car. He had drunk far too much to be safe behind the wheel and he half-longed to be stopped and challenged so that he could punch someone.

He had driven straight to Mag's house and confronted her but now that it was over, he felt deflated and sordid. It was too easy to vent his feelings on Mag and he felt small and mean for having done it.

He didn't want to go back to the garage or to his small flat above it. The guys would all be working and he couldn't face their pity, the solicitude in their faces. He drove around for about an hour, eventually pulling into a carpark where he sobered up while he stared out his windscreen. Several people gave him strange, questioning looks as they passed by but quickly looked away from his challenging stare. His phone rang. He looked at it. It was from an unknown number. He answered it.

'Yes,' he barked, hoping that his tone would discourage any concerned well-wishers.

'Dennis Byrne? Sergeant O'Brien here. A medical examination was conducted on your daughter this morning. The official results of an autopsy won't be available for some time but I do have some preliminary findings. Would you like to call into the station to talk?' O'Brien's cool, detached voice helped Dennis find a footing in normality.

'Yes, sure, I'm not far away. I'll be there in half an hour.'

The Jaguar sprang forward powerfully under Dennis's hands, his sense of purpose distracting him from his wounds. The Garda station in the small village of Enniskerry looked incongruously like a cottage from a fairy tale. It even had window boxes with yellow and purple crocuses in bloom. It had originally been built as a residential house but inside, it had been adapted to the working environment it now was. A counter separated the public reception area from the office. Behind it a young Garda in rolled-up shirt sleeves sat on a high stool reading a newspaper. When Dennis entered, he set the paper aside and looked at him questioningly.

'Dennis Byrne for Sergeant O'Brien. He's expecting me.'

A fleeting expression on the Garda's face told Dennis that he knew who he was. 'I'll let him know you're here,' he said.

A few moments later, O'Brien appeared at the front desk. He lifted the hinged flap of the counter top and invited Dennis to come through.

The tall red-haired garda from the accident scene was there, talking to another man over the photocopier. He nodded in acknowledgement at Dennis as they passed by. They entered O'Brien's office, a small white-walled room lined with shelves and filled with papers and files. O'Brien removed a pile of lever-arch files from the seat of one of the two assorted chairs just inside the door and sat down behind his desk. He indicated the newly liberated seat.

'Sit down, Mr. Byrne.'

Dennis would have preferred to remain standing but sat down anyway. 'You said that they did a medical examination this morning.' The image of a scalpel slicing through the unresisting skin of his daughter rose unbidden in this mind and he felt sick. 'What did it show up?'

'Nothing conclusive, I'm afraid. She had multiple wounds and contusions on her body, particularly on her face and head, most of which can be easily explained by the nature of the accident. We can also confirm that the accident did not result from Ciara having a heart attack or seizure of some kind. On that front, everything looked perfectly normal.'

Dennis swallowed painfully. 'Anything else?'

'There was some alcohol in her system but very little. She probably had less than a glass, not enough to push her over the limit.'

'So, where does that leave us?'

'Well, it's too early to be conclusive. We'll be looking at all the evidence before we make a judgement. There is one thing that did strike us as a little strange. It appears that she wasn't travelling particularly fast.'

'How do you know that?' Dennis asked.

O'Brien took some large photos from an envelope on his desk. He selected one to show Dennis. 'You can see here that the point of impact is very close to the edge of the mountain. If she had been travelling at fifty or even forty miles an hour, we'd have expected that the momentum of the car would have brought it out further forward than that. It's hard to be precise about it but the experts think that she was travelling at no more than twenty miles an hour.'

Dennis didn't know what to say. The question of suicide hovered unspoken in the air between them. It felt as though a lump of ice had formed in his chest, obstructing his breathing.

O'Brien looked at him with sympathy. 'I'm very sorry, Mr. Byrne. Would you like a coffee or a glass of water?'

Dennis shook his head.

The phone on the desk rang. O'Brien picked it up, answering with monosyllabic answers and questions.

While he waited, Dennis looked out the window over his shoulder. Two old men had stopped to greet each other on the road outside. Although he could only hear a mumble of voices, he could imagine their banal conversion and he felt excluded from any normality of life. It was as though he had shrunk slightly and the outer envelope of his body no longer fit him quite as snugly as it had before. He looked at his watch. At the same time yesterday, he had been working at the garage after dropping off Ciara at Mag's house. He tried not to think about that and shifted uneasily in his seat.

'What about the funeral?' he asked, when the sergeant had hung up.

'I see no reason why you can't go ahead and make the arrangements now. The body can be released for burial in the coming days. Your undertaker can get in touch with the morgue at Vincent's.'

Dennis examined the laces on his shoes intently and waited until he could be sure of his voice before speaking. 'You asked me to let you know if I found out where Ciara was last night.'

'You found out. Good. Well?' O'Brien said.

'She was at a party in the house of one of her university professors, a man by the name of McMurray.'

'Ah yes, I know him.' O'Brien became distracted by a pile of papers whose equilibrium had subtly changed and was now threatening to slide to the floor. 'He lives in Clonballa

House, that's the big old house not far from where Ciara had her accident. The entrance is a couple of hundred metres up the road. I'll call in and have a word with him, see what he can add to our understanding of what happened last night.'

There was nothing more to say and Dennis stood up to go.

O'Brien led him through the open office space to the main door. He shook Dennis's hand in parting. 'Thank you for coming, Mr Byrne, we'll be in touch.'

1973

The news Mag had given him had torn his world apart. Afterwards, Dennis went home and tried to figure out what he should do next. Dealing with a situation as emotionally tangled as this one was new to him and there was no one he could ask for advice. Should he charge over, demand to be allowed to enter her flat and force her to talk to him or should he wait until she had calmed down? In the end, he decided that decisions might be best taken with a cool head and after a good night's sleep for both of them. The following evening, as soon as he finished work, he knocked at her door, determined to make her understand that he would stick by her no matter what. Catherine, Mag's flatmate, answered the door.

'Catherine, is Mag in? Can I talk to her?' he asked.

'Sorry, Dennis, she's not here. When I got up this morning, she was gone already. She left a note on the table saying that she had to go home urgently. I hope there's nothing wrong with her parents. Did she say anything to you?'

'No, nothing.' Dennis tried to appear nonchalant. 'I might give her a call. Do you have the phone number of her parents' place?'

'No, I never had to get in touch with her there. I don't even know if they have the phone installed.'

'I'd better go; I have things to do. Will you tell her to call me soon as she gets back?'

He walked home instead of taking the bus and tried anxiously to work out how he was going to find her. It was frustrating to imagine that somewhere she might be making the most important decision of their lives and there was nothing he could do to intervene. He had never met any of Mag's family; he didn't even know their exact address or her father's first name.

The next morning, he persuaded the secretary at the garage to allow him to call the accountancy office where Mag worked. There, the receptionist, who seemed personally affronted at Mag's desertion of her post, informed him that Mag would not be returning to work. A cold wind of fear blew through him and he had to suppress a feeling of panic. During his lunch break, he went to the post office to consult the telephone directories. He tried calling four O'Donnell's who he thought might be Mag's family but without success.

In the days that followed, he thought about Mag all the time, imagining a hundred different scenarios that might have occurred between her and her family, but in all of them she came back to him; she told him that they said they wanted nothing more to do with her and so she needed him more than ever before; or she told him that her parents had accepted the situation and would help them; or she told him that she had made a mistake, that she wasn't pregnant after all. But in none of them did he imagine radio silence.

For the first week or two, he kept expecting her to reappear in his life as quickly as she had left it. After work, as he left the garage, he would glance around hoping that she would be there, waiting for him. Sometimes, he didn't even realise he was searching for her until his heart would leap as he thought he recognised her in a slim figure of the right height walking ahead of him, light brown curls swinging slightly from side to side, but it was never her.

He called to her flat every second day until Catherine told him that Mag had written to say that family matters had obliged her to leave Dublin, that she was very sorry for any inconvenience caused and had enclosed some money to cover the time it might take for her two flatmates to find someone else. But no letter came for Dennis.

The weeks passed, the days grew longer until it seemed as if the sun stayed up until almost midnight. Dennis started to work longer hours. He found it easier to bury his head under the bonnet of a car rather than go to the pub with the lads and pretend that he and Mag had just had a mundane lovers' spat, pretend that he didn't care, that there were lots more fish in the sea.

He discovered that he had a real affinity with cars. They purred under his touch like cats arching their backs into his caress. They spoke to him in growls and whines of their ailments and responded eagerly to his ministrations. He stayed late, working through mechanical problems as though they were puzzles to be solved, enjoying the sensation of replacing chaos with order.

It was a time when cars were starting to infiltrate society in a way they never had before. Until recently, they had been status symbols owned by the rich or the obsessed. They were practically unobtainable objects of desire for the young. Sometimes young, single men would splash a few drops of petrol on themselves before venturing out on a Saturday night in an attempt to insinuate that they were the owners of prized vehicles and so, inveigle their way, through a girl's nose, into her arms before she could discover the truth. Now though, cars were becoming normal, even commonplace, means of transport. People who knew nothing about cars and who, deep down, feared them, started to buy and own them. These customers, in particular, sought out Dennis to get him to explain to them how to look after these testy contraptions they had just acquired. It was as though his appreciation of their hunks of metal made them more manageable, less inexplicable. Mr Sweeney gave him more responsibility, tougher jobs to tackle. One evening, he pulled Dennis to one side.

'You're doing a fine job, lad.' he said, looking intently at Dennis while he scratched his thick, brown, untamed beard. 'You've got a knack with cars. I'm putting a few more bob in your wage packet from this week. Keep up the good work.'

He strode away without waiting for a response but a step or two later, he turned around as abruptly as he had left. 'But don't let me catch you doing any nixers for any of our customers. You'll be out of here on the toe of my boot if you try it.'

This gave Dennis, who hadn't even thought about this possibility, an idea. On Saturdays, he started to fix the cars of friends and neighbours and his reputation spread. He saved the money he made on these jobs although he wasn't sure yet what he'd use it for.

By the end of the summer, with no word from Mag, he had to accept that she had decided not to have anything more to do with him. His mental image of her was blurring. He could no longer recall the exact shade of her eyes, he forgot the pattern formed by the constellation of her freckles.

He started to go out with other girls but they were pale substitutes. He moved from one to the other in futile defiance. It was not as if she knew or could know, but he would have liked the insolence of his infidelity to reach her on angry, crackling waves.

One Saturday night, a bunch of them met up to go to the cinema. Francis, one of the other mechanics from the garage, brought his sister, Kitty, along. She was pretty in a confident, hair-flicking, taunting sort of way. Her audacity made the other girls giggle in nervous admiration. She made it clear she had set her sights on Dennis and Dennis was flattered. She sat beside him in the cinema and giggled at all his jokes until they were hushed by the people behind them. After that, they started seeing each other regularly. She was good company in an easy, uncomplicated way and the weeks passed unnoticed until the end of the year.

On New Year's Eve, Dennis calculated that if Mag was still pregnant, then the baby would be due around about then. He sent his thoughts out like searchlights sweeping through the darkness but they found nothing and so, he set out to furiously enjoy the last night of the year, laughing too hard, drinking too much, dancing too roughly.

Chapter 8

Word of Ciara's death spread and a steady stream of people called to Mag's house, bringing enough stews, cold meats, sandwiches and cakes to feed any number of people during either the siege or the invasion they seemed to anticipate. Mag found a strange kind of solace in their company. Their presence was a light that kept the wolves of depression at bay. But after everyone left she could no longer ignore the heavy weight in the pit of her stomach. How had her life, which had once seemed so full of promise, managed to twist on itself so that now it seemed to have been a pointless journey through a barren land? And now the one thing that had made it all worthwhile was gone.

Before going to bed, she opened the door of Ciara's bedroom. It was the smallest bedroom in the house but Ciara hadn't wanted to move into the one of the bigger ones as she got older and Mag hadn't pushed. Ciara had painted the walls a gay yellow, a colour that had seemed a little overwhelming to Mag at first but afterwards it had grown on her.

She looked around the room. It contained a touching mix of childhood objects and more recent adult acquisitions. On her bedside locker, there was a blue desk lamp with a funny face painted on it and a half-read novel. She opened the old white jewellery box whose ballerina twirled and danced when the lid was opened.

On the study desk there was a framed photo of Dennis and Mag on their wedding day. Mag picked it up. She was looking up at Dennis and laughing as a hail of confetti fluttered around them. Love illuminated her face and made her beautiful. Dennis, on the other hand, was looking directly at the camera with a serious expression. He was holding her close with one arm around her shoulders as if he feared that she might disappear again as she had once before. How was it that something which had seemed so united, so solid that day, had since unravelled completely, leaving just unconnected threads?

She turned to go to her own room.

The next morning, Dennis rang shortly after nine o'clock.

'Mag, it's me, Dennis. How are you feeling?' Without waiting for an answer, he ploughed on. 'That's a stupid question, I suppose, but I hope you got a few hours of sleep anyway.' It was obvious that he felt awkward about their confrontation the previous day but didn't know how to deal with it. As usual, he would ignore the problem until it disappeared or until he had outpaced it.

'I'm coping. Thank you for your concern, Dennis.'

If Dennis detected a note of sarcasm, he didn't refer to it. 'I met Sergeant O'Brien yesterday afternoon. He gave me some initial details of what they discovered in the medical examination. As far as I could see, it didn't show anything in particular. It doesn't look as if Ciara had much to drink and she wasn't even speeding. This accident has me baffled.'

Mag didn't respond.

'Mag?'

'Yes, I'm here.'

'Anyway, the main reason I rang is to discuss arrangements for the funeral. I presume you're happy to go with Carters as the undertakers.' He paused. 'We also have to decide where to bury her. I'd like it if it was in Glasnevin with my parents.'

'Fine.'

'Are you sure, Mag? We can talk about it if you want but it makes sense. Ciara is a Byrne. Also, it would be easier for us both to visit the grave,'

'No, let's go with Glasnevin.' Dennis's driven energy was wearing Mag down. 'So, what's the next step?'

'I've already spoken to Steven Carter and he said that he would meet us at the hospital later this afternoon to decide on the details for the funeral. Could you organise Ciara's clothes for him?'

'I will.'

'I'll pick you up in an hour.'

'I'll be ready.'

When Dennis called to the door, Mag didn't invite him in. She picked up her coat and bag and turned to lock the door. In the car, she hardened her heart to Dennis's nervous fidgeting. They didn't speak.

The undertaker was waiting for them at the main reception area. He led them to a small, bare room beside the hospital chapel. Steven Carter was a thin, grey-haired man with a calm manner who listened more than he spoke. His sympathy was professional and unobtrusive. The arrangements were made quickly and efficiently. The removal of Ciara's body to the church would take place on Tuesday evening and the funeral would be held the following morning. He had already spoken to the mortuary officials and he gave Mag a blue plastic bag containing the clothes, shoes and handbag Ciara had been wearing at the time of the accident. She, in turn, gave him the bag with the clothes she had chosen earlier that morning, the clothes Ciara would be buried in.

After Steven Carter left, Mag and Dennis walked down the corridor of the hospital back to the main entrance, their hollow footsteps resounding in their ears. Outside, they stood at the top of the steps without speaking. Dennis took a pack of cigarettes from his pocket and lit one. Meg glanced at him in surprise.

'I didn't know you were back smoking,' she said.

'I don't know that I am. I just bought this pack in the pub yesterday.'

Other hardened smokers, some attached to portable drip units and wearing striped pyjamas, huddled together on the steps warming themselves with the hum of conversation. The bubble of silence that enclosed Mag and Dennis made her feel conspicuous. Dennis threw his cigarette on the ground after two puffs, crushed it under his shoe and then tossed the almost full pack into the bin beside him.

'Will we go, so?' he asked. He walked down the steps.

'I was thinking of calling out now to see that professor in Enniskerry,' he said when Mag had caught up with him. They walked side-by-side to Dennis's car parked at the back of the hospital.

'What good do you think that would do?'

'I don't know, none probably, I'd just like to talk to him, find out more about what happened that night. Anything that could explain the accident to me. I'd also like to have a look at the road in daylight. Do you want to come with me? You're good at getting people to talk.'

Mag hesitated. 'I don't mind going with you but do you really think that it wasn't simply a second of misjudgement on Ciara's part? She wasn't infallible, you know, Dennis.'

'I know that, but still, she was a good driver. She knew both her own and the car's limitations.'

'I'm not sure how you can find out what really happened. Ciara is gone and there's no one else who can tell us.'

'That's why I want to talk to this professor. He was one of the last ones to see her. Maybe he can tell us something.'

Unconsciously, he started to walk faster and Mag had to quicken her step to keep up with him. She slipped into the cool leather passenger seat beside Dennis. The radio blared into life when he turned the ignition. Mag, self-conscious, folded her hands in her lap. The idle chatter and meaningless laughter of the radio DJ filled the car and felt as inappropriate as the sounds of children at play filtering into a silent church. Dennis reached out and switched it off. Stillness reclaimed the suddenly empty space. They took the dual carriageway out of the city before exiting and taking the quiet country roads.

In the quiet, Dennis cleared his throat. His eyes remained focused on the road ahead more intensely than seemed necessary. His voice was gruff when he spoke.

'Mag, I'd like to say that from my point of view, nothing changes with regard to our arrangements. With money and all that, I mean. Ciara is gone but I have no problem at all with things going on the way they were before, not a problem in the world.'

Mag quickly glanced at him but didn't speak. She stared out the windscreen at the road ahead.

'The garage is doing very well, we have more business than we can handle,' Dennis continued. 'Money is the last thing we need to worry about right now.'

'Thank you,' Mag said.

'Oh I didn't mean for you to thank me for anything. The garage was the two of us. You were as involved as me in getting it going; you don't need me to tell you that.'

Mag knew that this was as close to an apology as she was going to get from him. She relented and answered gently. 'I remember and I do appreciate it that you've never made money a difficulty between us. We've had our issues but money was never one of them.'

A muscle in Dennis's jaw rippled but he said nothing. They turned the final corner and arrived at the same spot to which they had come early Saturday morning. This time, it was devoid of people and action.

Dennis pulled into the verge at the side of the road and cut the engine. They got out of the car and crossed the road. They gazed down from the point where Ciara's car had tumbled over the mountain edge. Very little trace remained of the accident. The car had been removed and although the scrub was still flattened where the car had landed, it was already making tentative efforts to spring back and erase all signs of human tragedy. Mag shivered as she noticed pieces of broken glass glinting maliciously in the grass. A large bubble of resentment at nature's indifference rose within her. She tried to swallow it away but it jammed painfully in her throat, blocking tears from falling.

'I don't think I feel up to talking to anyone right now, Dennis,' she said. 'You go ahead if you want but I'd rather stay here.'

'Are you sure?' Dennis examined her face.

Mag nodded.

'Well, this probably won't take very long anyway. Why don't you walk back to Sinner Magee's? It's the pub we passed a few hundred yards back. I'll join you there when I get out of here.'

'Alright. Don't worry about me, I'll be fine,' Mag said.

As she watched the car pull off, Mag pulled her jacket tighter around her. She looked out over the mountain side across the fields below and on towards the edge of the sprawling city. The brisk spring breeze was cooler at this height. The sun filtered through the patchy clouds casting rapidly changing patterns of light and shadow over the countryside below. The day was fickle and indecisive, unsure of what mood it wanted to be in.

Around her, she noticed the onslaught of spring which, in recent days, seemed to have suddenly realised the passing of time and was rushing around rousing nature out of its winter torpor. The new leaves shone with the luminous green of abrasive youth, the wild dog roses were blooming tentatively and the heather and bracken were starting to produce their confident purple and yellow flowers.

But these observations could not distract her heart for even a second. She put her hands in her pockets and tried to breathe evenly. An overwhelming feeling of sorrow threatened to crush her. She was about to turn away when something small and shiny in the grassy verge caught her eye. She bent down and picked it up. A jolt of recognition ran through her. It was the little deer charm from Ciara's charm bracelet. She knew its every contour as well as she knew the shape of her own hands. The tiny ring of gold welded on its back which attached it to the bracelet was bent open, twisted. She turned it over in the palm of her hand wondering how it had ended up here. She marked the place where she had found it with a large distinctive mottled stone.

She walked slowly towards the pub, in no hurry to join the normal flow of human activity. As she walked, she tried to imagine how the charm could have been lost but she had difficulty finding a realistic possibility. The ambulance had not been parked anywhere near where she had found it, so it couldn't have been pulled off when they transferred her from the car.

Sooner than she wanted, she found herself in front of Sinner Magee's pub. It looked like an old sprawling farmhouse. The windows were small and the door was low. Some people were sitting outside on an old weathered bench, optimistically determined to enjoy the occasional flashes of sun that came and went at a whim. Inside, the pub was dark and gloomy as Mag's eyes adjusted to the change in light. It was late lunch time and the pub brimmed with life. Mag made her way through the crowd to a vacant seat near a window. She was chilled to the bone. She ordered a hot whiskey from a young boy who anxiously repeated her order to commit it to memory. She watched his gangly adolescent gait as he made his way to the bar. He looked about fourteen.

She felt the deer charm in her pocket and turned it over with her fingers. She took it out and looked at it: a small familiar thing transformed by circumstances into something more mysterious.

The boy placed her hot whiskey on the table in front of her. A paper napkin was twisted around the glass to prevent her from burning her fingers. She cradled it in her hands and let the hot, intoxicating fumes drift upwards into her face. She swallowed a mouthful and felt it travel through her throat along her oesophagus until it landed in her stomach radiating furious heat like radioactive matter.

A shadow fell over her and she looked up. It was Dennis.

1973 - 1974

It was four years since Mag had last met Aunt Lizzie, her father's eldest sister, but she had a memory of a dour, difficult woman for whom religion was both a crutch and a justification. She saw life as a harsh training ground where the more arduous the course, the better one's chances of achieving the necessary fitness for eternal life. Mag's first glimpse of her confirmed that Aunt Lizzie was just as she remembered. She was making her way from the house to the hen coop when Bernie's car crunched over the gravel of the driveway. She placed the two buckets she was carrying on the ground beside her and folded her arms under her impressive bosom. She made no move towards the two girls and as Mag shut her car door, she could see her hitch up her arms to shift her breasts into a more comfortable position. The gesture was reminiscent of a warrior redistributing his body weight in preparation for battle. Mag dilly-dallied over taking her bag from the back of the car to make sure that Bernie would approach her aunt first and provide some sort of shield for her.

Lizzie was a small dumpy woman of about sixty years with steel-grey, tightly-permed hair. She had a round face with deeply creased wrinkles. Her small blue eyes were motionless behind her pointed, heavy-framed glasses. Her mouth was a straight line, so tightly pursed that all of the red part of her lips was pushed inwards. None of her features was objectionable when considered in isolation but it was an arrangement that held no beauty. It was as though the muscles underneath had been moulded by bitterness into unattractiveness. Her stance seemed to defy the world to call her ugly.

'You're here early,' she said, her tone managing to make it sound like a misdemeanour. 'You didn't waste any time.'

'Hello, Aunt Lizzie. No, we didn't meet any traffic and we found our way no problem, thanks to your instructions last night.' Even Bernie was meek and placating.

'Hello, Aunt Lizzie,' Mag said. She made no attempt to kiss her aunt, barred from entry by the folded arms.

'Thank you for taking Mag in, Aunt Lizzie. You are very kind. We all really appreciate it,' Bernie said.

'Humph. Well, she needn't think she'll be lounging around the house while I dance attendance on her.' Lizzie spoke as though Mag were not present.

'Of course not, Mag will be happy to help out in any way she can.' This habit was obviously contagious.

'We'll see about that. I have to finish feeding the hens. Can't let them go hungry just because some daft girl got herself into trouble,' she said, as if the two girls were suggesting that she should.

Mag and Bernie watched her retreating back and then looked at each other, not sure if they should follow her, stay where they were or go into the house and finally, through indecision, ended up standing waiting for her to come back. Mag listened to the excited clucking of the hens and looked around the grim functional square block of a house unadorned by any frivolity. Her heart sank. She was dreading Bernie's departure already.

Minutes later, Lizzie strode out of the hen house and, without saying anything, led the way into the house where she lived with the two youngest of her five sons: Des, a fertiliser salesman, and Michael, who worked in a sausage factory in Tullamore. The three eldest sons were married. Mag barely remembered her uncle Mick who had died when she was small. Her vague memory was of a quiet old man who liked to crinkle a sweet wrapper in his pocket to attract the attention of children passing by and then slip them one with a wink while his wife wasn't looking. He had been much older than Lizzie; it had been a late-in-life marriage.

Mag followed her sister through the front door. The downstairs part of the house was comprised of a kitchen with a large Aga stove against one wall, aggressively radiating heat despite the relative mildness of the day; a back scullery where all the laundry was done; a bathroom recently installed and a 'good' room reserved for the reception of the parish priest or other notables of similar standing. Through the open door of this little-used room, Mag caught a glimpse of stiff, high-backed chairs, bristly brown carpet and picked up a musty, old-smoke smell as she followed her aunt to the kitchen.

Lizzie banged the kettle on the stove to make tea. The two girls looked at each other uneasily and then sat on two chairs at the kitchen table, keeping a gap between their spines and the backs of their chairs in case they might be accused of lounging. From the wall, the small flickering red light under a Child of Prague in full regalia commanded Mag's attention.

'Don't leave your bag there,' Lizzie barked. 'I'll show you where you'll sleep.'

'I'll wait for you here,' Bernie said in answer to the request for help in Mag's wild glance.

Lizzie marched up the stairs leading Mag along a long, narrow hallway. There was only one small window at the far end which made a very feeble attempt to dispel the gloominess. Her aunt opened the last door on the right to reveal a small stark bedroom. Against one wall was a single bed with a blue metal frame covered by a well-worn limp patchwork quilt. A narrow wardrobe and a white chest of drawers stood at the end of the bed. Over the bed hung a framed picture of the Virgin Mary dressed in white and blue, head tilted to one side, her eyes melting with sadness and anguish. Mag looked away.

'Thank you, Aunt Lizzie. It's very nice.'

Aunt Lizzie grunted.

After tea and a few more formalities exchanged, Bernie left. That night, Mag cried into her flat pillow for hours before falling into an exhausted sleep in the early hours of the morning.

The following days took on a dreary, depressing monotony. Aunt Lizzie would wake her at six-thirty and, after a quick breakfast of porridge, tea and bread and jam, she would start her day. Poverty had made Aunt Lizzie believe in self-sufficiency and so Mag had to tend to the vegetable garden and the hens as well as the household tasks.

In the evenings, she sat and watched television on a small black and white screen with her aunt before being sent to bed. Sometimes, Des and Michael were there and, despite their rough insensitive jokes, she enjoyed their company but more often than not they were out late or, in Des's case, travelling for work.

Summer came and Mag spent long endless days on the bog, saving the turf for the winter ahead. This activity was new to her as she had no experience with bogs in Meath and, in any case, her father, a wealthy farmer by local standards, would probably have disdained such laborious work to provide fuel that burned away so quickly. The process was done in several steps. Firstly, oblong sods of turf were cut methodically out of the bog face with the slane which looked like a strange L-shaped spade. The sods were dark, heavy, full of water and imparted an odour of ancient plants as they slowly decomposed into an unexpected form of fuel. Over the following weeks, they needed to be turned to allow the sun to dry them out thoroughly. Then, they would throw the hard, cracked lumps into a trailer and bring them back to the little shed behind the house for use during the winter.

Although it was becoming more difficult to bend over, Mag quite liked this work. The sun shone warmly on her shoulders, the ground underfoot was pleasantly springy and she enjoyed the companionship of others as they worked side by side and ate their sandwiches and drank their tea together in the middle of the day.

Towards the end of this summer, despite the fact that all the turf had not yet been saved, Aunt Lizzie decided that Mag should stop going to the bog as she feared that her rounded belly might raise suspicions in the minds of the neighbours.

From then on, Mag remained at the house preparing meals, feeding the hens and doing the housework and laundry. Aunt Lizzie firmly believed that hard work never killed anyone and that idle hands were a temptation to the devil.

One interminable Saturday evening, while Mag sat watching the Late Late Show with her aunt, she felt the baby move and kick her for the first time. She twitched in startled surprise on her chair but said nothing.

Aunt Lizzie glared at her. 'Off to bed with you now if you are going to be fidgeting like that,' she said.

From then on, Mag started to talk to her baby whenever she was alone. Sometimes she thought that the baby reacted back to her but as she had nobody to ask, she couldn't tell if this was just her overactive imagination.

Winter burst in on them like a rude unannounced houseguest in the last weekend of September and seemed to lose none of its bluster in the months that followed. Mag was torn between wishing away time so that she could put this ordeal behind her and construct some kind of life of her own, and holding on to each day as a measured bittersweet moment left in the company of this baby that she would never get to know.

On Christmas Day, she got a phone call from her mother but neither of them was able to say much to the other, one choked by a sense of loss and disappointment, the other overwhelmed to the point of not knowing where to start. As a Christmas present, Aunt Lizzie gave Mag a full-length, long-sleeved nightdress and when she wasn't looking, Des and Michael gave her a bottle of perfume along with abrupt, rough hugs.

Five days later, Mag felt a subtle change in her body. She felt stiff and could no longer walk as freely as before. She tried to talk to Aunt Lizzie about it but the look in her eyes froze the words in her throat. She went to bed early on New Year's Eve and cried herself to sleep. Sometime later she woke, a dull pain nagging her in the background. After a few minutes, she realised that it was the baby making its way into the world. She crept along the corridor and rapped on Aunt Lizzie's bedroom door.

'I think the baby is coming,' she whispered.

'Well, don't just stand there, go and pack a bag for the hospital,' Lizzie snapped. 'I'll wake one of the lads and get them to bring us.'

Des, who had stumbled into his bed only an hour earlier, managed to pull himself together sufficiently to drive them to Tullamore hospital but not enough to converse. Aunt Lizzie sat beside her in the back seat of the car but remained tight-lipped, frowning and tutting at Mag's lack of self-control whenever she gasped or moaned.

It was almost six am when they arrived at the hospital. Des and Aunt Lizzie stood on either side of Mag to support her through the corridor. Mag tried to walk steadily but every so often a contraction would take her breath away and cause her knees to sag. The hospital was starting to stir and the preparations for the day were being put in place. As Des pushed open one of the large double doors of the maternity ward, Mag wanted to turn around and run away. Except she couldn't run and even if she could, she had nowhere to run to. She felt small and powerless. Unlike the rest of the hospital, this department was already full of movement and the hustle and bustle terrified her.

A large imposing nun presided over Mag's transfer to the labour ward which was carried out by a young, intimidated nurse. Mag was taken directly to the labour ward, a room filled with what looked like shiny instruments of torture, and put lying on what looked like a table. The nun, Mag discovered, was the ward sister and remained tight-lipped with no sign of compassion or kindness. She pulled down an overhead lamp with a practised sweep of her arm and, after a brief examination, gave a grim, satisfied nod that nature was conducting itself properly.

The pain was now coming in waves and, at its peak, was so intense that it blocked out all possibility of thought. She could only clench her entire body and wait for the pain to wash over her and subside. With one particularly strong contraction, she screamed out and the nun told her sharply to control herself.

'Is it normal to have this much pain?' Mag gasped.

'Perfectly normal,' the nun replied shortly and turned to the young nurse who had brought Mag into the room.

'Nurse Maguire, come here. Once this patient is dilated to around six or seven, please call me or Dr Moore who is on duty this morning. If labour continues to proceed at this rate, I don't expect that you'll need us for a few hours.'

Without a direct word or glance at Mag, she rushed off to attend to some other more pressing duties and young Nurse Maguire relaxed enough to smile hastily at Mag.

'Everything looks as though it's progressing just fine,' she said. 'Another few hours and it will all be over.'

'A few hours?' Mag wasn't sure if that seemed like an interminable time to endure this pain or if it was the blink of an eye before the baby would be snatched from her and taken out of her life forever.

The nurse patted her hand. 'Try to be patient.'

'Can I have some water please?' Mag said.

'Oh no, sorry, dear, that's not possible.' Nurse Maguire reacted as though she had just asked for a gin and tonic. 'We can't give you anything in case you need a caesarean.'

Six hours later, Mag was still in labour. She was exhausted. Her hair stuck to her head in a matted, wet mess. She felt completely drained in body and soul. And still the pain came back again and again. Nothing mattered anymore except for the pain to stop so that she could quench this raging thirst. Never had water seemed so desirable.

The waves of pain succeeded each other, closer and closer, until there was no respite in between. Just as it reached a point where Mag didn't think she could take it anymore, the formidable ward sister returned, accompanied by the obstetrician, a small elderly man with a lined face and tufts of fuzzy white hair over his ears. They both rolled up their sleeves in a resolute way that worried Mag immensely. Her anxiety increased as they proceeded to attach ominously-shaped metal contraptions with straps and buckles to the end of her bed. They placed her feet in them and tightened the straps around them. At this point, their obliviousness of her as a person was a relief. She had tried to persuade herself that this was not really happening to her, that she could drift away from this body and come back to it when it had regained some semblance of dignity.

She was soon snapped back to order by the impatient tone of the ward sister. 'Push, girl, push.'

Nurse Maguire came to her side and helped her to time her efforts so that they would have most effect.

A few moments later, the baby plopped out in a slippery gush into the waiting hands of the nun. The umbilical cord was cut. The nun transferred the crying baby to Nurse Maguire's arms. A rush of unidentified emotion swept over Mag. She had thought that she no longer had the energy to feel anything but she was wrong. Her arms itched to reach out to the baby but no one was paying any attention to her.

'Nurse Maguire, we need to see to another patient so I'll leave you to do the cleaning up.' The ward sister was washing her hands briskly while she spoke to the young nurse. 'Don't forget, this is an adoption case, so as soon as the child is washed and dressed, you can take it out to the waiting room where someone from social services will manage the situation.'

As soon as she was gone, Mag dared to ask. 'Is it a boy or a girl?'

The nurse was pulling a tiny white vest over the head of the baby. She was nervous, obviously unsure of what the right thing to do was. 'A boy,' she muttered.

'Could I hold him?' Mag measured out her words as if any tiny lapse on her part might cause the nurse to clamp down on this possibility.

'I'm not sure that's a good idea.'

'Please, just for a minute. I promise I won't make a fuss. Just one minute. Please give me that,' Mag begged, terrified that she would say no.

The nurse hesitated, convinced that this was not the correct protocol but she was weakened by the strength of Mag's desperation. She glanced at the door and then placed the baby in Mag's arms.

'Just one minute then,' she said.

Mag hadn't expected that he would be awake but he was. He peered up at her with serious, searching eyes as though wondering if she could explain to him what had just happened. They stayed like that for a very long time, for a whole minute or maybe two, until his eyes faltered and started to close. She leaned down and kissed his cheek. It felt like nothing she had ever felt before, like kissing the warm softness of a sunbeam.

This gesture must have worried the nurse who was hovering nearby because it was then that she galvanised herself into action.

'I'll have to take him now,' she said. 'The sister might be back at any minute.'

She wrapped the baby tightly in a small white blanket and hurried out of the room.

Drained beyond tears, Mag leaned back on her pillows and stared at the ceiling.

Chapter 9

As he watched Mag's forlorn, hunched figure, Dennis regretted that she would not be accompanying him to the McMurray house. Somehow, Mag had a knack of getting people to talk while hardly saying anything at all. When he was ill at ease, he became garrulous, answering his own questions and jumping in to fill any uncomfortable silences. He resolved that this time he would listen to McMurray instead of talking.

He turned left between the stone pillars and drove down a short lane towards the large house ahead of him. The entrance was not paved; it resembled a country laneway more than a driveway. A narrow strip of grass grew down the middle but the path showed obvious signs of maintenance. The grass beneath the old oaks and sycamores on either side had been mowed and daffodils flourished around their trunks.

The lane veered to the right and continued around the house to the back. A large courtyard at the front provided ample parking space and Dennis could see that two cars were already parked there; a black 645 BMW and a new wine-coloured S430 Mercedes. He whistled in appreciation. Nice cars. He parked under the shade of an enormous oak tree at the edge of the courtyard.

The large grey house had a plain elegance. It was three stories tall and had a facade endowed with many small-paned windows. It was obviously a house with a pedigree. Ivy surrounded the pillars of the porch at the massive white front door. Dennis took a deep breath. He picked up the heavy knocker before letting it fall with a solid thud.

A long moment passed and he was hesitating to knock again when the door was opened by a tall attractive woman in her early forties. She had a narrow, fine-boned face with a sharp nose and prominent cheekbones. Her straight dark hair was perfectly groomed. She reminded him of the austere grace of greyhounds that Dennis admired but couldn't warm to. She looked pale and tense.

'Hello,' the woman said. 'I'm afraid now is not a good time and we don't need any services.' She was impatient to close the door and get back inside.

Dennis understood that his casual clothes, muscular build and calloused, stained hands had caused her to mistake him for a passing tradesman.

'Hello, you're Mrs McMurray, I presume. My name is Dennis Byrne. My daughter Ciara died in a car accident on the road near your entrance this weekend. I was hoping to talk to you for a minute.'

Her face lost its composure for a moment as she registered his identity and realised her mistake. She glanced at his outstretched hand and hesitated before taking it. He could feel the long, thin bones, loose and lean underneath her skin.

'I'm very sorry,' she said. 'I thought you were someone else. This has been a very upsetting time for us. Please come in.'

'Thank you,' Dennis said, and stepped into a vast crimson red hall with a marble staircase that spiralled upwards. The perfect setting was spoiled only by a rugby ball and sports bag thrown negligently at the bottom of the stairs.

'I'm so sorry, Mr Byrne. You must be devastated.' Mrs McMurray's hands fluttered with nervous energy. 'Please go ahead into the sitting room while I call my husband.' She turned the knob of the door beside her and pushed it open.

'Max, come down now and take your stuff out of the hall,' he heard her call.

The room was like a set piece from a society magazine. Persian rugs spread across the burnished parquet flooring. A marble fireplace capable of burning whole trunks of trees dominated the room. Designer sofas and armchairs sprawled in a fake casual arrangement. Dennis eased himself into a rust-coloured leather armchair with a triangular headrest. He reached behind and removed a small tasselled cushion that was digging into his back. Despite the studied informality of the room, its comfort felt contrived, like a maiden aunt inviting her guests to make themselves at home with the full expectation that they would refrain from doing so. The only personal note was a large photograph on a canvas over the fireplace. It was obviously professionally taken and studiously casual. It was of Caroline McMurray, a few years younger than she was now, standing beside the trunk of a large oak tree with a man who was obviously her husband, gazing fondly at identical twin boys who he guessed were about ten years of age.

The door opened and a man entered, followed by Mrs McMurray. He was a tall, broad-shouldered man with short dark hair turning grey. Dennis estimated that he was seven or eight years younger than himself but he had the athletic vitality of an even younger man. His tanned handsome face was clouded and his dark blue eyes were red rimmed.

'Hello, Mr Byrne, I'm Colm McMurray, you've already met my wife, Caroline, I believe.' His voice was subdued, respectful. 'I'm so sorry about your daughter. It's tragic. I still can't believe it.'

'Neither can we,' Dennis said, bowing his head. 'Ciara was the light of our lives.'

'I can understand that.' McMurray nodded. 'She was a wonderful girl, dynamic, full of enthusiasm. An exceptional student too.'

The husband and wife sat down side by side on the yellow sofa opposite him. Colm McMurray was wearing brown corduroy jeans and a beige polo-neck jumper. Caroline wore wide-legged grey silky-looking trousers and a shirt in muted purple. As a couple, they matched each other perfectly and Dennis was impressed by how photogenic they were.

'My understanding is that Ciara was here before her accident. Is that right?' Dennis said.

'That's right, unfortunately,' Colm McMurray responded. 'I've been the year head for Ciara's class since they started college. My module had just finished up so I wouldn't be teaching them again. I invited the final-years here for pizza and beer. With the exams next month, and then the Easter holidays I might not see most of them again, I thought a little get-together was in order.'

'How was she? What kind of mood was she in?' Dennis looked from one to the other.

Caroline opened her mouth to answer but Colm interrupted her. 'I'm afraid my wife wasn't here last night. She was on a shopping trip in London for the weekend and didn't get back until the following day. But as for Ciara, I didn't notice anything different about her. She seemed in good form.'

'Hmm, I met her for lunch earlier that day and I got the impression that something was bothering her. You have no idea what that might have been, I suppose.'

'Sorry, I can't help you there.'

'So, nothing happened while she was here, no incident, nothing that might have upset her.'

'Well, I did notice that she had an argument with one of her classmates. Vincent Connolly. They were in the hall. On my way to the kitchen, I overheard heated words between them but I didn't get involved and I didn't take it too seriously. Young Connolly can be a little bit hot-headed.'

'Was that at the end of the night?' Dennis asked.

'No, it was sometime in the middle. They both came back into the room and I thought everything was sorted between them. They were both a bit quiet afterwards but nothing else happened. I doubt if their little spat had any influence on her driving, if that's what you're thinking.'

'No, I suppose not. I'm sure there's a simple explanation but I'd feel better if I knew what it was.'

Caroline repositioned herself on the corner of the sofa. She uncrossed and recrossed her legs. 'What exactly is it that you think needs explaining, Mr Byrne?' she asked. 'My understanding is that this was a tragic, but fairly straightforward, accident. The roads around here are treacherous, especially for someone who isn't used to them and at night too.'

'Yes, I'm sure you're right, but there are just a few little details that seem odd to me, for example, Ciara wasn't wearing her seat belt, apparently and that's completely out of character for her.'

Colm McMurray's eyes glistened with unshed tears. 'It's human nature to look for a rational explanation when the unexplainable happens. Such a waste of young life.'

Caroline looked at him. 'The guards didn't seem to think that there was anything to be concerned about, did they, Colm.'

'The guards were here yesterday,' Colm explained to Dennis.

'They said they might,' Dennis said

'Just a routine investigation, they said. They wanted to know what time she left, if she'd been drinking, that kind of thing. I got the impression they saw it as a pretty straightforward case.'

'A straightforward case,' Dennis repeated. He felt lightheaded and realised that he had eaten nothing for a day and a half. 'Now that you mention it, what time did she leave? It's strange that none of her pals saw the accident happen.'

'It was around midnight. They all left around the same time but I can't say which car left first or last. She might have been the last to leave. It was dark, they probably didn't see anything and just passed by. It's not as if the car was on the road.' Colm looked down at his hands.

'Have the funeral arrangements been made?' Caroline asked quietly.

'Yes,' Dennis said. 'The removal will be to Terenure church on Tuesday evening and the funeral after eleven o'clock mass on Wednesday.'

'We'll be there, won't we, darling,' Caroline said to her husband who ignored her and nodded at Dennis.

'Of course.'

A sudden pain swelled in Dennis's chest. He needed to leave. He stood up. 'Thank you both very much for your time and help. I won't keep you any longer.'

Colm and Caroline stood up too.

'I'll show you out, Mr Byrne,' Caroline said.

'I'm sorry there's not more we can do. We're all so helpless in situations like this.' Colm McMurray held Dennis's hand in a firm compassionate grip.

Dennis followed Caroline McMurray to the front door. 'Goodbye and thank you again,' he said.

'Goodbye, Mr Byrne, take care.'

The weather had changed. Dull, grey clouds had drifted in. A chill breeze had lifted, stirring the high branches, stilling the birds. Atomized rain hovered on pillows of air and rested on his face and clothes as he walked through them. He felt hollow, confused. He had no idea what he had expected or hoped for here but whatever it was drifted narrowly ahead of him out of sight and beyond his reach.

He drove slowly to the pub watching out for Mag on the road but he saw no sign of her or anyone else. The car park at Sinner McGee's was almost full. As he opened the door of the pub, the warmth of the atmosphere hit him like a blanket thrown over his face. He made his way through the heat, the laughter, the burbling talk, looking over the heads of the crowd trying to locate Mag. He found her sitting near the window, self-contained and solemn. Her absorbed, thoughtful expression separated her from the liveliness around her. She didn't notice him until he was standing beside her. When she looked up at him, he could see that she was pale and worried.

He ordered a coffee and a sandwich from a passing lounge boy and sat down opposite her.

'You look like you've seen a ghost,' he said and then immediately regretted his choice of words. 'I'm sorry, Mag. Maybe I shouldn't have left you out there on your own.'

'I'm OK. I didn't feel worse there than anywhere else. How did you get on?'

'I saw them all right. They are a funny pair, surrounded by everything that money can buy but not a set-up that I'd like. As far as I can make out, he invited over a bunch of students from Ciara's class for a few beers to celebrate the end of the year. The wife wasn't there; she was in London.'

'Did he have anything to say about Ciara?'

'Nothing much. All he said was that she was in good form and that she left around the same time as everyone else. Oh, and that she had some kind of a run-in with a young lad from her class. Vincent Connolly was his name.' Dennis gulped down his sandwich in three mouthfuls, barely chewing it.

'I've heard the name. She was seeing him a little while back but they broke up before Christmas. She told me that he wasn't too happy about the breakup.'

Dennis looked up sharply. 'She didn't mention anything to me about him.'

'I don't think it was very serious and she probably didn't want you getting worked up over nothing.'

Mag put her hand in her pocket and held out a small gold object to him. 'I found something strange up the road from where Ciara had her accident.'

He took it from her and examined it. 'What's this?'

'It was Ciara's,' she said. 'It's from her charm bracelet.'

'Where exactly did you find it?'

'In the grassy verge by the side of the road.'

'How did it end up there?'

'I have no idea. It's obvious that it was pulled off her bracelet. You can see how the link that attached it to the bracelet was pulled open. She was still wearing the bracelet when I saw her in the ambulance, but I noticed this charm was missing. The funny thing is that where I found this charm wasn't where the ambulance was parked the other night.'

'That makes for a lot of funny things about this accident,' Dennis said grimly and stared out the window over Mag's shoulder. The wind was high and torn scraps of clouds in varying shades of grey raced across the sky.

'There's probably a simple explanation,' Mag said.

'Like what?'

'I don't know. My head is spinning; I can't think straight. Let's tell the Gardaí. They'll know what to do with it.' Mag took a hankie from her bag and wrapped the charm in it.

'I hope so,' Dennis said. 'I sincerely hope so.'

They didn't speak for a few minutes.

'Mag.' He paused. 'When I met her for lunch on Friday there was something she wanted to talk to us both about. Do you know what it was?'

'No, she wouldn't tell me, she just said that she wanted to tell us together.'

'She wanted me to come in with her that Friday afternoon but I wouldn't. I said I'd consider calling over on Sunday. If I had, might things have turned out differently? Maybe we could have helped her with whatever was bothering her and the accident wouldn't have happened.' Tension prickled his skin and he rubbed his cheeks vigorously to get rid of it.

'There's no point in talking like that, Dennis. You could come up with a thousand 'if onlys' and none of them will do any good. All we can do is what we think is best at the time.'

'I know but I can't help feeling that I failed her somehow.' His voice was barely a whisper.

'You didn't fail her,' Mag said. 'You never did.'

A silence fell between them. It was a long time since they had spoken to each other apart from hasty exchanges of formalities. Over the years, they had maintained a facade of civility for Ciara's sake but since their separation, it had never been more than that. It was strange that they were succeeding better now that their reason for doing so was gone.

He could feel the quicksand of sorrow and regret starting to drag him down and he pulled himself up briskly. 'Will you show me exactly where you found the charm?' he said. 'Maybe if I see where it was in relation to everything else, something might start to make sense.'

'No problem, I marked the spot with a stone.'

'We should walk,' he said. 'It's not very safe to park on that bend.'

Dennis pulled the collar of his jacket up against the chill wind and the light, spattering rain. He thrust his hands into his pockets and followed Mag down the road. He was glad that the narrowness of the road and the proximity of the traffic obliged them to walk in single file. It gave him breathing space, a chance to chase away the bad spirits. He watched Mag's back as they walked and wondered how she was feeling, if her heart was strong enough to withstand.

'Here it is.' Mag stopped abruptly and he almost collided with her. 'And as I remember it, the ambulance was parked there on that flat bit of grass.' She pointed to a spot about twenty metres further downhill. They walked to the place where the ambulance had been and looked over the edge.

'I'm fairly sure what they did was put her on a stretcher down there and then carry her up at this point. The ground is quite trampled here.' Dennis was scanning the area, looking for answers when he noticed Mag sway. He put his arm around her shoulders and pulled her back from the brink.

'It's OK, Dennis, just a touch of vertigo.' Mag closed her eyes and leaned on him for support. Her face was now tinged with grey and she looked older.

'We'll go now, that's enough for today. It's too cold to be hanging around.' He took one last glance around them. 'Wait here, I'll get the car.'

'No, I'm better. I can walk, it's not far.' Mag pulled herself upright.

In the car on the way back, Mag lay back on the headrest and closed her eyes. He didn't think she was sleeping but she didn't speak.

He pulled up outside her house, leaving the engine running. When he asked her if she would be alright on her own, she managed a weak smile and nodded.

'You keep the charm,' he said. 'I'll tell O'Brien about it. I'm sure he'll want to talk to us about it.'

Dennis waited and watched Mag walking up the garden path to the front door before driving away.

1975

Dennis groaned as the June sunlight beamed down on him through the thin unlined curtains. His closed eyelids were no defence against its unrelenting cheerfulness. He ventured a sliver of an opening but regretted it immediately. From the dead arm dangling from the top bunk on the other side of the room, he could tell that Gerry was even less ready for this day than he was. Seamus, on the other hand, was singing with gusto as he patiently tried to find matching socks in the cardboard box they kept on top of the battered white chest of drawers. He was holding up two socks of different shades of navy to the light when he detected the small sign of life coming from Dennis's bed.

'Great, you're finally awake. Come on, get up, we've a lot to get organised today. The sooner we have a start on it, the better.' Dennis opened one eye but found Seamus's grin offensive.

'Getting married is turning your brain to mush,' Dennis said and turned over on his other side to avoid looking at the pitiful sight.

'Not a bit. There's nothing wrong with trying to look your best for your wedding day. And I don't want my family putting me to shame either. So come on, get up, this is the only day the three of us have off together so let's get fitted for these suits today.'

'Why can't we go later? It's Saturday,' Dennis mumbled.

'No, we will not go later. We'll go now and get the first fitting over and done with. It can't be put off any longer, the wedding is in eight weeks.' Seamus tugged on Gerry's lifeless arm. 'Come on, Gerry, get out of the bed. We're leaving in half an hour.'

A little over an hour later, the three brothers set out on their quest. Seamus's ebullience was contagious and their spirits were high.

'Please. After you, Madame.' With an elaborately gallant gesture, Gerry swept open the main door of Clery's department store on O'Connell Street. Suspecting mockery, the woman clutched the collar of her jacket and sniffed at him. Dennis, taking advantage of the open door, strode through. 'Thank you, my good man.'

The section of the store of interest to them was on the third floor, to the right of the wide, elegant staircase, away from the main crowds. One tailor was vigorously commending a client on his excellent choice near the three changing rooms in the corner. Another, a small, stooped man, stood arranging ties in a display near the counter. He wore a measuring tape around his neck and an apron containing the tools of his trade. A thick carpet sank under their weight as they progressed past the rows of suits hanging from several rails. Some held sample suits in different cloths and styles to demonstrate to customers and some had ready-made suits. They were greeted by the small tailor, a bald man with impressively bushy eyebrows.

'Good morning, sir,' Dennis said cheerfully. He pushed Seamus forward and slapped him on the back. 'We've come to see if you can work your magic on this man. If you can create the illusion of handsomeness for his big day, we'd be immensely grateful.' He lowered his voice to a confidential tone. 'Now we're well aware of the challenge involved so let there be no shame in admitting you're not up to the job.'

The tailor drew himself up and stepped forward. He addressed Seamus. 'Don't worry, sir, we'll sort you out with a fine suit. No-one will recognise you.'

'Now, we're on the right track; unrecognisable is a good start,' said Dennis.

'Don't mind him, every family has one of them,' Seamus said. 'I'm here to get fitted for a suit for my wedding and my two brothers are my groomsmen so they'll need suits too.'

A protracted discussion ensued between Seamus and the tailor on styles, colours, fabrics. Dennis and Gerry were bored and looked around for an alternative form of entertainment. The other tailor had disappeared and after Seamus disappeared into the changing room to have his measurements taken, the two younger brothers were left on their own. They wandered around, examining the rails of hanging suits. It was then that they saw the suit. It was a suit like no other. It was the kind of suit that would have looked perfect on the lead singer of a showband, a lurid, shining suit in a luminous pale blue with a darker blue satin stripe running down the outrageously flared legs of the trousers. The same dark blue satin appeared on the wide lapels of the jacket which extended all the way to the armpits. Dennis picked it up and held the jacket against his chest in front of the full-length mirror. He spotted a frilled shirt with a swirling pattern on the shelf behind the counter and exchanged a mischievous glance with Gerry.

A few minutes later, he sauntered out of one of the changing rooms wearing the outfit.

Encouraged by Gerry's laughter, he undid another button so that the shirt was open halfway down his chest. He pulled his hair forward into a quiff over his forehead and put on an exaggerated swagger as if he was on stage. 'Oh, sugar. Honey, honey. You are my candy girl and you got me wanting you,' he sang. Jiggling his eyebrows, he shimmied up to an older woman near the stairs who glared at him and hurried on towards the linens department.

'Did you see that?' He turned to Gerry. 'Mad for me, she was. She could hardly control herself.'

From the corner of his eye, Dennis caught a glimpse of two girls coming down the stairs. As they approached, he held up his hands in mock self-defence. 'Now, ladies, take it easy. There's plenty of me to go around. No need to get carried away.' His voice trailed off. His ears buzzed and he swallowed hard.

'Hello, Mag,' he said, all originality abandoning him.

'Hello, Dennis,' she replied. 'I'm glad to see that you've overcome your crippling shyness and are getting out of yourself.' She smiled to show she was joking.

The prim, bespectacled girl beside Mag hitched her handbag further up on her shoulder. She cast a look of surprised disapproval at Mag.

'Oh, you mean this?' he said, looking down at the suit and wished that he had never set eyes on it. 'We were just messing around, myself and Gerry here. You haven't met my brother Gerry before, have you?'

Gerry grinned and nodded at her.

Dennis continued. 'We're here trying on suits for the wedding.' A sudden panic gripped him. 'Not mine, of course. No fear of that! Seamus, another brother, is getting married in August, so we're getting ourselves kitted out.'

He stopped talking. He felt like a fool. He hated the way his tongue was running away with itself but the flicker of amusement in Mag's eyes had brought back, in a flood, all of the old feelings he had thought dead and buried.

'Well, if it's a rock n' roll kind of wedding, you'll be hard pressed to beat what you have on. You'd turn Elvis himself green with envy,' Mag said.

Dennis glanced down at the suit and laughed. 'I think Seamus would sooner get married in his underpants than wear a suit like this.'

The mere mention of men's intimate apparel was sufficient to push Mag's companion over the edge.

'Well, I've a bus to catch.' She turned to Mag, hand on hip. 'Mag, are you coming or staying?' she said.

'You go ahead, Sylvia. I can always catch the next one. I'll see you on Monday.'

Sylvia disdained speaking directly to the two men, throwing only a haughty glance at them as she sailed by.

Dennis and Mag tried to hold in their laughter until she was out of earshot.

Gerry put his hands in his pockets and strolled with fake nonchalance back towards the dressing rooms.

'So, what are you doing here?' Dennis asked.

'I work here. I'm in the accounts department. I've been here almost a year.'

'Oh.' Dennis's face darkened. It was two years since he had last seen her and it was a blow to discover that she had been back in Dublin so long and had made no attempt to contact him. His attraction to her clashed with his pride and reached an impasse.

Mag fidgeted with her handbag. 'I wasn't sure you'd want to hear from me after everything,' she said softly.

'How could you think that?' His voice was low but urgent. He glanced around before continuing. 'I've spent the past year wondering what happened, what went wrong.'

'Let's not talk about it here, Dennis. If you want we could meet up sometime, somewhere else, somewhere more private and then I can explain it all.'

'And why don't we go somewhere right now?' Dennis held her eye boldly.

'We could, I've just finished work but I thought you were busy here, with your brothers and everything.

'Oh, that can wait. There's no panic for that.' Dennis turned and called to Gerry who was studiously examining the ties through the glass countertop. 'Gerry, I'm off. Tell Seamus I'll wear anything he wants me to wear and that I'll come in for my fitting one of the evenings after work.'

'Right you are! I'm sure he'll understand the shift in priorities.' Gerry gave them a cheeky wink.

'How about going to Conway's around the corner?' Dennis asked.

'Fine with me but if you're going like that, I might be a bit underdressed.' Mag lips twitched with suppressed laughter.

'Oh, right, I was forgetting. Give me a minute.'

A short while later, they sat facing each other in a dark corner of Conway's, their drinks and sandwiches barely touched while Mag explained the tumult of the past year.

'But why didn't you let me know? I hadn't a clue what happened to you. For all I knew, you threw yourself into the river.' The thin hard crust over Dennis's anger broke and it bubbled and seethed as though fresh.

'I know, Dennis, I'm sorry but it wasn't an easy time for me. I don't know if this makes sense but I didn't think I could hold myself together enough to go through with it if I was in touch with you, even if I let myself think about you. I couldn't see any other way out. I let everyone down around me. After that, the least I could do was not make things even worse.' Mag twisted a hankie in her lap as tears dripped from the end of her nose.

Dennis turned his glass around and around on his beer mat, at a loss for words. 'I missed you, Mag,' he said quietly at last.

She didn't seem to have heard him. 'I tell myself that the baby has a better life now than he would ever have had with me. They say there are no children loved as much as adopted children because the people want them so badly.'

'Mag, you didn't have much choice. There's no point in getting yourself all upset over what's past. The best thing is to move on.' He lit a cigarette and offered her one. She shook her head.

'I know that and, on the whole, it doesn't get to me too much. Sometimes though I wonder if there's any way things could have turned out differently. I don't know how, but well...it's good to talk about it.'

Dennis didn't know how making herself so miserable could be a good thing but he wasn't sure he would ever understand so he decided not to probe.

'Well, would you like me to buy you a new sandwich, so? You've cried so much into that one that the bread's gone soggy.'

Mag snuffled a laugh. 'No, it's all right. I'm watching my weight anyway.'

'Well, that's the greatest load of cobblers I ever heard. Why do all women want to turn into stick insects? I'll never understand them.'

Their conversation moved back onto more neutral territory but even so Dennis was aware of a sense of impending gloom as he thought about ending the conversation and parting company. He stubbed out his cigarette, picked up his beer mat and carefully folded it over so it broke neatly down the middle.

'So you're probably off to Meath this weekend, are you?'

'No, I'm staying in Dublin.'

'I suppose you have plans already made for tonight. Are you going dancing or anything?'

'It's a possibility,' Mag said. 'A few of the girls have been trying to get me out to the new Tivoli ballroom and I think I might go along. It's been a while since I went dancing.'

'There's a good chance I'll be there myself. You never know, we might have a dance, for old times' sake?'

'You never know,' Mag said.

Dennis's heart soared with joy. On the way home, he felt like dancing like Gene Kelly in the streets but instead he put his hands in his pockets and whistled softly to himself.

Chapter 10

Mag couldn't sleep. She tossed and turned in her bed, exhausted and yet alert. Life without Ciara stretched ahead of her like a bleak, gaping chasm and she longed to escape into sleep for a few hours. Even the sleeping tablets had no impact.

Years before, a dull lethargy had inched its way into her life, suffocating her heart, her mind, her soul. In the years that followed, she had managed to recover but it had been at a high cost and achieved with a lot of help. Now, that same old feeling was creeping up on her again. Except that this time, she didn't have anything to live for. She felt as though she were living the last moments of a plane crash, watching as plane and earth rushed to meet each other, accepting the inevitability of annihilation without fear or even curiosity.

As the sun rose and the light grew, her eyes became unbearably heavy and she drifted into something that resembled sleep. When she woke it was after nine o'clock but she didn't feel rested. She got up and, careless of how she looked, dressed in a pair of old jeans and a well-worn jumper. She dragged a brush through her hair without bothering to look in the mirror.

She took a mug of tea to the garden and sat on the log-bench beside the rockery. She scratched at the damp moss in the crevices and thought about the events of the past few days. Scraps of conversation and phrases uttered echoed in her mind; faces encountered appeared before her mind's eye but she felt unable to make them connect into any coherent pattern. She didn't allow herself to think about a time before the accident: she wasn't ready yet to cope with the stabs of pain that accompanied the happier memories of the past. She wasn't sure if she ever would be.

Instead, she occupied herself with making mental lists of things to be done before the funeral, lists of people she should contact, lists for shopping so that she could cater for the mourners who would call to the house after the removal and the funeral. She forced her brain to run around in endless circles so that she wouldn't topple into the black, bottomless core in the middle of her world.

She heard the distant ring of the phone; the first call of many that would punctuate the day. She took her time going back into the house to answer it. It was Dennis.

'Mag, I hope I didn't wake you. The phone was ringing for ages,' he said. 'Are you all right?'

'Yes, I was in the garden. I didn't hear the phone.' There was no point in going into detail with Dennis. Despite his concern, she was nervous of him and needed to keep her distance.

'I was talking to O'Brien this morning,' he said. 'He said he'd like to meet us to discuss what we found. He said that he could call in to your house on his way into town. Does that suit you?'

'Fine, I wasn't planning on going anywhere. What time will he be here?'

'He said it would be around twelve. I have one or two things to do here in the garage but I should be there in plenty of time.'

Mag hung up and went to the kitchen. Sunlight was pouring in through the patio doors and she felt momentarily dazzled. The note of worry in Dennis's voice and the memory of his supportive arm the previous day made Mag agitated. Was it merely the normal concern that any human being feels for another in a time of bereavement or was Dennis looking for comfort in a familiar haven? She had thought the old feelings of love completely extinguished but his concern had blown away the ashes and underneath a tiny spark still existed. Almost ten years had passed since that terrible day which had turned their lives upside down. Since then distant, veiled politeness was the best they had achieved. Would it take the death of their daughter for them to find forgiveness and tolerance in each other?

A cynical voice of reason mocked her. He probably feared that she was on the verge of another breakdown and that was the last thing he must feel like handling right now. And yet it helped to share these painful moments with someone who had loved Ciara as much as she had. It didn't feel right to speak in the past tense about loving Ciara. The love was still there, just as strong as ever. It hadn't vanished; it simply had nowhere to go anymore. It circled around inside her body ravaging her, gnawing at her relentlessly.

When she answered the door to Dennis later that morning, she was shocked at how this experience was affecting him. His face was drawn, his eyes dull and his shoulders drooped. She had never thought of Dennis as middle-aged but now she could see that time was taking its toll; his buoyant invincibility was crumbling.

'You didn't sleep, did you?' she asked.

'Not much,' he said. 'Did you?'

'No. Come on through to the kitchen. I'll make you something to eat. You probably haven't been eating either.'

'I couldn't, I've no interest in food, Mag. I don't think my stomach could take it.'

'Come on, you have to eat something. It'll serve no purpose to starve ourselves.'

It was easier advice to give than to take. She had subsisted on cups of tea and slices of toast since the first glimpse of Dennis's grim white face when he got out of his car early on Saturday morning.

At the table, Dennis automatically sat at the place he used to occupy before. Mag took sausages, rashers and eggs from the fridge. She put on the kettle and turned on the grill. She cut a couple of slices of the homemade brown bread dropped in by old Mrs Fogarty from around the corner who had hobbled to the door and pressed it into her hands with a heartfelt sympathy she couldn't express in words. She melted butter in a frying pan and cooked some small button mushrooms, adding a dash of lemon and a pinch of salt at the end. She put a mug of tea in front of Dennis while she continued to prepare the breakfast. She set the table and put two plates in the oven to warm. She put the teapot on the table swaddled by the funny-face tea-cosy Ciara had made years before in a home economics class. She divided the food between their plates, giving the lion's share to Dennis before sitting down.

Despite Dennis's protests, he ate everything on his plate as well as two large slices of brown bread. Mag ate one sausage, half-heartedly dipping a piece of bread into the runny yoke of her fried egg.

'I've often said it before and it can't be denied. You're a fine cook, Mag.' Dennis pushed his empty plate away and sat back in his chair.

Mag laughed despite herself. 'And I think there is a fair amount of agreement on the fact that you talk a lot of rubbish. I don't think that frying an egg and a sausage qualifies as a serious test of a person's culinary abilities.'

Dennis gave her a mischievous look. 'Well, I think I could move you up into my three-star category if there happened to be a slice of your tea brack available.'

Mag stopped laughing. She dropped her fork with a clatter and stared into her plate.

'Mag?' Dennis said hesitantly. 'I was only joking. I didn't mean it.'

'That's the problem.' She put her elbows on the table and covered her face with her hands. Her voice was muffled by the lump in her throat. 'How can we joke; how can we laugh when we've just lost Ciara? She was the most important thing in my life, Dennis, the best thing I've ever done? For a second, I forget that she is gone and then it comes back and hits me all over again.' She covered her face with her hands, her chin buried in her chest. 'I just don't know if I can cope. I just don't know if I can get through this,' she said quietly without looking at Dennis.

'What can I say, Mag? I don't know either. I feel guilty too for eating that food, for the fact that my stomach wanted it. I feel guilty for every 'normal' reaction I have. I don't know the answers; we just have to take things slowly, cope any way we can.'

Mag lifted her head. 'I don't even know what it is I want. On the one hand, I don't want to 'get on with life' but neither do I want this pain to continue forever. Sometimes, I think it connects me to her, that it's better than nothing and yet, I don't know if I can survive feeling this way for long. It's tearing me apart. I can't see any way out. Nothing can ever be right again.'

Dennis looked down into his plate, miserable and mute. Mag wished she hadn't said anything. She was making Dennis feel worse. Maybe he had the right attitude. Maybe the best thing was to focus on the present moment and not look either forward or back. Maybe he had always been right.

She pushed her chair away from the table with a noisy screech and stood up. She put the dirty plates in the dishwasher. Dennis started to clear the table. An embarrassed silence hovered over them and it came as a relief when the doorbell rang.

In the hallway, she took a quick look in the mirror and smoothed her hair down into what she hoped was a presentable state.

Although he wasn't wearing a uniform, the stocky grey-haired man on the doorstep exuded an aura of authority, of official presence. Mag remembered him from the scene of the accident.

'Come in, Sergeant O'Brien. Thank you for coming,' she said.

'It's not a problem, Mrs Byrne. I'm happy to come here if it makes it easier for you.' He waited politely for her to close the door and lead the way into the sitting room. Dennis joined them. The two men acknowledged each other with a nod.

'Please sit down, Sergeant,' Mag said. She sat in her favourite armchair, a high-backed chair which gave her a view of the garden through the large bay window. From the top of the piano, several photos of Ciara at different ages looked down at them; a small, chubby three-year-old; a delighted and proud five-year-old cycling her first two-wheeled bicycle; a young teenager, newly-developing and self-conscious, her hand at her forehead to shield her eyes from the sun; and a more recent one of a smiling and confident Ciara taken the previous summer when she had gone on holiday with friends. She moved the angle of her chair so she couldn't see them anymore.

O'Brien sat on the edge of the sofa and took a small flap notebook from the inside breast pocket of his jacket. Dennis, having difficulty deciding where to sit, paced the length of the room before installing himself in an old brown leather armchair.

'As I understand it, Mrs Byrne, from my conversation this morning with your husband, you returned to the scene of the accident yesterday. Is that right?'

'Yes, Sergeant.'

'And while you were there you discovered an item belonging to your daughter. Is that correct?'

'Yes, I found one of the charms from Ciara's bracelet. I saw that it was missing on the night of the accident when I saw Ciara in the ambulance...' Mag stopped talking and took a deep breath.

'Take your time, Mrs Byrne.' O'Brien looked up from his notebook. 'Where exactly did you find it?'

'In the grassy verge, close to where the accident happened,' Mag said.

Dennis interrupted. 'I estimated that it was about twenty or thirty metres uphill from the tracks where her car left the road.'

'I didn't think you were there, Mr Byrne,' O'Brien said levelly.

'I wasn't with Mag at the time that she found it but afterwards, she showed me exactly where she found it,' Dennis replied. 'What we thought was odd was that it wasn't anywhere near where the ambulance was parked. I can't figure out how it ended up there.'

'May I see the object in question?' O'Brien addressed Mag directly.

'I'll go and get it. It's upstairs.' Mag stood up and left the room. When she returned a minute later she had the impression that no word had been spoken during her absence. The two men were waiting for her in a reluctant truce.

She held out the charm to O'Brien who took it and examined it.

'It looks like it got torn off,' he said. 'What time was it that you found it?'

'I'd say it was around two o'clock yesterday afternoon.' Mag frowned. 'It was two-thirty when you got to the pub after seeing the McMurrays, wasn't that it, Dennis? And I found it about half an hour before that.'

O'Brien looked up sharply at Dennis. 'And what, might I ask, were you doing in the McMurray house?'

'I wanted to talk to them about what happened to Ciara the night of her accident.'

'That, Mr Byrne, is our job. You don't seem to realise that this is an official investigation.'

'Ciara was my daughter. I have a right to know what caused her death.'

'Indeed you do and you will be informed in due course. What you do not have the right to do is hinder and obstruct us in our enquiries.' O'Brien bristled at Dennis's indignation.

Mag looked from one man to the other and a sense of foreboding filled her. 'We're very sorry, Sergeant, if we have intruded. It certainly wasn't our intention.'

Dennis glared at her and turned back to O'Brien. 'Your enquiries? And what exactly do they consist of? As far as I can see, you asked a few routine questions and that's about it. We found the charm, not you. I don't get the impression that you are taking my concerns about Ciara not wearing her seat-belt seriously.'

'It is not our custom to discuss our investigative methods with the general public.'

Dennis looked ready to explode and Mag intervened. 'So what about the charm? The main question I have is: did it get there before or after the accident?'

'I couldn't possibly put forward a theory on that at the moment.' O'Brien was offended. 'All I can say is that we will be fully investigating the matter and all aspects of the case will be given due consideration and taken into account within the wider context of all information at our disposal.'

'You're hiding behind the jargon. Are you saying that you see something suspicious in Ciara's accident or not?' Dennis said impatiently.

'Suspicious is not the word I would use.' O'Brien encompassed both of them in his gaze. 'Let me make something clear to you both. This is an official investigation and I ask you not to interfere in any way. Involvement of this kind can only be detrimental to our work. And that means not interfering with any witnesses or other persons involved and not holding on to potentially relevant information for almost twenty-four hours before notifying us.'

'I understand your position, Sergeant. I apologise for any hassle we might have caused. Do you have any idea when the post-mortem or inquest will take place?' Mag said.

O'Brien turned to answer her question and as he did his gaze lingered for an instant over the photos of Ciara on the piano. His tone softened. 'It depends. I'm hoping that our investigation will be completed and our report prepared on time for the next scheduled hearings at the beginning of May. If not, then it could take a month longer. The purpose of the inquest is to pronounce the official cause of death but all of the details will be made known to you in advance of the proceedings.'

'So you'll keep us informed as you go?' Dennis asked.

'In so far as I can. Mr Byrne, we are fully aware of the trauma you are undergoing and you have our deepest sympathies but I respectfully ask you to trust us to do our job correctly.' O'Brien stood up. 'I'd better be off now. I have a meeting in Pearse Street Station. Thank you both for your time.'

Mag showed him to the door. As soon as it clicked shut, Dennis exploded.

'Bloody Gardaí. Good for nothing, a waste of space! I can't believe it. We find the charm and then he blames us because they didn't find it themselves.' He stormed through the room and slammed his fist on the oak cabinet at the other end.

'Calm down, Dennis. The man's doing his best.' Mag said.

'Well, his best just isn't good enough. All he cares about is ticking off the right boxes on the forms, filling in official reports until some judge stamps the whole thing and then they can file it away and forget about it. The last thing he wants is to complicate life for himself.'

'Dennis, I think you're being hard. He struck me as a man who takes his job seriously.'

'You would say that.' Dennis was pacing around the sitting room like a caged tiger. 'That's what you want to believe but they don't care about us, they don't care about Ciara. They don't care about knowing the truth. All they want is a peaceful life. For them, the sooner the better the whole thing blows over so that that they can get back to handing out fucking parking tickets or whatever it is that they do with the rest of their time.'

Mag wanted Dennis to go. His anger was stressful and she could feel the onset of a bad headache flickering over her right eye. 'Stop shouting. I think you're getting carried away, Dennis. It doesn't help to get worked up like this.'

'Worked up?! Of course, I'm bloody well worked up. How could I not be? I've lost my daughter and I want to know how and why. And if you cared about Ciara, you'd want to know too.'

That was it. He had gone too far. She was shaking when she stood up. 'How dare you question my feelings for Ciara? I've had enough from you, Dennis. You trample like a bulldozer over other people's lives and feelings just because for once it's you that's hurt. Go away and leave me alone.'

'That's right, run away like you always have. It shouldn't surprise me.' Dennis grabbed his jacket roughly from the coat-rack in the hall and fumbled to open the front door. Splotches of red had appeared on his neck and twisted veins stood out like ropes.

Mag was so choked with anger and bitterness that she could say nothing.

Dennis slammed the door shut and a moment later, Mag heard the Jaguar rev noisily in protest at Dennis's brutal acceleration.

She sank onto the tapestry stool beside the phone table in the hall. Her headache was now pulsing through her brain and she found it hard to think. She was even angrier at herself than at Dennis. She should never have trusted him. She shouldn't have let her defences down so quickly. What had made her think that he was changed, that now he might understand?

1979

Mag was sitting, feet tucked in under her, on the sagging sofa of her Baggot Street flat with a large mug of tea and the Sunday newspaper when the doorbell rang or rather trumpeted in short repeated blasts. It was Dennis.

'Come on.' A kiss landed on her lips. 'Get ready. I'm taking you to the sea for the day.'

'What on earth are you plotting now?' Mag said, half-delighted, half-bewildered by the appearance of this gust of energy whirling around her flat.

'Come on, get dressed, or I'll have to take these pyjamas off you myself and then we'll never get there.' He kissed her again. 'Hmmm, maybe we should move on to plan B in any case.'

Mag laughed and disentangled herself. 'I swear; you have a one-track mind. I wouldn't mind knowing what plan A is first. Where exactly are you planning on going?'

'Wexford. Kilmore Quay, to be precise. That's where my granny lived before she moved to Dublin. It's a fantastic place, you'll love it. Now come on, get ready.'

Mag could feel herself becoming infected by his enthusiasm. She leaned over the back of the sofa and pulled back the net curtains to look out the window. 'So what will I wear? Is it cold out?'

'Looks good for the moment but this is Ireland, Mag. There'll surely be a bit of rain, sun and wind so come prepared for the lot. And I'm giving you ten minutes, no more.'

In a rush of optimism, Mag wore a blue summer dress printed with flowers and butterflies. A warm, busy breeze lifted her spirits even further as she stepped outside. The old yellow Volvo Dennis had resuscitated the year before was parked outside her door.

As they drove and left the city behind them, Mag felt like a child whose school day had unexpectedly been replaced with an excursion. They rolled their windows down and waved indiscriminately at farmers in fields, other motorists, children sucking on long, coloured, plastic tubes of Mr Freeze.

'Every bit as good as a convertible, this car.' Dennis gave her a self-satisfied grin as her curls performed a lunatic dance in the breeze.

In Enniscorthy, Dennis stopped outside a small grocery shop. A confusion of plastic buckets, spades, beach balls and inflatable rings was piled high outside beside a display of apples and oranges and a dangling sign for whipped ice cream cones.

'A picnic is the only way to go on a day like this,' Dennis said. 'I'll pick up something to eat in here. Any special requests?'

Mag shook her head. She was content to let him take control of the day and to bask in the enjoyment. He came back with two ham and cheese sandwiches, a packet of Toffy Pop biscuits and a large bottle of Cidona which he put on top of an old plaid blanket lying on the back seat.

Half an hour later, they arrived in Kilmore Quay. It was a small village perched on the edge of the sea. White-washed cottages with low-hanging thatched roofs, brightly coloured half-doors and small windows deep-set in thick walls clustered together. Other, more recent houses wore pastel shades of pink, yellow and blue as if to compensate for their relative youth and lesser charm.

They parked the car in the village and took their improvised picnic and the blanket with them. They walked along the quay, past the moored boats to a rocky strand beyond. They laid out their blanket on a grassy flat above the stony beach and watched children run in and out of the waves shrieking with tortured pleasure as the cold water splashed over them.

'Let's go for a paddle.' Dennis grinned at Mag and peeled off his shoes and socks. 'Last one in has to do the washing-up for a week!' He took Mag's hand and dragged her up. They ran barefoot across the smooth pebbles to the narrow stretch of sand before the water's edge. Even though she had mentally prepared herself, the chilly clutch of the sea's touch knocked a gasp out of her.

'Wimp,' Dennis said, kicking spray at her.

'Oh, now you're looking for trouble.' She ran away from him in the direction of children who were dancing in and out of the waves a little further along on the beach. It took very little persuasion from her to get them to launch an all-out assault on Dennis. Outnumbered six to one, Dennis stood no chance and ended up drenched. His protests and threats only egged his tormentors on to greater zeal who sensed that there was no real menace in them. Finally, he charged commando-style at them and threw one little boy, screaming with delight, into the water. The others clamoured around him to be next.

'That was a low move, very low,' he said after he had managed to extricate himself, wet all over.

'It's your own fault. You started the battle but the one with the best strategy, as well as the best troops, won out in the end.'

They ate their sandwiches on the blanket and passed the bottle of Cidona over and back to each other. They lay back on the grass. Dennis lit a cigarette and blew trails of smoke towards the sky. Mag watched the thin clouds scuttle by overhead. A sense of well-being washed over her and time lingered in the moment.

In the early afternoon they stood up and walked hand in hand back to the quay. Confidence was building in the staying power of the day's heat. Startling white legs, abruptly revealed, strolled along the pier. Children carefully licked ice-cream cones all the way round to ensure that no drip would escape them. A family was preparing to take a boat-trip and the mother and father tried in vain to contain the excitement of their three children as they attempted to put yellow life-jackets on them. Beside them, a fisherman made adjustments to his equipment.

'Where are you off to?' Dennis asked.

'Round the Saltees and back again. We have room for two more if you want to squeeze in.'

Dennis turned to Mag. 'What do you think? Are you on?'

'I am,' she said 'Let's go.'

The two islands, the Great and Little Saltee Islands, lay clearly visible a short distance from the shore, rising low and elongated from the water. The boat chugged away from the quay. Mag and Dennis sat at the front prow, watching the islands grow in definition and detail. Although, from the shore, the islands had seemed very close, Mag felt that with every thrust forward they were moving towards isolation and wilderness, far from the world of the mainland.

The boat approached the islands and drifted for a while along their shores. From this new vantage point, Mag was surprised to find that the islands were not the oases of peace they appeared to be from a distance. Uninhabited by humans, the islands were hectic, bustling metropolises of the bird world. Thousands of cormorants clamoured for space on the rugged cliff face, screaming abuse as they hustled their way through the crowds. Puffins waddled on the rocks closer to the water, holding their heads high, their painted, sad-clown faces forlornly resigned to the mockery of onlookers. Gannets plunged like kamikaze pilots into the water only to arise triumphant like phoenixes, brandishing fish in their sharp, pointed beaks.

A few curious grey seals approached the boat, their pudgy faces framed by the sea like old women wearing headscarves. They examined the occupants of the boat with mild interest and then swam away with a dismissive flip of their tails. Waves lapped strongly against the sides of the boat, reminding them of how precarious their presence was and how ill-adapted humans were to this environment.

Mag breathed in the air as if it were from a different planet. She revelled in the escape they had made from the humdrum of daily life and she squeezed Dennis's hand in thanks for what he had given her. He squeezed hers back and they cuddled closer.

The boat slowly circumnavigated the islands. Towards the back of the boat, Mag could hear the vague rumble of the fisherman's voice explaining the history of the Saltees to the family, how the area had become a bird sanctuary and how that had affected the local fishing industry. Mag didn't want to listen. She just wanted the sensations of the day to sink deep into her bones so that later she could relive them at will. The wind lifted and Mag shivered. She leaned in against Dennis's side and pulled the blanket around their knees.

Afterwards, when they got back to shore, her legs felt strange and wobbly. Dennis put his arm around her shoulders to steady her and joked that this was how they would be fifty years later. Around them, the frenzy and excitement of the sunny day had calmed down and among the dwindling crowd there was a sense of regret at its impending departure.

'Let's walk,' Mag said.

They walked along the water's edge past the village until the beach came to an end where the cliffs spilled into the sea. They sat on the sand and watched the sun swell and burn red, the grand finale of the day.

'I really enjoyed today, Dennis. It was a great idea to come,' Mag said quietly.

'It's magic, this place. We used to come here on our holidays for a week every summer until I was twelve, before Granny got her stroke. We loved it here. We'd go swimming until all hours at night, lots of times we nearly broke our necks climbing the cliffs. We only went back to the house when we were either starving or it was too dark to see any more.'

'What happened to your granny?' Mag asked.

'She moved in with my aunt in Clontarf. She died a few years ago.'

Dennis put his arm around her. Mag let her head fall against his shoulder.

'I suppose we should go if we want to get back before dark.' Despite her words, Mag didn't make any move to stand up.

Dennis touched her cheek and gently turned her face to his. He kissed her. He ran his fingers through her hair and her stomach flipped. She slipped her hands inside his jacket and felt his skin, his muscles, warm and real, under the light material of his shirt. His lips and face tasted of salt. He was breathing deeply, close to her ear. Every hair on her body stood up, alert, longing to be smoothed down by his caress. His hand moved from her back to brush the curve of her breast under her arm before following every contour of her face with his fingertips.

He murmured softly into her neck. 'Mag, I never felt like this before. It just feels so good to be with you.'

'I think meeting you is the best thing that ever happened to me, Dennis.' This evening, even his name sounded different to her. Now, it sounded like a term of endearment, a soft, intimate sound to be whispered in private.

'Even after what happened before?'

'Even after that.'

Dennis pulled back from her so that he could see her eyes. 'I don't ever want to let you go. I love you, Mag,' His intensity was almost painful to her.

'I love you too, Dennis. I'm not going anywhere.'

'Would you marry me? I might not have a lot to offer but I love you more than I can say.'

'I know that and that's all I want. I'd be happy and proud to marry you.' Mag touched his forehead and smoothed away the lines of strain that had appeared as he tried to find the right words to express his love. If only he knew how plainly obvious it was in his eyes. There was nothing he had to say.

He held her face between his two hands and kissed her everywhere, on the nose, eyes, forehead, cheeks and finally on the mouth with a tenderness that said that they had all the time in the world.

On their way back to the car, he held her close to him. Every so often he skipped a silly little dance of joy. It was one of the things Mag loved about him: he seized happiness and cleaved it to himself without hesitation or fear. The sunshine of her own happiness was never so unambiguous.

They made plans in the car as they drove back to Dublin, frequently reaching out to touch each other to remind themselves that this was real, that they really were the luckiest people in the whole world. Mag touched the side of Dennis's face as he concentrated on the road ahead and felt slightly afraid of the strength of this feeling; of the risk that it exposed her to, the risk that it might become as essential to living as air.

She must have drifted off to sleep, lulled by the heartbeat of the car, because the next thing she remembered was Dennis gently shaking her awake outside her flat.

'We're back, Mag,' he whispered. It was dark and the old familiar smoky smell of Dublin was in her nostrils. It took her a second to realise that the day had not been a dream.

'Thank you for accepting to marry me, future Mrs Byrne,' Dennis said at the doorstep.

'Thank you for asking, Mr Byrne.'

She waited until his yellow Volvo had disappeared completely out of sight before closing the door.

Chapter 11

After the disagreement with O'Brien and Mag, Dennis drove back to the garage, not knowing where else to go. He missed Ciara with a savage, gnawing ache that dissolved his insides like acid. There was nowhere he could go that would give him respite from that.

He trudged through the following days and weeks unable to accept comfort or consolation from the company of others. The mechanics from his garage made an effort to tread softly around him, fearful of triggering off an explosion and yet keen to help him in any way they could. His second-in-command, Francie O'Mahony, an old friend from his apprenticeship days, did his best to support and look after him. Sometimes, Francie would try to persuade him to stop working and eat a sandwich with them at lunchtime but, at best, Dennis would take two bites and, after a few minutes of weighty silence during which one or other of the mechanics would try to make conversation, he would walk away and throw himself back into work.

Dennis had always had a good relationship with his employees. They respected him as a mechanic, as a boss and as a man. He was fair, flexible and his garage was a good place to work. Even his occasional outbursts of temper were easily forgiven as they tended to blow over quickly and his usual sunny good humour would come to the fore again. After Ciara's death, they doubled their efforts to make the business run as smoothly as possible and make their small contribution to Dennis's peace of mind.

But Dennis remained impervious to all contact. He built up a hard carapace around himself and allowed no one inside. He accepted bowls of stew, roasts, cakes from family, friends and customers with passive thanks. He put them in his kitchen where they stayed untouched for a week or two until a fuzzy mould started to grow over them and then he would transfer them to the bin.

His brothers worried about him and he knew that they had established a rota between them to call in to see him in the evenings and make sure that he didn't do anything crazy. He told them to go away and get back to their own lives. He stopped answering the phone. In the evenings, when the garage was empty and silent, he sat on his sofa in the dark and stared into the empty grate of the fireplace in front of him and drank whiskey until drunkenness overpowered his thoughts and submerged his pain. Often, he never made it to his bed and would wake in the armchair in the early morning, stiff, unrefreshed and thick-headed. The second bedroom, the bedroom where Ciara slept when she used to stay with him, remained closed and still.

He showered to clear his head of the fuzz of alcohol so that he could function and work at a level where he was not a danger to himself or his customers. And still he found that life was too clear, too sharp. He could see the concern and affection in the faces of others but he observed it dispassionately from the other side of a thick glass wall. He didn't want their love; he wanted Ciara's and anything else felt like a pale imitation that mirrored back to him the vastness of his loss.

He didn't see or speak to Mag during this time except at the removal and the funeral. The day of the funeral, he caught her eye once or twice but she quickly looked away. People were crowding around her offering their deepest sympathies, pressing her hands in theirs, hugging her. Her sister, Bernie, who was growing more imperial with age, hovered around her blocking or permitting access depending on how she judged Mag was holding up at that point in time. The hard glint in Bernie's eye when she addressed him allowed Dennis no illusions that any attempt on his part to approach Mag would be welcome.

Outside the church, he stood like an automaton, dry-eyed, unable to react, shaking hands and muttering 'thank you' at regular intervals to the endless flow of people who passed in front of him. The funeral was a huge one attended by family, neighbours, friends: hundreds of people Dennis didn't recognise. Colm and Caroline McMurray were there as promised. Even in dark clothes and with sombre faces they stood out as a strikingly handsome couple. They were discreet and unobtrusive, staying at the back of the church, approaching Dennis first and then Mag to briefly offer their condolences, before leaving quickly.

As Dennis watched them leave, enduring the greetings of the mourners, impatient for the procession to the graveyard to start so that he could escape, he noticed that they had come in separate cars and that no word was exchanged between them at the moment of splitting up.

A group of young college students – Ciara's friends no doubt – stood in a huddle, smoking and talking in low voices. They looked awkward, unsure of the funeral protocol. One of them was probably Vincent, Dennis thought. As he scanned the faces, he wondered which one had mistreated Ciara, given her hassle after she had broken up with him and even argued with her just hours before she died. Maybe he hadn't had the cheek to come to the funeral at all. He felt like walking up to them and demanding that Vincent identify himself but he knew it was not the right place for a confrontation.

The day was clear and bright but with a cold edge that took the mourners by surprise whenever a breeze blew through their ranks. Outside the church, Dennis's brothers stood protectively near him but they didn't know the words of consolation that might reach him and he had nothing to say to them.

Stephen Carter, the undertaker, approached him and, in the soft undertones of a man who had made a profession out of being invisible, asked him how he would like to travel to the graveyard. Dennis told him he would take his own car.

By the graveside, the words of the priest reached him in snippets. He felt as though the wind was blowing right through the empty, hollow space inside him. After the coffin was lowered into the grave, Dennis stepped forward and threw in a sprig of cherry blossom, its tiny pink blooms barely visible.

When the ceremony was over, Mag approached the Byrne clan and, without singling Dennis out for special attention, she told them that they were all welcome to come back to the house for a drink and something to eat. Seamus thanked her and assured her that they would go.

'Not me,' Dennis said after she had left and strode away to his car before anyone could stop him. On the way home he bought two bottles of Jameson.

Over the next few days he learned to barricade his emotions into the deepest part of him and keep them there by working zealously through long hours. He snapped easily at the other mechanics, demanding superhuman effort at all times and unforgiving of any slip-up.

Several times he tried to get in touch with Eamonn O'Brien but most of the time he was either out of the office or Dennis hung up before the phone could ring through. Only once did he speak to him and then he was told briefly that there was nothing new to report. A few days after that, the garda compound made contact with him to let him know that all the necessary tests had been done on Ciara's car and that it was available for release if he wanted to come and pick it up. Early the next morning, he took the tow-truck from the garage and brought back the small blue car, mangled and crushed beyond repair. He placed it in a corner of the garage yard and silenced with a withering glare any potential questions about what he planned to do with it. As he had expected, the results of the tests had shown no mechanical failure but, as far as he could make out, had given no precise indication of what had caused the accident.

Almost three weeks had passed since the funeral when Dennis received a phone call from Mag while he was at work. He had not been taking any personal calls but he happened to be in the office filling in a service form when Francie thrust the receiver into his hand before he could refuse it.

'Hello, Dennis. How are you?' she said.

'Holding up,' he said. 'And you?'

'Same, good days, bad days. Well, to be honest, not exactly good ones, just bad and not so bad.'

Dennis didn't say anything. He had lost practice with small-talk.

'Dennis, I got a call from the university asking me if I could come in sometime soon to clear out Ciara's room and take away her personal things. I told them I would do it on Thursday.'

'Do you want me to go as well?'

'No, I can do it on my own. No, the reason I'm calling is that the key to the room is on her set of car keys which I think you have.'

'Yes, they gave them to me when I picked up the car from the compound.'

'Can I call around for them?'

'I'd like to go with you. There's probably furniture and other heavy stuff.' Dennis felt an impulsive urge to accompany Mag. Any contact with Ciara, however distant, was better than none even if it felt like poking an open wound.

'OK, if that's what you want. We could meet at the front gate of Trinity at ten on Thursday morning?'

'I'll see you then.' Dennis was getting ready to hang up when Mag's voice halted him.

'Dennis. I was wondering if we should take the opportunity to see Vincent Connolly, the young fellow she used to go out with. What do you think?'

‘I thought that we weren’t supposed to talk to ‘witnesses’?’

‘I know, but it’s been three weeks and I haven’t heard anything from the guards. Have you?’

‘No.’

‘I have his phone number here. It’s in Ciara’s address book which was among the things they gave me back from the hospital.’

‘Right, let’s talk to him. If he has nothing to hide, he can’t object.’ Something in Dennis stirred for the first time in weeks. The desire to know what had happened rose to the surface again and became a target he could safely focus on.

‘I’ll call him and arrange to meet him then.’ There was a strain in Mag’s voice. He felt sorry for her but he couldn’t console her. Human contact was an activity he hadn’t exercised for a while and he had grown rusty at it.

On Thursday, Dennis got to Trinity early. He walked down Nassau Street along the rounded curve of the high railings that enclosed the Trinity buildings. The flat surfaces of the stonework and outer curves of the pillars shone a pale grey but the nooks and crannies were black where the oil-charged pollution of the heavy city-centre traffic had lodged itself. Dennis stared up at the massive twenty-foot-high front entrance carved in a thick, studded wood as solid and timeless as stone. The blue-faced clock above it indicated nine-thirty. He had time to kill before Mag arrived.

Students rushed and pushed each other through the smaller, more human-sized, round-topped doorway cut into the larger gates. Bicycles were brought to a sudden screeching halt at the entrance, walked through the doorway, a bottleneck of pedestrian traffic, and then were mounted again as their owners tried to avoid being late for their lectures. Their shaggy hair, androgynous, eccentric clothes and heavy rucksacks full of books made Dennis feel out of place, old. He passed through the chilly, time-laden passageway into Front Square. Here, the mayhem of the street was replaced with a different kind of busyness. The students seemed oblivious to the weight of history around them. With heedless ease, they chained their bicycles to railings, shouted at each other, raced across the knobbly cobblestones to their next class.

In front of the pillared Exam Hall, a group was forming in preparation for a graduation ceremony. There was an excitement in the air like static electricity. The graduates, in their long black robes and black square-topped mortar boards with bobbing tassels, were unable to stay still and darted from one friend to another. The parents, sharp and polished in unaccustomed finery, fussed over their offspring. A middle-aged man was dragging a black-robed girl away from her friends. He positioned her with the Campanile in the background, put his arm around his daughter and squared up his shoulders. Pride was oozing out of every pore. Beside him, his daughter squirmed with embarrassment.

'Now, Liz, press the button once, give it a second to focus and then press again. It couldn't be simpler. Make sure you get our feet and heads in the shot.' His wife, a small blond woman, was having trouble with a complex-looking camera. 'Take another few. I want to make sure to get a good one.'

Dennis turned away, his heart swollen. Never would he never stand in that man's shoes. Never would he have the opportunity to wallow in his foolish father's pride.

He walked back to the entrance, trying to chase away the regrets that seized his heart. Mag was there already, at the left of the entrance beside the heavy chain that separated the public area from the lawn. Her face was pale and in the weeks since he had last seen her, weight had fallen from her.

'Hello, Mag,' he said as he approached.

'Hello, Dennis.' She hitched up her handbag on her shoulder in a defensive gesture. 'I said we'd meet Vincent here before we go to her room.'

'What time did you arrange to meet him?'

'Ten. It's almost that now. He should be here soon.'

A few minutes later, Dennis spotted a young man coming towards them. On seeing Dennis and Mag, he paused for a split second and then continued his slow, bobbing walk. He was tall and skinny with short, messy, light brown hair. His face was thin with sharp, angular features. His clothes dangled on his bony frame.

'Hi, you must be Ciara's folks,' he said as he approached them. 'I remember seeing you at the funeral.' He made no attempt to shake hands. 'I'm Vincent Connolly.' His head bobbed in rhythm with his words.

'Dennis Byrne,' Dennis said and thrust out his hand in a gesture that somehow lacked friendliness.

'Cool,' said Vincent.

'Why don't you lead the way to Ciara's room? We can talk there.' Mag said.

'Cool,' Vincent said again. 'You have the keys?'

'Yes, I have them here.' Dennis said. 'Let's go'. Vincent was starting to rattle him already and he didn't want to lose his temper, not yet anyway.

They walked in silence past the Campanile, past the expansive Trinity tree, into the next courtyard. Vincent ambled along beside the row of tall red-brick buildings encircling the college before climbing the front steps of one of them to the front door. He pushed the door open and went in.

'Ciara's place is on the second floor,' he said. He shuffled up the stairs, not bothering to hold on to a handrail. He stopped outside a brown door and casually leaned his shoulder against the wall beside it.

'This is it,' he said. Dennis wanted to thump the airiness out of him. He took Ciara's bunch of keys from his pocket. He examined them to see which one might best fit the lock.

'It's the shiny one with the blue spot painted on it,' Vincent said.

Dennis gave him a warning look before opening the door. The room was tiny, no more than twelve by fourteen feet. It had a single bed against one wall with three shelves overhead. A study desk was set into the window which looked out over the central courtyard. There were two chairs in the room; a swivel chair at the desk and a chair Ciara had bought in a second-hand shop and painted blue.

Signs of Ciara were everywhere; her striped scarf thrown on the bed, the threadbare, black and white stuffed cat that had been a present for her third birthday, a Greenpeace poster of a blue whale with her calf on the wall over her desk, a pin-up notice board covered in cards, notes and a jumbled mish-mash of photos of her family and friends.

'You seem to know your way around well enough.' Dennis looked at Vincent.

'I stayed here for a couple of weeks back in November,' Vincent said.

A similar question crossed Dennis's and Mag's minds as they surveyed the cramped room, the single bed.

Vincent read their thoughts. 'Yeah, well…' He shrugged, embarrassed.

'Ciara never said anything to me,' Mag said.

'It was a temporary thing. I got in a fix. I was sort of seeing Ciara at the time and she helped me out.'

'What does that mean 'sort of seeing Ciara'?' At that moment, nothing could have given Dennis greater pleasure than to pick him up and bounce him off the walls.

'Hey, man, keep your hair on. I'm telling you how it happened. We were going out for a month or so at the time. Around then, I got pulled over with two ounces of pot on me. My old man's a Super and he kind of freaked the head. He kicked me out of the house and I had nowhere to go. I'd had it, I was going to pack the whole thing in,' - the wave of his hand encompassed the desk, the room, the college - 'but Ciara talked me out of it. She let me stay here until I got myself sorted with a part-time job in a pub and a place to stay. She was a good pal.'

'So why did you break up?" Mag sat down on the bed.

Vincent shifted position and kicked the leg of the desk feebly. His nonchalant façade was fading away. 'It was her who broke it off, but it was my fault. I know I behaved like a shit.' He gazed downwards, occasionally flicking a glance at Mag, never at Dennis. 'I didn't want Ciara to think that I was one of her hard-luck cases to take pity on...don't ask me why but I gave her a hard time. Maybe I didn't want her to think that just because she helped me it didn't mean she owned me. I copped on to myself but it was too late. By then, she didn't want anything more to do with me. I suppose she was right.'

'So, tell me what went on in your professor's house the night she had her accident.' Dennis let his clenched fist swing and tap against the wall behind him. 'I heard that you had some sort of a fight with Ciara. What was that all about?'

'It wasn't a fight. Hey, it wasn't that bad. We were only talking. I wanted to have a word with her so I followed her out of the room and we talked in the hall. I asked her to give me another chance but she said it was too late. When I asked if she was seeing someone else, she wouldn't answer me straight out and I got mad.' He glanced quickly at Dennis and then back at Mag. 'I know, I was stupid. I shouted at her and then, she got mad at me. Eventually she told me that she had met someone else, someone a lot older than me, more mature. She ended up telling me to just leave her alone. I hung around because I wanted to apologise but she wanted nothing to do with me so I left the party early and went straight into town on the bike.'

'After you left, where did you go?' Mag asked quietly after a second of silence.

Dennis glanced at her, surprised. He had assumed that Mag could see through this waster as he did but she looked like she was taking him seriously.

Vincent hooked his thumbs into the pockets of his jeans which fell low around his hips. 'I went to O'Neill's on Poolbeg Street. I thought I'd meet up with a few of the lads but there was no-one. I ended up getting pissed by myself.

At closing time, none of the taxis would take me home so I walked back. I had one hell of a hangover the next day and I spent most of it in bed. In the evening, I got a call from one of the lads to say Ciara was...had...well, you know.'

'Did Ciara give you any indication of who she was seeing?' Mag asked.

'No,' Vincent said but his hesitation implied that he knew something more. Dennis wondered what he knew or suspected.

A sharp knock on the door startled all three of them. Dennis was the closest to the door. He opened it. A short, stocky man in uniform stood on the other side.

'Hello there,' he said. 'I'm with security. I heard that there were people here. I'm just checking up on things.'

'I'm Dennis Byrne, Ciara Byrne's father. This is her mother. She arranged with the authorities that we would clear out her room today. We probably should have called in to let you know we were here.'

'No, that's all right, Mr Byrne. I was aware that you'd be coming.' He looked around the room. 'Will you be taking everything with you today?'

'I don't think so. I didn't realise there was so much.'

'We have a storage room downstairs if you want to leave some stuff there for a while.' He hesitated. 'I was very sorry to hear about your daughter. She was a lovely girl. Always a smile for everyone.'

Out of the corner of his eye, he noticed Vincent. 'Ah, you!' he said. He was going to say more but stopped. On his way out, he turned back to Dennis. 'Do you have boxes to pack up her things? They'll have any amount of them at the Buttery.' There was a hint of impatience in his tone when he spoke to Vincent again. 'Go on, make yourself useful, go down and pick up a few boxes for these people.'

Dennis found himself alone with Mag in the small room. He looked around, unsure of what to do next. So many things reminded him of Ciara. He would have liked to apologise to Mag for his outburst a few weeks previously, but the atmosphere, charged with Ciara's unseen presence, inhibited him. He walked to the window and watched the students in the grounds; some were racing to their next class or to an early lunch; others were hanging about in groups making the most of the April sunshine.

He turned to face Mag. 'What do you think he meant by that comment earlier? Was Ciara seeing someone else that I don't know about or did she just say that to get rid of him? Did you hear anything about an older man?'

'She said nothing to me about it if there was someone.' Mag paused.

'Maybe that's what she was going to tell us about the weekend she died.'

Dennis felt a wave of despair wash over him. What had been going on in Ciara's life? And even if he knew, would it make any difference?

Mag stood up. 'Come on,' she said. 'We may as well do what we came to do.' She started to remove the books from the shelves above the bed. Dennis made a half-hearted attempt to gather up the papers on the desk. Ciara's laptop was open in the middle of the desk. His eyes were drawn to the small yellow Post-it notes stuck around the edge, little reminders by Ciara to herself of projects to be completed and due dates for papers. A thought occurred to him.

'Mag, how about checking her email messages? They might help us to find out what was going on?'

'I don't know. Do you think we should?' Mag said.

Dennis didn't reply. Privacy was not a luxury that belonged to Ciara anymore. He pulled up the swivel chair in front of the computer and switched it on. Vincent came back into the room, carrying empty cardboard boxes.

'Seeing as you seem to know everything else around here, maybe you might help me to get into the email messages on this computer,' Dennis said abruptly.

'I don't know the password but give me a few minutes.' Vincent dropped the boxes on the bed. Dennis pushed his chair to one side to allow him to pull the other blue chair close to the screen. As soon as Vincent started tapping at the keyboard it was obvious that he knew what he was doing. Windows flashed open and closed, incomprehensible letters and numbers scuttled across a black screen only to be wiped away as Vincent's long fingers dashed over the keys. Five minutes of concentrated activity passed before Vincent hit the enter key with a flourish. 'There you go,' he said. 'The password is 'cgb17670', easy, her initials and her date of birth. People are crazy, man, may as well have no password.'

Dennis leaned back a little to observe him. 'You're a sneaky fucker, aren't you?'

Vincent shrugged and gave him a wry grin that gave Dennis the first inkling as to why his daughter might have been attracted to this scrawny, unruly young man.

'Now show me how to get into the emails and then you can switch it off. I'll look at them another time.' Vincent ran quickly through the necessary manoeuvres, losing Dennis but rather than make him show him again, Dennis decided to try and work it out for himself later.

The two men heard a sharp intake of breath behind them and turned around to see what had happened. Mag had been emptying the narrow wardrobe at the end of the bed, folding Ciara's clothes into a cardboard box. She was sitting on the bed with an old shoebox beside her, an envelope in her hand. Something had upset her.

Vincent stood up and shuffled uncomfortably on his feet. 'I'll leave you to it then.'

'Go on so,' Dennis said and then, brusquely, almost as an afterthought, 'Thanks.'

'What do you have there?' he asked Mag after the door closed.

'They're old letters Ciara kept. This is one I wrote to her from the hospital.'

Dennis turned away to re-examine the computer screen. An old uneasiness crept over him. The atmosphere in the room was starting to feel oppressive. 'We should pack up as quickly as we can.' he said. 'I'll come back over the next day or two with the van and pick up everything. I'll go and ask the security guard where that storage room is.'

Mag nodded. She put the letter back in a box and, avoiding Dennis's eyes, continued to pack away Ciara's belongings.

Dennis strode quickly along the corridor and down the stairs. At the front door, he breathed in deeply the welcome fresh air. Not far away, the security guard was in conversation with a tradesman carrying a toolbox. As the two men separated, Dennis called out to him.

'Anything I can do for you?' the security guard asked.

'Just wondering if you could show me where to put all the stuff from the room.'

'No problem. Come with me.' He led Dennis back into the building and showed him a small windowless room near the entrance. 'I can give you a hand if there's anything particularly heavy up there.' He paused. He nodded upwards to the room above. 'That young lad, he's not bothering you, I hope?'

'No. Why should he be?'

'No reason. I only mention it because I caught him a couple of times pestering your daughter, throwing stones at her window at night, that sort of thing. No real harm in him, I don't think, but still, I warned him off.'

'Thanks for telling me.' Dennis said. The two men lapsed into silence.

'Difficult times,' the security guard said, as though to no one in particular.

1980

It was a beautiful summer's day, a day of meteorological perfection rarely found in Ireland. The sun shone warmly in a clear blue sky and the merest wisp of a breeze brushed over the guests gathered outside the small country church. It lifted the flimsy pastel-coloured dresses confected in silk, organza, lace. It fluttered over the matching hats, whispered through the adorning veils, feathers and flowers causing the women to adjust them back into place with an imperceptible touch every so often. It brought gentle relief to the men, trussed in stiff, starched shirts, flawlessly calibrated ties and suits with razor-sharp creases.

Dennis drifted through the crowd, allowing vibrantly red lips to alight on his cheeks leaving a sticky memory of their passage. His right hand was crushed and shaken to the point of spasms by the weight of goodwill. A current of happiness surged through him every time he thought that today was the day he would marry Mag. Today, he would declare his love for her and from now on they would be an inseparable unit. He found it hard to anchor his thoughts to any conversation for long and often had to ask people to repeat their questions.

Later, when the idea of moving inside to take their seats was first proposed, it was received reluctantly by all except Dennis. The chilly solemnity of the church was an unappealing alternative to the warm sunniness of the open-air. The guests shuffled towards the doorway but were slowed down and distracted by the least comment or conversation. Eventually, under the threat of being caught outside when the bridal car arrived, they dragged themselves over the threshold. Exchanges became hushed and laughter muted in the gravity of a place of worship. They slipped into their places, nodding and making signs at those they had not yet seen or spoken to.

Dennis walked to the top of the church and took his place beside Gerry, his best man. In the pew behind him were his parents, his three other brothers and his sister-in-law, Seamus's wife, holding their year-old baby. His mother, a woman of width who took up at least two places on the bench, was mopping up copious tears that ran in a steady stream over the lush hills of her cheeks down into the valleys of her chins.

'I can't believe it,' she was saying. 'My little Dennis. It seems like only yesterday that I was beating him with the wooden spoon after he made Thomas eat those poison berries.' Her voice echoed through the first ten pews.

Dennis turned around in embarrassment. He patted her hand. 'Don't cry, Mam. Keep it down. It's not as if I'm going far. I'll be around to see you all the time.'

'Don't rub it in, Dennis. That's what has her all upset.' Thomas hissed.

Gerry turned around. 'Shhhh. We're not out of the woods yet, lads.' He cast his eyes around at the assembled faces on the other side of the aisle. 'We don't want to arouse any suspicions before the deed is done. If this falls through we'll never get rid of him.'

Their mother waved an ineffectual hand at them. 'Stop, boys. I don't know what I did to deserve you. You'll be the death of me yet.'

'Don't worry, Mam.' Darren wrapped an arm around the vast expanse of her and squeezed. 'Sure, haven't you still got the rest of us? We won't let you get bored.'

'Believe me, Dennis, this is the easy bit. It's uphill from now on.' Seamus was trying to remove half of his carnation from the baby's mouth with his finger. He howled when the baby, suspecting a game, clamped down hard with his brand-new sharp teeth and then gurgled in delight at his father's reaction.

As time passed, the crowd, initially subdued, adjusted to the holiness of the place and the noise level increased. Discussions took place in normal voices, teasing banter bounced to and fro and laughter became frank and outright. The acceptable delay of fifteen to twenty minutes had long been exceeded and people started to surreptitiously glance at their watches. The priest, who was also Mag's uncle, appeared at the door of the vestry and, after greeting Dennis and the other members of the family, conducted an inspection of the altar and the paraphernalia associated with the ceremony. When thirty minutes had passed. a subtle change came over the congregation. Suppositions and theories were carried on lowered voices and spread over the pews until their cold feet crawled up Dennis's spine. His stomach contracted to a small hard knot and his face twisted into a rictus of a smile in response to his brothers' jokes. He straightened his back and fixed a rigid gaze at the altar.

Father Malley was assiduously adjusting the bible, the hymn book and the mass booklet into precise alignment when his attention was drawn by something at the end of the church. He hurried down the aisle, a worried expression on his face, his robes swishing with officiousness. The simultaneous rubbing of stiff materials on hard seats, the shuffling of feet and the whispers told Dennis that everyone had twisted around to try to see what could be causing the commotion. He dared not turn around himself for fear of encountering knowing, sympathetic looks. He stared at his feet which seemed far away and shrugged off Gerry's concerned squeeze of his arm.

The priest returned to the top of the altar within a few minutes, brimming with contained news. 'Good people, we know not the day or the hour that misfortune can strike and not even a mechanic is immune to the negative impact of a motor-car breakdown.' He smiled benevolently at Dennis who was having difficulty deciphering his words. 'Margaret and her father encountered a problem of a mechanical nature with their motor car on their way here today but fortunately the Lord sent a Good Samaritan to assist them and they are here now. The ceremony can now proceed.'

'Thanks be to God,' Dennis said with heartfelt gratitude, louder than he had intended. Relieved laughter erupted in response. It came to a sudden stop, replaced with gasps of admiration and Dennis knew that Mag was there. He turned and saw her framed against the open door of the church holding her father's arm. Her cheeks were flushed red and she was trying to calm down her racing breath. She was wearing a simple white dress with long sleeves and a wide neckline which revealed the delicate scaffolding of her shoulders and neck. Her short brown hair shone under a short veil and she held a small bunch of pink rose-buds. She looked directly at Dennis, took a deep breath and started the long, slow walk up the aisle.

'I'm glad you waited,' she whispered when she was standing beside him.

'Not as glad as I am that you came,' he whispered back.

The priest called them forward and so began a ritual repeated in its every detail by thousands of couples every day and yet individual and unique to each one. Dennis felt proud and yet a little intimidated to pronounce the vows that would join him to this woman for the rest of their lives. He slipped the ring on her finger and her clear smile made his heart skip with joy.

They walked down the aisle, urged forward by the applause and encouragements of their friends and family and Dennis had a feeling that, despite a certain cynicism he had about the value of a wedding ceremony, they were leaving with something they hadn't possessed on arriving, something new that they had created together.

After posing for innumerable photographs, Mag and Dennis re-joined their guests at White's hotel where the reception was being held. The relief that they had something to celebrate seemed to have intoxicated everyone and they threw themselves with added gusto into the revelry.

Every so often while he waltzed, twirled and charmed all of Mag's aunts as well as his own, Dennis searched the room with his eyes to find Mag. He would locate her talking to an elderly aunt, laughing at one of Gerry's jokes, dancing sedately with his father, or accepting a drink from one of his cousins. The mere sight of her was his touchstone for happiness. She looked as joyful and carefree as he had ever seen her. Once or twice their eyes met. The look that passed between them made him glow and the distance between them didn't matter as long as he knew she was there. At the end of the night, when only the last few inveterate partygoers remained, Dennis was glad to climb the stairs, Mag's hand in his, and have her all to himself.

Chapter 12

Mag wasn't sure what woke her but in the middle of the night her eyes flew open and, all of a sudden, she was wide awake. Her clock made an almost imperceptible electronic hum, a noise that rasped not just on her ears but on all her senses.

She could hear the tap in the bathroom dripping, one drip every ten or fifteen seconds. She imagined the drop forming on the rim of the tap, growing, swelling with molecules of water until, at a point precisely designated by nature, the weight of the drop exceeded its grip on the tap and it fell, smashing against the cold, shiny enamel below; the sound of loneliness.

She got up to shut off the tap. On her way back to bed, she passed Ciara's bedroom and, after a moment's hesitation, opened the door. The cardboard box with Ciara's personal things, including the letters Mag had written to her daughter, sat on her bed where Mag had left it the previous evening. Dennis had taken the lap-top with him but the rest of her things had been transferred to the store-room until he could go back with the van to pick them up.

Mag shivered and pulled her dressing-gown around her. She sat on Ciara's bed and started to sort through the contents of the box beside her. It held a muddle of papers, letters, knick-knacks, pens, pencils, USB memory sticks, all the jumble of a life that had been stopped in its tracks.

It would soon be a month since Ciara died. If anything, she felt worse now than she had at first. It was as though grief was a bottomless pit she had fallen into, a pit with smooth sides and precarious ledges out of which it was impossible to climb. The dark shadows of depression were crowding over her, blocking out the light. She was afraid.

It's not over 'til it's over. That's one of the great things about life. A voice of reason rang in her ears, a voice that had been a lifeline to her in the past. Treasa Quinn. Treasa had become a good friend when they had met years before at the hospital, despite the twenty-year age gap between them. She felt a sudden need to talk to her old friend and decided to call her in the morning.

Mag picked up the letter she had written to her daughter so many years earlier and opened it. Her writing was almost unrecognisable; thin and scrawling. In it she had asked for understanding and forgiveness, afraid that these might not be within the capacity of a ten-year-old to give. Above all, she had tried to reassure Ciara that she loved her more than anything in the world, no matter how things might seem. It was painful to remember that time when her soul had been rasped raw. It distressed her that Ciara had preserved the letter. Had her daughter really bounced back intact from that difficult time or had she been damaged underneath it all, masking her own vulnerability behind a layer of exuberance and laughter, concentrating on the needs of others to disguise her own?

Mag put aside the letters and examined the other contents of the box. There were notes Ciara had written for college assignments, copies of scientific articles, scraps of paper with to-do lists written on them. Mag smiled at one which had 'get organised!!!' underlined at the top of the list. She found smooth beach pebbles, one with a face drawn on it with an ink-pen. She picked up the cork notice board and examined the items pinned to it; holiday postcards from friends; a number of photos of friends, some of whom Mag had met; a used ticket for the Trinity Ball; scraps of paper with phone numbers scribbled on them. In one corner, tucked under the frame was a card with a line drawing of wild flowers on the front. Mag unpinned it from the board. A photo fell from it. It had been taken in a pub and was of Ciara sitting at a table beside a man Mag didn't recognise. He looked quite a bit older than her. He had his arm around her shoulders and they were both smiling happily at the camera.

Mag read the card.

'Dear Ciara, Firstly, let me apologise for my reaction the other evening. I didn't mean to get mad at you. I understand your point of view but this situation is not an easy one for me either.

I honestly don't think I am harbouring any feelings of bitterness or resentment as you seem to believe. I'd like to meet and discuss the matter openly but if you think there is no possibility of a future relationship, I understand and I respect your opinion. But I would like us to continue to see each other no matter what. It's been a wonderful privilege to meet and get to know you.

I enjoyed our drink on Tuesday evening. Sorry that I had to run home so quickly. In fact, it turned out to be nothing, the baby's

temperature came down shortly afterwards and we didn't even need to take her to the doctor.
Looking forward to seeing you soon,
Love, Joe
P.S. I enclose a copy of the photo of us taken in Madigan's the other day.'

Mag picked up the photo and examined it again. This man, Joe, looked to be in his early thirties, at least ten years older than Ciara. Although they were sitting, Mag estimated that he was quite a bit taller than Ciara. His dark hair was thinning at the front and his face had deeply creased laughter lines. He was looking at Ciara, not at the camera, and he had a self-satisfied, proprietary look on his face. His left hand dangled over Ciara's shoulder and had a wedding band on the ring finger. Ciara was cuddling close to his side, her open, trusting smile making her look very young and innocent.

Maybe young but not so innocent, Mag thought harshly. She tried to grapple with the realisation that her daughter, always a young girl to her, was also a woman. Suddenly, her memories, her best memories of the generosity, the kindness of her daughter, of their complicity were drifting away from her, becoming less real. She had never thought of Ciara as underhand or secretive. She had never thought Ciara capable of taking her happiness at the expense of another woman's.

Then, her mind rebelled. No, Ciara was still Ciara. Nothing, nobody would take that away from her. Ciara would always and forever be the little girl who, when Mag was at her lowest point, had tried to push Mag's tears up her cheeks and back into her eyes, the girl who had cried herself to sleep after seeing baby seals being clubbed to death in a television programme on the environment, the girl who had always been the champion of the underdog, the girl who had made her laugh, the girl who had given her a reason to live. As a child, Ciara's enthusiasm has often caused her to make errors of judgement but even if those errors had become adult-sized ones as she grew up, that didn't erase her basic goodness.

Mag went downstairs to the sitting-room and took out the albums and boxes containing old photos from the oak cabinet. She hadn't looked at most of them for years and, as she spread them out in front of her, all her memories of the past came flooding back. She drank them in, welcoming the darts of emotion, however sad, they offered her. It gave her an obscure comfort to realise that death was not the worst thing that could happen. Towards daybreak, she crawled to the sofa and fell asleep under a blanket, a sleep that was almost peaceful for the first time since she had lost Ciara.

She woke after only three hours of sleep but feeling more refreshed than she had for a long time. She made a cup of tea and thought about calling Treasa. She had first met Treasa ten years earlier in hospital when she was suffering from accelerated osteoporosis. She was now sixty-eight and coped with her painful and debilitating disease with the same composure and cheerfulness she showed in dealing with all of the other crises in her life.

After her husband had died leaving her with large debts, she had coped, practical and good-humoured as always. She had been a support and an example to Mag during difficult times and a strong friendship had grown between the two women.

Mag picked up the phone and dialled Treasa's number. Treasa's calm, sympathetic voice reached her over the sound waves. She had not been able to attend the funeral as she had broken her hip in the early spring and was still house-bound but she had written a warm letter of sympathy that had touched Mag.

'Of course you're welcome to come over, Mag. I'd love to see you,' she said.

That afternoon, Mag knocked at the dandelion-yellow door of the small red-brick, terraced house in Portobello. Faintly, she could hear the slow tap and shuffle of her friend approaching the door, supported by her walking stick. Treasa hugged her and led her into her small, cosy sitting room. Mag insisted on making the tea.

'You must miss Ciara so much, Mag' she said. 'The world is a hard, empty place when someone we love is taken out of it. It takes a long time to adjust.'

'To be honest, I don't think I'm coping very well, Treasa.' Mag stared for a moment into her mug of tea. 'People think I'm doing OK considering but, underneath it all, I think I'm falling apart.'

'Sometimes behind the façade of normality, normality comes. Don't be hard on yourself, Mag dear, the wound is very fresh. It may never fully heal but you'll learn to live with it.'

'I'd like to believe you but I'm not sure.'

'Give yourself time. Don't expect too much too soon. How is Ciara's father doing?'

'Not well, I think. I know you've never met Dennis but you know that we haven't exactly been on speaking terms for the past few years. Immediately after the accident, I thought that we were getting on better but then we had a major argument shortly after Ciara's death and I haven't seen much of him since. He can be such a bully but despite that I feel sorry for him, I know how he adored Ciara, she was the sun, moon and stars for him.'

'Poor man.'

'He's got a bee in his bonnet about the accident. He thinks there's something strange in the way it happened and that the guards aren't doing as much as they should to find out more. In fact, that's what we argued about. He thinks I'm on their side.'

'What exactly did he find strange?' Treasa wedged a small cushion down the side of her chair to support her hip.

'One thing that bothered him was that Ciara wasn't wearing her safety belt. It's true that it's not like her. I've never known her to not wear it before but he seems to be blowing it out of all proportion.'

Treasa nodded slowly. 'Anything else?'

'Well, the day after her accident we went back to the scene and found a charm that had come off her bracelet. It was on the verge by the roadside a bit away from where the accident happened. We couldn't think of a good explanation of how it got there and when we showed it to the guards, Dennis thought that they didn't take it seriously.'

Treasa was listening intently. 'Is it possible that it came off when they were transferring her from the car to the ambulance?' she asked.

'We already asked ourselves that question but I can't imagine how. We found it more than twenty metres from where the ambulance was parked. Unless it got caught in the clothes of one of the guards and then it dropped off when they walked away. It doesn't seem likely but who knows.'

'I see,' Treasa said.

Mag continued. 'But I think that the real problem for Dennis is that something was bothering Ciara just before she died. There's something she wanted to talk to us about but never got the chance. Ciara was always so open and honest and she was very close to Dennis so he can't understand how she kept secrets from him.'

'She was growing up,' Treasa said.

'I'm certainly realising that. This morning I found something that shocked me. I was looking through some things we picked up from her room in Trinity and I found a letter. It looks like it was from a man, a married man who she was seeing in secret.'

'It's hard to accept that someone we love, especially our child, has a life we know nothing about. She was at that age when she was finding her way: the age of trial and error.' Treasa leaned across and squeezed Mag's hand in her own gnarled one.

'I know but she could have talked to one of us. We'd have advised her.' Mag pulled a tissue from her bag and blew her nose.

'What young person wants to live their life second-hand?'

Mag said nothing but she was thinking that she would give anything for Ciara to live her life any way at all.

'Sorry to be a bit slow, Mag but what was it that caused the accident?'

'That's just it, we don't know. The theory the guards seem to favour is an error of judgement on Ciara's part,' Mag replied. 'Of course, Dennis has a problem with that. Through his eyes, Ciara was infallible. Before he gave her the car for her birthday, he insisted that she went on one of those crisis driving courses and he was so proud when she did very well on it despite her age.'

Treasa threw a log of wood into the fireplace. Mag watched her, her gaze drawn to the flickering of the flames. 'And guards see nothing to be concerned about in all of this?' Treasa said evenly.

'I don't think so but we haven't heard anything from them for weeks. Why? Do you think there's something to worry about?'

'I'm not saying that you should worry but I can understand Dennis wanting to know more about the circumstances surrounding her accident. I certainly would want to.'

Mag stared at her. She never expected Treasa, of all people, to support Dennis's suspicions. She was the most level-headed, down-to-earth person Mag knew. She coped with life-changing events, both good and bad, with a natural composure that Mag admired. 'So you think I haven't been very supportive of Dennis then?'

'Oh Mag, far be it from me to pass judgement on you at a time like this. I simply think that this must be a very tough time for Dennis as well and that he has valid concerns.'

Mag traced her finger along the piping on the edge of Treasa's sofa and tried to gather her thoughts. She had, until now, considered that Dennis was being completely unreasonable but now Treasa was making her examine the situation from his point of view. 'I've thought a lot about that charm and how it could have ended up so far away from the accident. The most logical answer I can think of is that Ciara pulled over the car just before she had the accident and then lost it. But that doesn't make sense either. Why would she do that?'

'She might have stopped if someone flagged her down. Not necessarily someone with sinister intentions. It could have been someone with car trouble or a hitchhiker.'

'At two in the morning? I suppose anything is possible.' Mag felt as though her mind was playing one of those impossible children's puzzles where the mixed-up squares are shunted around an empty slot to try to create a picture. Nothing made sense and yet something had to because Ciara was dead and a chain of events had led to that.

'I'm sorry, Mag.' Treasa leaned forward and patted Mag's knee. 'I didn't mean to upset you. You have enough to deal with. There is an explanation for everything but you just don't know what it is at the moment.'

'No, don't apologise, Treasa, it's been a help to talk. I've been so wrapped up in coming to terms with the fact that Ciara is gone and coping with my own feelings that I've found it hard to look beyond that. You've given me an inkling of how Dennis must see things. Knowing him, he needs to understand what happened to Ciara before he can grieve properly.'

'Death is a funny thing. We all deal with it in different ways. Some of us are better equipped to cope than others but that's not a reflection on the quality of our love.' Treasa gave Mag a small, compassionate smile.

When Mag stepped out of the warm cocoon of Treasa's house into the bracing bustle of the city streets outside, she felt at the same time both more and less lost than when she had arrived. The fragments she was discovering of Ciara's life were making her more confused but she felt surer now that if she and Dennis wanted to find answers, they would have to find them themselves. How would she talk about all of this to Dennis? It was important not only to talk to each other but to hear each other.

She turned left into her street, a cul-de-sac. She was surprised to see Dennis's green Jaguar parked underneath the large oak tree that leaned over from the public park on the other side. As she drew up, Dennis was closing the wrought iron gates and walking back to his car. He looked haggard, an adjective Mag would never have used for him before. He looked up when he heard a car arriving and seeing that it was Mag, his jaw stiffened and he waited for her to park.

1980

On their wedding night, Mag lay looking up at the plaster ceiling-rose in the middle of the high ceiling of the honeymoon suite. It had been perfectly restored but from where she lay, she could still see the hole in the centre where the chandelier was supposed to hang. The building had started life as the manor house of the local gentry before being converted into a hotel and the original features had been preserved and restored except when they clashed with the comforts of modern living. Instead of the chandelier, the hotel had installed large table lamps on each side of the bed, on the table near the window and on the dressing table at the foot of the bed.

Beside her, Dennis snored gently. His chest rose and fell with each intake of breath. He was an untidy sleeper, lying at an angle in the bed with one arm thrown out from his body.

Mag propped herself up on an elbow to better examine his face. She loved watching him sleep. His face was loosened, cleared, like a blackboard wiped free of the scribblings of the day. His hair was flattened on one side where he had slept on it for most of the night. His lips were slightly apart. Mag leaned over and kissed them very softly. She ran her lips across his bed-warmed cheek. His breathing pattern changed as her touch intruded on his unconsciousness. He stirred and, without opening his eyes, said sleepily 'Good morning, Mammy. I'm getting up now.'

Mag punched his arm and pulled the duvet off him, allowing the cool air of the room to hit his naked body. 'For that now, you can freeze.'

'Ah, Mag, I was just messing with you, let me back in.' Dennis tried to grab an edge of one of the sheets and slide his feet underneath. 'Please. Honey. Gorgeous. You won't regret it. Besides, I have a surprise for you.'

'What's the surprise?' Mag asked, loosening her hold on the blankets.

'Let me in and I'll tell you.' Dennis burrowed headfirst under the covers. Mag squealed as his hair tickled her stomach.

Much later, after they had made love and Mag was drowsy with contentment, her head on Dennis's chest while he ran her fingers through her hair, she remembered the promised surprise. 'So, tell me,' she said.

'You know how we decided not to take a real honeymoon? Well, I reneged on our agreement.'

'What do you mean?' She raised her head so that she could see his face. He was grinning like a Cheshire cat. '

I mean that this evening we're off to Paris. Our flight is at half past six.'

'What?' Mag was stunned. 'How long are we going for?'

'Just four days. We'll be back on Tuesday.' Dennis was obviously under the impression that she would be ecstatic and was lying back, basking in anticipation of the glory to come.

His self-complacency irritated Mag. She stared at him.

'Dennis, have you gone crazy? How much did that cost?'

'Don't worry about the money, I got a good deal. This is our honeymoon, Mag, our one and only.'

She pulled back the sheets and stepped out of bed. 'I'm going to take a shower,' she said. She picked up her toilet bag and went towards the bathroom.

'Hey, Mag, what's wrong? I thought you'd be pleased.' Dennis's voice registered amazement.

'And I thought we had already discussed this but obviously that didn't count for anything.'

'Oh, Mag, you can be such a misery-guts at times.'

Under the shower, Mag tried to assess the reasons for her anger and frustration. It wasn't just the money although it was partly that. Together, they had decided that after the wedding they would save as much as they could so that they could get a garage of their own started as quickly as possible. But there was something else. This wasn't how she wanted her marriage to start. She wanted to be an equal partner, she wanted them to share the big decisions about their lives. She didn't want to be the weak, dependent one who was to be adored and pampered. And still, her objections felt petty even to her. She wondered if they would wither away under the light of open discussion, leaving her with a feeling of being ridiculous. How could she express this to Dennis when she found it so hard to formulate her discontent to herself?

The unresolved tension hovered between them for the rest of the day, disguised somewhat by the little time they spent alone together. Once Mag tried to hold his hand but he didn't respond and she let it go. They waved away the last of the guests, finalised arrangements with the hotel, packed their bags, took their leave of their families, all the while maintaining a certain distant politeness when they spoke to each other.

Despite herself, a stirring of excitement started to grow inside her as they dealt with the formalities at the airport. She had never left Ireland before and Paris was Paris, exotic, mysterious, truly foreign. She found herself trying to remember some of the French she had learnt in school. Scraps of phrases, unconnected words emerged unexpectedly from her memory. She glanced at Dennis's face, feeling suddenly foolish and trivial. His jaw was set in a hard line and even though he must have sensed her eyes on him he didn't look at her. She knew he was disappointed by her reaction but she didn't know what to do to diffuse the situation.

They flew into Charles de Gaulle airport, an enormous, bustling labyrinth that amazed Mag. Luckily, Dennis had struck up conversation with an older couple on the aeroplane who were regular visitors to Paris and they helped them to take the suburban train to the centre of Paris where they were staying in the Latin Quarter.

Night had already fallen when they emerged from the underground station of Saint Michel-Notre Dame. On their short walk to their hotel, they looked at the cathedral of

Notre Dame, the grave constancy of its lines at the front contrasting with the extravagance of its arches and curves on the other side; the wide, busy Boulevard Saint Michel; the Seine flowing languorously below her, and in that brief time, Mag already fell in love with Paris. All around her she heard people speaking a language that tripped off their tongues, as light as whipped cream, a language she had previously only had heard spoken painfully with great effort. Paris even smelled different. Perfume, cigarette smoke, pollution, the evening warmth rising from the pavements mixed together and made a distinctive combination that Mag's senses had never encountered before. Her head swivelled in every direction as she tried to catch and absorb the sensations that swirled all around her. Her gaze alighted on Dennis's face. He was grinning complacently at her.

She threw her arms around his neck. 'Oh, Dennis,' she said. 'This is wonderful. Thank you for taking me here.'

'Ah, so it's not such a torture to be here after all. Because if you want, we can get back on the train and go home straightaway.'

'No, no, I love it. Not that I ever doubted that I would.' Mag felt Dennis must think her crazy. In fact, she was beginning to think that herself. She continued. 'It's just that I would have liked to have been consulted.'

'But then it wouldn't have been a surprise.' Dennis held her tight.

'I know. Forget about it, I was just being silly. Let's not let anything spoil this holiday. I want to see everything there is to see in Paris.'

The next few days blended into each other so that they passed in the blink of an eye and yet also managed to achieve a certain continuity that threaded its way into their lives. In the mornings, they slept late in the small family hotel they were staying in, a fact which seemed to delight the middle-aged couple who ran it.

'Ah, les amoureux,' they would say each morning as though Mag and Dennis had just performed an admirable feat, guiding them to a table while they prepared a late breakfast for them. They had been thrilled when they found out that this was Mag and Dennis's honeymoon, slapping Dennis on the shoulder in encouragement and pinching Mag's cheek, giving them advice that Mag was glad she couldn't understand, given the winks and exchanged looks that accompanied it.

They visited the Louvre, the Eiffel Tower, the Sacre-Coeur, Notre Dame, the Arc de Triomphe and many other great monuments but what Mag enjoyed best was wandering around the narrow streets off the main boulevards until a little café caught their eye and enticed them to sit outside at one of its circular tables, so tiny that it could barely hold two cups of coffee. They took a boat trip down the Seine at night once and cuddled close in the front row of the outside deck while the lights of Paris dazzled them. She felt far from home, wrapped up in a new glamorous life where love and happiness were real and permanent.

When the time came to go back to Dublin, to normality, it was with a sense of regret but also of gratitude that Mag left.

Chapter 13

Dennis was on the point of driving away when Mag's car appeared around the bend of the street. He opened the gates for her and waited until she parked her car in the driveway. His impatience to talk to her made him feel that she was taking an unconscionably long time to switch off the engine, pick up her handbag and get out of the car. He joined her on the path outside the house.

'I'm glad you're here, Dennis,' she said. 'I was going to call you. There are things we need to talk about.'

'I know, there's something new, something I found out this morning when I examined Ciara's emails.' He wondered how Mag would react when he told her, if she would be as angry and disappointed as he was.

'It may be that we've discovered the same thing,' Mag said as she opened the front door. 'Come inside and let's talk about it.'

Mag took her coat off and led him into the kitchen.

'So should you start or will I?' she said.

'Read these first. Then we can talk.' He took two folded sheets of white paper from his pocket and thrust them at her.

'I printed them off this morning from Ciara's computer. It's pretty clear what was going on. Read them, you'll see.'

She unfolded them, flattened them out on the table and stared at the black printed letters on the page. She looked up at him before starting to read.

He watched Mag while she read the pages. Her lips moved slightly but her expression didn't show any signs of the shock he had felt when he had first read the words. Maybe she knew already.

He stood up, opened the patio doors and walked out into the garden. He pushed his hands into the bottom of his pockets to keep them steady. The air was mild and whispered that summer would soon be there. A lone thrush landed on the crossbar of the swing-set he had installed for Ciara's second birthday. It hopped to the end of the bar, tilted back its head and opened its beak. Its song was clear and distinct, detached from all other background sounds.

That morning, when he had switched on Ciara's computer he had not expected to find anything of real consequence. There were over one hundred new messages that Ciara had never read, most of them junk mail received over the past month. He examined specifically the messages received and sent in the couple of weeks before her death and it was then that he found a message Ciara had written to her professor, Colm McMurray. The words exploded on the screen, sending needle-sharp shards into Dennis's heart.

'Dearest Colm, I need to write to you to let you know what I think. Every time we talk, I seem to get all mixed up and not able to express my feelings properly so hopefully I'll be able to explain here.

When you suggested going for a coffee after our meeting with Dylan Macken about my research project in December, I never imagined that we would end up where we are now. Things seem to have moved very fast and even though I really do care about you, I can't go on like this anymore. You told me then that you were separated and that it was only a question of paperwork and time until you got the divorce and moved out into your own place but I'm not so sure anymore that that's quite true. I don't want to be part of destroying your family; that needs to be something that you need to deal with completely separately from me before there can be anything between us. When I saw you the other day with your sons in the lab, they looked so young and it gave me a shock and made me realise that these are real people that are being affected.

I have to admit as well that the secrecy is taking its toll. I hate not being able to talk about something so important to my friends and family, even though I know that it would have repercussions on your career if it was known. You said it's only a few months until I graduate but I still don't like how this makes me feel. That's why I'm going to step away and let you sort things out in your life without me. If and when you are free, then maybe we can start fresh but I don't want you to feel that I'm putting any pressure on you for that to happen. Ciara.'

After reading the message, Dennis had sat back, stunned. His first instinct was fury at Colm McMurray for using his position and power to take advantage of his daughter. What experience of life did Ciara have that might equip her against the advances of a lecherous, preying creep like McMurray? Of course she would fall straight into the trap.

He looked back through the in-box for messages from McMurray. He found a reply to Ciara's message sent later that same day, a few days before the night of her accident.

'*My darling Ciara, please give me just a couple of weeks more. You are the one I love and want to be with. There is nothing between Caroline and me anymore and there hasn't been for a long time. Please believe me. It's just that life is complicated and I know that it will be hard on her and on the boys. The only reason I was delaying is that they are going into their Leaving Cert year and I don't want to derail their careers. I just need to find the right time to tell them. They'll be fine in the end. I'm sure that Philip and Thomas would just want me to be happy and they'll love you once they know you. Just stay back after the party on Friday and we'll talk about everything. The boys are away for a rugby match in Cork and Caroline is going shopping to London. Just give me one last chance to explain myself. I love you with all my heart. Colm*'

Ciara replied to that message with the following: '*Colm, I don't think that's a good idea. I want nothing to do with the end of your marriage. That has to be something that you sort out without involving me. The boys and Caroline would hold it against me and see me as a homewrecker and I'd hate that. I'll be at the party on Friday because I don't want the others to wonder why but after that it's over between us. There'll be no need to be in touch because of college and I'm going to go travelling for a while to get away. Who knows what might happen in the future but if there is a future for us it has to start on good foundations with no deceit or lies. Ciara*'

Dennis found a few other earlier messages between them that tracked the progression of their relationship but the latest messages told him all he needed to know.

'Dennis,' Mag said softly. She was standing behind him.

'Well?' he asked but before she could say anything he continued. 'Can you believe that bastard? Can you believe what he was up to? I have a good mind to go over there now and punch the living daylights out of him.'

'Dennis.' Mag's voice held a note of warning. 'There were two people involved. We don't know exactly how this happened.'

Dennis stared at her in disbelief. 'How can you say that? She was only twenty-two and he's twenty years older. He was her professor; she was his student. He abused his position and, as far as I'm concerned, abused my daughter.'

'Twenty-two's not that young; she wasn't a child anymore.'

Dennis shook his head. 'Mag, this is Ciara we're talking about. Ciara. Our little girl.'

'No, not so little, Dennis.' For the first time, Dennis noticed that Mag had a card in her hand. She held it out to him. 'I don't know if there's ever a good time to show you this. I found it among Ciara's things last night.'

Dennis took the card from her hand. He opened it and looked at the photo inside; Ciara cuddled up to a man he didn't recognise. He questioned Mag with a look but she made a sign for him to read on.

As he read, a lump formed in his chest making it difficult to breathe. His rage at McMurray which he had used as flimsy self-protection was torn down by the words he read. He could exonerate Ciara of the blame for the affair with McMurray but two affairs with two married men went beyond his powers of defence.

He held the card and photo out for Mag to take. 'What the hell did she think she was doing?' he said, roughly. Mag had no answer to this question and he whirled around. He felt the rims of his eyes hot and stinging and strode along the path around the house until he turned the corner.

It was hard to see straight. He was lost, adrift in a sea without landmarks. A rod of anger flared up white within him. It was hard enough to lose Ciara in the present but now, it seemed that all contrived to rip her out of his past as well.

He didn't know her any more. He gathered his hand into a fist and punched the stippled wall in front of him. Pain surged up his arm. He stared at his hand and saw flecks of blood on his grazed knuckles.

Noiselessly, Mag approached and stood beside him. She touched his arm. 'I know how you must be feeling, Dennis.'

He blinked. He felt as though there was sand trapped beneath his eyelids scraping across his eyeballs. 'It's no good, I can't fight this anymore,' he said and it was almost a relief to admit it.

'I understand, Dennis but maybe you should stop lashing out at people around you and accept Ciara for who she really was. It's hard, Dennis, but please, don't blame her,' Mag said in a low voice. 'I agree with you that there are a lot of things we don't understand in all of this but one thing we can be sure of—you'll know it when the shock wears off—is that Ciara was the best daughter we could ever have wished for and a wonderful person. We had her for twenty-two years and we'll just have to make that last for the rest of our lives.'

'But what about all of this that was going on in her life, all the stuff that we knew nothing about?' Dennis opened his hands, helpless.

'This is not what's important. We know the real Ciara, we know who she was and we have to hold on to that. She was becoming a woman and it's not an easy journey. Maybe she made some mistakes but who are we to judge, we made them too.'

'I'm not judging her, I'm...I'm…' He trailed off.

'Disappointed?'

'Maybe. Maybe. This whole fucking thing is such a mess; I don't know how I feel anymore.' He looked down into

Mag's face. It was years since he had seen her this way. Her compassionate blue eyes enfolded him. He felt an urge to pull her close and hold her. It had been such a long time.

Mag picked up his bleeding hand and examined it. 'Come inside and let me patch this up.'

At the table in the kitchen, she swabbed his hand with disinfectant. He watched her brown curls bob with her movements. Threads of grey that he hadn't noticed before ran through them.

While she applied a bandage, she spoke in a low voice. 'Dennis, listen to me. We need to find out more about what was going on in Ciara's life. We can't go on letting these doubts and questions torture us.'

Dennis was taken aback. 'I thought you wanted to leave all that to the Gardaí.'

'I did and I still do, except that we're not looking for the same thing. We need to understand what was happening, what was going on in Ciara's life, regardless of the cause of the accident.'

'Obviously McMurray hasn't been straight with the guards or with us.' Dennis winced as he flexed his stiffening knuckles. 'Maybe it has nothing to do with the accident, maybe he just didn't want people to know that he was having an affair with a student or maybe he was still keeping it from his wife but it's obvious that there was a major disagreement between them and that might have contributed to the accident, whether maliciously or not. But it looks to me as if he was definitely the last one to see her.'

Mag nodded. 'And don't forget that Ciara was seeing someone else. Could McMurray have found out? You know, Dennis, that's the thing that bothers me the most about the whole thing. Ciara might have been impulsive and foolish but she wasn't devious. I can't imagine her leading two men on, lying to them, seeing them both at the same time.'

'Don't ask me. I'm seeing a whole new side of Ciara that I didn't even know existed.' It made Dennis uncomfortable even to think about it.

'In any case, we should go to the guards with this information. They should confront McMurray with it and see what he has to say.'

'I'll get in touch with O'Brien. I'll go in to see him. Tomorrow, if possible. I'd rather see him face to face, make him tell me what he plans to do about it.'

'I'd like to be at that meeting too,' Mag said resolutely. 'It's been a month. I'd like to hear what progress they've made.'

'Fine, I'll let you know when he can see us.'

'One other thing, do we tell him about this guy, Joe, as well?'

Dennis hesitated. On the one hand, he wanted to protect his daughter's reputation, especially from the guards and the media, people who had no other knowledge of Ciara to balance their prejudice and yet he didn't want to keep information that might be useful from the guards.

'Maybe we should find out what we can about him before we say anything,' Mag said.

'Let's do that. It's not as if there's any direct link between him and the accident, not yet, anyway, so it might not be of interest to them.' Dennis was glad to accept Mag's suggestion. He didn't want O'Brien or anyone else thinking less of his daughter.

He glanced at his watch. 'I'd better go. I promised Francie I'd give him a hand with a problem engine before it gets dark.' He stood up, not sure of how to take his leave. A hug or a kiss seemed too intimate and yet he didn't want to walk out without some sign after all that had passed between them. He hesitated in the doorway.

'Thanks for everything, Mag,' he said awkwardly. 'You were always a good listener.'

'Something that was never your strong point, Dennis,' Mag said. Her smile took the sting out of her words.

'No, I suppose not,' Dennis said.

1980-81

Dennis's hands were sweating. No matter how many times he rubbed them on his trousers they became clammy again within minutes. He didn't want to give away the extent of his nervousness straight away as soon as they shook hands. He glanced at the clock on the wall beside him. Three minutes had passed since the last time he had looked at it.

The young girl behind the counter noticed and smiled at him sympathetically. 'He shouldn't be much longer, Mr Byrne.'

The bank was busy. A discreet hum animated the pristine, regimented surroundings as smartly-dressed businessmen waited to discuss their financial affairs in private rooms and across the counters with the bank staff. Even in his best suit and white shirt, freshly-ironed by Mag that morning, Dennis felt intimidated. He opened the file he held in his hands. The numbers swam across the page before his eyes. He closed it again. Mag had tried the night before to explain them to him one last time but his brain had refused to absorb any more stock level estimations, breakeven points or sales projections. He was convinced in the depths of his being, without any need of figures, that he could make this garage work. All he needed was someone to believe in him and give him a chance.

'Mr Byrne?' A tall, sharp-faced woman appeared in front of him. 'Come this way. The manager will see you now.' Her tone was clipped and efficient. She whipped around on her heels and, without waiting for a response from Dennis, marched off, past the cashiers to the offices on the other side. Dennis rallied himself into action and hurried after her. She opened the door of the furthest corner office and ushered him in.

The manager, a thin grey-haired man lifted himself a few inches out of his seat and leaned over his heavy, mahogany desk to offer Dennis his hand to shake.

'Please sit, Mr Byrne,' he said. Dennis sank into the low chair opposite, feeling small and vulnerable, a schoolboy called to the headmaster's office.

'You have requested a loan from this bank for the purposes of establishing an independent activity specialising in car repair and maintenance, have you not?' The manager removed his glasses and began rubbing the bridge of his nose.

Dennis blinked. 'Yes, I'm planning on starting a garage.'

'I must warn you that it is rare that we would give a favourable response to applicants of your age with so little collateral.'

'Oh,' said Dennis.

‘However, I have studied the application you submitted and I must admit that I am impressed. It shows a level of foresight and maturity rare in young aspiring entrepreneurs.’

‘Thanks.’ Dennis desperately hoped that he wouldn’t be asked to discuss any of the details contained in the file prepared by Mag.

‘I see that you have already identified suitable premises. With living quarters.’ He looked up and gave Dennis an approving nod. ‘You have a number of committed customers. Your figures are detailed and appear to be based on reality. Therefore, after due consideration, I am pleased to inform you that we are willing to provide you with the loan you require for your project.’ He smiled broadly in anticipation of Dennis’s gratitude.

‘Thank you very much,’ said Dennis.

The manager proceeded to outline the terms and conditions of the loan but nothing he said made sense to Dennis. His voice was a drone, unintelligible over the buzzing in Dennis’s ears.

He raced back to the small flat in Rathmines where he and Mag lived to tell her the good news. That night, sweeping away all of her objections, he took her out to dinner in a fancy restaurant to celebrate. The taste of imminent success intoxicated him more than the champagne he ordered.

The following weeks were hectic but thrilling. They made an offer on the old, rambling, run-down coal-yard they had spotted in Templeogue and it was accepted. They both gave in their notice on their jobs and began the arduous process of turning the yard into a space suitable for the new business. Large high corrugated gates opened onto a yard large enough to leave room for expansion. On one side was a shabby two-storey building; on the other, a row of coal sheds. Coal dust had penetrated everywhere, leaving a layer of black talc on every surface so that it seemed impossible to remove fully. In the main building, they knocked down internal walls to create a space where they could drive in cars and installed offices on the right-hand side. Above the offices was a flat where they could live. A steep, narrow stairway on one side of the building led to it. There were two bedrooms, a tiny kitchen at the back and another room that was the sitting room, dining room and everything else.

They converted the old coal sheds into workshops with benches for the dismantling, assembling, oiling, welding, testing of the cars of their future clients. For months, they worked until after midnight every night, then washed off the dirt and grime of the day before collapsing, exhausted, into bed beside each other.

They waited anxiously for their first customers to approach them when they finally opened their doors to business, but the garage quickly established a reputation for good quality and speedy repairs and soon Dennis had more work than he could handle alone. He contacted Francie O'Mahony, an old friend with whom Dennis had done his apprenticeship in Sweeney's garage. Despite the fact that Francie was a talented mechanic, he was unemployed. He had lost his job when his alcoholism became a serious problem causing him to become increasingly unreliable. Dennis's belief in him and the offer of a second chance brought Francie back from the brink and forged a solid friendship between the two men.

Mag's domain was the office. She looked after all the paperwork, kept the accounts, ordered parts and dealt with customers. During the first year, they worked long hours but Dennis could feel that success was within their grasp.

Just before the first anniversary of the opening of the garage, Mag called Dennis into the office. Her eyes were shining and she was trying unsuccessfully to suppress a smile.

'I have news, Dennis,' she said. 'I've just come from the doctor's. I'm pregnant.'

For a moment, Dennis stared uncomprehendingly into her face and then whooped with joy. He whirled her around the room, heedlessly knocking papers to the floor. He felt like the richest, luckiest man in the world. He squeezed her tightly against him until she protested and he had a sudden twinge of concern for their baby.

In the golden weeks that followed the announcement, Mag divided her time between working in the office and preparing the second bedroom in the upstairs flat for the baby. To Dennis's eyes, she glowed with an inner radiance.

In the eleventh week of her pregnancy, Dennis was working at the garage when he got a call from the Coombe. Mag had gone shopping in town that morning and had miscarried in the public toilets. A taxi-driver had taken her, doubled over with cramps, to the hospital. Immediately, Dennis dropped his tools and rushed to see her. He found Mag, pale and shocked, sitting in the emergency waiting room.

'How are you, Mag?' he asked anxiously. He crouched down in front of her, trying to warm up her cold hands which lay motionless in her lap. 'How are you feeling?'

She looked up blankly at him. She shook her head, unable to talk. He left her to speak to a nurse who had appeared to call the next patient. She took Dennis to one side, out of Mag's hearing.

'Straightforward miscarriage,' she said briskly. 'It's quite frequent prior to twelve weeks. There's absolutely no reason why your wife shouldn't make a full recovery and start another pregnancy within a few months. A couple of days of bed-rest and then she'll be up and about as good as new.'

Dennis led Mag slowly to the car and helped her to sit in the passenger's seat. Her silence and lack of reaction made him nervous so he chattered on, trying his best to bring her out of her torpor.

'The nurse said that you'll be just fine. Don't worry about it. It happens all the time. The next time will be the right time. We'll have a baby next year, just you wait and see.'

He glanced across at her. 'Go on, Mag, tell me to shut up, tell me that I might know something about the insides of a car but I don't have a clue about the internal workings of a woman.' But Mag wouldn't respond as he wanted her to. He couldn't reach her.

Mag examined her hands. 'I didn't know what to do, Dennis.' A sob escaped her. 'I stood there for ages. Someone started knocking at the door. I panicked and then—I flushed the toilet.'

Dennis shook his head, trying to shake the image out of it. 'Don't think about it, Mag, you're only upsetting yourself.' He tapped steadily on the steering wheel before pulling a cigarette from the pack on the dashboard. He put it between his lips but didn't light it. He stole a furtive look at Mag's tensed face and tossed it back beside the pack. He squeezed her knee.

'We'll be home in no time and then you can go up to bed for a good rest. I have to get back to fixing that jalopy of Johnny Higgins's. I don't know why he bothers. I've told him before; I'd be as well off cutting a hole in the floor for him so that he can stick his feet out and run it along the road like Fred Flintstone.'

Mag was mired in despair and was not listening to him. 'What should I have done? I didn't know what else to do. The water came surging up towards me and no matter how hard, I tried I couldn't look away. I was so afraid I'd see something recognisable; eyes or legs.'

'You did the right thing, Mag, of course you did. It's pointless tormenting yourself over it. Listen, did you hear that Francie has an admirer? He was telling me this morning what happened when he went to drop off the O'Neill's car after work yesterday. Didn't Mrs O'Neill call him inside and tell him that there was nothing like a manly man with a bit of grease on his hands for setting a woman right? Francie was lucky to escape with his virginity intact, not to mention his overalls.'

Tears started to roll down Mag's face. 'Why do you think it happened? Did I do something wrong? Maybe I did too much lifting and carrying.'

'You did nothing wrong at all, don't be fretting, Mag. You'll feel much better after a good rest. Here we are at the garage. No, stay there. I'll open the door and help you out. Let me carry you up the stairs.'

'No. Thanks. I'm able to walk.' Mag staggered as she stepped out of the car and reached out to clutch Dennis's arm. 'Stop worrying, Dennis, I'll be OK,' Mag said.

He put his arm around her waist and helped her to the door. 'Glad to hear it. The garage would fall apart if you weren't here keeping tabs on us. For a start, we wouldn't get paid. And as for myself, I'd be totally lost without you.'

Dennis's uneasiness lifted slightly after he had installed her in their double bed and drawn the curtains; she was just worn out, shattered, she'd be back to herself in the morning.

Except that she wasn't. Days passed. She was pale and quiet. He could see that she was distant, not quite focused on what he was saying when he tried to cheer her up, telling her funny stories of happenings with customers or suppliers. He knew that she wasn't sleeping very well because, although he fell into bed most nights exhausted and was asleep within seconds, sometimes he woke in the night and could feel her awake beside him. There was no movement but she bristled with alertness. Because he didn't know what to say, he pretended he was still asleep.

Gradually, the shadows retreated and she came back. Her energy returned and she went back to work in the office with new enthusiasm. Dennis, delighted to see her smiling again, used any excuse to drop in to see her whenever he had a minute and banished these overcast days from his memory.

Chapter 14

Mag took the bus into the city centre for their meeting with O'Brien. It meant that she didn't need to try to find parking in a city whose arteries were getting more choked every day. And, in any case, she liked public transport. She found it reassuring that all around her the world went on, everyone preoccupied with their own concerns. It was like entering a shoal of fish, each one appearing to dart in a random, independent direction and yet somehow there was an overall purpose, a distinguishable pattern if only one could pull back far enough to see it.

The bus trundled slowly into town, unable to build up any speed, hindered as it was by bus-stops, traffic lights and traffic. Mag watched a group of giggling teenage girls in school uniforms climb up the steps of the bus, making conspicuous efforts to ignore the boys they had left behind at the bus-stop. A young mother, herding two small children, a baby in one arm, a folded buggy in the other, tried to clamber aboard. An elderly man, unconcerned by any delay he might be causing, fumbled for the right coins in his pocket. Cloaked in anonymity, it was comforting to feel that she was a small part of a bigger picture.

Mag got off the bus on Dame Street. She crossed the road at the front gate of Trinity and walked along the high railings around the university until she reached Pearse Street Garda Station where they had an appointment to see O'Brien at twelve. Dennis had phoned her the previous evening to say that O'Brien preferred to see them there as he had a number of other meetings arranged that day.

It was a large garda station and although Mag had passed in front of it many times, she had never been inside. The austere grey front and imposing steps intimidated her. Numerous garda motorbikes and cars were parked outside. A steady stream of young men and women flowed through the wide front doors, taking the steps two at a time. She felt uncomfortable waiting outside, standing still. She checked the time; it was just after twelve. She looked around and saw Dennis running towards her at a brisk pace.

'Sorry I'm late. Parking.' He was out of breath. 'Let's go in.'

Inside, the station buzzed with activity. Mag and Dennis were ignored as people rushed by, intent on their destination. They were looking around for someone to ask directions from when a familiar voice called out to them. O'Brien was holding up his hand to attract their attention and to signal them to wait for him where they were. He turned back to the man and woman with whom he was having a spirited conversation and brought it to a close before joining them. This time he was in uniform. He seemed distracted.

'Please follow me. We have a meeting room just down here.' He led the way down a long corridor to a small, sparsely furnished, windowless room with flickering fluorescent light. He invited them to sit. 'I'd offer you something to drink,' he said. 'Only I don't think I'd be doing you any favours. It's from a machine and you'd almost want to run a drug test to distinguish the tea from the coffee.'

'That's all right. We don't need anything,' Mag said.

'So, you wanted to see me?' O'Brien looked from one to the other.

'Yes, we did,' Dennis said shortly. 'First of all, is there any update from your side?'

'The investigation is progressing,' O'Brien said, weighing his words. 'We are hoping to have our report completed and ready for the inquest next week.'

'And what are the main findings in your report?' Dennis said.

'I'm afraid I'm not really in a position to go through the details right now but I will be in touch over the next few days before the inquest takes place.' O'Brien was pleasant but firm. 'Now, I believe that there was something you wanted to tell me about?'

'Yes, we wanted to show you something Dennis discovered on Ciara's computer,' Mag said. 'Yesterday, we cleared out her room in Trinity and afterwards Dennis checked her email messages and found these. We thought we should let you know about them.' Mag took the two printed pages from her handbag and laid them on the table in front of O'Brien. He picked them up and read them.

'Ah,' he said, as if the world had yet again conformed to his negative opinion of it. He placed the pages on the table in front of him.

'Is that all you have to say, Sergeant?' Dennis asked.

'Sorry, Mr Byrne, I was thinking. Thank you for giving me this.'

'So what are you going to do about it? Are you going to challenge Colm McMurray about this? Find out what he has to say for himself?'

'I don't think that's appropriate for the moment. There's nothing illegal in a relationship of this sort between two consenting adults.'

Mag feared Dennis's reaction. 'But what if it had something to do with Ciara's death? She did have her accident just after she left his house,' she said. O'Brien remained inscrutable.

'It is up to us to judge if any possible link might exist between your daughter's accident and this relationship. It may very well be an unfortunate coincidence.' O'Brien leaned across the table. 'And just in case you are getting any ideas, I am warning you both; neither of you is to annoy or even approach Mr McMurray; not at his home or anywhere else. Have I made myself clear?'

'Perfectly,' Mag said.

Dennis nodded curtly. 'I have a question,' he asked, holding O'Brien's gaze. 'Is your investigation leading you to believe that another person was involved in Ciara's accident?'

'And what is making you ask that question?' O'Brien looked from one to the other.

'There are a few things that bother us about this accident and we want to be sure that the Gardaí are taking it seriously,' Mag said.

'Rest assured, Mrs Byrne, we are taking the matter very seriously as we do all of our cases. Leave it with us.'

'So that's it then.' Dennis leaned back, hands apart in a gesture of renunciation.

'For the moment, yes,' O'Brien said politely.

'Right, then we won't take up any more of your time.' Dennis pulled his jacket on in preparation to leave.

'Just one final thing,' O'Brien said. 'I would like to arrange to see both of you next week to discuss our findings in advance of the inquest on Friday. We could meet here or, if you prefer, I could call out to you.'

'Whatever suits you,' Mag said.

'I'll give you a call early next week to fix a time if that's all right.'

Mag and Dennis left the station, subdued and silent. Dennis thrust his hands into the pockets of his jacket. His hunched shoulders betrayed his dissatisfaction with the meeting. Mag had also hoped for something more, some clarification, but they were leaving as much in the dark as when they'd arrived. Side by side, they walked down the street away from the garda station.

At the intersection of Townsend Street and Pearse Street, Mag noticed a dark-haired, gangly young man dashing recklessly through traffic. He was followed closely by a small, fair girl whom Mag recognised but had difficulty placing. Horns blared as they reached the pavement a few steps in front of Dennis and Mag, intact but careless of the risks they had taken.

The girl punched her companion on the arm. 'We could have been killed,' she said. 'You are a total lunatic, Andrew Tierney. Remind me never to get in a car with you.'

As she spoke Mag remembered who she was. She was from Ciara's year at college, a friend who had come to the house once.

'Hello. It's Rachel, isn't it?' Mag said.

The girl looked around at the mention of her name and noticed Mag. Her excitement faded and she became embarrassed.

'Oh, hello, Mrs Byrne. I didn't see you. Sorry. I didn't mean anything by that stupid comment.'

'I know that, don't worry about it,' Mag said. 'Dennis, this is Rachel. She was a friend of Ciara's, from her class in college, isn't that right?'

'Yes. We were both in her class. Andrew was, as well.' She glanced at the young man beside her. 'Andrew, these are Ciara's parents.'

He shuffled diffidently, unsure of what to say. 'I'm very sorry about Ciara. We all miss her a lot,' he said.

'That's for sure,' Rachel said.

'We know. We do too,' Mag said.

There was a moment of silence as the two young people contemplated how they might best extricate themselves from this awkward situation. Dennis spoke up before they could leave. 'Tell me, by any chance, were either of you at that party in the McMurray house the night of Ciara's accident?'

'I wasn't,' Rachel said. 'But Andrew was.'

Andrew confirmed with a nod.

'Would you mind if we asked you a few questions about that night?' Dennis said. Mag tried to throw him a warning glance but he avoided meeting her eye.

'No problem,' Andrew said. 'I'm not sure that there's much I can say though.'

'Maybe we could talk about it over a bite of lunch. Is there a place nearby you could recommend?' Dennis was reviving a little after their interview with O'Brien.

Rachel and Andrew looked at each other. 'Well, we were on our way to a pizza place around the corner. The food's not bad and the portions are big,' Andrew said.

'Sounds perfect to me,' Dennis said.

It was obviously a restaurant that had gained a certain reputation for value for money among college students: the place was thronged with them. Andrew, with a well-practised technique, pounced on a table that was being liberated and they squeezed around a tiny table that would have better suited two. A girl with blue-streaked hair, five or six earrings in each ear and two in her nose dropped a rag on the table in front of them. She expeditiously scooted the crumbs to the floor and into their laps. She tucked the rag over the belt of her apron and produced a small notebook. 'So?' she said.

Rachel explained that there were no menus, the choices of the day being written up on blackboards overhead.

'So did McMurray organise this kind of get-together often?' Dennis asked Andrew after they had ordered.

'Not really, but he does invite all the final year students every year for a few drinks at the end of the year. I think he thinks he's a bit of a cool dude, like he's in with us. Also, he has this big mansion of a house and I get the impression he likes showing it off,' Andrew replied.

'Jealousy will get you nowhere, Andrew,' Rachel said.

Andrew shook his head slightly and rolled his eyes. 'He has all the girls in the college crazy about him. I don't know, it must be the older man syndrome.'

'You wouldn't understand,' Rachel said. 'It's called charisma; you have it or you don't and let me tell you, the man has it in buckets.'

Mag followed the exchange between the two students closely. There was nothing in their manner that betrayed any knowledge of a special relationship between Ciara and McMurray and she didn't think they would speak so openly if they were aware of anything.

'I don't get it,' Andrew turned to them. 'Personally, I think he's a bit of a prick. But there's no accounting for taste, especially girls' taste. In any case, that was the only time I was invited to his place.'

'I couldn't go, I was at my cousin's wedding that night,' Rachel added.

'Did you talk to Ciara during the evening?' Dennis asked Andrew.

'Just for a couple of minutes. To be honest, I thought she wasn't in great form but I put it down to the row she had with Vincent Connolly at one stage.'

'I heard about that. What was that about?' Dennis asked.

'I'm not sure, I didn't overhear it myself and Vincent didn't want to talk about it afterwards but I remember the mood he was in when he came back into the room. He didn't talk much for the rest of the night; I think he was a bit cut up. He left early too, before the rest of us. Although, when we were getting into the cars, I noticed him off to one side in the dark smoking. I thought he was long gone but maybe he just wanted to be on his own for a while before he got on his motorbike.'

Mag frowned as Andrew spoke but at that moment, the food arrived. The young, blue-haired waitress jostled for space on the table and tried to find room for the four enormous pizzas. Mag gazed in dismay at the amount of food on her plate while the others delved into theirs with obvious enthusiasm.

'Did Ciara leave at the same time as everyone or did she stay back?' she asked Andrew.

'I can't really remember. I think we all left around the same time. There were a good few of us so I can't be sure. I think maybe we left first.'

'So, you didn't see anything? You didn't see the accident or Ciara's car?' Dennis asked.

'No, nothing. Sorry. It was very dark and we were all talking in the car. I was driving but I saw nothing. She could have been a few minutes behind me. The first I heard about Ciara having an accident was the next morning.' Andrew shook his head apologetically. 'I couldn't believe it.'

'I hope you don't think that the row with Vincent Connolly had anything to do with Ciara's accident,' Rachel spoke up. 'He's been upset about it ever since but I don't think Ciara would have let it get to her all that much; she knew how he was.'

'Don't worry,' Mag said. 'We're not making any assumptions. We just wanted to get a clear understanding of what happened before the accident. By the way.' She picked up her bag and started searching inside it: 'I wonder if either of you know who this person might be.' She took out the photo of Ciara with Joe and held it out to them. 'I found it among Ciara's things but I don't recognise him.'

'I've seen him before,' Rachel said slowly. 'I saw him with Ciara in Madigan's one evening. They were deep in conversation. I said hello but she kind of made it clear that she didn't want me to hang around so I just left them to it.'

'So you don't know his name?' Dennis asked.

'No, she didn't introduce him or anything. I was a bit surprised but I suppose she didn't want me to spoil a romantic moment.'

'Oh, so you got the impression that this was a romantic relationship?' Mag said.

'I suppose so.' Rachel shifted around in her seat, uneasy. 'They looked as if they were having a big serious conversation and at one stage I saw him holding her hand. I asked Ciara who he was afterwards but she didn't want to talk about it so I didn't push.' She examined the photo again and glanced nervously at Mag and Dennis. She handed the photo to Mag who put it back in her bag.

'How long before Ciara's death did this happen?' Mag asked.

'It was a week or so before, middle of March, I think.'

Andrew looked at his watch. 'We'll have to run. We have a lecture at two,' he said. He took out his wallet from the back pocket of his jeans.

'Go ahead, you two,' Dennis said. 'I'll deal with the bill.'

'No, no, we'll pay for ourselves.' The two students produced their money and tried to give it to Dennis who insisted that they keep it. Eventually they gave up and, in a confusion of thanks, hurried off to their lecture.

After they left, Dennis and Mag looked at each other, neither of them sure what to say next.

'Is that all you're going to eat?' Dennis asked.

Mag gazed down at her almost untouched pizza. 'I'm not in the mood. Have it if you want.' She pushed her plate away from her and ordered a coffee from a passing waitress.

'What do you think?' Dennis asked through mouthfuls.

'Well, it's what we already thought. It looks like she was seeing both men at the same time. It's so strange, I don't recognise Ciara in all of this.'

'Do you think their wives knew?' Dennis said.

'I wouldn't be surprised if Caroline McMurray suspected,' Mag mused. 'When I spoke to her at the funeral, she struck me as very tense, uptight. I got the impression that things weren't great between them.'

'And did you hear what the young lad said about Vincent Connolly?' Dennis passed his plate to the waitress who brought Mag's coffee. 'He said that he saw him outside the house when they were all leaving. But Connolly told us that he left early and went straight to the pub. I'd be interested to know why he lied to us.'

'I noticed that,' she said.

'I might try to have another chat with him.'

The restaurant had emptied over the past few minutes and now Mag and Dennis were the only customers left.

'I need to get back to the garage shortly,' Dennis said. 'My plan is to come back in after work to pick up Ciara's stuff. I might drop into Madigan's and see what I can find out. Could I have that photo, just in case?' Mag gave it to him.

'Do you want me to take you home?' he asked.

'No, don't worry about me. You go ahead, I'll take the bus,' Mag said.

She watched Dennis walk to the counter to pay for their meal. He even managed to extract a semblance of a smile from their impassive waitress.

She wrapped her hands around her coffee mug and, in her mind, tried to hold on to the Ciara that she had always known.

1982

'Hiya, Mag. Dennis was looking for me. Is he here?' Jimmy came into the main office, wiping his hands on a greasy rag. It was five o'clock.

'He's in the back, Jimmy. He'll be out in a minute. Let me finish totting this up and I'll give him a shout.' Mag sneaked a look at the wiry young man that they had hired earlier in the year. At first, he had been prickly and defensive, suspicious of any kindness but over time he had become a good worker, dependable and straight. Mag was sure that he would be deeply hurt by his impending layoff. She had felt awful persuading Dennis to let him go but it was the only way they were going to be able to keep their head above water. For over six months now, they had been having serious financial problems in the garage. They were finding it hard to meet their monthly payments to the bank and were taking no money themselves out of the business. The recession was affecting them badly, their customers were struggling to pay and they had stretched their credit to the absolute limit. If things continued this way for much longer, there was a good chance they would have to close down before Christmas.

They now had four employees, two qualified mechanics and two apprentices. It made sense to let Jimmy go: he was the last one to join them and he cost more than the apprentices. Mag had examined, scrutinised, juggled the figures in every direction but they still told her the same story again and again; their costs consistently exceeded their income and something needed to change. Dennis had not wanted to hear it; he was convinced they'd find a way out, that this was only a temporary blip for the garage but eventually he was forced to listen to what Mag was telling him. She knew that this was a hard decision for Dennis who saw the garage and the small family they had become as joined by more than mere financials on a page but she also knew that soon, the choice would no longer be his.

She went to the door of the storeroom. 'Dennis, could you come here for a minute please?' Dennis appeared, holding three spark plugs. 'Well, Jimmy,' he said as though they had not already spent an hour together earlier that day on an engine change.

'Something wrong, Dennis?' Jimmy was on his guard.

'No, no, Jimmy… Well, yes, there is but it's nothing to do with you…Although it does concern you.'

Jimmy's eyes narrowed and he shifted his weight between his feet. He waited and said nothing.

'I don't know if you've noticed but the garage hasn't been doing very well lately.'

'Nope, I'm not paid to notice, I'm paid to fix cars.' Jimmy was not going to make this easy on him.

'Well, we got burnt with a few bad debts and we lost a couple of contracts for fleet servicing and there's a drop in passing trade too.'

Jimmy remained stoic.

'I think what Dennis is trying to say is that circumstances are forcing us to make some changes in the garage.' Mag wanted to help Dennis who was floundering desperately but Jimmy flashed her a look that told her to keep out, that this was men's business. Mag walked back to her desk and sat down. She pulled a ledger towards her and began to work but kept a watchful eye on the two men.

Dennis battled on. 'It's only temporary. I'll have you back on the books as soon as I can. It's just that we can't keep going the way we are and as you are the last one in then it makes sense that you're the one to go. But as I say, it's temporary.'

'No, it's not, Dennis. I won't be back.'

'There's no need to take it like that, Jimmy. There's nothing personal, I've no problem with your work.'

'That may be, but the boss is still the boss and he'll shaft everyone around him before he'll lose out himself. More fool me that I ever forgot it.' Jimmy's bitter words stabbed Dennis to the core because, despite his efforts to get on with his staff, he was afraid that they might be true.

'That's not how it is,' Dennis said. 'I have no choice here.'

'Right,' Jimmy said in the tone of a man refusing to descend into argument.

'Well, it's up to you; you can work out your months' notice or you can take your severance pay and go when it suits you.'

'I won't be hanging around,' Jimmy said shortly.

'Let's not part on bad terms,' Dennis said and held out his hand.

Jimmy looked down at the greasy rag he was still holding and placed it in Dennis's hand. 'I'll gather up my tools. You can check my kit on the way out; if you want to make sure I'm not taking any from the garage.'

'No, no, not at all, why would I do that? I have complete faith in you, Jimmy.'

'Well, I'll go. Good luck to you,' Jimmy said with an undertone of sarcasm. He left the office, his narrow back held straight. Dennis turned the spark plugs over in his hands and without looking at Mag, he said in a gruff voice, 'I'd better go and fit these.'

All the warmth was sucked out of the air when he left and a leaden heaviness pressed on Mag's shoulders. She rubbed her hand over her belly as if to reassure herself and the tiny embryo inside that this was a passing cloud that would blow over.

At dinner that evening, Dennis said very little. Mag felt an overwhelming urge to apologise but she didn't know what for. Life wasn't taking the path they had mapped out for it but she couldn't see any way to divert it back on course. The garage, Dennis's dream, was sinking into the quicksand of debt and the timing didn't allow them to greet the news of this new pregnancy with the joy that it deserved.

Mag found herself unable to shake off the uneasiness that had taken a grip of her. Every evening before getting into bed, the thought came to her unbidden: 'Another day gained'. She didn't want to keep a tally of the days until the end of her pregnancy but yet each day, the new number flipped over in her brain like the clock in the train station.

Sometimes, she lay awake at night and tried to tune in to her body, to listen to the flow of its liquids, to interpret its signs and gurgles but all remained mysterious to her. When she tried to express this in words to Dennis, he suggested that she take another appointment with the doctor or even that she change doctor if she had any misgivings about this one. According to him, it was pointless worrying unnecessarily when there were so many real problems to worry about. She knew he was right but somehow an illogical demon had taken possession of her and was telling her that if she dropped her vigilance, even for a moment, something terrible would happen.

On the 8th of November, three days before their monthly bank payment was due with nothing in the bank to meet it, they secured a contract with Lyons for maintenance of their fleet. The tide was turning. Dennis was exultant. Mag produced some projections. It certainly improved their turnover and would allow them to operate for a while longer but it was not profitable business. They needed desperately to find more lucrative business if they were to stay afloat.

Dennis flared up at her when she ventured to discuss this with him, treating her as if she were a harbinger of bad news. He accused her of always wanting to throw a wet blanket over any good news and stormed out of the room.

His words took on the resonance of a prophecy the following week when Mag was woken in the middle of the night by agonising pains in the bottom of her stomach. She was miscarrying again. The realisation shocked her but didn't surprise her and she knew that she had been anticipating this all along. She slipped out of bed and went to the bathroom to cry. She had been there a few minutes before she heard a soft knock on the bathroom door.

'What's wrong, Mag? Can I come in?'

She unlocked the door and let him in. She could tell he was shaken when he saw her swollen, tear-stained face.

'Is it the baby?' he asked.

She nodded. He pulled her towards him and held her against his chest.

'We'll go to see the doctor. We'll go together and get answers. Maybe we need to see a specialist?'

'We don't have the money; we can't afford it.'

'To hell with money. You can't put a price on something like this.'

It felt good to lean on him, to be enveloped in his arms as though nothing bad could hurt her inside this charmed circle. Dennis led her back to bed and for the rest of the night, she lay with her cheek against his chest, listening to his heart beating.

The doctor told them not to worry, that miscarriages were very common, far more common than they might imagine since it was something that most people didn't talk about. He said that they happened so frequently that it was perfectly possible that two miscarriages could be a coincidence and that it was only after three that it would be advisable to consult a specialist. Mag watched his lips moving and wondered how there could be a link between these dispassionate medical facts and the emotional loss and primal yearning she was feeling. Dennis listened with interest and nodded while the doctor spoke.

Afterwards, Dennis said that he thought this suggestion made sense. Mag's voice failed her: it was her body that would have to go through this a third time, an experience that these men seemed to be treating it as if it were an interesting scientific experiment. It was in her womb, in the centre of her being, that a spark of new life would start to take form, sending her secret messages signalling its presence long before anything was visible to anyone else. It was a connection that couldn't be explained rationally. She couldn't argue with Dennis because she knew what he would say. He would ask what other options they had, he would say that it was the only sensible way forward, that it would all be worth it in the long run, that of course he cared, and that this was his child too. She would be able to offer no defence against these words, because he was right, but they were not the words she wanted to hear.

Chapter 15

On his return to the garage, Dennis was drawn into a discussion about the best way to dismount and replace the worn rack and pinion on a Citroen steering system. As the afternoon wore on, the constant activity of the garage prevented him from thinking too deeply about his conversations with O'Brien and Ciara's college mates. It was a relief to forget about the unanswerable questions that niggled him and to feel instead the strain of manual effort in his muscles.

At five o'clock he put away his tools, took a quick shower and changed into clean jeans and a shirt. He decided to take the garage's small Volkswagen van into Trinity, fill it with Ciara's stuff and then take it to Mag's house where it would be easier to store.

He drove to the back gate of Trinity and spoke to the security guard controlling entry. He paged his colleague whom Dennis had met two days earlier when clearing the room and arranged for them to meet at the front door of Ciara's building. Dennis drove through the campus and parked as near as he could to the red-brick building.

The warm, concentrated rays of evening sun had drawn the students out of their rooms and classes and a group of them sat laughing and joking on the steps leading to the front door. They shot openly inquisitive looks at Dennis as he stood nearby waiting for the guard to join him.

'Do you want to get past?' one of them asked.

'No, thanks, I'm waiting for someone.'

The security guard arrived, jangling a bunch of keys. 'Hello, Mr Byrne,' he said. 'Follow me, I'll open up that storage room for you now.'

Looks and whispers were exchanged in the group.

'You'll have to move from here,' the guard said. 'This man will be passing through with furniture and boxes and you'll have to make way for him.'

'You're not Ciara's dad, are you?' one girl asked.

'I am,' Dennis said. 'I'm taking away her things.'

'Do you want a hand carrying stuff?' Two young men stood up.

'Thanks, that'd be great,' Dennis said. He surveyed the faces around him, their youth an impermeable shield against the harshness of death. 'By the way, I was hoping to have a word with Vincent Connolly from Ciara's class. Do you know where I might find him? Would he be around here somewhere?'

'I saw him earlier. In the canteen. I think I know where he is. I'll get him for you, if you like.' A tall girl in an oversized Aran jumper stood up and hitched up a heavy rucksack on her shoulder.

'Thanks, that'd be great,' Dennis said as she strode off with a nonchalant wave to her friends.

With the offered help, it only took three trips to empty the storeroom of Ciara's belongings but it took a bit longer to arrange everything so that it fit in the van. Dennis was amazed that so much had been amassed in such a small room. He was trying to twist a chair around so that he could squeeze in the last box of books when he looked up to see Colm McMurray approaching.

He straightened up and waited. McMurray walked up to him, his hands in his pockets. He looked tired, as though all the energy had seeped out of him. Dennis waited for him to speak.

McMurray glanced at the contents of the open van. 'I heard you were here,' he said.

'I had to take her things away,' Dennis said.

'I came to talk to you because I presume you know. About Ciara and me.'

'I do.' Dennis turned back to the van and gave one of the boxes a vicious shove to wedge it into a small space.

'I wanted to explain.'

'What's to explain? She was a kid. Your student.'

'It's not that simple.'

'It's that simple to me. Next, you'll try telling me she threw herself at you and you couldn't resist.' Dennis turned away in disgust and slammed the doors of the van shut.

'If you'll listen to me, I'll tell you what happened.'

Dennis stopped and turned around. 'Fine. I'm listening.'

'Yes, Ciara was young but she was an independent young woman who knew her own mind. Neither of us intended for things to work out the way they did but that's how it happened. I don't know if it would have lasted; there was a lot standing between us but for all that, we had something real.' He cleared his throat. 'I cared a lot for Ciara.'

The words echoed for a short moment in the air between them before Dennis shrugged. 'Fat lot of good that did her,' he said. 'Don't come expecting forgiveness from me. You used my daughter and then lied through your teeth to save I don't know what – your marriage? Your reputation?' A sneer of contempt curled Dennis's lips as he spoke.

'The reason I came to talk to you wasn't to get your forgiveness, as you put it. Ciara was very special to me and I felt that I owed it to her and to you to try to put things straight. I know I didn't handle it very well the day you called but I was still in shock. It wasn't my intention to lie but I didn't know how it would help you to tell you everything. I needed time to think. And I didn't want to be unfair to Ciara, who wasn't there to defend herself.'

'Ah, so all that charade was for Ciara's benefit? How honourable of you?' Dennis's raised voice and sarcastic tone caused two students cycling past to turn and stare at him.

'Don't twist my words. That's not what I meant and you know it,' McMurray said. 'I wanted to leave for Ciara but I have responsibilities to my sons. They need me. It's not that easy.'

'That's what they all say,' Dennis said. 'Don't try that line on me. I'm not a twenty-two-year-old girl.' He turned away to leave but paused with his hand on the car-door handle. 'So, what really happened that night? How did Ciara have her accident?'

McMurray shot him a look. 'The accident? I already told you. The only thing I didn't mention was that Ciara stayed back for a few minutes after everyone else left. We talked for a couple of minutes but she left just like I said she did. I knew nothing about the accident until the next day. If only you knew how sorry I am that I didn't do something that might have changed the course of events of that night.'

'Well, nothing can be done now. You and I will just have to live with the consequences,' Dennis said. He opened the door, got in the van and drove away. In his rear-view mirror, he could see McMurray gazing after him, a hangdog expression on his face, as if he hoped someone would come along and sort out the mess he'd made of his life.

The blood was pounding in Dennis's arteries as he gave an abrupt sign of thanks to the security guard on the way out.

He slipped into the crawling flow of rush hour traffic and edged along Westland Row. He decided to call into Madigan's, have a pint and find out if someone there knew who this Joe was. If he let an hour pass, the traffic would have eased off.

Madigan's was not busy, with the usual smattering of people when Dennis entered. He sat on a barstool at the counter and examined a newspaper someone had left behind while he waited to be served. Two barmen were talking and preparing for the evening. One, a stocky, wiry-haired man of about fifty, was emptying a dishwasher of glasses and the other, a younger man, tall and thin with a sharp nose and narrow moustache, was pouring a pint of Guinness.

'What'll you have?' he asked Dennis from his position behind the taps.

'You can pour me one of those,' Dennis said, nodding at the settling pint of Guinness on the mat beside the tap.

'Coming up.'

Dennis glanced over the headlines of the newspaper, unmindful of the information in it while the ritual of pouring, topping off and skimming was performed on his pint. A trickle from the creamy head flowed over the fingers of the barman as he placed the pint on a beer-mat in front of him.

'Thanks.' Dennis took a mouthful. 'That hit the spot. Now, if you happened to have a sandwich that'd be great.' He put down his glass with a sigh.

'You're in luck. We have a couple left over from lunch. Will chicken salad do you?'

'Perfect.'

The barman brought him a sandwich and as Dennis took a note from his wallet to pay, he removed the photo of Ciara with the man named Joe.

'You wouldn't happen to know this man, would you?' he asked, showing the barman the photo. The man wiped his hands carefully on a tea-towel and examined the photo.

'Ah yes, that's Joe Farrell. I haven't seen him for a good while now.' He examined the photo more closely. 'As a matter of fact, I think I took this photo myself.' He handed it back to Dennis. 'I remember the girl. Joe asked me to take the photo for him. I can't tell you who she is though.'

'It's OK, that's my daughter,' Dennis said.

'So why don't you ask her about Joe?' The barman was curious rather than aggressive.

Dennis looked long and hard into his pint before replying. 'I would if I could but she was killed in a car accident. A month ago.'

'I'm so sorry to hear that.' He slowly and meticulously straightened the towel on the bar in front of him. 'She seemed a very nice girl. Joe was obviously delighted to see her. He wasn't involved in the accident, I hope.'

'No but we found this photo among her belongings and I wouldn't mind talking to him.'

'Well, he used to drop in here fairly regularly on a Friday after work—that's how I got to know him—but ever since he took that new job in Siemens I don't see him so often, apart from that time he was here with your daughter.'

'Do you know how I might get in touch with him?' Dennis asked.

'Sorry, I don't have his number but if he calls in, I'll tell him you were looking for him. What's the name?'

'Dennis Byrne. Thanks.'

'No problem,' the barman said. He indicated Dennis's almost empty pint glass. 'Let me get you another one. It's on the house.'

'No, thanks,' Dennis said. 'I should be going.'

It was close to ten o'clock when he finally left. His energy was sapped by the realisation that no matter what he did, no matter what he found out, nothing could bring Ciara back. He stood up and put on his jacket and went to his van.

It felt cold and vast outside after the warmth and smoky closeness of the pub. Dennis took a longer path than necessary back to where the van was parked; it wouldn't do any harm to walk off the pint and, in any case, no-one was waiting for him anywhere.

1983

'Put your coat on, Mag. Let's go. There's something I need to show you.' Dennis burst into the office while Mag was stuffing invoices into envelopes.

'Let me finish off here first. I want to get these off in today's post,' Mag said distractedly.

'No.' Dennis removed the envelope from her hand, swivelled her chair around and pulled her into an upright position. 'This won't take long. The invoices can wait.'

He took Mag's coat from the coat-rack inside the door and held it open for her. 'Madame,' he said with a flourish. The coat no longer closed over her middle but Mag refused to buy a special maternity one as she said it would be a waste for only a few months. She was now seven months pregnant. As the weeks passed, both Dennis and Mag had started to breathe more easily. Even Mag, who had remained circumspect long after Dennis had given in to buoyant optimism, was now speaking in the future tense rather than the conditional.

'I don't know what the panic is,' Mag said but slipped her arms into her coat anyway. 'Another ten minutes and the job would have been done. I want to be sure that the invoices get delivered before the end of the month.'

'Stop fussing, missus, the garage is doing just fine now. Things are looking good and a day later for the invoices is neither here nor there.' Dennis put his arm around her shoulder and guided her out the door. 'Francie, we're off,' he shouted at the feet sticking out from under a Toyota. 'Mind the shop while we're gone. Good man.'

'I don't know what you are up to, Dennis Byrne, but in case you haven't noticed, I'm in no fit state to go gallivanting around the country.' Mag was laughing as she sidled into the passenger side of the car.

'How could I forget? Don't worry; it's not far at all.' He leaned over and, rubbing her stomach, spoke to it directly. 'Hang in there, Bob. Don't mind your mother. When you get out of there we'll sort her out together.'

A few minutes later, Dennis pulled up outside a large two-storey house at the end of a cul-de-sac in Terenure. There was a railing around a small patio area at the front, obviously off a bedroom. A cherry tree stood in the front garden. The house looked a little neglected but it was a solid house with a garden gate on one side that led to the back. There were trees along one side where the road abutted a small park and they and the location made the house a green haven hidden away from the busy main roads.

'What are we doing here? Who lives here?' Mag asked.

'Nobody, at the moment,' Dennis said. He took a key from his pocket and showed it to her. 'Dan Lowry lent me this. He's the estate agent looking after the sale of the house. I told him that we were on the look-out for a place to buy and he thought this might suit us. So, what do you think?' He enjoyed watching her expression evolve through a spectrum of emotions to eventually settle on disbelief.

'We can't afford a house like this,' she said. 'Have you forgotten about the garage?'

'Wait until you see the inside. You might change your mind. It needs a lot of work. An old couple used to live here until recently but he died a few months ago and she can't live alone any more. They weren't able to do much with the upkeep. Come in and take a look.'

The house felt enormous after their small flat over the garage. Downstairs, there was a large sitting room with a bay window which looked out over the garden, a smaller room to the front that had fallen into disuse and a big kitchen which had the potential to be open and sunny but was currently dark and shabby. Upstairs, there were four bedrooms, all different in form and size. Throughout, the house was dilapidated and dirty. Although it had been unoccupied for only four months, the warmth of people living there had vanished and it had lost its sense of homeliness.

At the back of the house, there was a patio area with a sloping path that led down to the garden which was a wilderness of brambles, nettles and lost objects, but it was big and was catching the afternoon sun.

'I love it,' Mag said.

'I thought you might,' Dennis said. 'So will we make an offer then?'

'Hold on, Dennis, I don't know if we can afford it. What if we hit a bad patch with the garage again? Will we be able to meet the repayments?'

'Stop worrying about the garage. Those problems are all behind us now. Think, Little Bob will have a place to play and we need to start having a life away from the garage too.'

Mag looked around and took a deep breath. 'Ok then, you've convinced me. Let's go for it.'

Their first offer was accepted and the sale took place quickly. After the papers were signed and the keys were handed over, Dennis had difficulty persuading Mag not to launch immediately into the renovation of the house. She was in the last month of her pregnancy but, despite her bulk, was more enthusiastic and energetic than he had seen her for a long time.

Early one morning in June, she shook him awake. 'Dennis, wake up.' Her low voice barely pierced his consciousness. Dawn had just broken and the furniture and objects in the room were starting to take shape.

'It's time. We need to go to the hospital. The baby is coming.'

'What?' He registered what she was saying and sat up with a start. 'Right, right, what do we need to do?' In a state of alarm, he started to get dressed, heedless of the items of clothing at hand.

'Calm down, Dennis. We have time. Would you like some breakfast?'

'Breakfast?' He stared at her in amazement. It seemed a strange, incongruous thing to be concerned about just before such a momentous event.

'It might take a while.'

In the end, Dennis made tea for them both. He drank a few, scalding mouthfuls from a mug before pouring the rest down the sink. Every so often, Mag gasped and winced as the contractions came until Dennis could take it no longer.

'Come on,' he said. 'We'd better go. Do you want me to carry you to the car?'

Mag burst out laughing. 'I can walk that far, Dennis. In any case there's no way the two of us would fit going down the stairs.' At the hospital, Mag was examined and transferred to the labour ward. Dennis hovered around her unsure of what his role was to be in these proceedings. He felt bulky and cumbersome.

Everywhere he stood, it seemed that he blocked access to a machine or an instrument or hindered the movements of the nurses. He tried to stay close to Mag but with each contraction Mag appeared to withdraw from him, seeking strength internally. He fidgeted around her until she sent him away for a while. 'You're making me nervous, Dennis. Have a coffee, come back in an hour,' Mag said, in between contractions.

Dennis looked to the attending nurse for her accord before obeying her. Accustomed as he was to working outside, he was glad to escape the suffocating heat of the hospital. He went outside to smoke a cigarette. He bought a newspaper but his eyes skidded over the headlines and he couldn't make sense of the words.

Almost an hour had passed when he returned to Mag's side but he could see instantly that it had been a difficult hour for her. She was sweating profusely, her hair was plastered to her head and her face was lined in a concentration of pain. She was alone. Dennis rushed to her. 'Mag, are you all right? Do you want me to call someone?'

'No. Just stay with me.' Mag spoke the words with some effort. She held his hand and squeezed it tightly each time the pain reached its peak. She moaned quietly. Dennis felt frustrated and helpless. He sat on a tiny stool whose spindly legs spread out ominously when he sank his weight on it and tried to cool her down with a damp face cloth. He smoothed back her hair but all the time the thought ran through his brain that this had been a mistake, that the end result could not be worth all this suffering.

The midwife came back and, after a quick examination, gave Mag a congratulatory pat on her bare knee. 'Very soon now,' she said. 'Do you want to stay till the end?' she asked Dennis.

'I was there at the beginning. I might as well be there at the end,' he replied, not at all convinced he was right. The violence of childbirth, the raw barbarity of the act was a shock to Dennis. He realised that he far preferred the relatively clean functionality of an engine to the messiness of the human body.

The obstetrician returned in time to catch the baby who slithered out, covered in a mess of white, brown and red human secretions, into his waiting hands. He cut the umbilical cord and placed the baby on Mag's stomach. Dennis's first reaction was one of disgust. 'Congratulations to you,' he said to Dennis. 'It's a perfect little girl.'

'A girl,' Dennis repeated and stared down at the tiny, pinched, purple face. She had wisps of dark hair on her head, a mere bump for a nose and her mouth was wide open wailing in protest at this unsolicited disruption in her existence.

'Do you want to take her?' Mag asked faintly.

Dennis hesitated but then picked her up and held her in the crook of his arm. After a while, her cries lost some of their force and tailed off. She grasped Dennis's t-shirt in her fist and he was surprised at how difficult it was to dislodge her grip. With the same gesture she caught a grip on his heart that never loosened over time and, from that instant, Dennis, unexpectedly and deeply, fell in love with his daughter.

He looked up at Mag, sure that she was sharing this moment with him, but was surprised to see that her eyes were fixed on a point beyond him and the new-born, perhaps beyond the walls of the delivery room. 'Mag, do you want her back?' he said softly, suddenly conscious that he might have been hogging their baby. Mag made a slight movement of affirmation and Dennis placed her on the bed beside her.

A nurse swooped the baby up in a brisk movement. 'Now, I need to give her a little wash and dress her and then you can take her back to the room with you,' she said.

'Are you disappointed that it's a girl, Dennis?' Mag asked as the nurse left them alone. 'You always called her Bob.'

'Disappointed? Not a bit, I'm over the moon.' Dennis leaned forward to kiss her forehead, still clammy with sweat. 'Well done.'

After Mag and the baby had been settled into a room, Dennis lingered nearby, reluctant to leave. When eventually he left the hospital, his emotions were in a whirl. He was barely conscious of his feet propelling him forward. He went back to the garage and told everyone the good news.

He could hardly wait to go back to the hospital a few hours later. When he did, he found the baby wailing in a transparent cradle beside Mag's bed while Mag had turned her back to her, huddled in a ball in the bed.

'Mag, what's wrong?' Dennis took the baby in his arms and held her against his chest, her head tucked under his chin. 'How can you leave her to cry like that?'

It was then he noticed that Mag was shaking and crying. He sat in the chair beside her bed, the baby still in his arms. Mag's eyes were red and swollen, her face stricken with grief. 'My God, Mag, is there something wrong with her? Did the doctors say anything?'

Mag shook her head. 'No, she's fine.'

'Well, what's wrong, love, why are you crying?'

'I don't know.' Mag's voice was thick and slow as she spoke the words. 'Everything is just so heavy. Life feels so hard.'

A lash of temper snapped through Dennis. 'I don't know what more you could want, Mag. Things have never been better for us, our finances are good, we've just bought a house, we have each other and now, to crown it all, we have this perfect little girl. Why can't you just enjoy all that?'

Mag didn't reply, just curled more into herself.

He sighed, in an attempt to curb his impatience. He caressed her hair. 'Mag, explain to me what's wrong. Tell me the reason why you're upset.'

Mag shook her head.

The baby, who had fallen asleep, stirred and snuggled in to him. Dennis's annoyance subsided. He couldn't understand Mag but he didn't want anything to spoil this precious time. 'Here, Mag, sit up and take her. We still haven't given her a name. What do you think we should call her?' For the second time that day, Dennis put the infant beside Mag in the bed.

'What about Ciara?' Mag mumbled.

'That's not bad. Ciara. I like it. Would that suit you, little Ciara?' He gazed down at his daughter who had her fingers clenched tightly around one of his. She seemed perfectly content to leave the choice to them.

Chapter 16

Mag was trying to compose a shopping list over an early-morning cup of tea—these days, she needed a plan of attack to prepare herself for the confusion of the rows and rows of products on the supermarket shelves—when Dennis rang.

'Morning, Mag, it was too late last night for me to call around and drop off Ciara's stuff. I'm hoping to do that this evening after work, if that's all right. I hope there's room in the garage?'

'No problem, I'll be here. Did you go to Madigan's after all?'

'I did and ended up staying longer than I intended. The barman knows him, he told me the guy's name but not much else. But first I have to tell you: I met Colm McMurray in Trinity as I was loading up the van with Ciara's things.'

Mag's chest tightened. 'What happened? Did you argue?'

'No, not exactly,' Dennis said.

'O'Brien won't be happy if he finds out.'

'Well it's not as if I went looking for him, more like the opposite. He heard I was there.'

'So what did he say?'

'My guess is that O'Brien talked to him so he knew I knew. He was trying to cover himself and justify why he lied in the first place. He tried to tell me it was serious, for both of them, but I can't believe a word he says. He lied to Ciara, to his wife; he can't be trusted.'

'Did he say anything more about the accident?'

'Not much, I'll tell you when I see you but there's still something strange about the whole thing. We haven't got the full story yet. I have to get back to work here but just one last thing, could you give me Vincent Connolly's phone number and address?'

Mag glanced down at Ciara's address book beside the telephone. 'What are you planning on doing?'

'I haven't fully decided but I would like to know what he was up to that night?' Dennis said.

'Take it easy, Dennis, we don't want to step on O'Brien's toes any more than we already have.' She called out the address and phone number from Ciara's address book.

'Don't worry, I'll be perfectly civilised. I'll see you later.'

After Mag hung up, she rattled around the house for a while, cleaning and tidying to keep herself occupied. She pulled on her old gardening boots and ventured into the garden. It was showing signs of lack of care in recent times. Spring had gaily disregarded her sorrow and now the bushes were unkempt, weeds had advanced everywhere and the whole garden had an overgrown appearance. She worked without a plan, moving haphazardly here and there, weeding, re-tying an escaped climber to the fence, snipping back an exuberant shrub. Thoughts bounced around in her head, shunting back and forth like a pinball machine.

Finally, she took off her gardening gloves and kicked off her muddy boots. She found the telephone directory and skipped through it until she found the McMurrays' number. She needed to know what Ciara had been up to. She could not come to terms with her daughter as a hypocrite. Foolish, impulsive, reckless, yes, all that was possible, but not deceitful. O'Brien had warned them not to contact McMurray but, technically, he had said nothing about speaking to Caroline McMurray. She knew she was quibbling but she wanted to hear what Caroline had to say, to find out if she had an explanation for the question marks they had over Ciara's actions. Something about her manner at the funeral convinced Mag that she knew about her husband's affair but she couldn't decipher how she felt about it.

The phone was answered on the third ring.

'Hello,' Mag said. 'Could I speak to Caroline McMurray please?'

'Sorry, she's not here,' a female voice replied. 'She's in the office. You can get her there if you like.'

'Could I get her number please?' Mag asked. 'I really need to get in touch with her.'

With a sigh, the woman gave her the number, explaining that she was the cleaning woman.

When Mag dialled the number she had been given, an upbeat, professional voice answered. 'Finesse Interior Design. Good morning.'

After asking for Caroline McMurray, she was told that Caroline was in a meeting and couldn't be disturbed. Mag declined to leave a message. Dissatisfied and restless, Mag looked up Finesse Interior Design and found the address. She considered what to do next. She could try again later;

she could drop the whole thing or she could go to see her without an appointment. In the end, she decided to call in hoping that Caroline might see her.

She hurried up the stairs before she could change her mind. Under the shower, she washed away the layer of grubbiness from her work in the garden and put on the dress she had bought the year before for her nephew's wedding. In the shop, she had thought it too expensive and a bit too young for her but Ciara, who had been shopping with her, had insisted. The well-cut dress had a navy-blue background with a pattern of stars of lots of colours that Mag had thought a bit flamboyant but she had trusted Ciara. She took a look at herself in the full-length mirror in her bedroom.

The outfit looked better on her now that she had lost some weight. She leaned in towards the mirror and examined her face up-close. She looked colourless, drained. She rubbed some blush into her cheeks. She applied a little eye-shadow which immediately emphasised the deep blueness of her eyes and brushed on some mascara. She selected a rose-coloured lipstick and stood back to assess the outcome. Her reflection in the mirror wasn't too bad. Her hair was a bit long, she could do with a cut, but it would do.

She wondered if it was petty, superficial to feel better because of this external transformation but she pushed away her misgivings, grateful for the confidence and energy, regardless of the source. She held her head up, straightened her shoulders and went downstairs.

She drove to Caroline McMurray's business and parked nearby, pausing for a moment in the car to find the courage to confront not only Caroline McMurray but her own deepest held impressions of the person she had loved best.

Her doubts were like shadows hovering around the edges of her memories of Ciara. Shining a bright light on her daughter's actions might show up flaws in her character but at least it would chase the shadows away. The truth, no matter how harsh, would be easier to deal with than the multitude of possibilities. She almost drove away but she forced her legs to walk up the steps to the large Georgian door. Beside it was a brass wall plaque with curlicues around the word 'Finesse'. She pressed on the doorbell, gave her name and was invited to come upstairs to the first floor.

She pushed open the door and found herself in a high-ceilinged, sunny room. An explosion of acidic oranges and greens sat surprisingly well against varnished floorboards and cream-coloured sofas. An enormous vase of long-stemmed lilies stood on a large glass coffee table. The scent filled the room to the point of being overwhelming.

A pretty girl with short, spiky hair, extravagantly dressed in a long Chinese-style tunic and green flowing trousers, came into the room from the offices beyond.

'Hello,' Mag said. 'I wonder if it would be possible to have a word with Mrs McMurray.'

'I'll see if she's available.' The girl gave her a pleasant smile. 'Is it concerning an interior design project?'

'No,' Mag said. 'It's a personal matter. I think she'll recognise the name.'

Mag barely had time to sit down when Caroline McMurray appeared at the doorway. As usual, she was impeccably-groomed but too thin, Mag thought, with shadows under her eyes.

'Hello, Mrs Byrne, this is a surprise,' she said.

'Sorry to call in on you like this. I was hoping you might have a few minutes to see me. There was something I wanted to talk to you about.'

'Come into my office. We can talk there.' She led Mag into a large office and closed the door. It held a large highly-polished desk with a red leather chair and on the other side of the room, a round table with four chairs. Magazines, material samples, sketches were scattered on the table.

'Please sit down. I'm afraid I don't have a lot of time as I have to go out to a house for a consultation. Also, I'm not sure how I can help.' Caroline glanced at her watch with a touch of impatience. She gathered up the items on the table to make room for Mag to sit down. Mag was conscious of the incongruousness of their meeting. The only link between them was Ciara, loved by one, maybe detested or even feared by the other. But now she was gone and a void, very different for each, had been left in their lives.

'I won't keep you too long.' Mag sat up straight in her chair and taking her courage in both hands, launched into the heart of the subject. 'I'm wondering if you know that my daughter was in a relationship with your husband.'

'I do,' Caroline said, her face showed very little sign of emotion.

'Dennis and I were very upset to hear about it. We knew nothing about this beforehand; she never told us. But I'm sure it hasn't been easy for you either.'

'I only found out about it after Ciara's death, as you did,' Caroline said. 'I had no idea but my husband was very upset after the accident and he confided in me. It was as big a shock for me as it was for you.' She seemed calm except for a nervous gesture of twisting a thick gold bracelet around and around her wrist.

'So, if you don't mind me asking, what did he say about their relationship?'

'That's a private matter that I don't want to discuss but I will say that it was a foolish mistake on his part. She looked up to him as so many of his young protégées do but she just took it a step too far and my husband gave in in a moment of weakness.' Caroline looked down and noticed her fidgeting with the bracelet. She stopped, placing her hands firmly on her knees.

'That's not how we heard it.' Mag's head was spinning. It was hard to know where the truth lay. Every time she felt that she was coming face to face with it, the truth twisted into another shape.

'Well, that's what my husband told me. Obviously we are both hearing second-hand accounts of what happened but I believe my husband. I'm not saying that it's been plain sailing throughout our marriage but we've been together for eighteen years and not everyone can say as much.'

It felt like a snide dig to Mag but Caroline's face was smooth and unruffled. She looked straight at Mag with no indication that she realised that she might have said anything hurtful.

'So, your husband is saying that it was just a fling, something of no consequence?' Mag wasn't sure what she wanted to believe. Neither option was particularly appealing.

'Not quite. My husband did care for her but he knew perfectly well that there was no future. He regretted getting involved but when an attractive much younger girl makes it clear that she's offering sex on a platter with no strings attached, very few men would be able to say no.'

Dennis would have, Mag instinctively thought. Caroline might disdain her broken marriage but it had been more genuine than hers ever was. A flash of anger rose within her. 'I don't believe for a minute that Ciara threw herself at him. She has never done anything like that. I know my daughter.'

Caroline smiled a patient, tolerant smile. 'I can well imagine that it's a side of your daughter that you've never seen. I don't mean to criticise her memory but she was young and my husband is a very attractive man. We all make mistakes in life. My husband and I need to get over this one, also for the sake of our sons and I'm sure we will. I'm sure your daughter would have learned from hers and moved on if only fate had not so cruelly cut her life short.'

Mag wanted to smack the trite pity off her perfectly made-up face but she knew it would serve no purpose. She stood up to leave so that she wouldn't lose her temper. 'I should go. I've taken up enough of your time.'

'Yes, I should get back to work,' Caroline said, glancing at her watch again. 'But regardless of the circumstances, I do want to assure you of my deepest sympathy.' She held out her hand to Mag and it was all she could do to take it. She could keep her callous condolences, they brought no comfort or consolation.

In the street, Mag was furious with herself for going to see her. Although the encounter did have the effect of removing all ambivalence Mag felt about Ciara's actions. Her belief in her daughter was unconditional and would never again be shaken.

1984

The baby was crying again. Oblivious, Dennis snored gently beside her. Mag stared at the ceiling, knowing that she was not going to stop, knowing that it was better to go to her now before she threw herself into a paroxysm of fury from which it would be difficult to bring her back but inertia nailed her to the spot. As the screams moved up a notch in pitch, Mag managed to peel herself away from the bed and go into the room next door.

Ciara was red-faced and furious. The lack of emotion Mag felt as she gazed down at this helpless yet demanding creature frightened her utterly. It confirmed that she was, indeed, fatally flawed. For years she had harboured the surreptitious, almost subconscious belief that it was only the unfortunate circumstances she had found herself in that had prevented her from nurturing her lost son. She had held that illusion close to her like a fragile crystal ball but now it had been wrenched from her and smashed into pieces. This second chance was as much of a disaster as the first had been except that this time she could blame nothing and no-one but herself. She was beyond redemption. How could any normal woman have such a void of love for her own perfect child, a child that had been deeply desired?

It was a dark secret that she dared not confide in anyone; not her husband who doted on his daughter as though she were an angel in corporeal form and who had firmly blocked out any prior claim he might have to fatherhood; not her mother who had always conveyed impatience with impractical psychological dilemmas; not her doctor, a grumpy old man who saw Ciara for a check-up once a month and seemed to begrudge spending time on healthy patients when sick ones were waiting to see him.

Mag could see no way out. Failure as a mother was something society could not tolerate. She would be ostracised, despised. What made it even more difficult for her was that her perception of her own situation was so at odds with that of the world around her. Everyone envied her, told her how lucky she was, they all profusely admired her new baby, her new house. She was forced into adopting a mask of gratitude, modestly accepting all the compliments given to her.

Two months after Ciara was born, they had moved into the new house. The task of bringing the house back to habitable form struck her as formidable. The excitement she had felt a few months previously when faced with this challenge of starting anew had melted away and could no longer be retrieved.

Alone in the house after Dennis had left for the garage, she sometimes wandered aimlessly around, crushed by the enormity of the task. More often, she lay in bed in a midway world, moving only to do the minimum of tasks to keep her daughter and herself alive. Over time, she managed to carve out two small havens among the desolation of the rooms, the kitchen and her bed. Maintaining order and cleanliness in these two niches took all her energy.

After standing for a few seconds in the dim light of early morning she roused herself and picked up Ciara. She was moving downstairs towards the kitchen when she met Dennis coming out of their bedroom. He was still partly in the grip of sleep.

'Everything all right, Mag? I heard Ciara crying,' he said.

Guilt overwhelmed her. 'She's hungry. I'm taking her downstairs to feed her. You go back to sleep.' Nervously, she jiggled the baby, who was now crying in gulps. Their eyes couldn't meet.

Dennis turned to go back to bed. He said nothing but she felt the reproach that she had given up breast-feeding as strongly as if he had said it aloud. Everything she did these days disappointed him. She saw it in his eyes when he came home in the evening to find her still in her dressing gown. She felt it when she froze under his touch as he tried to make love with her in the weeks following the birth. He had withdrawn silently and she had wept inside. Part of her wanted desperately to be held, to be loved, to have his caresses given, not offered, but her fear of failure in yet another area of her life paralyzed her, cut her off from him. They, who had once felt that the days and nights were not long enough for all the outpourings of their hearts, now spent most of their time together in silence or in stilted conversation.

Ciara leapt on the teat of the bottle and guzzled down the contents greedily. Another pang of guilt traversed Mag as she remembered the frustrated and fruitless efforts by the tiny mouth to find sustenance in her breast. Dennis had been keen for them to keep trying. He had been convinced of the merits of breast-milk, urging her to persevere, convinced that it was just a question of time. She had persisted for a while, to please him, but once, driven crazy by the cries of her starving baby, she had given her a bottle. She didn't tell Dennis immediately but one of the days while they were still in the little flat over the garage he had run upstairs to get something and found Ciara sucking contentedly on the bottle. He took what he had come for and went downstairs without a word. The matter had not been referred to afterwards.

It took an enormous effort for Mag to leave the house and take the baby for a walk. She steeled herself when she passed neighbours, acknowledging their greetings but never stopping to chat. She knew they thought her snobby or cold but it was better than them knowing that she was a failure as a mother, a wife, a person. On the few occasions that she went to the garage, everyone was at pains to tell her that they were coping just fine without her, that the new girl in the office was doing a great job. She was needed nowhere.

The first burgeon of hope appeared when Ciara was four months old. Mag had left her in her cradle while she took a shower. She took advantage of the few minutes of peace to dry her hair properly, put on perfume and dress at leisure. When at last she looked in at her, she noticed that Ciara was playing with her hands, holding them up, turning them around and staring at them in fascination as though they were a sudden, unexpected gift. But even they were cast aside when Mag entered the room. The baby's whole face lit up in a smile of undiluted joy at the sight of Mag's face and her arms and legs wriggled in ecstasy at the prospect of her company. An arrow of emotion that resembled love shot through Mag. She picked up her daughter and tried to make her laugh. To her immense surprise, her every effort succeeded wildly. Even the tears of relief which poured down Mag's face were a source of amusement to Ciara.

That morning, while Ciara napped, Mag removed the dark, heavy curtains from the sitting room and stripped the wallpaper from one wall. In the afternoon, the sun shone and she walked to the butcher's where she smiled and said hello to two neighbours. Dennis, when he came home that evening, was surprised at the subtle changes.

Little by little, life regained its colours for Mag and became infused with pleasure again. An exchange took place between Mag and Ciara from which a relationship grew. Mag and Dennis returned to the construction project that was their life together but something had changed. Mag closed off a scarred fragment of herself from Dennis and he too held back like a man reluctant to put his full weight on a leg that had let him down before.

Chapter 17

Dennis did not feel at all comfortable about leaving his van near Vincent's flat. The house was on a quiet street between Mountjoy Square and Dorset Street, a part of Dublin that the rising tide of prosperity had submerged rather than lifted. The weeds in the patch of garden at the front of the house were choked by plastic bags, crisp wrappers, and scraps of newspapers. The door, originally blue, did not appear to have been painted in Dennis's lifetime and the wood at the bottom had rotted and splintered so that a gaping hole at one corner allowed the wind to whistle into the hall.

A young girl, who still retained traces of prettiness despite her efforts to eradicate all femininity, opened the door to him. She was wearing a large man's jumper, her hair looked as if it had been hacked away with a blunt carving knife. She half-opened the door, hindered as she was by the presence of a motorbike and two bicycles in the hall, a parking choice which did nothing to reassure Dennis about the security of his van.

She waited for him to explain his presence and then yelled Vincent's name up the stairs. A moment later, he appeared. On seeing Dennis, he threw himself downstairs, expertly avoiding a stair in the middle where a plank had given way.

'Hey, man,' he said to Dennis, bobbing about in his peculiar way. 'Thanks, Bee,' he said to the disappearing back of the girl who had answered the door. She threw up a dismissive hand over her shoulder without turning around.

Vincent was barefoot. He was wearing an ancient tee-shirt with a hole under one arm and sagging jeans that emphasised the skinniness of his frame.

'There's something I wanted to discuss with you. You might be able to explain something to me,' Dennis said.

'Sounds serious. Do you want to come up to the flat?' Vincent said.

Dennis squeezed inside, closed the door behind him and followed Vincent up the stairs.

Vincent's flat was, in reality, a poky bed-sit. On one side of the room was a single unmade bed. A two-ring cooker-top, a paint-stained sink and a fridge were crowded into a corner on the opposite side. In between, was a small kitchen table, one leg propped up by a piece of folded newspaper to keep it steady and two wooden chairs. An old fireplace had been bricked-up and on the chipped mantelpiece was an ashtray with the remains of a joint indicating that Vincent's eviction from home had not cured him of that particular vice.

'The rent's cheap.' Vincent shrugged as he watched Dennis gaze around the room.

Dennis sat on one of the chairs. Vincent leaned against the mantelpiece, waiting for Dennis to speak.

‘I don’t think you’ve been telling me the truth, the whole truth and nothing but the truth,’ Dennis said.

‘How do you mean?’ Vincent’s discomfort showed as he ran his fingers through his uncombed hair.

‘I seem to remember you told us that on the night of Ciara’s accident you left the McMurray house early and went straight to a pub in town. You said you didn’t see her again after you left the house.’

‘And that’s true.’

‘Not according to your friend Andrew Tierney who tells us that he saw you hanging around outside the house when he was leaving later on that night.’

Vincent picked up a pack of cigarettes and fidgeted with it.

‘Shit, man. Hey, it’s not how it looks. Don’t get the wrong end of the stick.’

‘So why don’t you tell me exactly what you did do, and no lies this time.’ Dennis sat back in his chair and held him in his gaze.

‘After we fought, I wanted to talk to Ciara. I didn’t want to leave things the way they were but I didn’t want to discuss it with all the guys around, listening to us. So yeah, I hung around outside after I left the house to catch her when she was leaving. I wasn’t going to cause any hassle, I just wanted to talk.’ Vincent took a cigarette from the pack, lit it and offered one to Dennis who shook his head. He inhaled deeply before continuing. ‘I had a smoke or two. Then after a while—I can’t tell you how long—I saw the others leaving. I stood back under the trees. I didn’t think they saw me but obviously Andrew Tierney did. Anyway, I couldn’t see Ciara and after they had all gone I saw that her car was still there so I held on a bit longer. I thought she'd be out any minute but in the end I left before she came out. I got pissed off; I was freezing, so I gave up. I wanted to get out of there so fast I nearly crashed into the back of a Beemer pulled in at the side of the road. I went straight to the pub when I got into the city like I said and had a few pints.'

'Let me get this straight,' Dennis said. 'You didn't see Ciara at all once you left the house even though you waited for her outside.'

'That's about it.' Vincent's eyes slithered away from eye-contact and he stubbed out his cigarette. In the moment of silence that ensued, he crumbled. 'Hey, man, I'm sorry. I didn't tell you this shit before but I didn't want you getting the wrong end of the stick. Things were cool between me and Ciara even if it didn't look that way, I just wanted to talk, make sure she knew where I was coming from. I didn't tell you about hanging around because you're her old man and I didn't want you thinking that I'm some kind of crazy stalker. But when that cop asked me, I told him exactly the way it happened.'

Dennis looked up. 'Who are you talking about? A guard?'

'Yeah, the guy who was going around asking everyone questions.'

'What was his name?'

'I don't know; I keep my discussions with the guards to a minimum. O'Brien, I think.'

'What did he want to know?'

'What happened that night, when I arrived and left, what we talked about with Ciara, that kind of stuff.'

'Why did he want to know that?'

'Hey, why the third degree? How would I know? I don't go around quizzing up the guards. That's the best way to piss them off. Learned that fairly fast with the old man. Answer the question, say no more that you have to and move on as fast as you can, that's how I play it.'

'So, when did he talk to you?'

'A couple of weeks ago, I don't know. Hey, I don't have a watch. For sure, I don't keep a diary. All I know is that he came to the college asking a whole pile of questions about Ciara and not just me.'

Dennis stood up feeling agitated. He needed to move, he needed to think. What did this mean? Was this routine procedure or did O'Brien think there was something odd about Ciara's death?

'I'd better be off,' he said. 'Thanks for the info.'

'Right so,' Vincent said, thrown slightly by this sudden departure. 'Keep it cool, man.'

Dennis's thoughts were in turmoil as he left Vincent's flat. Despite his own feelings of uneasiness about the accident he had been sure that O'Brien had seen it as no more than an unfortunate incident. If he had the same doubts as Dennis himself, then this confirmation of his fears made him nervous.

He drove the van to Mag's house but if he had been asked afterwards he couldn't have remembered the route he had taken. It was the end of the evening and the colours were beginning to seep out of the day. He rang the doorbell, standing in the warm light cast through the windows in the hall.

Mag looked better, younger, more like she used to look. 'Hi Mag, I've got a vanload of stuff here. Where do you want me to put it?'

'I've cleared out some space in the office at the front. You can put it there for the moment, I'll sort through it later.'

He backed the van up to the door and started unloading. 'Leave it to me,' he said when Mag started to help. 'It won't take long and you're not exactly dressed for it.'

When he had finished she offered him a drink which he accepted gladly and she led him through to the sitting room. She had not yet drawn the curtains of the large bay windows, the patio light was on and the garden looked well. He had always liked this room; it had a peaceful atmosphere, it was easy to relax there. He sank into one of the large armchairs.

He felt his brain slow down and his body warm up with the first swallow of whiskey. She poured a gin and tonic for herself and sat on the sofa opposite.

'So, you met McMurray yesterday,' she said. 'How did it go? What did he have to say about Ciara?'

As he told her about his encounter with Colm McMurray, he found his anger and frustration melting away. He then proceeded to tell her about his conversations with the barman in Madigan's the previous day and with Vincent earlier that evening. She listened calmly until he had finished talking.

'I did something a little crazy myself today,' she said. 'I went to see Caroline McMurray.'

'What?' Dennis sat up straighter.

'I know, I'm not sure if I should have but I wanted to hear her side of things.'

'What did she say?'

'She told me basically that Ciara threw herself on Colm McMurray and, sure, what could the poor man say? No?'

Dennis laughed loudly and, as he did, the bubble of Mag's indignation burst and they laughed together.

'Either McMurray lied to her, or he lied to Ciara or she lied to you,' he said eventually.

'Well, in any case, one thing I'm sure of is that Ciara was not the liar.' She sat up with the force of her words.

Dennis picked up their glasses and walked to the cabinet to pour them another drink.

'A small one for me, Dennis,' Mag said. 'I can already feel the effects of the first one.'

'So where do you think this guy, Joe Farrell, fits in?' Dennis handed Mag her glass.

'I haven't a clue. I wonder if he and Colm McMurray knew anything about each other.'

'The first thing we need to do is find out who he is ourselves. Hold on, let me check the telephone directory,' Dennis said. 'Where is it?'

'It's on the telephone table in the hall.' When he came back she had slipped off her shoes and curled her feet under her.

He found four Joseph Farrells in Dublin in the phone book. He called the first one. It was answered by an old woman with a tremulous voice. She told him that her husband was out playing bridge but would be back shortly if he wanted to call back. The second call was answered by a man.

'Joe Farrell?' Dennis questioned.

'Yes, speaking.' The man waited for Dennis to continue.

'Joe Farrell who works in Siemens Electronics?'

'Yes. Who is this?' The man's voice betrayed impatience. Dennis could hear the babbling sounds of a child playing in the background. 'Sorry, I've made a mistake,' he said and hung up. He looked up at Mag.

'I think that's him,' he said.

'So what do we do now?' Mag asked.

Dennis looked down at the directory. 'He lives in Dundrum. How about if I call out to his house? As soon as I see him, I'll know if he's the one in the photo.'

'And what'll you say to him?' Mag said. 'I think we should go together.'

'That's fine with me. What about going tomorrow? It's Saturday, he probably won't be working.'

'OK.' Mag yawned. 'Sorry but I think that gin is sending me to sleep.'

'I'll go and let you get to bed. I'll pick you up at ten, it'll only take us twenty minutes or so to get there.' Dennis rose to his feet and stretched. He picked up his empty glass and carried it with him as if to take it to the kitchen. Mag walked with him.

'Don't worry about that. I'll deal with it,' she said and as she took the glass from him, her hand brushed against his.

Her touch triggered a reaction in him, like a snake uncoiling and stretching itself in his body. She stood half a head below him. The smell of her shampoo, her perfume and underneath it all the old familiar smell of her drifted into his nostrils. He reached out and touched her hair. He pulled one of her curls straight and released it, letting it spring back into place. He stroked her cheek with the back of his fingers. She backed away from him. She was pale and he thought he could detect fear in her expression.

'Mag, I'm sorry. I shouldn't have done that. I didn't think.' Her reaction hurt him as if a hand raised in play had caused a child to flinch.

'It's ok,' she said but it didn't sound as if it was.

'I'll go now,' he said. He needed to leave immediately; he wanted to be gone already. He felt coarse and clumsy. How could he have made such a blunder? And yet, it was strange that something which had once been so close, so natural, had now swung so far out of his reach. Had his impression of a new proximity between them been a misjudgement, an illusion created by a combination of loneliness, alcohol and night time? He was turning to go when he stopped. 'How did it all go wrong between us, Mag?' he asked.

'I don't know,' Mag said, her arms folded across her stomach. 'I don't think it was just one thing. Maybe we were too different. Neither of us was able to be what the other wanted.'

'But I didn't want you any other way. All I ever wanted was for you, us, to be happy.'

'That was part of the problem, Dennis. There was no room for sadness or distress with you and yet for a long time that's what I felt. I felt that I was letting you down if I let that show through.'

'I'm sorry if that's how you saw it.' Dennis shifted his feet awkwardly. 'I certainly didn't mean it. You know that I loved you a lot.'

'I don't think it was love we lacked, it was understanding.' Mag said. 'Somehow, love came naturally but understanding took effort. We covered up our problems with love until eventually that wasn't enough. After a while the cracks between us started to show until they widened into a rift that we couldn't bridge anymore.'

'I wanted to but I didn't know how.'

'No, Dennis, you didn't try. I was in trouble and that frightened you. I was drowning in depression and, rather than jump in to save me, you turned away.'

Dennis felt the sharp sting of the accusation. 'What are you saying? What should I have done?'

'I don't know, Dennis but let's not mull over the past; we can't change it. What's done is done. Now we need to move on, not look back.' Mag hugged herself as if she were cold.

'So, all this time you think I abandoned you? I thought I was doing my best. I tried everything I knew to make you happy but nothing worked until eventually I was convinced that you'd be better off without me. I saw Ciara torn between us and I thought, for her sake as well as for ours, we'd all be better off apart.'

'Why didn't you talk to me? Why couldn't we have discussed it?'

'I was hurt too, Mag. At first it was all too raw and then, as time went by, it became too hard to go back into it again. I didn't want to hear that I had failed, that I had made you miserable.'

'It wasn't about you. It was me. I needed help.'

Dennis searched her face, trying to understand, but he was stumbling on unfamiliar, foreign ground. He had never been one for analysing his feelings and he wasn't sure how he felt now. There were no words big enough to contain what he wanted to say. In the end, Mag broke the silence between them.

'Go home, Dennis,' she said quietly. 'We both miss Ciara, we're vulnerable right now. Why don't we forget about this and get on with our lives as best we can?'

Dennis looked at her face. 'Sure, I'll go now. Sorry again. I'll see you tomorrow,' he said. He fumbled with the latch of the door and closed it behind him, cutting her goodbye in two.

He took a few deep breaths as he walked to his car but it took longer than that for his pulse to calm down to a normal pace and for the glowing embers of his embarrassment to lose their heat. His head swirled with questions, questions he had never asked himself before.

1990

Dennis had his head buried in the engine of an old Citroen. After examination of its condition, he would normally have diagnosed it as terminal except that he could see that the owner had developed an attachment to it which went beyond a mere means of transportation.

A voice called him out of his mechanical preoccupations. It was Mag. 'You're wanted on the phone,' she said. 'It's Niall Grennan from Clontarf Motors.'

'Great, I was hoping he'd call. I'll be right there.' Dennis finished screwing in a nut on a wheel before stretching his back. He watched Mag returning to the office. It was good to have her back at the garage; it made life there much easier. She dealt with all the aspects of the business that he found a headache and as the garage had grown over the past few years, the paperwork, accounts and personnel issues seemed to take up a disproportionate amount of time.

Even though Mag only worked in the mornings while Ciara was at school, she managed to keep the office organised in a way that he couldn't. But even apart from the work she did, her presence had a positive impact on the atmosphere in the garage. She brought what Dennis thought of as a 'woman's touch'. All the lads liked her and turned to her for advice on their taxes, savings as well as girlfriend issues. For two of them, she had even organised a loan through the garage, deductible from their wages, to give them a deposit to buy a house.

Their own relationship had evolved but perhaps that was inevitable; they were no longer newly-weds. There were moments when Mag was unpredictable and sensitive but he had learned to ignore her moods and eventually she would come out of it.

He entered the office. Ciara was installed at one end of the desk Mag was working at. She was sticking stamps on a pile of letters in preparation for posting. She looked bored and her head picked up in interest at Dennis's arrival. She was on Easter holidays from school and had come into the office with Mag that day so that Mag could finalise the tax returns.

'Great job you're doing there, honey-bun,' Dennis said and gave her a gentle poke in the tummy. He took the phone from the desk. 'Niall. Good to hear from you,' he said. 'Yes, that's the very one. I know one man who'll be delighted with that news. I'll call over and pick it up later on.'

'The part for Cosgrove's Land Rover came in eventually,' Dennis told Mag after he had hung up. 'I'll go to Clontarf and get it. You don't need me for anything here, do you?' He took the keys of the old four-wheel-drive Jeep belonging to the garage from the drawer beside her and put them in his pocket.

'No, I should be finished here in about an hour or so and then we'll go home,' Mag said. 'I think Ciara's had enough.'

'I don't want to go home, Mammy,' Ciara said. 'I want to go somewhere else.'

'Where would you like to go?' Dennis licked one of the stamps and stuck it on her nose. He picked up a pen and, tilting her backwards in her chair, prepared to write on her forehead. 'Go on, tell me where you'd like to go and I'll post you there.'

Ciara giggled at his trickery and her gurgling laughter triggered off another geyser of love inside him. He loved it when she laughed at his silly jokes; it made him feel like the most powerful man in the world. What did money or business matter when he could make his little girl laugh?

She followed him into the yard and tugged his hand. 'Can I come with you, Daddy? Wherever you're going. Please.'

He looked down at her earnest, freckled face. She was impossible to resist. 'I don't mind, you can come if you want, but I warn you it's not going to be very exciting. I'm only picking up a spare part.'

'I want to come,' Ciara said.

'Well, ask your mother. If she says it's OK, then you can come but I'm leaving in a few minutes.'

Ciara danced away. Dennis exchanged a few words with Francie about the repairs on a crashed Volvo which had just come in and then sat into the Jeep at the back of the yard. A millisecond after he had turned the ignition, Ciara appeared in front of him waving her arms frantically. 'Wait for me. Mammy said I can go.'

He opened the door and let her clamber into the back-seat. The Jeep was not a thing of beauty or elegance and evidence of its long, faithful service was clear but it was mechanically sound and Dennis felt a bit adventurous every time he drove it.

He turned on the radio and as he drove through the city, he and Ciara sang along in joyful but tuneless harmony to all the hits as they came on. Between songs, Ciara chattered non-stop, asking him questions. They crossed the Liffey, made their way up O'Connell Street and on to Dorset Street. As they approached Clontarf, the smell of the sea mingled with the usual smells of city life. The stately old houses along the sea-front at Clontarf faced the horizon with dignity, confident in their enduring grace.

At the traffic lights where Dennis was supposed to turn left to go to Clontarf Motors, he turned around in his seat and looked mock-seriously at Ciara. 'Tell me, what age are you now?' Ciara giggled in delicious anticipation.

'You know what age I am, Daddy. I'm six and a half, nearly seven.'

'Six and a half. Imagine that, six and a half,' Dennis repeated to himself. 'Well, it's high time you learned to drive, Ciara Byrne. Let's go.'

When the lights turned green, he drove straight on instead of taking the left. A little while further along the coast road, he turned right on to North Bull Island. A huge expanse of sandy beach lay in front of them. In the far distance, two people were walking their dogs but otherwise the beach was deserted.

'Now, come in here to the front and sit on my knees,' Dennis said.

Delighted, Ciara climbed over the back of the seat and sat into position. After a brief explanation of the mechanics of driving, Dennis put the Jeep into gear and gave Ciara control of the steering wheel. They inched slowly forward.

'Can we go a bit faster, Daddy? Please?' Ciara asked after a few minutes of this snail's pace.

'Faster, you say? Faster? Well, all right then, seeing as you asked so nicely.' Dennis capitulated. He moved into third gear and pressed on the accelerator. The Jeep responded almost immediately and reared forward like a nervous horse. Ciara shrieked half with glee, half with terror. The wheels spat sand behind them and the car tore across the strand. The rough terrain and absence of the usual markers made their speed seem all the more impressive.

'Now, u-turn, Ciara,' Dennis yelled over the noise. He put his hands on top of hers and swerved to the right towards the waves. Ciara squealed again as they appeared to be driving straight into the sea at top speed but Dennis veered away just in time. After several more minutes of high emotion, Dennis stopped the Jeep and they tumbled out the door onto the sand. They rolled about and laughed outrageously until it hurt. They were not sure what exactly they found so funny but their laughter had an impetus of its own and ran away with them. Each time one of them managed to tame it to some extent, one look at the other would set them off again.

'We'd better go and get that spare part, Ciara,' Dennis said eventually. They brushed the sand off their clothes, every so often liberating a ripple of giggles when they caught each other's eye. When they got to the garage in Clontarf, the piece was waiting for them at the office. In no time they were back on the road but it was obvious that neither of them felt like going home or to work.

'We could go to the zoo,' Ciara said as they passed a sign for the Phoenix Park. 'It's in there. We have plenty of time.' Dennis hesitated only for a moment. He couldn't remember the last time he'd been to the zoo and if he couldn't take time off when he wanted to then what was the point in being his own boss.

'I'll go only if you promise not to let them keep me, no matter what they say.'

'You're silly, Daddy.' Ciara laughed.

The zoo felt like another world, not like Dublin at all. The gorillas held a particular fascination for them both until the large male gave them a bored look of condescension and turned his back to them so that he could scratch himself in peace. The tiny spider monkeys tilted their heads curiously at them and nibbled at grains of food with bizarrely human-like movements.

They ate ice creams not because the weather was really warm enough to tempt them but because it felt like the right thing to do. They arrived at the elephant enclosure on time to see them being fed. The elephants held back their heads with their trunks up in the air and, with surprising accuracy, caught the apples and bananas thrown to them in their mouths. It was starting to get cold and Ciara slipped her hand into his. He put both of their hands into the pocket of his jacket.

'We should go home now, Ciara. It's getting late.' Dennis looked at his watch. Ciara didn't resist; he could tell she was tired. He carried her on his shoulders to the car. On the way back they played an animal guessing game which got more ridiculous with each turn. It was almost six o'clock when they got home. Mag came running out of the house as soon as Dennis pulled up. Something serious had happened; she was pale and frantic.

'What's wrong, Mag?' Dennis asked as soon as she came near. Ciara slunk out of the car on the other side and closed the car-door quietly. Mag spotted her and turned on her.

'Has she been with you all this time? I have been worried sick. Why didn't you tell me?' Dennis had rarely, if ever, seen Mag as furious.

'I sent Ciara to ask you and she told me you said it was OK for her to come with me.' As he said the words, a penny dropped and Dennis understood what had happened. Before he could say anything more, Mag grabbed Ciara by the shoulders and shook her. 'Don't you dare lie like that ever again,' she screamed into her face. 'Do you have any idea of how worried I've been? I thought anything could have happened to you.'

All Dennis could see was Ciara's petrified face, her eyes wide with terror. Instinctively, he pulled Mag away and stepped between them.

'That's enough, Mag,' he said. 'Leave her alone.' Ciara threw herself against him and pressed her face against his stomach. 'Let's go inside,' Dennis said and picked up Ciara in his arms. She sobbed into his neck. Mag followed them, a few steps behind.

Dinner was a deadly silent affair, in stark contrast to the chatter and laughter of the day. Ciara refused to eat anything and Mag didn't insist. Afterwards, Dennis put Ciara to bed and stayed with her until she fell asleep.

On his way down the stairs he heard Mag's voice on the phone. 'No, she's home now. She had gone off with her father. I didn't know.' After a brief pause, 'Thank you, Garda. I'm sorry to have bothered you.'

Dennis felt a flash of compassion for the fear Mag must have felt while he and Ciara had frittered the day away. He put his hand on Mag's shoulder and squeezed it sympathetically but she shrugged it off and, without a word, went back to the kitchen.

Chapter 18

Mag woke early after an uneasy sleep. The episode with Dennis the previous evening had unsettled her and left her nerves tingling. Maybe she was reading more into a simple gesture than it merited but she couldn't rid herself of the feeling that she had played with fire and had almost been drawn into it. Had he reached out to her impulsively in a spontaneous need for comfort or did he really believe that they could revive something more permanent between them? In either case, it was typical of Dennis that he grasped what he wanted from life without considering how reasonable or feasible it was.

She dithered over what to wear; she wanted to look smart, in control, but she didn't want Dennis to think that she had made an effort to look good for him. In the end, she selected a plain white blouse and rust-coloured suede trousers. She glanced at her reflection in the mirror but didn't allow herself to linger. She made sure to be ready early and as soon as she heard the doorbell ring, she stepped outside to join Dennis. He was self-conscious, anxious not to refer to the subject of the evening before. He was making a big effort to appear at ease and unperturbed.

'Are you needed back at the garage later on this morning?' Mag asked as they walked down the path together.

'Not especially. I'll have to get back at some stage but Francie is there. He's well able to manage without me.' To Mag's ear, their voices sounded false as though they were both acting out designated roles.

In the car, Dennis was nervous, adjusting his seat back, fiddling with the heating. 'Sleep all right, did you?' he asked after a moment's silence.

'Not great,' she said.

'Mag, about last night,' Dennis started. 'I didn't mean to raise old ghosts. Can we forget about it?'

'No problem. We'll leave it at that.' Mag was trying her best to be calm but her insides were a kaleidoscope of different emotions swirling and spinning into ever changing patterns. How stubborn the heart was; it persisted in believing and hoping even when all logic told it that it was pointless. She waited for the turbulence to pass before speaking again. 'We haven't discussed what we're going to say to this man, supposing he is the right one. It's not as if we can walk in and discuss the matter openly in front of his wife.'

'We'll see when we get there,' Dennis said. 'We have his number. We could call him and ask him to meet us somewhere.'

'I hope we're not making a mistake here,' Mag said. 'Maybe we'd have been better off telling O'Brien first.'

'Too late now. We're on our way.' Dennis's jaw was set hard with determination. Mag said no more but a feeling of anxiety persisted.

It was a bright, sunny day that gave a foretaste of summer. There was a sense of exuberance in the air of the suburban streets. There was a bounce in the step of the couples out walking with their babies; people were getting their front gardens ready; others were washing their cars.

They found the house without too much difficulty. The street was a quiet cul-de-sac off the busy main street running through Dundrum. Number five was a small, two-storey, red brick house in the middle of a pretty terrace of identical houses. At one time, it would have been considered simple, unpretentious; now it probably cost a fortune.

Dennis parked across the street and switched off the engine. He rested his hands on the steering wheel and looked at the green door of the house. 'So what do you think?' he asked.

`We could ring first and hope that he's the one who answers the phone,' Mag said. 'There's a coffee shop on the corner back there. If he's not on his own maybe it would be easier if he joined us there.'

'Let's give it a shot.' Dennis flipped open his mobile phone. He composed the number but, just as he pressed the green send button, the door of the house they were watching opened. A young blond woman stepped outside. She was holding the hand of a small girl, who looked to be around four. A tall, broad-shouldered man followed her with a sleeping baby collapsed against his shoulder. Mag felt her chest catch. It was obviously the man from the photo.

The woman was telling him something while she opened the door of a Ford Focus and started to install the little girl in a car-seat. The man turned around, distracted, and went back into the house. Through the open door, they heard the distant sound of a telephone ringing and, belatedly, Dennis cut off the call from his mobile. When the man reappeared, he was no longer holding the baby. He kissed his wife, waved at the little girl through the car window and waited until they had driven away before going back inside.

'Bastard,' Dennis said in a low voice. 'It's him, isn't it?'

Mag nodded.

'Well, he's on his own now. Let's go and talk to him.' Dennis put his hand out to open the car-door.

There was an uncomfortable fluttering in Mag's stomach. She reached out and held Dennis's arm.

'What's wrong?' he said. She looked at his pale and determined face but didn't know what to say.

'Nothing,' she said and let him go.

'You don't have to come,' Dennis said. 'You can stay here if you like.'

'No, I'll go with you.' She got out of the car.

They crossed the street and Dennis knocked on the door. The man opened it. He smiled expectantly at them.

'Hello, we wanted to talk to Joseph Farrell.' Dennis said.

'That's me. What do you want?'

'Could we talk about it inside, please?' Dennis said brusquely.

'Who are you?' The man stared at Dennis, displeased at the intrusion. Then a look of understanding crossed his face. 'Did you call me last night and then hang up?'

'Yes,' said Dennis. 'I can explain.'

The man hesitated.

'We wanted to talk to you for a minute about Ciara Byrne,' Mag said, quietly. As the name registered in his brain, he looked from one to the other. Finally, he opened the door wider and let them in. He led them through the small hall into a kitchen where the breakfast things still lay on the table. He moved a Barbie tricycle to one side by way of offering them a seat but they remained standing. Mag looked around. It was a large room that had been extended into the garden. At the garden end was a yellow sofa and armchair with a liberal sprinkling of toys.

'Excuse us for intruding,' Mag said. 'We saw your wife leaving a minute ago and we thought it would be a good moment to speak to you.'

'Right?' Farrell was dubious.

'You knew Ciara then?' Dennis said.

'Yes, I can't say I knew her very well, I met her a few times, the first time was a few months ago. Why do you want to know?'

Dennis ignored that and followed his own line of questioning. 'Are you aware that she was killed in a car accident a month ago?'

'I know that. I was very sorry to hear it.'

'I'm sure you were,' Dennis said sarcastically.

'I was, actually.' Joseph Farrell's stance stiffened. 'Now, would you mind telling me who you are?'

For the second time, Dennis ignored his question. 'So what kind of a relationship did you have with her? When did you last see her?'

'Sorry, but I don't see why I should answer your questions. You've come into my house uninvited. Before we go on, I'd like an explanation.'

Mag could sense the mounting tension between the two men and tried to intervene to diffuse it. 'You're right, we haven't been very clear. We are Ciara's parents. The reason why we called is that we found a letter from you and a photo among Ciara's things.' She paused.

Dennis leapt in. 'We thought we'd give you a chance to give us an account of yourself before we pass on the information to the guards.'

Joseph Farrell raised an eyebrow. 'The guards? And why might they be interested in what I have to say?' His cool, detached tone was a fan to Dennis's fire.

'Why don't we leave it up to them to decide,' Dennis said. 'Of course, your wife might also be interested in hearing this story.'

Joseph Farrell drew himself up to his full height. 'I'm not sure I like your attitude. I don't appreciate being threatened in my own house.'

Mag frowned at Dennis, willing him to calm down, to allow the man to speak. Dennis caught her glance and made an effort to compose himself.

'It's not a threat but we are under an obligation to tell the guards about anything or anyone who might have any involvement with Ciara's accident,' he said in a more reasonable voice. 'So, why don't you tell us about your relationship with Ciara and then we'll go away and not bother you anymore?'

There was a silence as the man seemed to be considering what Dennis said. 'Fine. If you want to know, I'll tell you. I contacted Ciara in January earlier this year after I discovered that she was my sister,' he said. 'I was adopted in 1974 and…'

A pounding in Mag's ears made it difficult for her to hear. She was afraid she would faint and reached out to grip the back of a chair. His words spilled out, flowing through her brain, devoid of meaning. She looked around for something to anchor her to reality. She latched onto a child's drawing stuck to the fridge door, the red dribble on the outside of the jam-jar on the table, the grinning face of Winnie the Pooh on the cereal box.

'...never thought of looking up my biological parents before... I only met Ciara few times but she was a wonderful person...I'll miss her very much.'

Before she knew it, he had stopped talking. He looked at them, expecting a reaction. She sensed that Dennis was scrabbling to regain his equanimity which this revelation had cut from under him. She tried to swallow but her mouth was dry and her throat wouldn't react. Even if she were capable of speaking, she felt that any words she could have said would be useless, feeble things; confetti in the gale that was blowing through her.

As the silence grew, Joseph became brisk, business-like. 'As for Ciara's accident, I was on a business trip in Germany at the time and I only found out about it a week later when I tried to contact Ciara. That's why I didn't attend the funeral.'

'So, that's all that was going on between you?' Dennis managed to say eventually.

'Yes, that's all,' Joseph said dryly. He paused for a moment. 'Now, if that answers all your questions, I really do have things to get back to.'

Dennis stirred himself. 'Of course. We'll go now.'

Panic fluttered in Mag's stomach but she was unable to react. Joseph led the way to the front door. Dennis followed him and, as if she were walking through water, she took one slow step after the other. At the front door, she looked into the hard, closed face of this unknown man. A plaintive baby's cry rang out and he glanced behind him, impatient to close the door.

'Well, that explains certain things,' Dennis said with finality when they were sitting in the car. He sounded stubbornly passive. Mag withdrew into a cocoon trying to absorb what had just happened.

Over the years, she had often tried to envisage how the baby she had given away might have grown up but the details of his face, at one time imprinted in her memory, had faded and disappeared. Now that she knew definitively what he had become, all the other possibilities were swept away. She had given him a thousand faces, a thousand personalities but here was the only one. It was strange to think that her baby had become a child, a tall sturdy boy. He had gone to school where he had done well. He had become a teenager, probably keen on sport. He had gone to college, gotten a degree, met someone he loved, married her, had had children. He had done all this without her, without even knowing that she existed. Until now.

As they drove away, a crushing wave of remorse overwhelmed her. She turned in dread to Dennis. 'We didn't even acknowledge that he was our son, Dennis. We never said anything, we just left.'

'Mag, he's not our son. He became someone else's son a long time ago. We have no claim on him.' His face was firm, set.

Could he be right? Was that it? Nothing more. Would each of them continue to live their lives separately in a parallel universe?

'What about Ciara? He called her his sister, he said that they had met a few times.'

'A sister is different from a parent. Ciara had no part in giving him away; we, on the other hand, abandoned him, or at least that's probably how he sees it.'

Mag twisted her hands together in her lap. 'But he did try to find us. He wanted to see us.'

'He didn't look to me like a man overjoyed at the reunion,' Dennis said grimly. He glanced at Mag's face and spoke more gently. 'Mag, I have nothing against the man. Yes, I suppose we gave him life but it takes an awful lot more than that to be a parent. Ciara was my daughter; he's not my son.'

Yet again, she found herself faced with Dennis's implacable logic which was hard to resist but this time she had to rebel. When they arrived at her house, she sat for a moment in the stationary car before speaking from her heart. 'Dennis, you may be right when you say that he will never be our son but one thing is certain for me; I will always be his mother.'

1993

'Hello, Mrs Byrne. Mag, isn't it?' Mag felt a light touch on her back as she listlessly contemplated the colourful array of blemish-free vegetables in the supermarket. Each one of the tomatoes, carrots, peppers, courgettes was a shining example of perfection in both colour and form and yet the overall impression disheartened Mag. Surface was everything. What was underneath mattered nothing. It was the same for people. Society was even more harsh and unforgiving than nature.

She turned around and found Liz Lynch standing behind her. Mag knew her vaguely as the mother of a little boy in the same class as Ciara. Her son, Derek, was at her side now; a small, skinny, freckled nine-year-old.

'Hello Liz,' Mag said, suddenly ashamed of her greasy hair and old clothes. She had been unable to muster up the interest or the energy to have a shower that morning and she was now only too aware of how neglected she must look. She had dragged herself out of the house to go shopping because there was nothing left in the fridge but it had been a major effort.

'Hello, Derek,' she said. For an instant Mag saw that the time delay in her acknowledgement of the boy had disconcerted Liz. Yet again, she felt out of sync with the world. Sometimes, it was as though she were moving in slow motion, out of time with everyone around her who moved instinctively in a graceful dance of which she had forgotten the steps.

Liz quickly brushed over her lapse with a friendly smile. 'We saw Ciara at school earlier on when we dropped off Laura. Poor Derek is out sick at the moment. He had his appendix out last week.'

'Appendix,' Mag repeated. The word struck her as strange; sharp bristles on the outside, smooth and shiny on the inside, like a conker. Its meaning became disconnected from its sound. She couldn't think of anything else to say so she said goodbye and walked away. Behind her, she heard the boy say something to his mother who hushed him. As soon as she left them she realised with a flush of embarrassment how rude and strange her behaviour must have appeared but it was too late now to go back and change anything.

She picked up the few groceries she needed, keeping her head down in case someone else might recognise her. As she manoeuvred her way out of the car-park a man made a rude gesture at her and shouted some unintelligible, angry words. She must have done something wrong but she didn't know what. She drove home, frightened and trembling. She unpacked the groceries and then collapsed on a chair in the kitchen. She had learned to live with this presence which, for the past few years, had cast a shorter or longer shadow over her life depending on the moment, never disappearing completely. This time, though, the gloom seemed to have increased to the point of obscuring all light. She felt as disposable as a tissue, indispensable to no-one, least of all to herself. Even as a rational part of her mind suggested that this feeling would pass, an unshakeable conviction told her it would not.

She decided to go to bed and try to sleep. Sleep was a fickle friend these days which brought elusive oblivion only after teasing her mercilessly. She poured out a measure of whiskey from the bottle in the cabinet in the sitting-room and swallowed it down quickly. Then, as an afterthought, she brought the bottle upstairs with her. She took off her clothes and looked for her nightdress. She couldn't find it and gave up the search. She flipped off the lid of the box of sleeping tablets by her bedside and took one, then another one with a gulp of whiskey. She tottered on the brink of a decision, she felt light-headed with the choice. Before she could think any further, she tilted out a handful of the little diamond-shaped pills into her palm and swallowed them with another glug of whiskey. The whiskey tore at her insides. Damaging herself felt like the right thing to do. She lay back on the bed, closed her eyes and waited for peace.

Ciara's small face floated across the reddish darkness in front of her. It was then that a jolt of panic roused her. What had she done? No, she couldn't do this to Ciara. She tried to get out of bed and walk to the bathroom. If she could get there she would be saved. She stood up. Her legs felt heavy, immovable, her head light as a helium balloon. Or maybe it was her legs that were light and her head heavy. She couldn't tell any more. The bathroom was far away, very far away. She took a few staggering steps into the no-man's land between the bed and door and then threw herself on the handle to the bathroom door. Relief. The door opened. Hard diamonds of light sprinkled through the obscured glass of the bathroom window and hurt her eyes. She blinked. The washbasin shimmered and swayed, a mirage in the desert. Only a few more steps. Then she heard a sickening crack and a lightning-bolt of pain blazed across her eyes. She fell to the floor, unable to move and just before she lost consciousness, her last thought was that Ciara would never know that this was not how she had intended it to be.

She was aware of movement, of being lifted before disappearing again. Then, disembodied pain called her back into the world. She tried to locate the pain before she opened her eyes. It was in her throat, an ache stretching down to her stomach. There was also a throb in her nose. She was in a hospital room. A nurse had her back to her, arranging flowers in a vase. Mag tried to speak but a croak emerged instead.

The nurse turned around and smiled. 'So, Margaret, you're back with us,' she said.

Over the next couple of days, little by little, Mag discovered what had happened. She had fallen against the washbasin and broken her nose. She had lost consciousness and shortly afterwards Ciara had come home from school to find her almost naked in a pool of blood. Believing her mother dead, she had phoned her father in the garage and, almost incoherent, had begged him, through tears and sobs, to come home. When Dennis arrived, Ciara was in a state of shock, cold and shivering. The ambulance had arrived within minutes and taken Mag to the hospital where they had pumped out the contents of her stomach and saved her life.

She was amazed at how calmly everyone in the hospital seemed to absorb what had happened. No-one seemed to find her actions contemptible or shameful. She allowed herself to be treated like a baby, sleeping a lot and drinking mostly fluids. At the end of her second day in hospital she started to feel stronger and managed to sit up in bed. A doctor, a middle-aged man, came to see her. He pulled up a chair and sat beside her. She knew that he was a psychiatrist but it was still a shock when he mentioned the words 'attempted suicide'. She wanted to tell him that it wasn't how it was but she wasn't sure he would believe her. Gently he prised out of her how she had been feeling in the previous days, months and even years. She found his nodding acceptance a relief and resigned herself to his care.

On the third day, she started to panic about how Ciara must be feeling and asked to see her. She was aware that discussions were taking place between the medical staff and Dennis and she was delighted when later that evening, Ciara shyly entered her room, followed by Mag's sister Bernie. Bernie, for once, showed unusual diplomacy and left them alone once she saw that Mag was awake and alert. Ciara seemed reluctant to approach her and kept looking at the bandages covering Mag's nose.

'I must have given you a terrible fright, love,' Mag said. Her voice was still scratchy and new.

Ciara nodded.

'I didn't mean to do that at all. The doctors here have explained to me that I was sick, that I am sick, but they are going to make me better. They have special medicines that will cure me so that when I come home I'll be different. You'll see. I'll be even better than I was before.'

'I don't want you to be different, Mammy,' Ciara said. Mag held out her hand to her and Ciara approached the bed timidly. Mag tried to hug but it was difficult to do properly, hindered as she was by the tube running into her wrist and the throbbing of her nose. Her heart was breaking at the idea that, through her own fault, she had brought misery into the life of this wonderful little girl.

Bernie poked her head around the door. 'We'd better not tire your mother out too much, Ciara. We can come back another day and stay longer next time.' Ciara disentangled herself and joined her aunt. 'Go out to your Uncle Tommy there. I'll just have a quick word with your mammy.'

Bernie entered and closed the door. 'Now, Mag, I'll not stay long but I've had a word with the doctor and I think the best thing is for you to come home with me once they let you out. Fresh country air and decent meals are what you need to get you back on your feet.'

Mag smiled faintly and opened her mouth to speak.

'No, we won't argue about it. The boys are all gone, we have plenty of space. It'll do you good to take a break and focus on getting well.'

Mag nodded and let Bernie have her way.

During the time she stayed in the hospital, Dennis did not come to visit her but she knew from the nurses that he had phoned them a few times to find out how she was doing. She struck up a friendship with a woman she met in the television room, Treasa Quinn, a real friendship built on openness and mutual acceptance at a difficult time in the lives of the two women.

On the day before her discharge, Bernie offered to go to Mag's house and pick up whatever belongings she needed and, weakly, Mag accepted. She spent almost a month in Bernie's house and with every day that passed she felt better. Her prescribed medication banished the clouds over her and she started to feel more normal. In all that time, she heard nothing from Dennis and didn't try to contact him. She would ask for his forgiveness later when she was stronger.

Chapter 19

Street lights cast a dim orange light over the deserted yard of the garage below. A white, disembowelled Mercedes glowed eerily. A row of cars awaiting attention lined the back wall. It seemed bigger, more spacious when it was empty of the people who occupied it during the day. The silence was dull and stifling.

Over the years, the garage had grown into a stable, profitable business that provided a living for at least ten families. The bank would judge it a commercial success but, for the first time, Dennis considered it through cold, critical eyes. It was little as a life's legacy. The events and revelations of the last few weeks had shaken him profoundly. His natural ebullience had deserted him. He had always believed, or rather assumed, that his choices and decisions in life had been based on solid reasonable logic. Now he wondered if his priorities had been the wrong ones, if everything he had built had been on quicksand.

The action of the past few days had been a distraction, a diversion from his grief but now it tumbled down around him again. He felt he had mishandled the situations with Mag and with Joseph Farrell but he was at a loss as to how he should have done things differently. This self-questioning was alien to him and undermined his self-confidence.

He tried to shrug off his bleak thoughts and turned away from the window. The only sound in the room was of water bubbling around potatoes on the cooker. Dennis tested them; almost done. He had decided to make a decent dinner for himself and, even if it was only boiled potatoes, a pork chop and heated-up baked beans, it was better than anything else he had managed over the past few weeks.

His mobile phone rang. The sound came from the pocket of his jacket hanging over the back of a chair. He pulled it out and returned to the window overlooking the garage yard.

'Dennis Byrne?' The voice was crisp and efficient. 'Sergeant O'Brien here. Sorry to call at this late hour. Hope I'm not disturbing you. I was waiting for a response from the coroner before getting in touch. Would it be possible to arrange a meeting with you soon?'

'Oh, right, you mentioned that the other day. Is it to give us the latest update prior to the inquest? 'Dennis said.

'Yes, well. It looks like the inquest might take a little longer to schedule than we originally thought.'

'Why is that?' Shadows crept over his heart and it grew cold.

'I'd rather discuss that in person, if you don't mind. I've been in touch with Mrs Byrne and I've arranged to call to her house tomorrow morning at ten o'clock. I was hoping that would suit you and I could see you both together.' O'Brien sounded busy and, in any case, Dennis was too weary to question him further.

'No problem, I'll be there.'

'Thank you. I'll see you tomorrow then.'

'Good night, Mr. Byrne.'

Dennis stood thinking until a smell of burning drew him out of his thoughts. He hurried into the kitchen and removed the pot from the heat. The water had boiled off the potatoes. Where the skins touched the pot they were burnt black. The upper side had burst open allowing the soft, white, fluffy insides to spill out. It didn't matter: he wasn't hungry any more.

Dennis woke early the next morning, still unable to shake the feeling of impending doom. His thoughts raced around his head, twisting and tangling around each other like a pit of snakes. Unable to focus on anything for a useful length of time, he decided to call over to Mag's early.

Two days had passed since they had been to Joseph Farrell's house and, since then, they had not had the opportunity to talk. Although, even under the cold light of retrospection, he believed that he was right in what he had said to Mag about their role in this man's life, the reappearance of this son he had never known and to whom he had never given any thought before now, created niggling doubts which were harder to shake off than he liked to admit.

He told himself repeatedly that his only contribution to this man's existence was a single cell, a mere coincidence of nature, a concurrence of circumstances that was a totally insufficient basis for any kind of relationship. He understood that it was different for Mag who had borne him and even seen and held him as a baby, if only for the briefest of moments, but it did no good to brood over what was past history and could not be changed.

Melancholic as his mood was, it was a surprise to see that Mag seemed resolute and bright, almost cheerful, when she opened the door to him. He had thought that the shock of coming face-to-face with a past they had considered long-buried would have overwhelmed her but she seemed to be coping better than he was with the emotional flux.

'You're early. Come in, I was about to make tea.' She led him into the kitchen where she moved around in a buzz of activity.

'You seem to be in a good mood,' he said as he watched her.

'Today isn't the worst,' she said. 'I'm sure that'll all change when Sergeant O'Brien gets here. Did he tell you that the inquest is likely to be postponed?'

'He did.'

'What do you think that means?' Mag put the teapot down in front of them.

'I don't know but we'll find out soon enough. It may mean that they need more time to investigate Ciara's death.'

'So then they also think there's something wrong,' Mag said.

'Well, there's got to be. Even apart from finding the charm, there's something really odd about the whole thing. Ciara wasn't drinking, at least nothing that would impair her judgement, and yet she drove over the edge of that mountain without a seat-belt on. But when you add on top of that the charm from her bracelet that somehow ended up on the road, more than likely before the accident, then it definitely doesn't add up for me.'

'So what do you think did happen?'

'I'm not sure but I think someone else was involved in the accident, someone who hasn't said anything about it. I think Ciara stopped her car before she had the accident, talked to someone, lost the charm in some way, got back in her car and then had the accident. That's the only way that makes sense to me,' Dennis said.

'You've been convinced of that since the beginning, haven't you?' Mag leaned towards Dennis and touched his hand.

Dennis withdrew his hand, ostensibly to raise his mug to his lips but in reality to keep a cap on his sadness and prevent tears from falling. 'I've thought about it a lot. I've gone around in circles trying to work out what could have happened but I keep coming back to the same idea.'

'So then O'Brien may be on the same train of thought if he's delaying the inquest.'

'Maybe he has other information we don't have. He's been playing his cards very close to his chest. He's never said directly that there was something dodgy about the accident but he hasn't said there wasn't either. And now we know that he's going around asking a lot of questions.'

'So who do you think could have stopped Ciara after she left the McMurray house?' Mag frowned. A thought crossed her mind and she went pale. 'Dennis, she wasn't molested, was she? It's not possible that she was stopped by a weirdo or rapist, is it? Oh God, I couldn't bear the thought of anything like that happening to Ciara.'

Dennis gave Mag's hand a squeeze. 'No, Mag, I don't think so. O'Brien couldn't have kept it from us if there had been any evidence of that in the autopsy. It would be too obvious; he'd have had to tell us. And, in any case, her clothes would have been torn, at the very least. You have all the clothes she was wearing at the time, don't you?'

Mag looked up, startled. 'Yes, everything is still in the bag I got at the hospital. I haven't been able to look at it since. It's in her bedroom. I'll get it.'

She returned with the bag and handed it to Dennis. 'You open it,' she said.

Dennis forced his hands not to tremble as he untied the knot in the blue plastic bag. He tipped the contents out on the table. He put her boots side by side and laid her leather jacket out flat. There was also a long denim skirt and a flimsy blue and green button-through top. He picked up the top and examined it. It had dark stiffened patches of blood and, for a second, he thought he might vomit. He waited a second for the feeling to pass and then examined the top for rips or tears. There were none. A small zip-lock plastic bag held Ciara's earrings, a gold chain and the charm bracelet. Dennis took out the bracelet and examined the gap where the deer charm had been.

'No, Mag, I feel sure that Ciara was not stopped by a stranger. I think that it was someone she knew. And, for what it's worth, my money's on McMurray.'

'Why would he do that?' Mag asked.

'Well, it looks like he was the last one to see her, all the others had left, his wife wasn't there. He says that she left on her own and that he didn't find out about the accident until the next day but for all we know they may have argued and he may have followed her.' Dennis warmed to his theory. 'He already lied about them being together until he was forced to admit it. He could very easily be lying now.'

'What about Vincent? He wasn't exactly straight about his movements that night either. When you think about it, we only have his word that he didn't talk to her after she left the house.'

'I suppose,' Dennis was reluctant to consider other possibilities. 'But I still think it's far more likely to have been McMurray.'

'That's your prejudice talking, Dennis. You have a problem with the notion that Ciara could have been in love with a man nearly your own age.'

'Maybe but you have to admit that if McMurray was involved or even witnessed Ciara's accident he'd have every reason to keep quiet about it.'

'I couldn't see Vincent coming forward either, he's not exactly on the best of terms with the Gardaí.'

'So, you think Vincent had something to do with it?'

'No, I'm just acting as devil's advocate. To be honest, I'm happy to rely on the guards to find out what happened now that we know they are taking it seriously and now that we have a better understanding about what was going on in Ciara's life.'

'But do we understand?' Dennis knew she was right but he dreaded the moment when he would have to accept that nothing more could be done or known.

'I think we have to face the fact that Ciara was seeing a married man, no matter how inappropriate that relationship might seem to us. I think she got caught up in something—maybe there was some hero-worship involved. As for him, he took advantage of that. At least now we know that we got the wrong end of the stick about Joseph Farrell. It's a minor consolation but I feel better knowing that Ciara wasn't seeing the two men. I could never get my head around the idea of Ciara being sneaky or deceptive. I can understand her falling under the charm of McMurray, she was only twenty-two after all, but playing one man off the other didn't seem like her at all.'

'All the same, I'd like to know exactly how Ciara's accident came about.'

The ring of the doorbell cut through his words.

'Well, let's hope that that's what O'Brien will tell us. That must be him.' Mag went to answer the door.

She let O'Brien in and he followed her to the kitchen. Gravely, he shook hands with Dennis and refused Mag's offer of a cup of tea.

'Ciara's things, I assume,' he said, looking at the clothes on the table.

'Yes,' Dennis said. He folded them away and put them back in the plastic bag.

'I'd appreciate it if you'd allow me to take them away with me. You never know, there may be something there that might help us.'

'Of course, you're welcome to take everything but, if I may ask, Sergeant, help you with what?' Mag asked.

'Let's sit down and I'll explain from the beginning.' O'Brien pulled out a chair. He took out a notebook and a ballpoint pen, placed them on the table but then ignored them. He cleared his throat. 'First of all, as I mentioned to you both yesterday, the inquest has been adjourned. Following a garda recommendation to do so.'

'And the reason for that?' Dennis could feel his scalp prickling with tension.

'In the light of certain findings, we felt that further investigation was necessary into the circumstances surrounding your daughter's accident in order for us to present a fully consistent case to the coroner.'

'What findings do you mean?' Dennis asked.

O'Brien hesitated, gathering his thoughts. 'A certain number of points puzzled us from the beginning, none of them particularly remarkable when considered in isolation, but when several things strike us as odd in a case then it tends to send off warning bells. Firstly, it was obvious from the position of the car that your daughter was not travelling very fast when she went over the edge of the mountain. It was night-time but it's strange that she lost control travelling at that speed. Then, during the inspection of the vehicle afterwards it was noted that it was only in second gear. These facts combined with the discovery of the charm from Ciara's bracelet at the side of the road signalled to us that there might be an aspect to this accident that we had not fully understood.'

'Are you saying that you thought something was wrong from the beginning?' Dennis was amazed. He had been so convinced that O'Brien was fobbing him off.

'Let's say, I was keeping an open mind,' O'Brien gave him a humourless smile. 'I'm sorry to have been so cautious with you, Mr Byrne, but I was afraid that if I had been totally honest you might have jeopardised our investigation by reacting rashly.'

Dennis looked down in embarrassment, unable to refute the good sense of what the man was saying.

O'Brien continued. 'When we met, you emphasised that Ciara was a careful driver and that she always wore her seat-belt. This information was at odds with the evidence we had about the accident and so we decided to look more closely at all the aspects of the case.'

Dennis glanced at Mag. Her eyes were fixed on O'Brien, her face pale and worried.

'As I already told you,' O'Brien said. 'The autopsy revealed that Ciara had been drinking very little but what I didn't tell you is that it also referred to a fresh scratch on Ciara's face that didn't seem entirely compatible with the injuries sustained as a result of the accident.'

'So what does all this mean, Sergeant?' Mag's voice was tight with anxiety.

'I wish I could tell you that, Mrs Byrne, but I'm afraid we don't have all the answers yet. Please don't worry too much about it though, we're working on it,' O'Brien said.

'You've questioned Colm McMurray, I assume,' Dennis said.

'We have, and his wife, and most of the people who were at the party that night.'

'And what did McMurray have to say?'

'I'm afraid I'm not at liberty at this stage of the investigation to divulge any discussion we've had but, rest assured, I will let you know our conclusions as soon as I am able to do so.'

'When do you think that's likely to be?' Dennis asked.

'Soon, I hope,' O'Brien said. 'I know that this is difficult for you and we will be doing our best to resolve the situation as quickly as possible but I'm sure that you can understand when I say that I can give no guarantees.'

'You mentioned a scratch on Ciara's face. Does that mean someone attacked her?' Mag asked.

'I'd prefer to say that we are keeping an open mind on that for the moment. The scratch is not a very deep one. That night before she left, can you confirm that she didn't have a scratch on her face?'

'Definitely not,' Mag said.

'Well, it may have nothing to do with her accident. However, in the light of other issues we need to keep it in mind.'

'She had some sort of a fight with a young fellow at the party, Vincent Connolly, although I'm sure we'd have heard if it had come to blows,' Mag said.

'We're aware of that incident,' O'Brien said.

'Our understanding is that Ciara was the last one to leave and McMurray was on his own in the house. He must have been the last one to see her alive then,' Dennis insisted, hoping that O'Brien would relent and reveal where their suspicions lay.

O'Brien looked from Dennis to Mag. 'That seems to be backed up by the statements of the other young people at the party and we have confirmed that Mrs McMurray was in London at the time; her flight didn't get in until the next morning. However, I would counsel you against jumping to conclusions. Let us proceed with our enquiries and I'm sure the situation will be clarified in due course.'

'One last thing,' Dennis said. 'In conversation with young Vincent Connolly, he told me that he waited outside the McMurray house for Ciara to come outside so that he could talk to her. I don't think he meant any harm but I thought you should know.' Dennis stifled a guilty pang at betraying Vincent but it couldn't be helped.

'I've interviewed that young man and he told me that already,' O'Brien said sternly.

'A large part of the reason I have been so frank with you today is to discourage you from meddling in our investigation. Hard as it may be, you will just have to stand back and resist the temptation to get involved. I came here today hoping that if you were aware of our efforts, you might allow us to get on with the job.'

'We've got the message loud and clear.' Dennis exchanged a glance with Mag. 'You don't have to worry about us.'

'Now, if you would excuse me, I need to be getting back to the station.' He put away his unused notebook and pen and picked up the blue plastic bag containing Ciara's belongings.

While Mag was letting him out, Dennis walked to the patio doors and watched the play of sunlight on the lawn. He could hear the murmur of voices from the hall. In the silence that followed the closing of the door, he became aware of the ticking of the clock and the faint hum of the fridge motor. His eyes were fixed, without seeing, on a blackbird hopping on the lawn in search of something to eat.

Mag's soft voice broke into his reverie. 'So, it looks like you may be right, Dennis.'

'I'd rather I wasn't,' he said.

'I know,' she said. Thoughts of Ciara forced their way into his mind and squeezed his heart in a vice-grip of anguish. The idea that someone might have deliberately hurt his little girl was burning through his insides like a corrosive acid.

'McMurray,' he said through clenched teeth.

'All we can do now is wait,' Mag said, putting her hand on his sleeve.

'In fairness, I seem to have underestimated O'Brien. It looks like he's covering everything pretty well. Let's hope it won't be long before the whole thing is sorted. Not that it will bring Ciara back to us.' All of a sudden Dennis was tired, he wanted to leave and try to put all these hypotheses and theories out of his mind.

'Dennis, I've made a decision.' The seriousness of her voice made him stop. He waited for her to go on.

'I'm going to get in touch with Joseph Farrell. I'd like to see him again.'

'See him about what?'

'I'd like to talk to him, hear what he has to say, maybe explain how it came about that we gave him away to be adopted.

'We? *You* gave him away.' The correction left Dennis's lips before he had time to consider what he was saying. Although he had not intended to hurt her, she flinched. 'And there's not much to explain. Ours was a fairly typical situation: we were young, naïve, penniless and totally unprepared,' he said.

'But at one time, he did try to get in touch with us, through Ciara, even if it didn't work out that way in the end.'

'He only wanted to know who we were and now he knows. He's a man, an adult, he can contact us if he wants to but as far as I'm concerned we gave up any claim we had on him thirty-two years ago. We don't have the right to impose ourselves on his life without an invitation.'

'But that's exactly what we did the other day.'

‘That was before we knew who he was. And besides, look how that turned out.’

Dennis was not unsympathetic to Mag’s desire to go back in time and change the outcome of the past but it was not realistic. What was done was done.

‘He has done just fine in life, Mag, he’s perfectly happy, he doesn’t need us.’ He felt ill-at-ease, awkward in his attempt to console her but, in any case, she wasn’t listening.

She avoided his gaze, gathering her thoughts. ‘Dennis, I’m sorry I cut you out of the decision about the baby. I should have allowed you to have your say, it was your baby too, after all.’

Nervously, Dennis put his hands in his pockets and looked down at Mag’s bent head. ‘To be honest, Mag, that was never the issue for me. When you disappeared without a trace, I was hurt and angry that you didn’t give me a chance but all I cared about was you; the baby didn’t exist for me. In my mind, it wasn’t a baby, just an obstacle. I didn’t give it much thought then or afterwards. Maybe I was selfish but I was eighteen and hadn’t the faintest idea what fatherhood involved.’

‘That’s how I felt when I found out I was pregnant; I couldn’t imagine being a mother but over the nine months something changed. I was turning into a mother despite myself but it was too late to change my mind and when I gave him away it was a wrench that I didn’t expect. I tried to forget about it and move on but I never fully succeeded,’ Mag said quietly.

‘I know it must have been tough for you but I thought it was for the best not to talk about it. I didn’t want to revive painful memories when there was nothing we could do about it.'

A tear fell on the floor and it took a second for Dennis to realise what it was because there was no sound from Mag. 'Here, sit down,' he said and pulled out a chair. He pulled out his hankie, gave it to her and sat down opposite her. He didn't know if what he was saying was making things worse or better.

'All the same, we should have talked about it. It might have helped. You must have thought about it sometimes. Didn't you ever wonder about what might have been?" Mag said.

Dennis gave her question serious thought before answering. 'Every so often, I suppose it did occur to me that it would be nice to have a son, someone who might work with me and take over the garage but that's not how it was so I didn't waste a lot of time thinking about it, it was just a pipe dream. And I certainly don't think I ever associated that notion with the baby you had so long ago. For me, I became a father with Ciara. Over the years, I learned what being a father was through her and I can't see how a heedless act over thirty years ago when I was only a kid myself could have made me into one.'

Mag sat up straighter and her voice was firmer. 'So what you are telling me is that you think we should leave him alone. Even after the way things went the other day.'

'OK, I agree there was a bit of misunderstanding between us but that doesn't change the basic facts. He's met us, he knows who we are and if he wants to see us again, then that's a different matter. Let's leave it at that.'

'Except that I don't think I can.'

'You're reading too much into this, Mag.'

'I don't know what the right thing to do is, Dennis, but something tells me that this is an opportunity for me—not to put things right, nothing can do that—but it's a chance to explain what I did, what we did. That might not mean anything to him but I don't want to let that chance go.' Mag's tears had dried and she looked at him with a determined face.

Dennis sat back in his chair. 'Mag, you decide what the best thing to do is for you. I can't tell you what that is but you must understand that this man is not looking for another set of parents, or even friends; he wanted information, knowledge, that's all. I'm afraid you might get even more hurt than you already have been. Why can't you live with the fact that you made a decision a long time ago, a decision that was the right one at the time, and one that can't be changed now?'

'I just don't want to have any more regrets, Dennis. If I end up getting hurt, so be it, but at least I can feel I tried.'

'Well, if you're sure, then go ahead. I'm not going to stop you.'

'So, if I arrange to meet him, you don't want to come with me?' Mag looked at him with a steady gaze.

'No,' Dennis said. 'It's not my way.' He reached for his jacket. He left the house, sad and tired. He accepted Mag's interest in this new-found son but he was concerned that she might be building up false hopes of some kind of replacement in her heart for Ciara, a place that he knew with certitude could never be filled by anyone else, ever.

1993

'Independent, I-N-D-E-P-E-N-D-A-N-T,' Ciara called out. She was sitting at the kitchen table with her school books around her while Dennis cleared up after their dinner. Her copybook was propped up on the counter in front of him. He glanced at it every so often while he worked but his anxiety made it difficult for him to concentrate.

'Good. Now, decoration,' Dennis said.

'Daddy, that was wrong. What I said. It's e-n-t, not a-n-t. I knew you weren't paying attention. How am I supposed to get ten out of ten in my spelling test tomorrow if you don't correct me properly? I only got seven out of ten and six out of ten the last two times and now Marcella Delaney is way ahead of me.'

'Sorry, Ciara, I was thinking of something else,' Dennis said. 'Go on, do 'decoration', and then we'll go through them again.'

The door-bell rang. Ciara leapt out of her chair as though ejected from it and ran to the door. 'It's Mammy, it's Mammy,' she shrieked.

Dennis slowly folded the tea-towel, left it beside the sink and followed her. He shrank from seeing Mag again. His telephone conversation with her two days earlier had been short and factual. After one month of recovery spent in her sister's house, she had told him that she was ready to come home.

'Fine,' he had said in a neutral, noncommittal tone. Neither of them had expressed any of the emotion that lay behind their words, leaving by silent mutual agreement that discussion to a face-to-face meeting. Hearing her voice had removed any lingering doubt that might have remained. His decision was made and it was final, forged under the molten heat of his anger and hardened with time. Their marriage was over. For years he had tried his best to make things better between them but nothing he did was of any use. Instead of pulling her up, she was dragging him down—this last incident was proof of that—and he couldn't take it anymore.

Mag stood in the doorway, unable to enter because Ciara had thrown her arms around her waist, immobilising her. Behind Mag, stood Tommy, her brother-in-law, a suitcase in either hand.

'Come on, Ciara, let your mother and your uncle come inside.' Dennis put his hands on Ciara's shoulders and tried to pull her back from Mag.

Mag entered and looked around the hall as though checking for any changes that might have taken place in her absence. It felt strange to see her there. She looked the same and yet subtly different; her hair had grown and she had put on a little weight. She looked nervous. Dennis avoided looking at her directly.

Tommy followed Mag inside and put the cases down at the bottom of the stairs. 'Dennis,' he said in acknowledgement as he held out his hand. 'Hello, little miss,' he said to Ciara but Ciara had eyes for no-one but her mother.

'I'll be heading straight back, Mag.' Tommy was a man of few words which Dennis had always thought was a lucky thing, given the woman he was married to.

'No, Tommy, come in and have a cup of tea at least before you leave.' Mag was insistent.

‘Do, Tommy,’ Dennis said but without the same level of warmth. He didn’t feel like coping with the small talk that would entail.

‘No, I’ll go. It’s not a good time for me to be away from the farm. I still have a few cows left to calve. Good luck to you all.’ Tommy’s steady expression betrayed no trace of opinion or judgement.

After he left, even Ciara was infected by the crackling tension that lay in the air between Dennis and Mag. She chattered away, trying to fill the void. She pulled her mother’s hand to drag her into the kitchen.

‘Have you not finished doing your homework yet, Ciara?’ Mag asked when she saw the books on the table.

‘We’re coping as well as we can. It’s not always easy after a day’s work.’ Dennis couldn’t help the barb escaping him even though he had promised himself that he would say nothing in front of Ciara.

‘I didn’t mean it as a criticism, Dennis.’ Mag was flustered and picked up one of Ciara’s copies to cover her awkwardness.

‘Don’t look at that, Mammy.’ Ciara tried to pull it back out of her hands. ‘I didn’t do very well in my last few tests but, tomorrow, I’m going to try and get ten out of ten for you in my spellings test. And in my sums test.’ She smiled a radiant smile at her mother who said nothing, just pulled her close and pressed her small head against her breasts.

‘It’s great that Mammy’s home, isn’t it, Daddy?’ Ciara turned to Dennis.

‘Yes, great,’ Dennis said. ‘Now Ciara, I think it’s time for you to go to bed. Your mother and I need to talk. You’ll have to be good and refreshed if you want to beat that Marcella

Delaney tomorrow.' Dennis made a half-hearted attempt at bluff good humour but its failure was underlined by Ciara's overly enthusiastic reception of it.

'All right but Mammy, will you come up and stay with me for a little while after I've brushed my teeth and I'm in my pyjamas?' Ciara had difficulty leaving her mother's side as though she was afraid she might leave if she turned her back.

'Of course I will, love,' Mag said. 'Call me from the top of the stairs when you're ready.' She started to tidy away Ciara's school books.

'It feels strange being back. It's been a while' Mag said, quietly. She put her hand on Dennis's arm but he pulled away.

'Yes, it has,' he said. 'If you want to eat, there's a bit left over.'

'No, that's all right,' she said. 'I ate in Bernie's before leaving.' They looked at each other properly for the first time. Ciara's voice rang out, calling for Mag's attention.

Dennis was relieved to be left alone. He went into the sitting-room and poured himself a whiskey.

A while later, Mag joined him. She looked tired. 'She seems in good form,' she said.

'Hmmm,' Dennis said. 'She's getting better but it's taking time. She's been having nightmares.'

'I can imagine. I must have given her a terrible fright.'

The understatement acted as a bellows to the cinders of Dennis's anger. Was she even conscious of what she had done? 'Fright isn't the word for it. She was petrified, shocked beyond recognition. You haven't seen how she's been for the past month. She really believed you were dead. So did I, when I first saw you. She hasn't slept in her own bed for a full night since. Every night she wakes up and comes in to me, crying and shaking.'

'I'm sorry, Dennis, I really am. I wasn't well but I'm getting better. I'm sure we can sort everything out.'

Dennis continued as though she had not spoken. 'She thinks it was her fault. She thinks that if she had been better behaved, if she'd been a 'good girl', then you wouldn't have done it.' He stopped to look at Mag to see if she was taking in what he was saying. 'School hasn't been easy for her either. She doesn't know how to deal with all the whispers and rumours.'

'I know all that but it has been a very tough time for me too.' Mag started to cry.

'I don't care how tough a time you've had,' Dennis exploded. 'It hasn't exactly been easy for me but I don't care about that either. What I do care about is Ciara. She's only nine and you have put her through hell. She did nothing to deserve that.' Dennis was no longer able to stay seated. He stood up and paced the room with his hands in his pockets. 'For God's sake, Mag, didn't you know that she would be the one to find you? She got off the bus and came home to find you in the bathroom, unconscious, smashed up and covered in blood.'

Instinctively, Mag touched the side of her nose. 'I didn't mean…'

'I don't know what you meant but it was an incredibly selfish thing to do, Mag.' Dennis felt the bitterness ooze out of him like pus from a festering wound. 'You can't just wipe it away by saying sorry. Anything that might have been left between us, you destroyed. It's over. I can't go on this way.'

'What do you mean?' Mag crumpled in her chair.

Anger flashed through his words like light glinting off the blade of a knife. 'I'm going to move out. I'll move back into the flat over the garage. You and Ciara can have the house. Ciara can come and stay with me in the flat whenever she wants.' A protective layer was stripped from Mag's face showing the raw emotion underneath. Dennis felt a tug of compassion but hardened his heart when he remembered Ciara's white, shocked face as she watched the ambulance drive away taking Mag to the hospital. In that instant he too had realised that he might never see Mag alive again. The blaring siren and penetrating blue lights had drawn the neighbours out on the street. Feeling small and exposed, he had picked Ciara up and retreated inside. He had tried to reassure Ciara but he was too shaken inside to be convincing.

Later, when he realised that Mag's life was no longer in danger, the bitterness set in and grew like a gangrene in his soul. To prevent it from consuming him, he decided that he had to cut it out and discard it, and if that meant cutting Mag out of his life, then so be it.

'Don't worry, you won't be short of money, I'll sort that out. I'll move out tomorrow,' he said.

Mag scanned his face before speaking. Her tears had dried, her face was haggard 'So that's it then,' she said flatly.

'That's it.' Dennis drained the remains of his glass and left the room.

That night he slept in the spare bedroom. He left for the garage early the next morning before Ciara and Mag were up, although he could hear from the soft sounds coming from the bedroom that was once theirs, that Mag was not asleep.

Chapter 20

Mag laid the telephone directory on the table open on the correct page, Joseph Farrell's number underlined in red. In orderly alignment beside it was a blank sheet of notepaper, a pen and the cordless phone. She had given a significant amount of thought as to the best time to call. The evening seemed better than the daytime or even the weekend but should she call before or after the children were in bed? If she called too late, he might think her inconsiderate but if she called too early, then he might be too preoccupied with the little ones to speak to her.

In the end, she decided to phone early in the evening and then offer to call back later if she sensed that he was too busy to talk. She vacillated over the exact words she should use, testing them aloud. She prepared alternative speeches depending on whether it was he or his wife who answered the phone. She agonised over how to address him; Mr Farrell sounded too formal; Joe, too familiar; Joseph Farrell, too pompous. She would try to avoid using his name as much as she could but would use his first name in full, Joseph, if obliged. She looked at the clock; it was a quarter past seven;

Wednesday evening. There was nothing to be gained in putting it off any longer.

She picked up the phone and, consulting the directory with deliberation, she composed the number although she now knew it off by heart. Her fingertips felt big and bulky and spread over the sides of the buttons as she pressed on them. Then a sorting sound told her that each digit of the code she had just tapped out was being taken into account and directing her call to a phone in Dundrum. The ringing signal made her heart jump and it took all her willpower not to hang up.

Hello.' A small voice answered.

'Hello,' Mag said. Before she could say anything else, the little girl spoke.

'Nana,' she said, delighted. 'I got a new toothbrush today. It's got Winnie the Pooh on it.'

Mag swallowed with difficulty. 'I'm sorry, pet, this isn't your Nana,' she said. 'Is your Daddy there? Could I talk to him?'

'Daddy's upstairs.' The girl's voice was puffed up with the satisfaction of conveying important information. 'He's changing Fiona's nappy. She did a big poo that came out the sides and everything.'

'What are you doing, Katie? Who's on the phone?' Mag could hear a muffled voice in the background.

'It's not Nana,' Katie said.

A shuffle of activity ensued and a woman's voice travelled down the line. 'Hello?'

'Hello, Mrs Farrell?' Mag said. 'I wonder if it would be possible to speak to your husband, please?'

'Who's speaking please?' the woman asked.

'My name is Mag Byrne. Previously, Margaret O'Donnell.' A pause, as brief as the time it takes to inhale, told Mag that the woman knew who she was.

'Hold on, I'll see if he can come to the phone,' she said and put down the receiver.

An eternity passed. Mag wondered if they had forgotten about her. Then, abruptly, a voice took her by surprise. 'Hello? Joe Farrell here. What can I do for you?'

All of Mag's pre-prepared speeches left her head.

'It's Mag Byrne here. I wanted to apologise for the other day, for barging in on you the way we did. We have been very upset by Ciara's death. The past few weeks have been difficult, we must have seemed very rude and unresponsive when we met but we were having trouble absorbing what you told us. I'm very sorry.'

'Apology accepted,' Joe said. 'Don't worry about it, Mrs Byrne, no hard feelings at all. My deepest sympathy to you and your husband and I hope that, over time, you will be able to come to terms with your loss.' Despite the kind words and courtesy, there was a distance and finality in his voice. He was obviously preparing to hang up. Mag felt a surge of panic, she was desperate not to let things finish like this. Fear uncovered a reservoir of courage and she found her voice.

'Well, there was another small thing. I wonder if it would be possible... if you would consider meeting me. Maybe we could meet somewhere in town and we could talk. I don't know if you're interested in hearing what I have to say but I could explain to you about... the past.' She was afraid to stop talking, to allow the man the space to answer. 'Of course, if you'd rather not or if you'd rather wait until later, when you're ready, I could give you my phone number and you could call me whenever it suits you.'

She forced herself to stop rambling and time stood still for the second that passed before the man on the end of the line spoke again. She shut her eyes tightly and sent out an unformed prayer or wish.

'I don't see why not,' he said cautiously. 'If you'd like to meet up, that's fine with me. Some evening after work would suit me best. When would you like?'

'Oh, anytime at all, tomorrow or Friday or next week.'

'Let's meet tomorrow then. How about the bar of the Shelbourne? Six-thirty?'

'Great, great, perfect. I'm looking forward to seeing you.' She ran out of steam.

'Goodbye then, Mrs Byrne, see you tomorrow,' Joe said and put the phone down.

Mag felt as though she had just run a race; she was hot and flushed and her heart was racing. She was embarrassed that she had dealt with the conversation like an infatuated teenager not like a mature forty-nine-year-old woman but at least the outcome had been what she had hoped for.

The following day, it was raining as Mag got off the bus. The rain shower appeared out of nowhere brought by harried clouds which had paused in their scurrying across the sky to spill their contents on the surprised crowds below. Mag had not thought to bring an umbrella and ran from the bus-stop to the Shelbourne. She slunk through the elegant foyer of the old Georgian hotel, trying to make herself as inconspicuous as possible and made her way directly to the ladies' toilets to try to repair the damage. She combed her hair and reapplied her lipstick but her reflection persisted in looking bedraggled. While she was drying herself off as best she could under the hot air of the hand-dryer, a glamorous young woman with impeccable blond highlights and a long cream coat that swayed just inches from the floor entered and gave her a look of condescension before leaning closer to the mirror to verify her own perfection. Mag gathered her belongings together and hurried out.

The bar was busy, full of young men and women in business suits. They gathered in clusters close to the bar, around high tables, laughing confidently, the men with loosened ties to show that they were off-duty, the women sipping white wine from long-stemmed glasses.

Mag installed herself at a table at the edge of the room and put her coat on the chair beside her. She was wondering if there was any lounge service at this time or if she would have to make her way to the bar to order a drink when Joe walked through the large oak doors. He was wearing a dark navy suit with a pristine white shirt and in this formal attire he looked even taller and broader than she had remembered. He walked across the bar, looking confident and handsome, unapproachably so, Mag thought. He didn't see Mag at first so she stood up and waved at him. He strode over to her. He greeted her and noticed the absence of glass on the table

'You don't have a drink,' he said. 'What can I get you?'

'I was just about to get one. I only arrived a few minutes ago.' Mag was flustered as if he had caught her out in an indiscretion.

'Don't worry, what would you like?' He waited for her reply with the polite formality of a stranger which, after all, is what he was. She would have liked to order a gin and tonic but was afraid of betraying her apprehension even more under its influence. 'I'll have a coffee then, thank you.'

While he waited for their drinks at the bar, she glanced every so often at his back. She tried to prepare what she wanted to say but it was impossible to arrange her ideas in a coherent order.

He placed the coffee cup in front of her along with milk and sugar and went back to the bar for his pint of Guinness. He took off his jacket and sat down across from her.

'I hope you didn't get caught in that downpour, Mrs Byrne,' he said but she recognised it as a holding tactic while he waited for her to speak. It was she who had asked for this meeting but she no longer knew what it was she wanted to talk about. She saw now that Dennis was right. What had she been thinking of? What fairy-tale had she invented for herself? She was just a frumpy, middle-aged woman who had believed that she could turn back the clock. Now, confronted with the absurdity of her delusions, she wanted to get up and leave.

'Oh, I'll dry off. Please call me Mag. I hope I'm not putting you out too much by asking you to meet me. You must have a lot to do at home with two little girls.'

'They keep us busy,' he said shortly.

'Well, I suppose I should get to the point. It has been a bit of a shock for me to meet you. I never thought I would after all these years. It wasn't easy to give my baby up for adoption but I felt at the time as if there was no other choice.' She hesitated, afraid that it sounded as though she was whining. 'I don't know if you have any questions you wanted to ask me.'

This conversation felt surreal. It was hard to connect the baby she had held for such a short while with the man sitting in front of her. The world now belonged more to him than to her.

'Maybe I'll think of some later. But I'd be glad to hear your story, Mag, if you want to tell it. But don't feel that you owe me an explanation; you don't owe me anything.' He was polite and considerate but his tone kept her at arm's length.

She swallowed dryly and continued. 'We were just eighteen, and we'd only just met. I suppose you could say we were in love but we were too young to know it. When I got pregnant, we had nothing; no money, nowhere to live, I was still on trial in my job and Dennis had only an apprentice's pay.' She stopped for a moment, remembering. 'And Ireland was different then. In those days, we didn't make up our own minds. We all did what we were told, what was expected of us.' Said like that, her story sounded banal, common, one of thousands.

'I understand and I don't judge your decisions. It's hard for anyone to know what they would do in the same circumstances,' Joe said. 'You had your reasons. As for me, I've been very lucky; I was adopted by a great family. My parents gave me everything I needed.' He reminded her of Dennis in the way he said this.

A man approached them and slapped Joe on the shoulder. Joe looked up in surprise. 'Alan,' he said.

'Joe. It's been a while. Sorry to butt in but I'm on my way home. Give me a call one of these days and we'll have a game of squash.' Mag picked up a sugar sachet and fidgeted with it until the man had left. 'See you around, Joe,' he said and was gone.

'Joe,' Mag repeated softly, listening to the sound of his name; like a soft hush followed by an echo. 'I would have called you David.' Her voice was barely audible.

A silence formed. It was hard to speak with the lump in her throat. She continued. 'Nobody ever gave any thought in those days to the psychology of the thing, all anybody talked about was how much better off the baby would be with people who were in a position to look after him, you. I believed them.'

Joe leaned forward and squeezed her hand. The tide of strong emotions rose and a tear spilled out and rolled down her cheek. She tried to wipe it away as discreetly as she could.

'Please don't cry, Mag, you've nothing to blame yourself for. I'm sure you couldn't have done things any differently. I certainly don't hold anything against you.'

'If only I had the courage to stand up for myself and say no but I didn't realise that, as time passes during the pregnancy, a mother starts to care for her baby, even before she sees him. The day you were born I held you in my arms and you looked straight up at me as if you trusted me to make everything right. When they took you away, I felt as though I was letting you down but I was too afraid to resist and then it was too late.' The shame of her failure, that had always simmered under the surface, flared up now and burned her face.

'How did Dennis feel about it?' Joe asked.

'He didn't know. I ran away as soon as I found out. That was my mistake; I thought the answer to the problem lay with older, more experienced people, I never dreamed that we might have found the answer ourselves.'

'Please don't get upset, Mag. Hindsight is a wonderful thing but it's not very useful.' Joe smiled at her in an effort to cheer her up.

She smiled back 'You're right. Now, tell me more about you. I'm so glad that life has been good to you. Tell me about your family, your parents.'

'I was very lucky; I couldn't have asked for better parents.' His face clouded over. 'Unfortunately, my father died last year, just after Fiona was born. Cancer. But my mother is in good health, she still manages to play golf most weeks despite a touch of arthritis. She'll be seventy next year.'

'Is she the one your daughter calls Nana?' Mag said, remembering her telephone conversation with Katie.

'She's the one.'

'Does she know about me? I mean, have you told her about our meeting up?' Despite her nervousness, the idea that she might be having an illicit conversation with her son unknown to his rightful mother struck her as funny.

'She knows that I decided to find out about my biological parents last year. Until then it was never something that interested me and I suppose deep down I was afraid that it would hurt Mum and Dad if I did. Then, with Dad dying and when I became a father myself, I wanted to know more about my own origins. I talked to Mum about it and she had no objections. But funny enough, once the decision was made, I kept putting off the search; I was nervous of what I might find out. Eventually, Emer, my wife, pushed me into it.'

'How did you find us?' Mag was curious as she would not have known where to start to find him.

Joe loosened his tie, drew it over his head and put it in his pocket. 'It was easy, in fact. I got a copy of my original birth certificate and as the names of both of you were on it, it wasn't too difficult to track you down. Except that once I knew who you were I wasn't sure what to do next. I had no idea how you would react, if it would be a big shock or if you would be glad to see me. I considered phoning or calling to the door or writing a letter but in the end, I decided to write to Ciara. At that stage, I hadn't met her but I thought that, being one step removed from the situation, she could advise me on the best approach to take. She rang me afterwards and we met a couple of times to talk about everything. It was as simple as that.'

New tears threatened to fall but Mag blinked them back. 'How did she take it? I never told her about you, you know.'

'She was great. It didn't seem to shock her at all. In fact, I think she was delighted. She said that she always wanted a brother or sister and now she had one. The only thing that concerned her was how you might react, Mag.' Joe paused. 'She told me about the problems you've had in the past with depression. She wanted to make sure that we broke the news gently. She wanted to tell you herself first to prepare you before we met. She was planning to tell you and Dennis the weekend she died.'

'So that was what she wanted to talk to us about.' Mag felt her heart pinch with a pang of love for Ciara.

'When I got back from Germany and tried to get in touch to see how she got on, I was shocked to hear about her death. I had only known her a short while but already I was starting to see her as my little sister. I was very fond of her. Knowing how devastated you must have been, I decided not to get in touch with you. I'd waited over thirty years so one more wouldn't make a difference. Then out of the blue, as you know, you arrived on my doorstep.' Joe gave her a stern look but his eyes were teasing.

Mag made a grimace of apology. 'We weren't very diplomatic, I know.'

'We were all caught on the hop. When I realised who you were, my defences were up straightaway, especially when I saw how Dennis was reacting.'

'It was hard for him. You see, we found a letter and a photo from you among her belongings and we jumped immediately to the conclusion that she was having an affair. Dennis was very upset because he had also found out that she was seeing a married professor, one of her lecturers.'

'She told me about that.' Joe said. 'I advised her against it. I think she was coming around to that idea herself anyway. I don't think he had been honest with her and she was finding out that he wasn't the man she thought he was at first.'

As time passed, Mag felt more and more at ease in his company and she imagined that he felt the same in hers. He produced photos of his little girls and told her funny stories about them. While they talked, Mag realised that she was proud of him, ridiculous as that might seem. It was not as though she had been a part of his growth into this successful young man and loving father. All the glory for that belonged to another woman, his mother, the one who had taken him and cared for him since birth. Still, in a secret corner of her heart, she rejoiced in his successes and claimed them as her own.

His mobile phone rang, startling them both.

'Emer. Sorry, I didn't realise what time it was. I should have called. I'll be home as soon as possible. See you later, honey.' He ended the call and replaced the phone in his pocket. 'Mag, I'm going to have to leave but, if you like, we could meet up again another time.'

'I'd like that very much,' Mag said. She stood up, unsure of how to say goodbye.

Joe leaned down and kissed her on the cheek. 'It was very nice to meet you, Mag,' he said.

Mag felt tears well up again. She nodded, unable to speak. She didn't want to embarrass him or herself with another show of emotion. After he'd left, she touched the spot where he had kissed her. She ordered a brandy and an unfamiliar feeling of wellbeing, of living fully in this minute and no other, filled her.

1994

Mag gazed in dismay at the leaden rainbow reflected in the small pool of oil on the driveway outside her house. She knew that she should get the leak sorted out as soon as possible but her heart shrank at the thought of facing Dennis. Still, putting it off didn't help and it was ridiculously petty to consider going to any other garage to sort it out.

She took a deep breath. Maybe it was just as well. Maybe it was what she needed to force her to work something out with Dennis; she'd been putting it off for long enough. Three months had passed since Dennis had left the house and they had not had a proper conversation since. She noticed that he continued to transfer money onto her bank account but had never discussed it with her in any way.

Regularly, Ciara asked when Dennis would be coming back home but Mag couldn't tell her. She wanted to be honest but she didn't know the answer herself so she avoided any finality in her responses. Mag explained that they had come through some difficult times and Dennis needed some time before he could forgive and forget. Ciara agreed to be patient but Mag was left with a lingering sensation of guilt that she was concealing something from her daughter that she had a right to know.

A gap had stretched out between her and Dennis, a gap so vast and wide that it deformed their perceptions of each other. Mag didn't know if it could still be bridged but she did know that, for Ciara's sake, she had to try. Enough time had passed to allow Dennis to cool down and yet, if she waited any longer, separation could become a hard habit to break. No, now was a good time to talk. Besides, the circumstances were right; it was Saturday and Ciara was spending the day in her friend Sonia's house. Dennis would be working at the garage. She could call him beforehand and they might be able to have lunch together and discuss things.

She rang the garage. A young girl answered. Yes, Dennis was there but he was in the middle of a job and couldn't be disturbed, did she want to leave a message?

Mag declined and hung up. What to do now? Now that she had mustered up the determination she didn't want to give up. She decided to go to the garage and try to see Dennis. If he was too busy to go to lunch, then she always had the excuse of the oil leak to justify her presence. She sat into the car before she could change her mind.

The garage hadn't changed. It was as though she had left it only the day before. Pat O'Connor was laughing at some quip by Michael Noonan while they lowered an engine into the bonnet of a Renault. Francie was earnestly explaining some procedure to the new apprentice, Jason, but Dennis was nowhere to be seen. Was it her imagination or did they seem disconcerted to see her, as though she wasn't welcome? She straightened her shoulders and prepared to brazen it out.

'Hello, Francie. How are you? I just dropped in because I have a minor problem with my car, an oil leak. I was wondering if someone would take a look at it,' she said.

'Mag. Good to see you,' Francie said although he was not exactly wholehearted in his enthusiasm. 'Leave the keys in the ignition and I'll have a look at it straightaway. If you want to go and do some shopping in the meantime, it'll be ready when you get back'

'Well, actually, I wouldn't mind having a word with Dennis if he's around.'

'He's in the workshop, welding a piece. Come with me, I'll bring you to him.' He put down the spare part he was holding and prepared to lead Mag across the yard to the row of workshops on the far side.

'I know the way, Francie.' Mag said. 'But, I think I'll wait for him in the office, if you wouldn't mind telling him I'm here.' Francie's discomfort increased and it irritated Mag. The dispute between her and Dennis had nothing to do with him; he didn't have to take sides. She was making her way back towards the main office building when Francie stopped her.

'I don't know, Mag, it might be better if you went to see him in the workshop.'

Mag looked at him in surprise. They had always gotten on well and it disappointed her to see this change in his attitude.

‘I’ll be in the office, Francie,’ she said coldly. ‘If you have a problem with telling him I’m here, I can ask someone else.’

Francie was miserable. ‘No, it’s all right, Mag, I’ll tell him.’

Mag was glad to escape from the blinding glare of the oblique looks from the mechanics. She acknowledged them as a group with what she hoped was a breezy wave and retreated into the office. She noted with mean satisfaction that the office was a lot less organised than when she had been in charge. Files were stacked on top of each other in a higgledy-piggledy pile on one desk and, on another, at least a month’s worth of unattended paperwork had accumulated, almost tumbling over the side onto the floor.

She sneaked a look at one of the files but put it back quickly when she heard the door of the upstairs flat open. Francie must have been mistaken. Dennis must have been upstairs rather than in the workshop. She could hear his footsteps on the stairway beside the office. At the bottom of the stairs, there were two doors, one straight ahead which led to the yard and the street and one on the left which led into the office. She tried to assume a calm, neutral expression and touched her hair in preparation for his arrival. Her mind had created a visual image of Dennis even before the door opened so that she was taken aback when the figure that appeared didn’t match. It was a woman, a woman she knew, a woman she had met on several social occasions. It was Kitty O’Mahony, Francie’s sister. Kitty was just as surprised to see her. She froze. Her arms were raised, tying her fair, shoulder-length hair back in a clip at her nape. Usually, Kitty dressed with the self-assured elegance of the single woman who has both the time and money to make the most of herself but this time she looked a little rumpled, her cheeks still held the pink flush of sleep.

It took Mag a while to register what she was seeing but then Kitty's shamefaced expression triggered a sudden rush of understanding. She blushed, embarrassed at her own naivety. Of course. It had happened before, years before, before Dennis and Mag had married. Of course Dennis would turn to her again when he was alone. Kitty had no attachments; she was a successful, single businesswoman who had progressed through the ranks in the Bank of Ireland. Her face burning scarlet, Mag turned to leave the office without a word.

'Mag. Stop.' Kitty called after her. From the door, Mag could see Dennis crossing the yard from the workshop. She stopped and, for a second, she met his gaze but could read nothing there. Hastily, she continued walking towards her car. Kitty had followed her to the door and, out of the corner of her eye, Mag saw her shrug in apology at Dennis. Out of the corner of her eye, she could see Dennis trying to catch up with her but she kept looking forward, head high as she got into her car and turned the key in the ignition. Mag's movements were awkward, jerky. She desperately did not want to stall. Already, she felt like a fool in front of everyone and wanted to leave as quickly as possible holding on to some shred of dignity. As she drove away, a self-protective anger descended like steel reinforcements through her humiliation. Her anger was directed mostly at Dennis for betraying her, for allowing that betrayal to be so public but also at the others for their complicity.

Later that evening, she sat down with Ciara and explained that Dennis would not be coming back, ever. Ciara was frightened by the new, unbending determination in her mother's voice. Mag softened and told her that both she and Dennis loved her dearly, them more than anything in the whole world but that, between them, things had changed and it wasn't possible for them to live together any more.

'You don't want him to come back, that's it, isn't it?' Ciara screamed. 'It's your fault. You've spoiled everything. I hate you.' She ran upstairs and slammed her bedroom door. She refused to come down for dinner and Mag sat alone at the table, pushing her food around her plate, unable to eat.

As the days passed, drifting into weeks, then months, the distance between Mag and Dennis hardened into permanency. But, after a while, something changed in Mag. The shame and anger she experienced acted as grit under the wheels of her life, bringing her forward, no longer whirring uselessly as they might have done before. She forged new friendships, took cookery classes, joined a walking group, found a new energy for gardening. On the inevitable occasions that she and Dennis were obliged to meet, she maintained a frosty politeness and he, an irritable pride.

Even after he and Kitty parted ways, (a development enthusiastically relayed by Ciara who saw this as a breakthrough) Mag gave no indication of any change of heart. Sporadically, Ciara would try to revive their interest in each other but Mag made it a rule not to ask even the simplest question about Dennis and in case she might raise some futile hope in Ciara's imagination.

Chapter 21

Dennis recognised the gait before he recognised the face, clad as it was in a black motorbike helmet. He wiped his hands on a rag and approached Vincent who emerged tousled-haired from the helmet, reminding Dennis that despite his blasé manner he still wasn't fully grown up. His shabby jeans hung far down over his skinny hips and Dennis wondered momentarily if this was a deliberate fashion choice or if it was merely the best he could afford. One thing was sure, he wasn't the first owner of the black leather biker's jacket he was wearing; it was impossible that the level of deterioration inflicted on it had been achieved within Vincent's short lifetime.

'Well, Vincent, what brings you here?' Dennis fixed the young man with a stern gaze while Vincent shuffled uneasily.

'Howaya, man? I dropped in because I wanted a quick word with you about this business with Ciara. After you came to my place it made me think that there was something dodgy going on, what with the cops asking me questions and then you. The cops said it was just routine but since then, I heard that they've been asking a lot of people a lot of questions.'

'Get to the point, Vincent,' Dennis said, stuffing the oily rag into the back pocket of his overalls.

'The word out is that this is an official investigation and that the cops think that Ciara's accident was not so simple and straightforward. I know it probably doesn't look good to you that I hung around that night to talk to Ciara but, hey, I want you to know that I had nothing to do with the accident. I didn't even see her.' He paused in his fidgeting with the straps of his helmet. 'I know now why she was the last to leave. I'm sure you've heard about her and McMurray. The news is fairly widely broadcast by now.'

Dennis nodded. 'We know about that.'

'Did he have anything to do with Ciara's accident?'

'Let's leave any suppositions of that sort to the guards. Nobody is being accused of anything for the moment, the guards are merely being thorough in their enquiries.'

Dennis had the good grace to smile internally at his own words, so contradictory of his thoughts and actions of recent weeks.

Vincent took a pack of cigarettes from his pocket and silently requested permission to smoke from Dennis.

'Go ahead but watch where you put the butt, this is a garage,' Dennis said.

'She told me that she was seeing someone else, someone older but I thought it was just a ploy to get rid of me. I never dreamed she was seeing McMurray. Although I suppose I should have guessed, when I saw the way his wife got so upset outside his office.'

'What do you mean?' Dennis asked.

'It was the week before Ciara's accident. I was waiting in the corridor to talk to McMurray to ask if he'd allow me to resubmit an assignment that I did badly in. But anyway his wife was just outside his office waiting to see him as well. Then she walked away and stumbled against the wall. She looked like sh… I mean, she didn't look great. She was really white and I thought she was going to faint so I went over to her and asked her if she was OK, if she wanted a glass of water but she said no. I was going to knock on McMurray's door to let him know that she wasn't well but she flipped the lid and told me to leave well enough alone. She said she just needed some fresh air and to be left alone. The thing is that the door wasn't closed completely and I could hear that Ciara was in there.' He was about to toss the end of his cigarette behind him when a glare from Dennis stopped him. He crushed it underfoot, then picked it up and held it.

'At the time, it never dawned on me that there was something going on between them but now I feel like a thicko for not seeing what was under my nose.'

'Forget about it, they kept it secret from more prying eyes than yours,' Dennis said.

'I won't keep you any longer, man. You probably want to get back to work. Just wanted you to know that Ciara meant a lot to me. I'd never have done anything to hurt her. I loved her.' Vincent squirmed and looked away as he mumbled these last words. His embarrassment at revealing his feelings to another man was clearly visible. Dennis felt a twinge of sympathy for this awkward young man and decided to let his admission go.

'Go on,' he said gruffly. 'If you've done nothing wrong, then don't worry about it. The guards know what they are up to.' He clapped Vincent on the shoulder in parting and relief filled the young man's face. He put back on his helmet and roared away in a storm of noise and fumes.

Dennis stood for a moment, thinking about what Vincent had told him. There was something he had said that bothered him, something that didn't quite fit with his previous impressions. He had a vague notion that Caroline McMurray had not known about her husband's affair until after Ciara's death. Where had that idea come from? Mag. She had said something about that.

He strode into the office and rang Mag. 'I've just had Vincent Connolly here at the garage,' he told her.

'Oh, did he call for any particular reason?' Mag said.

'Apparently there are rumours spreading like wildfire all around the university. The guards are questioning anyone with any links to Ciara and by now it's common knowledge that Ciara was seeing McMurray. Vincent came to reassure me of his good faith and of his attachment to Ciara.'

'Do you believe him?'

'As a matter of fact, I think I do,' Dennis said. 'But there's something else he said that puzzles me. Tell me, Mag, when you talked to Caroline McMurray, when did she say she found out about Ciara and McMurray?'

'She said her husband told her after the accident. He was upset and confided in her, she said.'

'That's what I thought. Well, according to what Vincent Connolly says, it looks like she knew a lot earlier. She overheard a conversation between Ciara and her husband in his office at the university, a conversation that obviously upset her a lot. Vincent saw her in the corridor and offered to tell her husband but she got mad at him. He didn't think much of it at the time but now that he knows what he knows, he's putting two and two together and assuming that she found out about the two of them at that time.'

'That's strange, why would she tell me that she didn't know anything until much later? Why lie? What difference could it make?' Mag said slowly.

'I have no idea.'

'Has Vincent told this to the guards?' Mag asked.

'I don't know, possibly not. At the time he thought she was taken a turn but now he's thinking that she was probably devastated after finding out about the affair,' Dennis said.

'And at the thought of losing her lovely house and top-of-the-range BMW,' Mag said with uncharacteristic bitterness.

'That's a bit harsh....' He broke off. 'Hold on, Mag, you've just reminded me of something. When I called over to Vincent's flat last week, he said something. It didn't register with me until now. I remember he said that he nearly broke his neck on the back of a parked BMW. I wonder where exactly that BMW was parked.'

'Are you suggesting that it might have been Caroline McMurray's BMW?'

'Maybe McMurray used it while his wife was away, I think it might be worth asking the question in any case.'

There was a pause as Mag considered the matter. 'Let's ask Vincent where the car was parked and if it seems in any way relevant then we should tell O'Brien.'

'I'll talk to Vincent and check it out.'

'Let me know what he says, won't you?'

'Of course.'

As soon as he hung up, Dennis tried calling Vincent on his mobile. The call went straight to the answering service but he didn't feel like leaving a message. It was frustrating but there was no point in discussing it with O'Brien until he got further information from Vincent.

He worked all afternoon, stopping only to make fruitless calls to Vincent's mobile. The air was charged with an ominous dread and he found it hard to talk to the other mechanics. Machines were so much easier to deal with than people; no matter how complex they might be, there was only one right answer, only one correct way of functioning. His employees seemed to sense instinctively his need to be alone and they avoided him, allowing him to distract his anxious brain with mechanical intricacies. The next time he looked up, evening had arrived, rounding off the corners of the day. The mechanics were getting ready to leave. They waved goodbye at him from across the yard before melting away out of sight. Dennis plugged away at the engine of a well-travelled Saab until it emitted an even hum that gave him a grim satisfaction.

He tried phoning Vincent several times throughout the evening and was taken by surprise when he got an answer on his last attempt before going to bed.

'Sorry, I left my mobile in the flat. I just got in,' Vincent explained.

Dennis got straight to the point. 'I have a question. It occurred to me after you left here this morning. It's about something you mentioned in passing the day I called to your flat.'

'Yes?' Vincent's voice was hesitant and slightly defensive.

'I seem to remember you telling me that, on the night of Ciara's accident, you left on your motorbike and that, on your way back to the city, you almost crashed into the back of a parked BMW.'

'Yes, I had to swerve to avoid it. It had no lights on and in any case I had my mind on other things. It didn't help though; it being black. But what's that got to do with anything?' Puzzlement replaced defensiveness.

'Never mind that for the moment. Can you tell me where exactly it was parked?'

'It wasn't far from the entrance to the McMurray house. There's a bend there where the road widens a bit and there's just about enough room for a car to pull in off the road near the edge of the mountain. It was parked right there, the rear still sticking out on the road. I managed to swing around it but it was close enough to set my heart racing. Do you think it might have been the cause of Ciara's accident?'

'Did you tell the guards about this?' A frisson of apprehension ran through Dennis.

'No, I don't think so. No. It didn't come up and it never dawned on me that there could have been any connection.'

'Did you notice anyone in the car? Or standing nearby?'

'No, I didn't stop to look. It gave me a bit of a fright and I wasn't in the mood to talk to anyone. At that stage, I wanted to get back to town as fast as I could.'

'Did you notice anything more about the car? The model, the reg, anything?'

'Sorry, it was a BMW for sure, I recognised the back, but after that I can't tell you anymore. I was on top of it before I knew it and then within a second I was past it. Does it mean something to you? Do you have an idea whose car it was?'

'A vague idea, that's all. I'll pass on the information to the guards. Thanks, Vincent.'

'So are you going to tell me what's going on?'

'Not right now. You'll find out in good time.'

Adrenaline rushed through Dennis's veins. Sleep had been washed out of his system. He wanted to talk to O'Brien immediately but it was too late. He would have to wait until the morning, an eternity. Instinct had told him that McMurray was mixed up in this and now, even though the exact ties were not clear, it looked like he was right. He paced the length of the room a few times and, despite his anxiety, went to bed. He didn't expect to sleep but he woke the next morning to bright sunlight streaming in through the window.

He called the Enniskerry garda station but he was told that O'Brien was out on official business in Pearse Street station. He rang Pearse Street and, after long minutes on hold, was told that O'Brien was busy and could not be disturbed. He left a message asking O'Brien to call him back.

Francie arrived early that morning and they had a silent companionable coffee together before they got down to work. Dennis tried to put the matter out of his mind and to focus on the work on hand but, despite his best efforts, his ears pricked up each time he heard the phone ringing in the distance. Each time he paused, expecting to be called to the phone to speak to O'Brien but each time he could only hear the even mumble of voices as the secretary dealt with customers and suppliers.

Finally, unable to ignore the steady hum of thoughts and questions circling around his brain, he decided to go to the garda station and talk to O'Brien personally. He had to pass on this information and ensure that O'Brien had as many of the pieces of the puzzle as possible.

He parked close to the station paying no heed to the parking metre and took the steps up to the front door two by two. The entrance lobby was a hubbub of activity. It was lunchtime and guards were leaving for and returning from lunch. Dennis brushed through, ignoring the conversations, the camaraderie of lunch arrangements being made around him. He went directly to the receptionist.

'I'd like to speak to Sergeant Eamonn O'Brien, if I may,' he said.

'Sorry, that won't be possible. He's busy,' she said.

'It's important. My name is Dennis Byrne. If you could tell him I'm here he might find the time to see me.'

She peered at him. 'You left a message for him this morning, didn't you? Please take a seat, I'll let him know you are here but I can't promise anything.'

Dennis sat on one of the plastic, linked seats which lined the wall and settled down to wait. He wished he had brought a newspaper, not to read but to hide behind. The girl at the switchboard was speaking quietly into the microphone on her headphones. She made an apologetic face at him. 'He really can't be disturbed right now,' she said. 'I'll try again in a little while.'

'I'll wait,' Dennis said. While he watched, the stragglers in the central lobby thinned out. An hour wore on and it became more of a passage-way than a meeting place. Gardaí, wearing blue uniform shirts and navy ties bustled through the area from one office to another. The relaxed lunch atmosphere that had pervaded when he arrived was replaced by a sense of activity, of efficiency.

After an hour had passed, Dennis was preparing to ask the receptionist to ring O'Brien again when two men, speaking in low, intense voices came walking down the corridor towards him. One of them was O'Brien. He was talking to a tall, thin man in a dark suit who was clutching a battered leather brief-case. Dennis stood up to go towards him but then stopped. Behind them, hidden from view until that moment was Caroline McMurray. A uniformed guard walked by her side. Automatically he looked around for McMurray himself but there was no sign of him.

Caroline McMurray was the same and yet very different from the woman he had encountered on other occasions. Her cream shirt and check skirt looked as expensive and elegant as always but they no longer had that crisp freshness. Her hair, usually sleek and perfect, was dull and untidy. But the biggest change was in her face. Fear had stripped away her veneer of self-possession, her polished poise. She looked much older than the last time Dennis had seen her. She was staring down at the floor ahead of her, avoiding meeting anyone's eyes. She was not crying but her eyes were red and blood-shot from old tears. She must have felt Dennis's stare because she glanced up at him before they reached him. It took her a second to register who he was. She flinched. As if by telepathy, in the second that their gazes collided, he understood what was going on. She was the one who had caused Ciara's death. He glanced quickly at O'Brien and his realisation was confirmed.

O'Brien stopped. 'Go ahead. I'll join you,' he said to the others. 'What are you doing here, Mr Byrne?'

Dennis stared at Caroline McMurray's back. He shook himself and turned back to O'Brien. 'I came because I had some information to give you but it looks like I might be too late.'

'Come with me,' O'Brien said, touching his elbow. He led him away down the corridor to an empty office. On a filing cabinet behind the desk, a coffee machine with a half-full coffee-pot hissed.

'Sit down,' O'Brien said as he poured coffee into two mugs. He opened the top drawer of the filing cabinet and took out a naggin of brandy. He poured a generous slug into one of the mugs and handed it to Dennis. 'Drink that,' he said. 'You need it. I got your message this morning but I didn't have time to call you back. I didn't know you were here.'

Dennis drank a mouthful of the reinforced coffee and felt his blood warm up. 'I wanted to tell you something, something Vincent Connolly told me when he called to see me at the garage yesterday. He said that he saw Caroline McMurray outside McMurray's office in the university. She was very upset after overhearing a conversation between her husband and Ciara.'

'Yes, that's how she found out about their affair initially. She told us that,' O'Brien said. 'Later, unknown to him, she read his emails and found out that Ciara was coming to the house the night of the accident.'

'Vincent also told me that he had seen a black BMW parked not far from the McMurray house on the night of the accident. But I suppose you know all about that already. I thought at first that Colm McMurray might have taken her car and followed Ciara but it was her, wasn't it?' Dennis

'It was. I think we have a fairly clear idea now of what happened that night.' O'Brien walked around the desk with his coffee mug in his hand and sat on the edge of the radiator under the window.

Dennis waited for him to go on.

'On Friday morning, Caroline McMurray dropped off her sons to school—they were going on a rugby weekend afterwards—and then drove on to the airport as planned to go shopping in London. She parked it in the carpark and flew out. After she found out about the affair and that Ciara was coming to the house that evening, she had bought another plane ticket and flew home on Friday evening. She drove out to the house and planned to walk in on her husband and Ciara after all the others had left but while she waited to make sure that they were all gone, she heard Ciara leaving. She could hear McMurray shouting, asking her to stay so her plan wasn't going to work. She was parked on the side of the road near the house so she moved her car out to prevent Ciara from leaving. Ciara got out of her car and the two women talked. Well, argued, more like.' O'Brien took a deep breath, looked intently at Dennis to check how he was taking this before continuing. Dennis nodded to tell him that he wanted to know.

'Ciara said that it was over with McMurray, that she was sorry but apparently, Caroline asked Ciara to abandon her plan to do a masters in Trinity so that she wouldn't have any contact with her husband. Ciara refused and Caroline slapped her on the face. That's how Ciara got the scratch. It also must be when the charm was pulled off Ciara's bracelet but neither of them noticed in the dark. Ciara ran to her car and locked herself in. Caroline banged on the window. Ciara must have been frightened and started the engine to drive around Caroline's car. Caroline got into her own car. She says that her anger took over and she accelerated and bumped into the back of Ciara's car. She didn't realise they were so close to the edge and she got a fright when Ciara's car went over.'

'She didn't check if she was still alive or call an ambulance or anything?' Dennis stood up and paced the room.

'No. She says that she looked down and could see that there was no way she could have survived so she didn't think and just drove away. She drove to the airport and parked the car again. Then she pretended that she had come in on the morning flight as originally planned.'

'She told you all this?' Dennis asked.

'Well yes, she tried to deny it at first but, in the end, she didn't have much choice. We have flight log records as well as CCTV footage of her at the airport so she couldn't deny it. We also found traces of paint from Ciara's car on the front bumper of her car.'

'What made you suspect her?'

'We had our doubts about this accident early on. We looked for what might have provoked the accident and couldn't see anything. There was a fresh scratch on your daughter's face that didn't seem to have been caused by the accident. Your comment about her not wearing a seat-belt struck a chord and we looked further. Then, when you found the charm, it was another element adding to the mystery. Finally, young Vincent's statement about the BMW parked nearby raised more suspicions. There were just too many things that didn't make sense.'

'I thought you weren't taking it seriously. So you were looking into it all along. Why didn't you tell me?'

'I had no proof, nothing concrete. And I was afraid that you would barge in like a bull in a china shop and mess up our investigation. People who think they are getting away with something tend to make mistakes.'

Dennis made a face: there was more than a grain in truth in O'Brien's assertion. 'So what made you think it was her?'

'Once we found out about the affair, Caroline McMurray became a person of interest, along with her husband. We checked flights and when we saw that she had booked a flight on Friday evening, we requested CCTV footage at the airport. We only got that back this week. I also asked for a DNA analysis of the clothes Ciara was wearing after I took them back from you. After that, we called her in for an interview and confronted her with what we had.' O'Brien's pride in his investigative process was starting to show despite his efforts to remain dispassionate. 'She finally broke down and confessed to everything.'

Dennis closed his eyes. At that moment, he hated Caroline McMurray in a way that he had never hated anyone.

'Was McMurray involved?' he asked through gritted teeth.

'We don't think so but we'll be fully exploring that possibility.'

Dennis put his head in his hands and took a deep breath. There could never be an easy way to lose Ciara but to have her snatched out of his life in this way somehow made things worse.

'Will she be arrested?'

O'Brien approached him and put a hand on his hunched shoulder. 'My best guess at the moment is that she'll face charges of dangerous driving leading to injury or death but leave this with us. Go home, Dennis, look after yourself. We'll be in touch.'

The red-hot desire for revenge that had fired up in him faded. She could never pay for taking Ciara away; no price was high enough. Weariness overtook Dennis. Words would change nothing; there was nothing they could do to soften the rock-hard truth underneath.

'Right. Well, thanks for everything you've done.' He stood up and held out his hand to O'Brien.

O'Brien took it. 'There's no need to thank me, I was only doing my job. We'll be in touch.'

It was a relief to be out in the open air, to feel the warmth of the sun on his face. Dennis drove through the city streets, barely aware of what was going on around him. Without realising it, he took the old familiar route towards the home of his childhood. It was an ordinary narrow, red-brick house, identical to all the others in the terraced row and even to the other houses in the maze of streets nearby. It had been sold years before, after his mother's death. He parked outside and remembered the times he had breezed through the door after school and work, the times he had sneaked in, shoes in hand, at five or six in the morning in the vain hope that he might fool his mother into thinking that he was already in bed. He remembered how she had doted over Ciara, her adored granddaughter, after having raised five boisterous sons.

The house had changed very little. The new owners had painted the door bright blue and planted a rosebush in the minuscule patch of green at the front. A few wilting tulips lined the short path to the front door but other than that it was still the same place where the future had seemed enormous and his worries tiny. A woman opened the window of what had once been his bedroom and shook a quilt out of it. Dennis caught her eye and felt embarrassed as if he had been caught out spying on her.

He took the coast road and drove on to North Bull Island. He sat on one of the dunes and watched the endless motion of the waves. It was high tide and the end of a warm, sunny day. The coldness of evening was starting to creep in from the sea and a mother was trying to drag her two small children away from the joys of the beach for their tea. Dennis trickled the sand through his fingers.

Ciara's voice echoed in his mind. Memories of her paraded in front of him like one of those old-fashioned slide projections. But he wasn't afraid of them, he didn't run away any more. He held them against him and allowed the pain and sorrow to seep into his bones. The layers of anger, frustration, disappointment, resentment, desire for revenge had all been peeled away and he had reached the pure core of his loss. For the first time, he thought that he might, one day, be able to face all the good things that Ciara had brought to him.

He would go to see Mag and tell her about these latest developments but later. For the moment, he allowed himself to sit and lose himself in a different time and space. Eventually it became too dark and cold to stay on the beach any longer and he got up to leave. He walked heavily back to his car, his feet retained by the loose sand.

Chapter 22

While she peeled the apples to make an apple tart, Mag mentally ticked off what she had done and what still remained to do before they arrived. Two days earlier, she had issued a tentative invitation to Joe to come with his family for tea and, to her surprise, he had accepted. Now that the anticipated time of their arrival was drawing near, she wanted to make sure that everything was prepared so that this visit would go as well as possible.

No matter how hard she tried, she couldn't rid herself of the feeling that this was a test, an interview and it made her nervous. She sliced the apples into the pastry base and sprinkled sugar on top. She folded over the rolled out pastry on top and with a deft hand shaved off the excess. She made a few deft nicks across the top of the apple tart and slid it into the oven.

She washed her hands and took stock of her surroundings. She had spent most of the previous day cleaning and tidying the house and it gleamed from the unaccustomed attention. Her next task was a tougher one.

She had decided to go up into the attic and bring down some of Ciara's old toys for the children to play with.

Access to the attic was by a sliding ladder which Mag pulled down through a trapdoor. An enclosed, musty warmth enfolded Mag as she released the trapped heat of the past few sunny days. She stepped inside. A bare bulb glowed in the pyramid-shaped space and illuminated the carcasses of old furniture, lamps and cardboard boxes stacked there. In thick black marker, Mag had noted the contents on the sides of the boxes. They held Christmas decorations, papers and documents, relegated ornaments, objects from her parents' house that she couldn't bear to part with, Ciara's old school books and drawings, clothes she had grown out of and somewhere among them all, toys that Ciara had played with when she was a little girl.

A brief search located a couple of boxes of toys in a far corner. Mag had given most of Ciara's toys away a long time ago but she had held on to certain favourites, sure that one day Ciara's own children would be happy to have them. There was enough here to entertain Joe's children. Through the gaping top of one of the boxes, Mag recognised a blond-haired, blue-eyed doll that one Christmas had been Ciara's pride and joy and beside her a golden, one-eyed, tattered teddy whose popularity had endured a little longer. A memory, bringing with it equal parts of intense pain and joy, flashed before Mag's eyes of Ciara's chubby, dimpled hands trying to stick a plaster on the threadbare fur of the beloved bear.

She took the boxes downstairs and left them in the sitting-room. A detour by the kitchen and a glance in the oven told her that the apple tart was cooked. She took it out and went upstairs to get herself ready. She had lots of time to spare but she wanted to be ready and at ease when they arrived.

She was standing in the sitting room checking for any oversights or last minute improvements she might make when she heard the slamming of car doors and the animated blend of adults' and children's voices outside the house. Despite all her forethought and planning, Mag's heart beat faster and she had to make a conscious effort to regain her composure. She opened the door before they reached it. Joe was holding his little daughter Katie's hand. His wife was carrying the baby. Katie was wearing a purple dress with a frill at the bottom and an embroidered heart on the front. Two glittery clips held her hair back. Mag's throat tightened with hope and longing when she noticed the efforts that had been made to dress up the children.

'Hello, Mag, how are you? This is Emer, my wife,' Joe said. 'And this is our big girl, Katie and the baby, Fiona.'

'Hello, Mrs Byrne,' Emer said.

'Please call me Mag,' Mag said. 'Here, let me carry that for you.' She rushed forward to take the changing bag from Emer's hand. She led them inside and settled them in the sitting-room while she went to the kitchen to make tea. When she came back, Katie had already discovered the boxes of toys. Glimpses of fascinating treasures made her itch to investigate. Only her father's physical restraint held her at bay.

'You can let her have them, Joe,' Mag said. 'I took them down especially for her and Fiona to play with.'

'Were they Ciara's? Are you sure you don't want to keep them safe?' Joe asked.

'Yes. Don't worry about it, that's what toys are for.'

'That's very kind of you. Thank you, Mag,' Emer said.

Mag took an instant liking to Emer, a small, outspoken woman with a strong and frequent laugh. While Mag poured tea and served the apple tart, Emer explained that she was a science teacher, that she had taken a year off after the birth of Fiona and was planning to go back to work in September. She chatted away to ease any awkwardness between Mag and Joe.

Later, Katie approached Mag. Clutching the blond-haired doll under her arm, she examined Mag with open curiosity. 'My daddy said that you used to be his mummy before he got another one, the real one. How come he got two? I only got one,' she said, slightly aggrieved.

Mag wasn't sure how to respond; she wasn't sure what role, if any, Joe saw her fulfilling in his children's lives but she was pleased that he had acknowledged her as his mother even if it was as a 'pretend' one. She looked to Joe and Emer for help.

Emer intervened. 'Katie, don't annoy Mag. We'll explain it to you again, but later.'

'I have two grannies, though,' Katie continued as though she hadn't heard. She paused; a new thought had crossed her mind. 'Does that mean that I can have three now?'

'Maybe I could be an extra bonus granny? That's if you and your mummy and daddy don't mind.' Mag gave Joe and Emer an anxious look, hoping that she wasn't overstepping the limits.

'Hmmm,' Katie said, as if she would give it some thought and went back to playing.

Fiona, a chubby, placid fourteen-month old baby, was busy practising her walking. She walked around the coffee table, the piano stool and armchairs dropping to her knees to crawl when the distances were too great to reach across. In her dark blue eyes framed by dark eyelashes, Mag thought she could see a resemblance to Ciara but she said nothing.

Someone knocked at the door and Mag excused herself to answer it. Dennis stood on the doorstep. He looked tired, deflated. His usual energy seemed to have seeped away.

'Come in, Dennis,' Mag said. 'Is there something wrong?'

'I called around to let you know the latest.' Dennis stepped inside. He squeezed his temples together, covering his eyes with one hand. 'I was at the garda station earlier. There's an update on Ciara's accident.'

Mag stared at him. She didn't feel ready to hear this but when would she ever be? At that moment, the door of the sitting-room opened and Joe came out holding Katie's hand. She was walking awkwardly, clutching her dress. Taken by surprise, Dennis gave him a gruff hello and Joe nodded in acknowledgement.

'Excuse us,' Joe said. 'Mag, could you tell me where your toilet is? We have a little urgent matter to deal with here.'

'It's right there.' Mag indicated the appropriate door and Joe and Katie hurried through it. 'Joe is here with his wife and their two little girls,' Mag explained.

'Do you want me to go? Maybe now isn't the time. I can come back later.' Dennis shifted about uncomfortably.

'No, tell me quickly. I want to know.'

'It was Caroline McMurray. She came back early from London and waylaid Ciara as she left the house. They had words. She attacked Ciara. Ciara tried to get away but

Caroline McMurray drove into the back of her and pushed her over the edge. It looks like she'll be up for dangerous driving leading to death. O'Brien's dealing with it.' Dennis's shoulders were hunched over and his voice was low.

Mag shuddered as she thought about Ciara's last seconds before she hit the mountain side. In the brief silence, the door of the toilet opened noisily and Joe shooed Katie briskly into the sitting-room before closing the door behind them.

'I went to the station to tell O'Brien what Vincent told me but he was on to her already. She was there, Mag.' Dennis stopped before going on. 'They took her in for questioning.'

'Did you see her?'

'Yes.' Then Dennis lifted his head and forced energy into his voice. 'So that's it. We pretty much know now. I'll go home, Mag. We can talk more tomorrow, if you like,' he said.

'Why don't you stay, Dennis?' Mag caught his arm and held him back as he moved towards the door. 'Come in for a minute.'

Dennis hesitated. He looked at the closed door of the sitting room and raised his eyebrows in doubt.

'Come in and say hello to Emer and the girls. It'd be rude to leave without that much. You needn't stay very long,' Mag said.

Dennis blew the air out of his lungs in a noisy sigh. She would have preferred to arrange a meeting at another time; he was too downhearted to be sociable but chance had imposed this encounter and she could only hope that it went as well as possible. He shrugged in concession and followed her into the sitting-room.

'Emer, I'd like you to meet Dennis. Dennis, this is Joe's wife, Emer. Of course you've already met Joe, and here are Katie and Fiona. Sit down there, Dennis, I'll pour you some tea before you leave. Will you have a hot sup, Emer?' Mag chattered on, trying to smooth out the wary tension that lay between Dennis and Joe.

Dennis murmured the necessary greetings and sat into an armchair.

'I'm very sorry for your troubles, Mr Byrne,' Emer said. 'Obviously, I've heard about your daughter's car accident. It's a tragic time for you both.'

'It hasn't been easy,' Mag said. 'And one of the hardest things is that it could have been avoided.' She looked at Dennis for permission to tell them what they knew. Her eyes prickled with unshed tears.

'Let's say it was provoked,' Dennis said. 'I was at the Garda station earlier and they've taken someone in for questioning in relation to the accident.'

'The wife of the man Ciara was seeing,' Mag added in explanation.

Dennis threw her a quizzical look before turning back to Joe and Emer. 'She waylaid her and caused her to crash.'

Instinctively, Emer glanced at her children. Katie was instructing Fiona, who was totally uninterested and just wanted to bite on everything, how to insert shapes into the appropriate holes in the back of a plastic tortoise. They didn't seem to be paying any attention to the adult conversation.

'That's awful. I suppose they'll charge her,' Joe said.

'We'll know more soon. It's in the hands of the gods now. And the guards.' Dennis sounded flippant but Mag knew it was a cover for deep emotions.

A sombre silence fell over the group which attracted the attention of the children more than conversation had done. Katie moved closer and made an open, frank examination of Dennis from the safety of her father's side. When Dennis looked directly at her, she quickly buried her face in her father's jumper.

'At least now we know,' Dennis said. 'There's nothing more we can do except move on.' His words convinced nobody, they were merely a thin skin of bravado.

'We should go, Mag. Thank you for your hospitality but it's getting late for the girls; we should get them to bed shortly,' Joe said.

Fiona had grown bored with the toys and hauled herself up into a standing position behind Dennis' chair. She toddled around the armchair holding on to the arm and then continued in the direction of the coffee table gripping onto Dennis's leg until she realised that this warm prop was attached to a person. She looked up in interest at its owner. Dennis leaned down to her. He showed her his fist with his thumb wrapped inside. He tapped it with his other hand and, all of a sudden, his thumb popped out and waggled at the little girl. Fiona stared in amazement and then gurgled with laughter. Dennis played the trick again to his appreciative audience. Drawn by this new potential source of entertainment, Katie approached him and observed the action.

'Why are your hands all black?' she asked after a while.

'Oh, that's because I had a big fight with a dragon earlier today. Dragons are very dirty animals, you know, with all that fire and smoke.'

Katie's eyes opened wide in delight and astonishment before reason intervened. 'You're joking. Dragons don't exist.' But a little doubt remained. 'Do they, Daddy?'

'Well, I've never seen one.' Joe was smiling.

'Right so,' Dennis said. 'The next time I see that dragon I'm going to tell him that he doesn't exist. I'll tell him you said so.'

Katie giggled.

'Come on, Katie, we have to get ready and go now,' Emer said. 'Here, put on your cardigan.'

While Joe and Emer gathered their belongings, Katie went to pick up the blond-haired doll. 'Can I take her home? Please?' she asked Mag.

Before Mag could answer, Joe interrupted. 'No, Katie, leave her back,' he said firmly.

Katie's bottom lip slipped out and started to hang over the edge. Tears were not far away. Her mother rubbed her head. 'Katie, you can't take her away. This is her house. You have lots of dolls at home but if you leave her here then she'll be here for you to play with the next time you come back.' Emer's words warmed Mag's heart. Next time.

She stooped down to Katie's level. 'I hope you'll come back soon. I'll save all the toys for your next visit,' she said.

'OK,' Katie said, recovering fast from her disappointment. Katie kissed her on the cheek automatically and then turned to Dennis to kiss him goodbye too.

'Do you live here too?' she asked.

'No, I don't,' Dennis said.

'That's enough now, Katie.' Joe put his hands on her shoulders. 'Thank you very much for inviting us over, Mag. Next time, you'll have to come to us.'

That such a thing could be mentioned so casually and naturally brought a lump to Mag's throat and she could only nod in agreement.

'Goodbye, Dennis.' Joe held his hand out to Dennis.

'Goodbye, it was nice to see you all.' Mag was encouraged by the warmth in Dennis's voice.

After they had left, the house seemed quiet and empty. Mag tidied up and put the cups and plates in the dishwasher while Dennis stood at the window watching the light fade. Faint evening sounds filtered into the room from the garden.

Mag spoke. 'Do you think she did it deliberately?'

Dennis considered her question. 'I don't know but I think there's a good chance. If only Ciara had kept her cool.'

They stared at each other, unable to talk about it anymore.

'Would you like to stay for something to eat, Dennis?' Mag asked at last.

'I wouldn't mind. I don't feel like going home right now.'

Dennis followed her into the kitchen and watched her while she started to prepare dinner. She was conscious of his eyes following her around the room and she asked him to set the table to keep him occupied.

She had bought steaks just in case Joe and Emer had decided to stay for dinner and she took them out of the fridge. She ground some pepper on them and seasoned them with salt. Both she and Dennis were absorbed in their thoughts and worked together in silence. The ease with which they slotted into the familiar routine reminded her of older times.

'What else can I do to help?' he asked when the table was ready.

'Take the lettuce from the fridge for me. But you should give your hands a good scrubbing first.'

Dennis examined his oil-stained hands and smiled. 'Katie is a funny little thing, isn't she? Full of chat. She reminded me of how Ciara was at that age.'

Mag smiled at the memory. She took out a glass salad bowl and tore the leaves of lettuce into it. She chopped up half an avocado and added some pine-nuts.

'I don't seem to remember your cooking being that fancy before, Mag. I'm very impressed.'

'I've taken some cooking classes in recent years with Kathleen Dwyer and a few other friends. Every so often we meet up and make dinner together.' Dennis looked over her shoulder as she mixed up oil, vinegar and mustard for a dressing.

'You see, that's what makes all the difference. I'd probably have put a blob of salad cream on it, if anything at all.'

Mag laughed. 'I should invite you over some day for a proper meal. I could test out a few new recipes on you.'

'Feel free to use me as a guinea pig. I'd be ready, willing and hungry.'

As they waited for the potatoes to cook, Mag opened the patio doors and stepped outside to escape the heat of the kitchen. Dennis came outside to stand beside her. It was still bright enough not to need to turn on the outside lights but night was starting to bleed the colours from the garden.

'Is it hard to stay here where there are so many memories of Ciara?' he asked quietly.

'Yes and no. Everything reminds me of her but at least I feel close to her. Maybe later, it won't hurt so much.'

For a few minutes, they listened to the mysterious rustling and hooting as the animals of the night emerged. The quietness of the night smothered their voices and they spoke quietly about common friends and the garage before going back into the kitchen to eat.

'I'm thinking of going back to work, Dennis,' Mag said later.

'Why would you do that? There's no need. The garage brings in more than enough and as I've said before, you're as entitled to it as I am.'

'I want to work. It would do me good to get out and about more. And in any case, what you say isn't quite true. I haven't had anything to do with the garage for more than ten years and even then it was part-time.'

'The garage wouldn't be there if it wasn't for you and you got more done part-time than most people could do full-time and don't forget you had Ciara to look after as well. Anyway, do what you want but you don't have to.'

Mag stood up to clear the dinner plates, partly to hide the tears that began to flow upon the mention of Ciara's name.

'So you got in touch with Joe, after all.' Dennis spoke with fake casualness. 'He seems a decent enough guy.'

'Yes, I like him. This evening was my first time to meet his family. It's a good sign that he agreed for me to meet them.

'He works in Siemens, doesn't he? What does he do there?'

'He's an electronics engineer. Why all the questions, Dennis? Do I detect some interest in getting to know him?'

'No reason. I'm just asking. Do you think you'll see more of them?'

'I hope so. We'll see. There's no point in rushing anything.' Mag picked up a bowl of fruit and put it on the table in front of them. 'Have a piece of fruit. I have nothing else for dessert.'

Dennis started to peel a pear. 'Good for you. Maybe it is possible to change the past after all or at least maybe we can go back and keep some of the good parts of it. That might even be true for other things as well.' He grinned at her and Mag shook her head at his obvious insinuation.

She smiled and took an apple from the bowl. 'Dennis Byrne, you'd think you'd have learned your lesson by now.'

'I'm a slow learner. It's taken me over thirty years to get this far but I might finally be figuring it out.' He lifted his hand. She thought he was going to touch her; she held her breath but then he put it down on the table beside his plate.

An owl hooted in the garden and sounded the depth of the silence that enfolded them. It reminded them that it was getting late. Dennis looked at his watch. 'I'd better go.'

Mag stood up and walked to the door with him.

'Thanks for dinner, Mag. I'll talk to you soon.' His eyes flashed; the old irrepressible Dennis was resurfacing.

She closed the door behind him and leaned back against it. A conflict raged inside her. How much of the past could be repaired? Was it courting disaster to attempt to exhume it and breathe life back into it? Or was something that had been precious, once upon a time, worth taking risks to salvage? Conflicting answers danced in and out of her mind. She closed her eyes and banished the thoughts. She smiled to herself as she thought about what Ciara would think but her losses were too fresh and too great to allow her to gamble right now. She needed to retreat to allow her wounds to seal over before deciding which battle to fight and which to concede.

Acknowledgements

Thank you, Mathilde Viret and Fiona Kearns for all your work on the beautiful book cover for Love Lost, Mathilde for the illustration and Fiona for the design. You have been incredibly patient with me when I didn't know what I wanted but knew very well what I didn't.

It's impossible to thank everyone to whom I owe thanks. But I'll try. First of all, my family, both the one I landed in and the one I made. As with every family, we have our ups and downs but underneath it all is a thick mattress of love that allows us to bounce back. My sisters and brothers have encouraged me, bought my books for friends, put up with me banging on about bookish things that I'm sure they have little interest in but, most of all, they show their love by being there, slagging me in the good times and stepping in in the times of need.

My four daughters are amazing, kind, intelligent, funny, compassionate women who make me laugh and educate me about so many things, both serious and silly. Thank you for being you!

I have been so lucky with my friends. I joined a wonderful bunch of people in the College of Marketing and Design who are still a joy to spend time with when we reunite. Thank you to the Dead Ants for your love and friendship over the decades.

After seventeen years living in France, my French friends will always be in my heart: Elizabeth and Xavier, the two

Sylvies, Francois, Isabelle and Philippe and of course, my Franco-Irish contingent: Tracy, Nordine, Jackie, Gilbert, Lorraine and Gilles.

After moving back to Tullamore, I couldn't have been luckier with the friends I found: Clodagh, Noreen, Tricia, Andrea and Joan. Thank you so much.

My Dublin friends are too numerous to name (I knew I was stepping into a minefield): the friends made during the MBA; the friends made in my evening Spanish classes; the ones made volunteering in Vision Ireland in Terenure; the writing buddies that create a community where we can all be nerdy about writing and books together. I'll just mention two in particular: Ger—a treasure of a friend—and Marie, who encourages me with her generous heart and quick brain.

Printed in Great Britain
by Amazon

57145278R00185